Praise fo

What We Kept to Ourselves

"Kim's second novel is hard to put down, unique, haunting, and beautifully written, as the author slowly weaves layer upon layer in an intricate, mysterious web."

—*Booklist*, starred review

"*What We Kept to Ourselves* is both a suspenseful page-turner and a poignant family drama. Kim's beautiful, thoughtful prose illuminates themes of immigration, identity, love, and loss. A gorgeous, thrilling read!"

—Jean Kwok, *New York Times* bestselling author of *Girl in Translation*

"Bursting with yearning, twists, and secrets, *What We Kept to Ourselves* is about the difficult questions that die in our throats when it comes to asking our loved ones. A triumph!"

—Frances Cha, author of *If I Had Your Face*

"A powerful tribute to the bonds between the least privileged. Each page of *What We Kept to Ourselves* pulses with stunning detail and deep insight. I couldn't put it down."

—Margaret Wilkerson Sexton, bestselling author of *On the Rooftop*

"Layers after layers of mystery are revealed with each chapter of this exquisitely written novel. *What We Kept to Ourselves* is a compelling, poetic, important, thought-provoking, and unforgettable read. Nancy Jooyoun Kim is a master storyteller who has the power to keep us spellbound and reminds us what we must do to make this world a better place."

—Nguyễn Phan Quế Mai,
internationally bestselling author of
The Mountains Sing and *Dust Child*

"A gorgeous literary novel featuring poetic prose and a propulsive mystery. *What We Kept to Ourselves* is a moving story about immigration, family secrets, and human connection. Truly a masterpiece that I couldn't put down."

—Emiko Jean, *New York Times* bestselling
author of *Mika in Real Life*

"Nancy Jooyoun Kim has crafted a moving, propulsive story about a family haunted by secrets. *What We Kept to Ourselves* spans the intimately personal to the urgently political to investigate how the traumas of the past shape the human experience. This is a probing, sharp novel about family, loss, desire, grief, the search for justice, and so much more."

—Crystal Hana Kim, author of *If You Leave Me*

"Nancy Jooyoun Kim's *What We Kept to Ourselves* illuminates the glacial secrets among a family that crackle under a glass lens. Through the brushstrokes of tragedy and grief and mystery, Kim interrogates how a forgotten past bleeds into the choices we make in our everyday lives."

—E. J. Koh, author of *The Liberators*

"*What We Kept to Ourselves* is a nail-biting thriller with hairpin turns, a generational saga, a love story, an unsparing look at belonging and unbelonging in America today and the joys of food, family, forgiveness. I can't stop thinking about the Kim family. A glorious achievement!"

—Marie Myung-Ok Lee, author of *The Evening Hero*

"A propulsive mystery about yearning, loneliness, and duty (but to and for whom?). Kim is a masterful wordsmith, tackling brittle topics with grace, urgency, and, most importantly, hope. This book is a call to action, and a reminder that it's never too late to live the life you've always wanted."

—Carolyn Huynh, author of
The Fortunes of Jaded Women

"Those of us who love Southern California know it's an entire universe, where people's dreams and loves and families orbit and dance and collide in neighborhoods as diverse as the world. Nancy Jooyoun Kim knows Los Angeles so deeply that her novel brings to life loquat trees, the melancholy of staying where new roots sometimes cannot flourish, and the geography of neighbors and strangers whose loyalties turn into what might be love."

—Susan Straight, National Book Award finalist
and author of *In the Country of Women*

"*What We Kept to Ourselves* is an intricately crafted mystery and a heart-wrenching family saga. Nancy Jooyoun Kim writes with a piercing moral clarity, suffusing every page with emotional depth. Fiery, bittersweet, and complex, this is a novel of incredible conviction and empathy."

—Michelle Min Sterling, *New York Times*
bestselling author of *Camp Zero*

"*What We Kept to Ourselves* is a breathtaking literary force of a novel. With melodious prose, Nancy Jooyoun Kim has crafted a page-turning mystery with thoughtful meditations on family, love, and connection. This novel is a searing portrait of how long-buried secrets, desperate hopes, and blind compromises shape the decisions that affect generations to come. Kim is a master storyteller!"

—Catherine Adel West, author of *Saving Ruby King*

Also by Nancy Jooyoun Kim

The Last Story of Mina Lee

WHAT WE KEPT TO OURSELVES

A Novel

Nancy Jooyoun Kim

ATRIA PAPERBACK

New York London Toronto Sydney New Delhi

An Imprint of Simon & Schuster, LLC
1230 Avenue of the Americas
New York, NY 10020

First Atria Paperback edition July 2024

ATRIA PAPERBACK and colophon are trademarks of Simon & Schuster, LLC

Simon & Schuster Celebrating 100 Years of Publishing in 2024

For information about special discounts for bulk purchases, please contact Simon & Schuster Special Sales at 1-866-506-1949 or business@simonandschuster.com.

The Simon & Schuster Speakers Bureau can bring authors to your live event. For more information or to book an event, contact the Simon & Schuster Speakers Bureau at 1-866-248-3049 or visit our website at www.simonspeakers.com.

Interior design by Alexis Minieri

Manufactured in the United States of America

1 3 5 7 9 10 8 6 4 2

Library of Congress Cataloging-in-Publication Data
Names: Kim, Nancy Jooyoun, author.
Title: What we kept to ourselves : a novel /Nancy Jooyoun Kim
Description: New York : Atria Books, 2023.
Identifiers: LCCN 2023004268 (print) | LCCN 2023004269 (ebook) |
ISBN 9781668004821 (hardcover) | ISBN 9781668004838 (paperback) |
ISBN 9781668004845 (ebook)
Subjects: LCGFT: Detective and mystery fiction. | Novels.
Classification: LCC PS3611.I454545 W43 2023 (print) | LCC PS3611.I454545 (ebook) |
DDC 813/.6--dc23/eng/20230519
LC record available at https://lccn.loc.gov/2023004268
LC ebook record available at https://lccn.loc.gov/2023004269

ISBN 978-1-6680-0482-1
ISBN 978-1-6680-0483-8 (pbk)
ISBN 978-1-6680-0484-5 (ebook)

For my father

WHAT WE KEPT TO OURSELVES

1999

The night he found the body behind the loquat tree in his yard, John had driven home from work like on any other evening, weighed down by the usual worries. These troubles had become so familiar that he never questioned them anymore, and because he never shared them with anyone, they would forever go unchallenged. It was *his* misery after all.

These days his concerns hinged on the apocalyptic flavor of the moment—Y2K, or the Millennium Bug—like a futuristic disease or a line dance at a wedding. How could John protect his two children from something he didn't understand? Asteroids and floods, all that biblical stuff, made more sense than technology, this internet, which was spooky, invisible, and everywhere at once.

But they weren't even children anymore. His daughter Ana was already an adult, a college graduate living in Berkeley—leafy streets crunching underfoot like granola in the fall and dimly lit coffee shops with dogs snoozing at people's feet—less than four hundred miles away, but much too far in his mind. And his son Ronald had already finished half his senior year in high school.

The house was quiet with them no longer on the phone, vaporized by this thing called email and AOL. After John had spent over a year saving up for the Packard Bell PC tower, all he could hear now from his son's bedroom were the robotic chirps and static fuzz of the dial-up, an occasional burst of laughter, his fingers chicken-pecking the keys. Their thoughts and feelings now traveled in wires, through air, like ghosts.

Once, months ago, John had asked his son to show him how to use the computer. Instead of the cardboard signs around the plant nursery that he had handwritten with a giant Marks-A-Lot, he decided he would have them printed and laminated at Kinko's. More professional, like a big-box store. But as he cupped the mouse awkwardly, Ronald hovering by his side, John couldn't figure out where anything was "saved" and why he couldn't just print everything out. His son argued that it was better in the box because you could go back and fix things without having to waste paper.

But that isn't life, John wanted to say. *That isn't the way life works.*

The machines were lying to us. And because of them, we were all going to die. So why burden his sixty-one-year-old brain with these advancements? Around every corner, something seemed to be falling apart or ready to implode on itself. Trash littered roads on which people drove too fast, blasting music. Graffiti covered street signs with phalluses, the hieroglyphics of spoiled children. Homeless encampments, piles of tents, shopping carts and garbage, like the flotsam of a shipwreck, gathered under freeway overpasses, harkening back to the refugee camps of his youth.

Until the end of the world, John still had his plant nursery, his teenage son at home, a daughter coming to visit for the holidays, his Sunday-morning hikes, and his wife to honor on the one-year anniversary of her disappearance. At first, he had told his children that she had probably embarked on a vacation, that she would be back. But as he sat nearly six months later with his son at the dining room table, he had lied, not the first of its kind: *Mommy died.*

Death was so much easier to explain. Death was the period at the end of a sentence. A disappearance was a question mark. You'd always be left waiting for a response. Much like how the war had kept him separated from his mother and sister and brother, who still might be alive somewhere in Korea across the border between the North and the South. He never knew what happened to them either. A part of him hoped they had lived and that they would reunite one day, but the rest of his being wished they had died. Because what would be the point of a life separated, cracked in two?

In preparation for Ana's visit, he had gotten her a bag of fancy Coffee Bean & Tea Leaf ground coffee. Her favorite was Peet's, but at least this was better than his Folgers. He bought a glass pitcher called a French press that the nice young lady with a nose piercing recommended to him. He entered a thrift store for the first time in his life in West Hollywood and purchased Ana some hippie tapestry to hang on the wall of her bedroom. People in Berkeley liked that kind of stuff, he thought. On her whiteboard, which she hadn't used since high school, he drew a peace sign and wrote "WELCOME HOME ANA" above it, as a parent on television would. Maybe he'd never get rid of his accent, which was like a thick scar on his tongue, but he could act like that TV dad. He could try. He would. If only she gave him another chance.

And when the world ended, he'd go out sitting on the living room couch with his two children beside him, the twinkling lights of the artificial Christmas tree they'd assemble that weekend reflected on his tear-streaked face, and a photograph of his wife, Sunny, from their wedding day clutched to his chest. How beautiful she was—her brown eyes, tender and soft, behind a veil attached to a circular hat polka-dotted with tiny pearls, which resembled a little cake on her head and matched her long white dress. She was glamorous, yet covered her charming, crooked teeth whenever she laughed. And he had always wanted to grab her hand and say, *You are perfect the way you are.*

But she was gone. He'd have to live with this broken heart. If he hurt enough, she might return. If he hurt enough, she might be able to sense how much he needed her.

John pulled into the driveway and cut the engine of his Eldorado, inhaling the musty smell from the vents and exhaust. He collected his leather briefcase from the passenger seat. His neck and back muscles ached from lifting plants, bags of compost and mulch, all day. He massaged his shoulder with his free hand and pushed open the car door to go inside the house, where his son waited for him to make dinner.

As he approached the front door, he caught sight of a ragged cat, which shat in his yard and slinked away toward his neighbor Rodriguez's lawn. Despite its plainness and low chain-link fence, he loved this bandage-beige house with its grass mowed biweekly, its single row of roses that bloomed in reds and hot pinks and perfumed the air in the long, dry summer heat, and the hodgepodge of ceramic pots with a collection of cacti and succulents on the brick steps leading to the front. The least he could do was keep his wife's plants alive.

But the backyard—a future project of hers—was now a total mess, had become overgrown in parts and completely barren in others, with garden tools and a shovel caked with dirt, abandoned. No one went to the rear, where the garage stood in silence, filled with their kids' old schoolwork and mementos, the books and notebooks he kept from his days long ago in graduate school, and Sunny's art supplies. He'd rather not think of it at all, the structure itself like a large delete button.

With his girlfriend's T-shirt draped over his face, Ronald bathed in her favorite scent, Juniper Breeze. The perfection of that evergreen was unlike the seasonal high-school fragrance variations on American desserts—peppermint sticks and gingerbread and sugar cookies.

His parents never baked; ovens were for storing pots and pans. Many of the immigrant kids, or the children of immigrants like himself, who came from predominantly Latino and Asian families, didn't have homes filled with pies or cupcakes. Yet everyone at school wanted to smell the same way, longed for the comfort of some common nostalgia, whether it belonged to them and their histories or not. But comfort to him smelled of his mother in the kitchen, her hands in plastic gloves, massaging red pepper flakes, salt, a dash of white sugar, garlic, and saeujeot into the chopped leaves of a napa cabbage. He would stand beside her at the counter, and every time she taste-tested the kimchi, she'd place a child's bite-sized portion in his mouth, careful not to deposit the scarlet paste on his face, her plastic gloves crinkled on his lips. She'd ask, "What do you think?"

But nobody in America celebrated the smell of kimchi. The only non-Korean he knew who actually loved kimchi was his girlfriend Peggy, who was Filipina and stopped at the Korean market every time she was in town, where she'd load up on her favorite banchan—kkakdugi, seasoned spinach, and jangjorim.

A week ago last Friday, Ronald had strummed his fingers against the warmth of Peggy's stomach, along the bottom edge of her pale pink bra with the tiniest bow between her breasts, as his mouth touched the cup of her perfect navel. At first she flinched at the coldness of his fingers, then smirked, her eyes closed in pleasure. He kissed her lips, which were smooth and small and ripe, the color of berries.

They had met back in middle school in Hancock Park, where her family had lived about two to three miles away from him yet worlds apart, with its distinctive multimillion-dollar residences, formal hedges, country club, and healthy white people. But her family had fled four years ago to La Cañada for the obvious—the lack of crime and homelessness, the better schools, the serene isolation of the foothills by the Angeles National Forest, and the full amenities of neighboring Pasadena and Glendale. Her father was a doctor, and her mother, some kind of manager or administrator at the VA.

And he loved her. Peggy Lee Santos. They loved each other still. Even though he could not follow her to the fancy places she would go, the private universities that she researched with her seemingly infinite hours on AOL, he would drive to the end of the world for her in his father's beat-up, ugly Eldorado.

Pots and pans clattered like sad cymbals less than ten feet from his door in the kitchen where his father prepared dinner. Frustrated, Ronald pulled Peggy's T-shirt off his face and switched on his desk lamp, washing in glare the import-car posters—images of shiny modified Hondas flanked by models—around his bed. He didn't even know why he had these posters anymore. For a little while, before he could actually drive, he had been interested in cars—the speed, the acceleration, the women—but now these images, curling at the corners, functioned only as distractions to cover the emptiness of the dirty white walls.

In a photo that his older sister Ana had framed for him on his desk, Ronald and his mother posed after his middle school graduation. Her face glowed as she clutched him with manicured fingers around his shoulders. She never had the time to do her nails, but she'd painted them that morning in front of her vanity. He remembered how much pride she exuded that day, but he could also sense—because he and his mother always had this way between them—her sadness over his growing up so fast.

How embarrassed he had felt that day beside her, as if he was too grown to be babied by his mother. But what he would give to hold her hand now. How much they could say to each other without words, how much they knew about each other in a squeeze of the shoulder, a quiet observation of one another through an open door, a mirror, a glance. His father, on the other hand, had always been unknowable, opaque, a dull stone worn smooth by time.

He didn't believe his father's claim that she was dead. There was no body. There was no proof.

Ronald had the itch to log on to see if he could find Peggy or any of his friends. Although they had already made plans to meet up in Pasadena tonight, he needed an escape now. But his father always got angry when he clogged up the phone line before nine p.m. Who knew who could call the house? They should all be available—just in case. But his father never acknowledged for whom or what they had been waiting.

Instead, their lives were a constant away message.

His father had set the breakfast nook for dinner—paper napkins, metal chopsticks, spoons. They hadn't used the dining room table since his mother disappeared. Ronald slid onto the bench in front of the oxtail soup, the meat and bone and mu which had simmered for hours last night in a garlicky salt-and-pepper broth. Steam delicately painted the air with the rich and oily smell of gelatin and beef. Even if his father underseasoned and never bothered to brown anything, time and low heat performed most of the work.

"Did you sell all the Christmas stuff at the shop?" Ronald asked.

"What, the garlands?" John set his bowl of rice in front of Ronald, then winced as he bent to sit.

"The poinsettias. The ones you were making such a big deal about."

"Yeah, yeah. Almost gone. More come in the morning," his father said.

The soup was too hot, so instead Ronald sampled the baechu kimchi that his father bought. Without his mother, no one bothered to make kimchi at home. His mother would prepare jars and jars that they'd eat from almost every night, which his sister Ana found to be repetitive and dull. Sure, Ronald craved cheeseburgers and fast food too, but Ana claimed to dislike all the spice, and she hated the chopsticks, always using a fork instead. She had to make everything some kind of protest. No wonder why she liked Berkeley.

"Can I take the car out tonight?" Ronald asked.

"How long?"

"Couple hours." He spooned the tender meat off the knobby bones, which he discarded onto his napkin.

"Your homework?" his father asked.

"It's Friday." Ronald hated his father's voice—the graininess from all his years of smoking, the heaviness of the tone, the accent, which wasn't quite Korean but distinctly foreign. His sister had once explained that since their father had immigrated in the early sixties, he'd picked up his accent from speaking English with Chinese Americans, Black customers, and Jewish shopkeepers who were then prevalent in the areas of South LA where he'd worked. But whatever the reason, his father's accent always embarrassed Ronald. He was embarrassed *for* his father. His mother could hardly speak English, but he preferred her voice to his whenever she tried. She could play off anything through her tact and charm, her sense of humor. Her laugh, a *ho, ho, ho,* which she covered with her hand.

"And?" his father asked.

"Can I borrow the car?" Ronald said as clearly as possible.

His father sucked the meat from between his teeth. "Bring the car back before midnight." His purplish lips frowned. "No drink. No smoke. No pregnant, uh, okay?"

After dinner, the neighborhood cats scratched the roof, which John had patched himself last year, strapped to the chimney with rope around his waist. His wife Sunny had fed and talked to the cats like children. She would stand at the back doorstep making kissing sounds. John once found her outside with a pair of tweezers and a struggling yellow cat between her legs, its limbs everywhere, like an asterisk. She pulled a splinter from its right front paw and winced when the cat mewed in pain. She spoke to the cat in Korean as if it could understand her: "Be calm. I'm trying to help you. Can't you see I'm trying to help you?"

Remembering these words, his brain hurt. He wanted television.

On the tan-colored pillow-top couch in his pajamas, his hair smoothed to the left in a perfect part, his dentures removed, he flipped on the television to Los Angeles's local multi-Asian channel (Vietnamese and Cantonese and Tagalog during the weekdays, Japanese and Korean at night). He disappeared into the news and commercials. A public service announcement on the conservation of water reminded him of the bills in the mailbox. He was so forgetful these days.

After slipping on a pair of old loafers, John shivered as he stalked down the driveway, knees aching. Their mostly quiet street ran east to west following the sun's blazing arc across the sky, which melted into a citrus-colored acid every night. Sirens and cars zoomed blocks away down Pico Boulevard, a swift-flowing thoroughfare connecting the city's dense, bustling interior to the Pacific Ocean. Despite the smog, the air smelled sweet and clear in this neighborhood of lawns and palm trees that swayed like slender hat-wearing ladies.

In this gentle darkness, his next-door neighbor Rodriguez, who always donned a white tank top despite the December chill, draped Christmas and icicle string lights on the towering prickly pear and succulents at the edge of his lawn. He waved as a form of silent solidarity between homeowners. John had rarely spoken to him, but he knew from Sunny that his family was from Mexico and he'd grown up in LA. She had contended that she could read a person by looking at the things for which he got his hands dirty. She once deemed Rodriguez, with his thick graying hair and faded neck tattoos, a hardy minimalist who was soft inside, much like his beloved cacti, in contrast to the junglelike foliage, the twining vines, jasmine and passionflower that hopped the fence between their backyards.

"That Rodriguez is an artist," she'd said. "Look at the arrangement of his plants." She added the next part in a vain attempt to make John feel inadequate: "The other day I caught him smelling one of the blooms off his prickly pear. And then—you know what he did? He reached down and pet one of my kitties. Right on the head."

One of her cats, a splotchy tortoiseshell, the same one John had seen earlier slinking down the driveway, now lay beneath the streetlight in front of the house. Separated from him by at least fifteen feet and one waist-high chain-link fence, the cat gazed contentedly at him and then strutted out of sight. John reached inside the mailbox for the envelopes, the junk mail, and the weekly advertisements (pizza coupons, an ad for window blinds, personal check orders, a takeout Thai food menu). His heart sunk. Another trial CD for AOL, a plastic disc with delicate rainbows on its mirrored belly. He didn't care if it was free; nothing was free, and it would keep the phone line busy. Who knew if Sunny would call one day and need help? But again there was nothing, no letter from her tonight.

Airplanes at a great distance blinked and painted trails lit by the sliver of a moon in the sky. Ana would be here, finally, tomorrow. He always loved the warmth and clean smell of her every time he hugged her, which was now only twice a year, when he met her at the gate of the airport and when she left. He adored the way her hair felt under his chin, the thick texture like her mother's. Even if only for a few seconds, those seconds mattered very much to him.

He had to convince her to move back. She didn't need to live at the house. There was so many places in LA with young people and coffee shops and bookstores, all those things she liked about the Bay Area. He could even plant her some trees if she liked them so much. On Sundays, they could go hiking together. She had already quit her job.

"Why?" he had asked her last weekend over the phone. "Didn't you just start?"

"It's too stressful," Ana said.

"*Stressful?*" He knew the literal meaning of the word but couldn't comprehend why in the hell an office job could be so stressful. Try working at a bread factory like he had all those years ago while in a PhD program in a foreign country called America. Had she ever stood for ten hours, baking hot, without even a break for water? His head would spin and spin and spin, and an infinity of glistening loaves that looked like long butt cheeks would streak by on rattling conveyer belts that smelled like rubber and WD-40. And his job wasn't even as bad as the ones with the mixing machines, their industrial cruelty doled out in the name of hamburger buns.

"Yeah, it's too much work," she said.

"Too much work?"

"Not everyone is made like you, Dad." Annoyance permeated her voice. "I'll find something else."

Find something else? His kids were spoiled. What made them think that they could find another job whenever they "felt" like it? Maybe it was her degree from a fancy American college, which he had never gotten because he'd dropped out of grad school. Was that it? Get a degree and when things were too stressful, you quit? His kids were soft, hadn't gone through war like he had at thirteen, hadn't lost their family and home, too. They didn't know what it was like to climb over dead people, bodies bloated and rotten, or to steal from the dead because you never knew when you could get another pair of shoes. They never had to wear another man's socks, with another man's blood on them. They didn't know what that was like, that smell, all those bodies, the shit and urine, those maggots and flies. These American kids would never get it.

Whatever the reason for Ana quitting her job, now was the time to show her that Los Angeles was her home. They didn't have to settle for those twice-a-year hugs. Her father would guide her through this transition, take care of everything, provide some soft landing as he had always done.

With the mail still in his hands, he made his way up the driveway. A fog of breath expelled from his mouth. The cat sprinted a couple feet in front of him and disappeared behind the house. "Son of a bitch," John said, toothless, his dentures fizzing in their cup for the night. He'd scare the cats away for good this time.

He shivered as he trudged down the gravel path that ran alongside the house toward the backyard, his eyes adjusting to the dark. Something crunched beneath his loafers. He stepped down from the concrete pad in front of the garage and made his way through weeds, feeling the hard, compacted soil beneath his feet.

On the other side of the freestanding garage, behind the adjacent loquat tree, a pair of shoes, beat-up and broken, emerged from the darkness where vines dangled over the fence from his neighbor's yard.

"Excuse me," John said. His heart pounded as his breath clouded the air. Sirens howled in the distance. The snap of a twig. "Excuse me," he said again, voice rising. His anger grew as he gripped the mail in his hands in a fist. He was angry, mostly because he was terrified of those shoes, those legs. In a sense he was furious with himself.

But the man, facedown, did not move.

John approached slowly, wondering if he should first run back into the house and call the police.

With his foot, John nudged the man's leg and shouted.

Of course, the man was dead.

And nearby lay a white envelope with the words "Sunny Kim" on it.

1977

Sunhee lay down beside her husband, who was perched on the edge of the bed, bathed in the amber glow of the lamp on their single nightstand, calculating his week's earnings in his notebook. The crickets played their legs in a fever outside, as alley cats mewled through the open windows from which a gentle breeze, that nonetheless smelled of trash and smoke, caressed her face. He gripped the pen and nodded as he focused, counting as if to a rhythm, but there was no music; there were only money and bills. *How dull*, she thought.

The mattress squeaked and groaned as she adjusted her now cumbrous body, almost seven months pregnant. She frowned at the sour smell underneath her arms. It was too hot. How she missed slumbering on her floor mat at home in Seoul, longed for its firmness against her back. She didn't understand why her husband insisted on this soft, noisy mattress as if to sleep on the ground, like they had always done in Korea, would be some kind of regression. Even the squeaking of the springs as they had sex embarrassed her. What a pathetic sound. But they were Americans now.

Sunhee inched closer to her husband. "Could you get me some pickles?" She craved the slices of cucumber she had salted herself without seasoning or dill like the local brands. She preferred the simplicity of her own homemade pickles, the way her mother made them, before sautéing them in a pan with garlic and sesame oil and red pepper.

"Huh?" He squinted at her through the dimness of where she lay.

"Pickles, a bowl of them." She cleared her throat. "I finally found a comfortable position and I don't want to move."

He sighed, smiling as he rested his notebook on the nightstand. He got away with it all because of that smile, didn't he? That smile had mischief in it. He didn't smile enough these days.

"Okay, okay," he said. As he stood from the mattress, her body tilted like a canoe. She pondered the crooked calendar on the wall, which displayed the month of October. She realized it was already July now, nearly August, and for whatever reason, neither she nor her husband had bothered to turn the calendar pages or even replace it with a new one for this year, as if time had been frozen during that month they had first met last autumn in Seoul, and in a way it had. How time flew. She could hear him rummaging in the kitchen like a visitor struggling through some foreign land—the refrigerator, the pantry, the cupboards.

Through an initial arrangement between their families, she had married Kim Jung Ho, the son of a law school professor, in November, following a month electrified by courtship—elegant boxes of tawny pears that crunched in the mouth, chocolates wrapped in sensuous golden paper like a tiny blanket by Gustav Klimt, and a lavish bouquet of red roses, tight unripe buds that bloomed after days in water and reminded her of rococo and John Waterhouse, women of opulent dresses and swanlike necks. Tall and lean, Kim Jung Ho possessed a handsome face, long but squared off at the chin; and full, wavy black hair, almost blue like a cormorant's wing. With his tan, chestnut-colored skin from all that sun in California, he was easy to look at, even glamorous. And unlike her other suitors, he offered her the adventure of a lifetime, a chance at another country. America.

He had immigrated to Los Angeles on a student visa for a PhD program in English literature in the early 1960s, although he eventually dropped out, which made him a bit of a renegade. He had claimed that he always loved books, and as a teenager after the war, displaced and alienated by his experiences of violence, his unexpressed feelings about his separation from his mother and siblings, he had been particularly drawn to foreign stories, faraway lands in which the tragic flaws of great men, who had reminded him of his father, had been shaped into lyrical language and forceful, heartstopping drama. In other words, Shakespeare.

When she had asked him why he left school, despite his clear passion for the subject, he'd said in a somewhat cool, detached manner: "In America, there are so many ways to make a living. There, we don't have to do what our parents say. We can be anyone we want. We can be free from their expectations, free from history. I love it so much." He claimed to now "work in oil," which she hadn't understood at the time meant *gas station attendant.*

She had imagined them cruising in a convertible on a highway beside a stretch of sand and infinite blue waves to a faint horizon, and dancing under gem-colored lights at a smoky Hollywood nightclub, far from what had become the most dreadful, complicated place—Seoul. Despite the growing economy after the brutalities of the war, which she herself had lived through as a baby and young child, there were protests and civil unrest against the president and government almost every day, news of students killed, police violence, murders and disappearances. She was tired and yearned for some stability now that she was in her late twenties. She needed marriage, a family. A new lease. A different story.

But after she had married Kim Jung Ho and boarded an airplane for the first time in her life, stopping only once in balmy, green-and-teal Hawaii, she had been thrust into this alien world of wide streets and concrete and fast cars. She never said this out loud, but she'd regretted her decision immediately. Sure, they had gone to the beach a couple times. He had even tried a ballroom dancing class with her, but he was unable to quickly grasp the steps and claimed to be too busy to learn.

She had taken for granted the click-clack sound of her heels on the old stone paths in Seoul. Just the memory thrilled her. The open-air markets teeming with life and sound, the gruff voices of the women who worked in the stalls, the fresh octopus, clams, and mussels that smelled of the ocean, their home. The fish eyes glistened like the mother-of-pearl inlaid on an enamel box. And the bins full of banchan—every namul imaginable, from chives to mugwort to dandelion. There was always so much variety in color and texture and smell, while in America, food appeared to be simply brown and white and dry, slices of pale vegetables coated in more cream sauce. Did Americans like color at all, besides the unnatural hues of mustard and ketchup?

Once her husband returned to the bedroom and handed her the bowl of pickles, Sunhee said in a regal declaration, "I have thought of a name." She had been meaning to have this discussion but he was too busy, didn't like to be distracted at night, except right before they fell asleep and he nuzzled his face into her neck, rubbing her now round stomach with his hands from behind.

He picked up his notebook. As he sat down again on the bed, the legs of his boxers scooted up, revealing the muscles of his thighs, lightly covered in hair. She loved his body, long and strong, but not in a way that was overly muscular or overbearing. He had a gracefulness, a leanness about him that reminded her of men in the movies. He had been striking on their wedding day in his dark suit and crisp white shirt. She'd worn a heavy winter dress with a high neck and long A-line skirt embroidered with tiny pearls, as if she had emerged from the ocean as a virgin. But she wasn't. She smiled. Neither was he.

"Anastasia. Anastasia Kim," she said in English, like a proclamation from a queen.

John laughed, shifting his weight on the bed. "What are you talking about?" He lifted his head. "How many syllables? Pick something simple. Something that makes more sense. I can't call my daughter that."

"No, no, dummy. Not her. *Me.*"

"What?"

"Me, me."

"You're kidding." He closed his notebook. "Who do you think you are? A Russian princess?"

She smirked.

"If you're going to change your name, you should pick something closer to your own. Look, let me help you. Your name is Sunhee, right? Well, pick *Sunny*. Close enough, right? Do you know what that means?"

"Oh, you have no sense of glamour, no sense of poetry. I want to be Anastasia."

"Queen of Complaints?"

"Shut up." She chuckled, then sneezed. Her allergies. Too much grass in this country. "At least I'm original. I'm sure it required imagination for you to think of 'John.' Just like the Americans say it, 'John Doe.' You might as well have kept 'Jung Ho.'"

"I like Sunhee, or even Sunny, better than Anastasia."

She smiled and rubbed her stomach. "Anastasia could use a foot rub. Anastasia is tired."

"Okay, okay," he said, balancing the notebook on the edge of the nightstand beside the lamp. "But my turn next." As he grabbed her foot, pressed his thumb into the arch, she closed her eyes, savoring his hands, his fingers on her skin. She purred and laughed as he inadvertently tickled her now very sensitive toes. But in less than a minute, his motions became mechanical, harried, as if his mind had ventured elsewhere already, rather than remain in that moment, in those seconds beside her, inhaling the life that they had—both its mundane beauty and sadness—that was still, when considered under a certain light, miraculous. So many people had died in the war. So many people lost. So many families torn apart. Literally. And here they were—*feeling* something. All their senses, their limbs intact. Alive.

As he massaged her calves, her thighs tingled. She shut her eyes, struck by the memory of her college art studio in Seoul where she had spent so many hours pressing globs of paint straight from the tube onto the palette, colors with strange names like Cadmium Green, Napthol Scarlet, and Raw Umber. She remembered the prickle of excitement as she presented her paintings to her favorite professor, Cho Myunghwa, who had been in her late twenties and had studied at Beaux-Arts de Paris and could speak four languages. Her father had been a diplomat. Never pretentious or too precious, she had a gentle seriousness about her, a relaxed and open face, bright and round as a full moon, and a very solid but slim stature like a dancer's. When considering her work, Professor Cho leaned in close and Sunhee caught the scent of cigarettes, ashy but intoxicating, although none of the students had ever seen her smoke. She didn't know if she wanted to be Professor Cho, or if she simply wanted to be near her to absorb her confidence and untouchability, what Americans would describe as "cool."

The last time she had seen Professor Cho had been two months before she had met her now husband, years after she had graduated from college. She chanced upon the professor at the gallery show of one of Sunhee's friends, a ceramicist of mostly whitewall, rich and creamy porcelain inspired by the Joseon era. As Sunhee contemplated the subtle peach undertone of a moon jar's glaze, she felt a finger tuck a lock of her own hair behind her ear. She couldn't help but jump a little at the sight of Professor Cho next to her, wearing a slinky aubergine dress with billowing sleeves split at the shoulders, like Diana Ross, arms exposed. Sunhee had been accustomed to seeing her in studio clothes, loose cotton work pants and chore jackets, unaffectedly androgynous, functional. Here in this impressive gallery space, she was a disco queen with arched eyebrows and hair voluminously coiffed.

"The color of that jar," Professor Cho said, "reminds me of skin." She tilted her head as if to take in a different angle. "That smear, the peachiness of it. As if the jar itself is a face, painted white, and someone had taken two fingers and simply removed the makeup right there." She made a funny kissing sound into the air.

Sunhee could see it too. And the narrow base of the moon jar was a neck.

"What are you painting these days?" Professor Cho asked. "Besides your lips."

Sunhee laughed, self-conscious. Years ago, Professor Cho would have never joked with her former student this way, nor would she have ever touched Sunhee's hair and ear the way she had just done, startling Sunhee with a tiny zap of static.

She didn't know how to say this to her former professor, but she had no desire to paint the still lifes and landscapes she had specialized in. They bored her now. She wanted to do something else, but what? She yearned to invent something different, define a style for herself. Something dark and fashionable that would express not how accurately she could mirror or idealize the world, the goodness around her, but what she felt inside. It was the 1970s after all. There was often a disconnect between the reality she shared with the world and what was in her mind. Surrealism—the unsettling of images, strange juxtapositions, such as Magritte's two lovers kissing, shrouded as individuals in white cloth, the darkness and its humor—made sense. But nobody would understand that, especially her family. They would tell her to go back to painting peonies and cherry blossoms, cranes and Mandarin ducks. Maybe she was never meant to be an artist like her father, and it was just a way to lure a future husband, the way some women played instruments or sang simply to impress guests at dinner parties. Maybe Professor Cho would've understood, but if Sunhee opened one door, she might never be able to close it again.

She could feel her husband staring at her with his handsome face, his thick, straight brows, and she smiled in an attempt to hide how complicated her feelings had become. He had, in a way he would never understand, saved her from herself. If he knew, if he ever understood, he would leave her. And that would be the worst fate of all. A woman's role was to encourage, to inspire. She was his companion. Who was she to think that she deserved her own life? But some days she wanted, she yearned, to show and share something more—as if she had been trapped within a single chapter of a story.

1999

In the heart of Koreatown, next to a wide, nearly treeless intersection where cars stampeded through green and yellow lights, star jasmine twined through Sunny Nursery's rusted wrought iron fence. Watering a line of ficus, shaggy and weeping in the dark, Ronald yawned. He hadn't slept at all last night. After hanging out with Peggy and her friends in Pasadena, including a drive-through run for curly fries they'd dangled like ribbons into their mouths, laughing, he had come home later than expected. He'd planned to creep through the front door, past his father's bedroom to his own, and close his eyes before his Saturday-morning shift. But as he approached the house, which glowed from behind with an eerie bluish-white light, like the setting of an alien abduction, he noticed two police cars out front.

Breathless, he said, "Oh shit" to himself. Something had happened. The first thing that crossed his mind was that his father was dead.

He had a heart attack or stroke.

This was it. Now Ronald and Ana had no one left.

As he parked on a side street, heart beating like the wings of a moth, Ronald repeated to himself, *What am I gonna do now?* He almost fell, tripping over the bottoms of his baggy jeans as he ascended the slope of the concrete driveway. A technician in a jumpsuit passed him without a word or eye contact when Ronald asked, "Hey, what happened, man?"

Ronald's sneakers crunched on the gravel of the path running alongside the house toward the backyard, cordoned off by yellow tape and filled with strangers. Both he and his father had avoided the problems in that yard for so long, the overgrown weeds, the thorny vines. Despite the distraction of a photographer's flash, he searched for someone or something familiar in this unknown version of his home, the frightful spectacle, the scene of a crime.

His father sat on the steps down from the house's back door that led to the kitchen, head in his knobby hands. "Thank God," Ronald said, panting. The fog of his breath billowed out of his mouth. "Dad? What happened?" A cramp twisted like a knife in his ribs. "Are you okay?"

His father gazed up at him, then he closed his eyes. How lost and confused his father appeared. Stunned and childlike. Ronald had never seen his father like this.

"Somebody died in our yard," his father said. "Fruit tree. Next to fruit tree."

"What?"

"Somebody homeless. Homeless man." He gestured toward the garage. "Go inside, okay? Everything going to be okay."

"But—"

"Go inside. Inside house." His face hardened. The boy who had appeared a minute ago disappeared. "Police do their job. Working now."

He was indeed the father that Ronald had always known. But Ronald sensed the callousness of his father's words was a cover-up for his father's particular and endless brand of desolation. They had never needed the police before, the police who did not find their mother, who must've thought of her as another dead or missing woman in a working-class area, a victim of a negligent and unkempt household. The police did not save their father's gas station or any of the surrounding small businesses where immigrants had poured their entire lives, which had been burned and destroyed during the riots. What would the police do for them now?

Leaving his father outside, Ronald sneaked onto Instant Messenger and found Peggy's away message: "Sweet dreams." The luxury of having your internet on at such odd hours. But who had been the intended audience? Definitely not him since she knew how restricted his time on AIM had been—despite those damn free CDs. Why did his father have to be so cheap? Ronald needed someone to talk to, but who would be up at this hour? His sister would be asleep. He would be seeing her tomorrow. Then again, how could she even help him make sense of what was happening in his backyard? His father would find some dumb way to blame him, that Ronald had left the gate unlocked when he had taken out the trash earlier, that it was all his fault someone had died outside their house like a wild animal. No wonder why his mother ran away. His father's temper had been constant enough to become boring, pitiful, and banal. But his private intensity made him terrifying, like a volcano always threatening to erupt with its signals of smoke trailing off the skin of the earth. His father had never hit him, but he had grabbed him before, pulled his arm and shoved him against a wall. Even if Ronald was now stronger, he still flinched at the daggers in his father's face. The bullets in his eyes. His mouth, a loaded weapon.

How did his mother ever love his father? Love required soil-like softness to take root.

And who was the dead stranger next to the loquat tree? Ronald had an urge to see the body, to know who this man was. What would a homeless man be doing in the backyard? Most of the homeless people lived in more commercial areas of the city, like downtown, or at gas stations or freeway exits. How could something like this happen behind their house? Why here? Why now?

Eventually Ronald fell into a fretful sleep. Hours later, after everyone had left, his father knocked on his bedroom door, startling him awake.

In the darkness, Ronald asked, "What happened?"

"I find him," his father said. "Look like sleeping."

"So he was just dead?"

"We talk later."

Ronald knew there was more to the story, but his father treated him like a child. He was seventeen already—almost an adult.

"Don't tell your sister about this, okay?"

"Why not?" Ronald asked, surprising himself. "Why should we keep this from her?" When his father didn't respond, Ronald said, "Are you scared that she'll never come back, that you'll give her more reasons to hate this place?" His voice cracked.

The silence was overwhelming. Ronald could almost hear his father's heart breaking. Why did he have to say that? She didn't necessarily hate this house; she just couldn't stand it here anymore after their mother had gone. No one could stand it, the oppressive quiet her absence left behind.

His father sighed. "She's . . . your sister is very stressed, too much. Let's make nice. Okay?"

Remembering those words now at Sunny Nursery, Ronald watered the one-gallon shrubs in the morning's purplish tint, as the sun began its ascent, leaking light in the east through cloud and haze. He pulled his hood off his head. He would never admit it out loud, but his father was right this time. What would be the point of telling Ana all of this when she arrived today? They could wait until tomorrow, let her settle in, relax. The last time he had spoken to her, weeks ago, she had been distressed about her job, about the life she had chosen for herself. She needed them to be strong for her. He had to protect her. That was what his mother would want.

Dirty water from the containers sprayed on the old sneakers he wore at work. He enjoyed the job at the nursery despite the early hours, and how his father, who this morning had been oddly quiet, usually nitpicked and bossed him around. The plants thrived in this haven where water trickled over rocks in a small stone fountain with a spout made of bamboo, a ceramic frog on a lily pond. Behind the nursery were older homes with security bars over their windows and patchy lawns, some of which had been replaced entirely by concrete in order to accommodate more cars behind fences. Across the street, a strip mall served as a bustling location of commerce and congregation—a bridal shop with a white dress behind the always-dusty plate glass, a Korean bookstore, a billiards hall with neon signs and tinted windows, a bakery with delectable cream puffs (Ana's favorite). He'd make sure to grab a few before they headed home. What else would his mother have done? She would've cooked something nice for Ana. She would've made her all her favorite foods—haemul pajeon, japchae, bibimbap. She would've spent the last week or so preparing more kimchi and banchan for her arrival.

That's what he'd do. Ana would understand that he was trying—finally, maybe. For once, he had only to find the right language.

The sun baked Ana's face through the rectangle of powder-blue sky as she flew home to Los Angeles, perhaps one last time before the end of the world. Beside her, a boy of about eight or nine contemplated her like a museum piece. She imagined herself from his point of view: her fresh-shorn hair and the buzz cut that revealed, much to her dismay, an indentation at the back of her skull; her eyes rimmed with heavy liner; the flamboyance of the amethyst pashmina around her shoulders; her dull black combat boots. She had studied hard in school her entire life, become an expert on seeing the world through *their* lens—white, straight, and male. And she had spent her time in Berkeley as an English and ethnic studies major, "decolonizing" herself, yet still she knew how to put herself in the boy's shoes, not only in a sort of clinical sense, but with empathy and grace, something this world seemed to have so little of for her, and her mother especially.

Before she went missing a year ago, her mother had already been invisible in so many ways—immigrant, working-class, middle aged, foreign, and with the permanent scar of an accent. When she evaporated from their lives, no one had any answers. From what Ana could tell, the police could do nothing. To set up rewards their family would have needed private funds, which they didn't have. Ana leaned back, shutting her eyes, taking long breaths in through the nose and out through the mouth, quelling her travel sickness for the hour-and-a-half flight.

Although her mother had been on an airplane only a handful of times, she had loved flying, admitted that she dreamed of being a Korean Amelia Earhart in one of those open-top planes with a pair of fogged goggles and an aviator cap. Ana had only learned about this the one time they had all traveled by air together when accompanying Ana to college four years ago. Her mother had requested to say hello to the flight crew in the cockpit. Her father had fumed and asked that she please sit down, while Ana and Ronald squirmed in their seats. Ana couldn't tell who embarrassed her more: her mother with her childlike charm or her father with his lack of humor.

Chewing her already short nails in her fingerless gloves, Ana relived, as if it were just yesterday, the morning she had found out her mother was missing. Ana had been in her apartment, which smelled of the fresh dark-roast coffee she had brewed, poured for herself. A second cup. She creaked open the lid of her gray Toshiba laptop, which was the thickness of Ronald Takaki's *Strangers from a Different Shore*. The phone rang.

"Ana?" her father asked. His breathing, loud and steady, the engine that she, despite her frustration, loved possibly more than anyone. How she had always secretly yearned to make him happy, whole.

"Yes?"

"Mommy." His voice cracked.

The tenderness of that word. *Mommy.*

"Yesterday night, Mommy go out."

"What happened?"

"She go out. No home, not home *yet*." He corrected himself.

"What?"

"She come back."

"What do you mean? What time did she leave?"

"Ten or eleven. Ten. I don't know."

"I don't . . . I don't understand." The dam broke. She burst into tears. "Where was she supposed to— What?" She had the sudden urge to throw the receiver against the wall as if it had betrayed her. Ana had planned to be back home in two days for Christmas break.

"Where's Ronald?" she asked as if he were gone too. "Is he there?" The tone in her voice suggested: *I can't trust him with you.*

"He is in his room."

"Is he okay?" She sat down on her bed and wiped her face with her T-shirt collar.

Her father never answered.

"What happened? I don't understand. Why was she— What was she out doing so late anyways?" She could hear his breathing, short and quick, as if for the past few minutes, he had been laboring to preserve himself, his calm and steady tone, but he couldn't handle it anymore. She worried for her father too at that moment. "Did you get into another fight?"

Her father didn't answer, and she gritted her teeth. Of course the answer was yes. But now was not the time, was it? He could have a heart attack. And *she* would be responsible for that.

Covering her mouth with her hand, she closed her eyes and sat down on her bed. The phone cord stretched as far as it could reach. She wanted to scream. She couldn't help but imagine her mother slumped in the driver's seat of their beige Oldsmobile, bruised and splashed in red. But there was nothing abstract about this expression. The body was the most actual. Her mother, who beamed in black-and-white photos beneath a diaphanous hanbok, the billowing skirt the size of her heart, had been beautiful and bright once—before she came *here*. Ana would never forgive this country. She'd never forgive her father, despite how much she loved him.

It was *him*. *He* did this. Blood on his hands.

"I'll find a way to get there today. I have to pack now." Ana hung up the phone and curled herself on the bed, hiding her face from the morning light, wan and gray, but too bright. She had so much to do now. She'd have to call the airline and change her ticket. She couldn't find a tissue within arm's reach, so she stripped her pillow of its case, held it to her face. "Umma. Umma," she said, like a child lost on a crowded street. "Umma," she screamed, surprising herself when she realized that now her mother was that child lost. She didn't care if anyone heard her. She had been her mother's daughter, yes, but in many ways, as an American-born child, she had been responsible for her parents as immigrants. She carried the weight of being the translator, the interpreter of their dreams, not simply a body who moved through space, one life, but an entire continent of all the times her parents closed their mouths or looked away, had been spat upon in different ways, had toiled in silence without pay or a single acknowledgment by the world that they mattered, they were irreplaceable. They had not simply been casualties of war, chess pieces to be played, workhorses who should not complain, immigrants and refugees; they were her mother, her father. Inexplicable. Singular in every way.

On the plane now, almost one year after that phone call, after the grief of their lives had become concrete, palpable, a mother gone, a family of four minus one, Ana wiped the tears from her eyes with the end of her sleeve. Her mother would've been in the kitchen busying herself—pickling, stewing, frying pajeon in a skillet, which she'd stack on a plate for them to reheat whenever hungry. She always planned and prepared for them, their needs. The home that Ana would return to would never be the same.

In this cramped vestibule that smelled of honey-roasted peanuts, socks, and aftershave, Ana reached into her purse for her copy of Adrienne Rich's *The Will to Change*. She stared absently at the lines and wondered how her father would ever understand that, since her mother had disappeared, she hated going home because she still blamed him. He was in his sixties now, with high blood pressure and cholesterol. She couldn't lose him. As much as she resented him, he and Ronald were all that she had left. They still needed each other. She loved him.

She knew her mother was dead but could never say it out loud. Her brother still believed that their mother would return one day. It was obvious. And who knew what her father really believed, despite his declaration over the summer that she had probably died. He was a pragmatist. Practically, a survivalist. But his heart, the truth of it, had always been a mystery.

After he rubbed his face dry, John caught himself in the plant nursery's bathroom mirror, splotched from sprays of soap and water. Tears blurred his eyes, slipped down his nose and onto his lips, which he licked and wiped. Ronald was working with him today, and John kept his sobs quiet to avoid his son overhearing. He had not cried in years, not when his gas station, his entire livelihood, had been destroyed during the riots. Not even after his wife's disappearance. But last night . . . the man's shoes, the white envelope with his wife's name on it . . .

John hiccupped as his face burned. He seated himself on the grimy laminate floor and leaned his back against the toilet bowl. After he had discovered the body, he had placed the letter to Sunny in his pocket and bolted for the house, inserted his dentures, and fumbled with the phone as he called 911. A man was in his yard. He was not moving. Did he check for a pulse? No, he was too terrified. He could not go back out there. A man was dead. He was Black. He couldn't tell how old he was. Please come help. He didn't want to touch him. He smelled of urine and waste. He was probably homeless.

Outside, his neighbor Rodriguez had responded first, flashlight in hand. His royal-blue robe draped down on the ground as he crouched and nudged the leg of the man beneath the loquat tree.

He shook his head and said, "He's dead," before rising to stand.

When the investigators arrived, Rodriguez stood on the sidewalk and waited for John. His Christmas decorations twinkled in the chaos of the police's flashing blue lights.

"Homeless people. They're everywhere these days," Rodriguez said.

Despite the burgundy windbreaker he wore, John shivered in his thin pajamas.

"I need another fence," John said. "A taller one, I think."

"I know a guy who can do it for you. Maybe I need one too. Not a chain-link. Too easy to climb. Like a metal one, you know? Who knows these days."

"Yeah, I will wait until January. Maybe the world end."

"Ha, you believe in that shit?" Rodriguez asked.

John envied Rodriguez, who had never married or had kids and lived by himself. Occasionally, family members or a friend would visit, but never a girlfriend or spouse. He knew very little about Rodriguez except that he worked as a contractor in construction of some sort. His large white truck always had two-by-fours, building and paint supplies in its bed. John assumed because of his tattoos that he had been some sort of gang member, but his life appeared simple, easy, and nonviolent. He spent the majority of his free time gardening—weeding and pruning and propagating his impressive cacti and succulent collection.

Now, outside the bathroom, the nursery's phone rang. John hoisted himself off the floor with a hand on the toilet lid and sprinted toward his office, hoping it might be the wholesale truck, which hadn't arrived this morning as expected.

"Mr. Kim? It's Detective Coleman. Los Angeles Police Department."

The detective from last night—a man in his fifties who appeared to be Latino despite his English last name. He had shown up a couple hours after the initial police officers had arrived, even though John had overheard that the death appeared to be an accident, a head injury incurred after a fall. So the words "Los Angeles Police Department" alarmed him. What more could they want? John had spent so much time last night already with the bright lights, the investigators in his yard.

"I have some more questions about the man who was found on your property. Ronald Jones."

John gripped the receiver, his knuckles white. The stranger shared a name with his son. The envelope beside his arm had been addressed to John's wife.

"I'd like to come by again today if that's alright?"

But John needed to pick up his daughter in a couple hours. His little girl. His Ana. And now she would have to know about what happened. Before they had left, the investigators had even done an excellent job of cleaning up after themselves in the dark, removing the yellow tape and leaving John to hose down the yard. He hadn't planned on telling her until after a couple days, didn't want to sully her arrival with such terrible news, a dead man behind their house, homeless and probably hungry. "I wanted to come by while it's still light out."

"My daughter is coming home today," John said.

"Do you understand what I'm saying?"

Now he'd have to leave work early with Ronald and Ana to meet Detective Coleman. He couldn't even spare her from this tragedy.

After he hung up the phone, John rubbed his head as if to erase his thoughts.

"Everything okay?" Ronald appeared in the doorway, startling him. "Are you gonna leave to pick up Ana soon? I can do it if you're too tired."

"No, no, that's okay." John would tell them about the detective once everyone was together.

Ronald stood in front of him for a moment too long, then finally said, "Do you think on the way home we could stop by the market? I was thinking of making some banchan, kimchi while Ana's here."

"*Kimchi?*" John almost laughed. Someone had died in their yard last night. Suddenly his son had cooking ambitions? "You know how to make kimchi?"

"I think so. Maybe."

"How do you know how to make kimchi? Mommy teach you?"

"Forget about it."

He could feel his son boiling. Something cracked inside his chest. "We have to go home right away, okay? Police come over."

"Again?"

His throat was dry. "We can go . . . later. We can go after dinner, okay?"

"Forget about it. I'll do it myself." Ronald slammed the door behind him.

John remembered all those hours Sunny had spent in the kitchen as she had prepared banchan and kimchi that would last them for weeks, even months. He had caught glimpses of her sometimes with the children in front of the stove, or at the kitchen counter, the cutting board. He never realized how hard it had been to feed everyone, how much she had put into those meals, which he could never re-create. How many dishes she had washed, how many pots and pans scrubbed under the water that dried her hands despite the fact that she covered them with oversized magenta rubber gloves. It wasn't easy, but she always made it look that way. She never wanted them to worry about her. And now his son planned to prepare something for Ana, welcome her home, not as if they weren't missing their mother, but to say, *We still have this place; we still have time together.*

Maybe his son had been paying attention after all. Maybe it was John who wasn't. His dreams had been so big, but now he felt small. He was like a child again, a thirteen-year-old who'd fled, who couldn't even make the choice to stay behind with his mother. His ears rang with the whistles of bombs dropping overhead. *Keep running. Faster, faster.* He wept in his hands. He couldn't help himself. *Coward.* A man had died behind the home they had built.

When John had caught a glimpse of the flimsy rectangle of paper, splotched with liquid, a few feet from the stranger, he had assumed that the man had stolen their mail, a letter to Sunny, his wife. John snatched the envelope and hid it beneath his mattress before he dialed 911. It remained there, unopened.

But the detective didn't need to know about that. No one would.

1981

While her daughter read books in their bedroom, Sunny scrubbed the Harvest Gold of the vinyl kitchen floor, stopping only to wipe the sweat off her brow with her forearm. The ground of their cramped one-bedroom apartment had become the canvas of their lives, splattered with pieces of food from the mornings when she rushed to prepare her husband and daughter their favorite American breakfast of bacon and eggs, the afternoons when she sliced and sautéed banchan for dinner, and the evenings when she boiled jjigaes and guks, frying gulbi or mackerel on a skillet.

For lunch, her husband insisted on buying fast food—greasy cheeseburgers and fries, hot dogs smothered in the kind of chili that permanently stained clothes, a deli sandwich wrapped in white paper or a teriyaki plate, gleaming. She couldn't understand why he would want to eat a stranger's food when she could pack him something more nutritious, a dosirak or kimbap stuffed with vegetables sautéed and danmuji, bright and yellow as the petals of mustard flower. But oh, how he adored the food in America.

She closed her eyes and inhaled as deeply as she could. Her nausea made everything, even the simplest tasks, so much more tedious. So she relied on only a rag and a bucket of water, the bright lemon-scented dish soap for the kitchen and bathroom.

She needed air. She wouldn't tell her husband about her pregnancy until she knew for sure that she would keep the baby, welcome the child to this world with open arms.

She slowly stood up from the damp floor, supporting her lower back with her hand, and stepped around books and toys strewn all over the living room to open the balcony door. A warm breeze greeted her as well as the banda music, the bump of its brass, from another open window. She hummed and tapped her feet and moved to the rhythm by herself. How free she felt outside. How free she felt listening to other people's music.

On hot and dry days like this—despite it already being autumn—Sunny craved naengmyeon, the slurp of those cold, chewy noodles that stretched from the mouth, the tartness, the tingle on the tongue. Time had slipped by like soft white flour between her fingers. Ana had become so big and strong since those first hours nearly four years ago, when she had glowed in the glum light of the hospital room, eyes closed, soggy-looking and tender, wearing the tiniest hat above that smooshed face, a full moon. The brightness, the gravitational pull of her. The sweet smell of cream, the delicious powder. Sunny could stare at and kiss her cheeks forever. And the love overwhelmed her, submerging her like a high tide along with any regrets she might have had about marrying Kim Jung Ho, about moving to this country, displacing herself for this city of heat and smog. Here breathed and cried and laughed the most perfect person in the world. Sunny was honored to be her mother, grateful and humbled.

But no one had warned her about how lonely she would feel—giving and giving and giving and still never feeling like she was enough. Or perhaps she was the only woman who experienced this ache. Perhaps she was a terrible person. Perhaps she had not been cut out for motherhood at all. Too selfish, loved pleasure too much, loved herself too much. Despite all the years that had passed, her hand cramped with the memory of holding a brush, the grinding down of mineral and vegetable and glue in the pigment sticks for watercolors, the dark colors bleeding gently into paper, the lick of the horsehair brush on inviting mulberry sheets like the first snow of winter. All of her supplies remained in a box somewhere inside their bedroom closet. There was no time.

Soon after she had given birth to Ana four years ago, her father had died of pancreatic cancer. Sunny had never even truly understood him being gone, except that he was no longer available to answer the phone back home in Korea. She couldn't travel for the funeral. She had to take care of her daughter, who was less than two months old, and her husband first. She missed so much about her father—the beauty of his long face, the quiet stillness of his large brown eyes beneath the tweed or wool flat caps he always wore, the elegance of his crossed legs, his reluctant smile, and how he sketched and painted her with love. She had adored the privilege of watching him work in his studio, the odor of those oil pigments, reds and blues and yellows, squeezed from precious little tubes. He mixed them into the earthen tones that reminded him of the dirt and the land that he had left behind in the North when they had fled during the war, his sisters enshrined in his art, their geometric faces that reminded her both of Modigliani and Picasso. How his brush, his palette, his canvas carried the weight of history. Art made our hauntings not only tolerable but communal, and therefore powerful, like trauma transformed into treasure.

Tears spilled out of her eyes as she gripped the balcony railing, which was covered in dirt and dust, and sat herself down on the bumpy stucco of the balcony floor. Sunny was so tired she couldn't even hear the music anymore, just the pumping of her heart in her chest. The nausea. She didn't care if anyone could see her—a mother alone, a housewife crying by herself, an immigrant who missed her family back home.

Over the past five years, Sunny had made many friends at church, but most of the women lived in the suburbs and, during the week, spent their days at work—their convenience or clothing stores, restaurants, and dry-cleaning businesses—where they could bring their children on days off from school. Since her husband still worked for wages at a gas station, an unsuitable environment for kids anyways, Sunny had no choice but to stay at home until her daughter started preschool or kindergarten. She had kept in touch with her classmates and neighbors in Korea, but the phone calls and letters had been too expensive to keep up, a luxury to connect over such a great distance. Once a year she received a long letter from Professor Cho, which she would sign at the end with two fingerprints that had been dipped in peach paint, a reminder of the moon jar and its glaze. *What are you painting these days?* she had asked. *Besides your lips.* And the answer now was nothing. Absolutely nothing. Sunny cleaned and scrubbed. She picked toys off the ground.

The only person Sunny could count on was an elderly neighbor, Mrs. Lee, who had immigrated to Hawaii in the 1920s to work on a sugar plantation, then moved to Los Angeles to reside closer to the families of her adult children. They lived in Orange County's Garden Grove, but Mrs. Lee preferred Koreatown where she could walk everywhere. With her thin, long face, wrinkled and beaming from her partially toothless smile, Mrs. Lee watched Ana for a couple hours so that Sunny could ride the bus to the post office or buy groceries and housewares from the Korean market.

"Hello, little bulldozer, hello," Mrs. Lee would say when Sunny dropped Ana off at her apartment, one floor down from theirs. She bent over and tried to pick up Ana but could not. "She is getting heavier and heavier every day."

"Grandma, please be careful. Don't strain yourself."

"Who, me?" Mrs. Lee laughed. "Oh, honey, I gave birth in a dirt hole three times in the fields. Each time I went right back to work. I was in the strikes. I threw rocks at police. Don't worry about me."

In the few months that she had known her, Sunny grew to love Mrs. Lee like her own mother. Despite the difficulties of Mrs. Lee's life, her eyes had remained delightful and bright behind the mask of her weathered skin. Unlike the other grandmothers Sunny knew, Mrs. Lee did not dye her white hair, proud of her years and the wisdom and dignity that came with them. She inspired Sunny into believing that despite her hardships, her loneliness, she could still find sources of pleasure and magic in everyday life.

America was still a strange country to Sunny. She was convinced that she could never learn the language. She tried. She folded laundry and cleaned the apartment while reciting English phrases from the television or out of an instructional book. "Hello, how are you?" "My name is Sunny. What is yours?" "See you in a while, crocodile." "Welcome to [insert franchise here]. How may I help you?"

But she went only to the Korean grocery or home goods store, and even when she mailed letters or packages abroad, the post office in Koreatown had Koreans working behind the counter. Her husband paid the bills and completed any official documents or transactions that required English. Despite his accent, he was fluent. So, how could she learn the language? How could she adjust, melt into the larger culture? Where were the opportunities to do so? The only non-Koreans that she encountered on a regular basis were their neighbors, Mexican and Central American immigrants who struggled with English themselves. She would almost be better off learning Spanish, the language of the music that bumped through the walls.

She couldn't stand this apartment, which always smelled a little moldy despite how hard she scrubbed, the dim lighting from the alley of garbage bins, the closed curtains of the neighboring building. This country, this loneliness, her husband's work—six days per week, gone for almost twelve hours per day—was killing her slowly, tearing her apart, piece by piece, cell by cell, dismantling her as if she were being sold for parts.

She longed for her family in Korea, for the snow that crunched beneath her boots, the hot chestnuts sold by vendors along wet streets back home, the sounds and smells of the market, of fish scales frying on pans, mounds of kimchi and squid, women and men bartering and slurping with chill-burnt faces and laughter. There was so much to feel, to taste, to touch. Perhaps because of the war, so much loss and death in their lives, people didn't take their senses for granted.

Maybe she would tell her husband that she needed to visit Korea. She could take Ana. It would be important for Ana to meet Sunny's sister and mother, who, like Sunny's father, could pass away any day now. It would be important for her to know her heritage and culture.

Maybe tonight Sunny would tell him the news. *I'm pregnant.* Maybe another child would glue them together. Maybe another child, a boy for him, would help them hold on to their lives a little more. All of them. Maybe tonight.

"Daddy is here," Ana screamed. John hoisted her off the ground, his arms streaked with grease, muscles straining. Sunny wished he would take a bath before touching their daughter. She turned away, covering her mouth with a half-closed fist at the smell of gasoline on her husband's clothes. Did he even notice how weak and light-headed she had been lately? The room melted around her and she steadied herself on the arm of the couch.

"You are so heavy," he said in English, beaming as he returned Ana to the ground. John unbuttoned his khaki work shirt, stripped himself down to his white tank top and underwear, before hopping in the shower. Sunny went to the narrow kitchen and clicked on the stove to reheat the miyeok guk with its dark gelatinous leaves of seaweed in a beef broth, sesame oil shimmering on the surface. She never even liked cooking much. Her mother always had such poise and command in the kitchen. Yet here in America, preparing banchan and jjigaes and guks not only fed her family but reminded them to hold on to their pasts, the creativity that allowed them to survive not only winters and storms but war and every attempt other countries had made to erase them—their language, their customs, their names—from this earth. There was fire in this food, a burning personality, dogged persistence. She didn't care if her husband coveted the cheeseburgers and sandwiches and slices of pizza he ate at work. Cheater.

He could take whatever he wanted away from her, but he'd have to cut out her tongue.

She laid out the banchan—seasoned spinach, stir-fried fish cake, mak kimchi—for the two of them, since Ana had eaten dinner earlier by herself. She ladled the miyeok guk into the bowls with a pattern of mustard-colored butterflies and flowers on the outside edges. She always ensured that John received the most beef brisket that flavored the broth.

John emerged from the steamy bathroom, rubbing his thick mane, touched with gray at the temples. He rested on a dining chair with a towel draped over his shoulder. On her stomach, Ana squeezed herself beneath the long coffee table, impersonating an anteater, which she had learned about in one of the many books they had gotten from the library. Her tongue flicked in and out of her mouth. Sunny remembered that Ana, too, would need a bath tonight after how much applesauce she had gotten into her sticky hair, how Sunny would have to bend down again despite her back pain. She loved Ana's face when she splashed in the water with the pile of foam on her head, but Sunny felt weak, heavy, and tired. She wanted to sleep for days.

Before she could gather the courage to tell him about her pregnancy, another baby unplanned, John said with an almost childlike joy: "I bought a gas station."

"What?" Sunny asked. She had known about the bank loan he had applied for, but she hadn't heard about the approval yet, or that he would or could move so quickly on purchasing his own business, a first. Troubled by the prospect of another child when they were already scrambling, working so hard to survive, she had forgotten about his dream of ownership. John would have even less time for her and the children. And he would never allow them to help out at a gas station. It would be too dangerous. If she were to get a job herself in Koreatown, they'd have to pay someone to watch the baby, which they couldn't afford to do either. Why should she have this baby, then? Why should she even tell him? It was her body anyways.

"This will be so much better for us," he said. His eyes gleamed. "I can make my own hours. I can hire help. Eventually, it'll pay itself off."

She stood, nearly knocking over her seat. She needed air. Another baby and a new business without even a place to really call home—only this dark, cramped apartment with the mold growing in the grout, only the music and the neighbor's voices muffled through the walls. It was too much for her. It was too much for anyone. She remembered now how for weeks after coming home from the hospital, Ana had howled for seemingly hours on end, how Sunny had rocked and bounced her until her arms grew numb while a burning sensation shot down the back of her leg. The baby seemed to be crying on behalf of all of them. How Sunny's mind collapsed with the repetition—the feeding, the diapering, the laundering—as if she rode a delightful yet deranged merry-go-round with no exit. How many days she had gone without sleep, without eating a full meal, or without showering in order to keep her child clean, nourished, and well rested while her husband squeegeed windshields and filled up tanks and tires to support them all on his wages from the gas station. And how did she survive at all? She needed family. She needed extra hands. There was never enough time to scrub and wash and bathe and soothe. She hardly recognized herself in the mirror. The light had left her eyes. She had evaporated somehow.

But where was she? Where had Sunny gone?

She was trapped in a painting, *The Lovers*, kissing through fabric, lips shrouded in white. A preparation for burial. It was someone else's art. It wasn't even her husband's, was it? It was bigger than them. It was bigger than God. It was America. She had never before felt this inadequate, despite how well-meaning, hardworking she could be.

"What about a house?" Her voice broke as she stared out the balcony at the beige exterior of the next building, illuminated by a security light. A neighbor's television broadcast the news. "Don't you think we should first focus on a larger place for—"

"We'll focus on that next. I promise, okay? It'll be better once Ana starts preschool. It won't feel so small. We will save. And then we'll have room for another—"

"Where is it?" she interrupted, wiping away the tears that slid down her cheeks before he could see them. She knew what he was about to say—*baby*.

"It's in South LA."

Why couldn't he have told her in advance? Maybe they could've found a business that they could run together—a dry cleaner or a corner store in Koreatown—so that she could get out of the house more often, or bring the children by. Eventually, they could help too. She didn't want to stay at home full-time. It wasn't for her, and never would be. She'd have to change herself too much. But instead she asked like a knee-jerk reaction: "What kind of an area is it in?"

"What do you mean?" he asked.

"Do you know how much I will worry?" she asked. "You have a child now. A family. You'll have to work longer hours. At night—"

"I don't want to talk about this." He gazed into the bowl in front of him, pressing his lips together. "It's very expensive to start a business here. It was the only place I could afford."

"But what about us?"

"I do everything for you and Ana," he said.

Sunny didn't know how to respond. She believed him, but why couldn't he realize that she mattered too? Buying a business was a long-term decision, and he either thought she wasn't intelligent enough to be part of the process or that she didn't have a particular point of view. He should've known better.

"All you do is work," she said. "It's too dangerous for you. You'll have to work at night I bet." She sat down at the table with her head in her hands. "What kind of an area is it in?" She knew that *he knew* what she meant. *Is it mostly Black people too?*

He didn't answer. Instead, he streaked the condensation off his glass. "How could you judge people that you don't know a thing about?"

"The women at church talk about them all the time." Maybe once or twice they had, but nonetheless, she said, "They destroy their own neighborhood. They're angry." She couldn't identify the exact source of what she parroted now, but it felt powerful to say these words out loud, as if her voice could disappear into the safety of a vicious, well-rehearsed chorus. It was so much easier to blame other people, people you didn't know. Because *she* was angry all the time.

John hurled his glass of water like a grenade toward the kitchen, where it shattered on the floor, the vinyl she had spent so many hours on her knees wiping and scrubbing down.

"Daddy," Ana screamed, panic in her voice.

Sunny closed her eyes, trying to calm herself. There wasn't a victory worth hurting her daughter.

"Don't you remember the things that we went through?" In the kitchen, John crouched down, picking up the glass. He was referring to the war, and not only the war, but before, when Korea had been a colony of Japan, when they had been forced into another language, new names, the erasure of their histories, their families, and they lived like ghosts without bodies to call their own. "People are people, everywhere," he said. "We all want the same things." He dropped the shattered cup into the trash. "We all want a better life." His voice broke. "That's what we all have, that's what we all want. A future. A future for ourselves, our children."

"But it's the present that I hate the most," Sunny said, surprising herself. Tears streamed down her face as if to water the seeds, the words she could not take back now. How much of a failure Sunny felt like here, where she'd always be inadequate to everyone she loved. She couldn't even fulfill herself let alone her child, her husband. She never felt like enough. Perhaps her husband could be comfortable with this, this perpetual sense of scarcity, but she could not. She longed for a life that was lived in the movement of her hand, the movement of a brush licking paper as she swayed to music with her lips upturned into a smile, the smell of the pajeon in the markets frying on a winter night, the sound of her mother singing and singing. Two fingers pressed into the side of a white moon jar, two fingers that revealed the color of its flesh, the peach. How even through the most terrible of times—war, hunger, death—Sunny always found the strength to admire every scrap of beauty she could find with the most tender parts of her mind, from the persimmons that danced as they hung from twine after they had been plucked from trees, the clack of her heels as she ran away on stone-cobbled streets, the sheets on their heads as they played peekaboo with Ana, the lovers shrouded like death while they kissed. They could not see each other and we could not see them.

Ana cried in the corner of the living room, where she had huddled into herself. John rushed to pick her up off the floor. Her hero.

He carried her to the room they shared, comforting her as best he could. He said in English, "I'm sorry to scare you. Daddy was wrong, okay?"

Sunny's heart broke. She knew that in a way he was talking to her too. When did he stop being able to really speak with her? Maybe they had become terrified of each other, terrified of hurting and being hurt by each other. Maybe he regretted his decision, but she could feel it was too late. She wanted to say, *I'm losing my mind. I miss my family back home. I never even got to say goodbye to my father. I miss walking down the street and not feeling so alone. I'm terrified of this world.* Instead she scanned the now-empty room and sat down in front of her miyeok guk, which had already gone cold. He hadn't even taken a single bite. She should've known that he had probably eaten already, filling himself on fast food. But this life, this dream of his, was consuming her alive. She picked up the bowl and forced the broth down her throat, feeding their unborn child. She ate and ate until she no longer felt anymore.

1999

Hair shorn down to an inch of her head, Ana had been hardly recog- nizable to John, despite the familiar combat boots worn year-round, and the purple shawl around her shoulders, which softened the edges of her face, as well as her personality that, in adulthood, had gotten quite hard. Although she was tough in so many ways now, he remembered her most as a charming, dimpled child with a bright smile and sparkling eyes. Without her long locks, which she usually wore in a ponytail or braid, she appeared vulnerable, like a featherless baby bird. How he missed being able to scoop her off the ground, the way she'd sit in his arms and play with his face, rub his stubble and giggle. She had the squishiest arms that reminded him of fresh tteok, doughy and warm. He could gobble them up.

Now Ana laughed at his stare, rubbing her head with her hand. "What? You don't like it?"

"I like it." John embraced her. She smelled herbaceous, almost minty, like the chaparral on his Sunday hikes.

As they drove home from the nursery with Ana in the passenger seat and his son slouched in the back, he told her about the man he had found dead behind their house. Ana herself had worked in housing services, so of course the idea of a homeless man dying in their yard would disturb her. Someone that vulnerable, tired, and hungry struck a different nerve. He could understand that. But the man could've also been a threat to their safety. Who knew how long he had been in their yard, watching them? Who knew what he could've stolen? Maybe even a life.

"And he was just dead?" Ana asked. "So now this cop, he's going to come by and what?"

"He wants to talk. I don't know."

John thought of what the detective had said. That the stranger's name was Ronald Jones.

Ana sighed out loud. Worry clouded her face. "I can't believe that happened," she said, breaking the tense silence like a pickax.

In front of their bandage-colored house, a white Ford Bronco was parked. Detective Coleman emerged with a notebook and a heavy-looking file. In his navy blazer, scrunched in the back from having sat too long, he appeared different under what had been left of the day's light—a boyishly square face, irregular and mottled, printed with the faint outline of a shaved mustache and a permanent smirk. John wanted to like him, but, for whatever reason, could not.

"Either of you here last night?" Coleman asked, gesturing toward Ana and Ronald.

Before they could answer, John said, "No, no, she come this morning. Berkeley. UC Berkeley. My daughter Ana. My son, not here, out. He go out at night."

Coleman tilted his head at Ronald. "What was your name again?"

"Uh, Ronald Kim." He tugged on the stretched-out neck of his oversized gray T-shirt.

Coleman lifted his brows as he jotted this down. There was anger, maybe frustration in his face, his forehead and brows. It was a difficult job, John understood this. Dangerous. Everyone painted the police as the bad guys, the pigs, but the horrors these men must experience on a daily basis were like a war that would never end. Even if Sunny pointed out how little they had protected their family's livelihood during the riots, and how law enforcement officers harmed people with such intensity because of the color of their skin, the lack of consequences, John always reminded her that the stressful nature of the police's responsibilities made mistakes inevitable. If she knew or encountered criminals like he had at the gas station on a daily basis, she would understand.

And it was strange to think now that Sunny had once been such a different person. When Ana was young, before Ronald's birth, she had believed that the area he had bought his first gas station in would be too dangerous. *They destroy their own neighborhood. They're angry*. He remembered the distinct shame and satisfaction of shattering his glass of water on the ground.

After all his years in America, as a small business owner and the victim of calamitous losses such as the destruction of his gas station in the riots, John now believed that lawful citizens knew to stay out of the police's way, pay their bills, keep their heads down. Sunny and his children had been too sheltered and idealistic to understand how difficult it was to maintain law and order when desperation, anger, even boredom drove people to vandalize, murder, intrude.

"And *your* name?" Ana asked, crossing her arms in front of her chest. Her tone embarrassed John. Couldn't she show him some respect? The officer had a gun under his jacket. They could all see that. Who did she think she was? Berkeley graduate.

"Coleman. Ernesto Coleman. Would you like my badge number too, young lady?"

"No, that's okay. Maybe I should go grab a notebook myself."

Coleman shook his head, snickered. "And who were you out with?" he asked Ronald.

"My girlfriend, Peggy. I was in La Cañada the whole time. Uh, I left around eight? I got back late."

Did Coleman think his son could've been involved? Sweat glided down the side of John's ribs. Sure, his son wore baggy jeans and didn't get good grades, but he never hurt anyone. Never. His son was innocent.

After Ronald had given the detective as much information as he could, John motioned for his kids to go inside the house, while he followed Coleman to the backyard. Coleman surveyed the loquat tree, dusty and thick leaved, where John had found the body. He dug through the dense passionflower vines on the fence that separated their property from Rodriguez's. John kept his distance. Coleman tested the side door on the garage, which had been untouched and locked for years.

"Any indication of burglary?" Coleman asked. "Anything missing? Did you notice anything different yesterday?"

"No," John said, as sweat streamed down his neck. The letter, still unopened. He had snatched it from the ground, *his* ground. And only John would ever know.

The detective puffed air out of his mouth, stepping on a pile of cat shit, which he didn't even notice. "I spoke to your neighbor, Mr. Rodriguez, a little while ago. Do you mind if we talk inside?"

To John's relief, Coleman slipped off his shoes at the door. They sat as far as they could from each other on the soft tan couch, which Sunny had purchased after they had saved enough money almost fifteen years ago. He remembered the stress of all that furniture shopping, how they had never spent so much money in their entire lives, and what a luxury that had been, two refugees, children of war, who had learned to run to save themselves, now rooted to this place through this great big American home.

Coleman scanned the room, hunched a little over his open knees, fingers laced. His eyes appeared dull, as if he might be hungry or exhausted. It had been a long night for him too.

"Something to drink?" John asked. "Water? Tea?"

"No, no thank you."

John couldn't help but notice, from the detective's point of view, the tidy living room with only touches of personality and charm once created by Sunny—a bouquet of dried red roses in a glass vase, some doilies, two of her father's oil paintings, and framed photographs of Ana and Ronald as children. How long had it been since a stranger, or anyone outside of his family, entered this house? It must've been well over a year, since even before her disappearance.

"Is there a Sunny Kim here?" Coleman asked.

"No, no, no." John shook his head.

"Gone? Passed away?"

"She disappeared." The words ripped his heart out of his mouth. "My wife. Last year." John couldn't tell him now about the envelope with her name on it that he had found beside the body. He should've told the police about it last night.

But it belonged to him. It *was* his. He hadn't even read it yet. And no one else needed to know about such a personal matter when the man's death was an accident.

Coleman glanced up and down the walls, stained by hands over time, sloppily repainted through the years. He scrunched his face at a family photo on the wall. "Mr. Kim, the man you found in your backyard was homeless," Coleman said. "His name was Ronald Jones, but he went by RJ. Since your yard is bare and very dry, there are no footprints or indication of where he might've entered. But I suspect he had been spending the night and climbed the fence when he heard your approach. He would've slipped or fallen and hit his head." He knocked on the wood coffee table with his knuckles. "Hard as a rock."

John flinched at the sound. He couldn't understand what exactly Coleman wanted, but he had been prying into their lives unnecessarily. RJ was a stranger who happened to die on his property.

"He had a notebook on him with her name and your address in it. *Sunny Kim*. Know about this?"

"Notebook? No, I don't understand," John said.

"Kind of a coincidence, right?"

"I don't understand." His head pounded.

"That he died here. And he had *your* address in his notebook. Even if it was an accident. Strange, wouldn't you say? Like they knew each other. RJ and Sunny."

"No. Maybe he steal name. Maybe he *use* name. I don't know him. I don't know."

Coleman adjusted himself in his seat, which revealed his gun, heavy and sagging, secured in a black holster. John had never gotten rid of his own snub-nosed revolver, which he kept below the counter in a fireproof safe at the nursery. Maybe now that he had found a dead man in his yard, he needed one here. A Glock, like the detective's. Who knew who was lurking out there in the dark? He should move the gun to his bedroom at least. He needed to protect his children at the end of the world. Who knew who could die next?

"Have you seen anyone else in your backyard?" Coleman asked.

"No, never," he said. "One time, maybe long time ago, a dog. Always cats. Lot of cats."

Coleman coughed as if covering a laugh, but John was serious.

"And you've never spoken to or seen this man before in your life? I have some photos from when he was young." Coleman held up a color photocopy of RJ in front of a nondescript administrative-looking building. He wore what appeared to be a janitor's uniform. The brash midday sun created shadows and obscured the details of his face. He could've been anyone. But the light had been distinctively Southern Californian, pure and harsh. "This was from when he worked at one of our stations down south. Vista Park. In the seventies, early eighties, he was a custodial attendant."

"*Custodial?*" John asked.

"A janitor for the police department."

On the coffee table, Coleman placed another image of RJ in front of a dusky view of Los Angeles. With his wide-set eyes, long face, his tidy beard and mustache, he was as attractive as an actor or a movie star. John couldn't believe that this had been the same man, the man who died, thin and gray in his backyard.

"Your son's name is Ronald," Coleman said.

"Yes, we named him, my wife name him because Ronald Reagan. President." The last one John had actually voted for.

"Good man," Coleman said with a nod of his head. "Miss those days."

John couldn't agree more. Things had been simple back then.

"I already spoke to your neighbor, Mr. Rodriguez. And Mrs. Clemsey, your other neighbor, the elderly woman next door. Nice lady. Mr. Rodriguez had been out front and didn't see anyone last night except you, when you retrieved the mail, and your son earlier when he left. He said he appeared to be in a hurry. So the only other way to enter your property would be from the rear, over the fence. Do you know who lives back there?"

"No." John couldn't even imagine who they were. So many of his neighbors had become old and reclusive through the years, with children or grandchildren moving in and out of houses. He couldn't keep track of all the people, only recognized a different car parked now and then, here or there. The neighborhood had always been in flux. Once, he'd even observed a young white couple unloading a moving van a few blocks away, white people who stood out like pale aliens that lived in the television set, or reminded him of the US military during the war. Except these white people had no muscles. He'd wondered if they were destitute or lost. Why else would they live here? But then he realized they had made the house "attractive," with its dark sage paint, a custom-made fence of rusted steel, exotic plants he had never even seen before despite owning a nursery, and heavy-duty string lights intended to be up all year.

"Might he have dropped anything that we could've missed? A backpack? A bag?"

"No. I don't know." John picked up the color copy of RJ in front of the city. He too had once been handsome and young, and now how did they all appear? He squinted as he held the image at arm's length. John, a taxpaying, law-abiding citizen, had nothing to do with him. "I don't know him."

Coleman brushed the front of his slacks as he stood up from the couch. His knees cracked. John couldn't move, but a wave of relief washed over him as Coleman stepped toward the front door.

"If you happen to remember or find anything, give me a call, alright, Mr. Kim?" He slipped on his shoes. "You know, sometimes stuff happens and we forget or block it out. Especially as we get older."

The photographs remained in front of John. "The photos. You want them?"

"No, you can keep those. They're copies. Ask your neighbors. Ask around if you have time."

John's legs trembled beneath him. "Was he . . . were you, uh . . . looking for him?" he asked.

"You might say that. Sure." Coleman smirked and slipped a cigarette out of a packet. "If you find anything, let me know, okay, Mr. Kim? Don't want to mess with any of this." He pulled a lighter out of his navy blazer pocket, which once again revealed his gun.

As he watched Coleman drive away in the dark, John fumed at this invasion. The dead man in his yard must've been wanted by the police, a criminal. As if John didn't have enough to deal with at the end of the world.

From underneath his mattress, he retrieved the letter. The rectangle of paper, dappled with water, its security print—a crosshatched blue soaked at the corner—had been addressed in a fluid cursive to none other than her. Sunny Kim. A stranger's handwriting.

Clearly, the person who wrote her name didn't know that she had been missing for almost a year.

There was so much anger and regret in him these days, and he didn't know what to do with it. Regret and regret and regret. That was all he could feel. It had taken over his life. The burning. But no fire would be enormous enough to erase his emotions, his memory. The things he wanted to forget. Once, an American GI had taunted him and his father with a bar of chocolate that they, laughing, threw on the side of the road as they drove away in their truck. Stomach bloated from starvation, he bit into the candy only to be struck by the foulness of human shit inside. His father smacked him on the side of the head, an explosion of stars, and yelled that he'd leave him behind like his mother if he kept getting sick.

The betrayals of that time. The calamities of a war that turned a family against itself. Even though he had died long ago, his father's bony but powerful hand, the grin on the soldier's face, the air raids and the napalm that lit children on fire, boiled them alive, had been imprinted on him.

In the living room, John ripped up the unopened envelope along with the copies of RJ's photos and threw them into the trash can he kept for recycling near the front door. He didn't care about this man, what he knew, or why he was in his backyard.

Get out of my house, he wanted to scream at them all. *What if my wife comes home? Get her name out of your mouth.*

After her father stormed to the kitchen, Ana scrambled from where she had been hiding next to the living room doorway and pocketed the pieces of paper that she had just witnessed him tear apart. She found her brother in his bedroom and shared the parts that she had been able to overhear of their father's conversation with the detective—that although RJ had died by accident, there had been suspicion regarding his whereabouts, his belongings. *Might he have dropped anything that we could've missed?* Their mother's name and their address had been in his notebook.

On the soft carpet of her brother's bedroom, Ana and Ronald taped together the letter and photocopied images of RJ while their father prepared dinner in the kitchen. Some words had smeared from liquid or water and were unreadable.

DEAR SUN ____________________ GRATEFUL WE _____N INTO EACH OTHER. A MIRACLE. YOU HAVE SAVED ME MORE THAN ONCE AND YOU DON'T EVEN KNOW IT.

I'VE BEEN WORK____ ON ______________ AND HAVE COME BY YOUR HOUSE FOR ____________________. I TRIED CALLING BUT ______________________. I ALSO NOTICED YOUR CAR ____________ MISSING. I WANTED TO LEAVE THIS LETTER SO YOU'LL KNOW I WAS HERE, AND TO __________________.

I AM NEVER IN ONE PLACE BUT IF YOU NEED TO ___________, FIND JANET WHO WORKS AT THE LIBRARY ON DERBYSHIRE. I'LL CHECK IN WITH _________________________.

I HAVE ALSO BEEN USING YOUR ADDRESS FOR A LIBRARY CARD. I HAVE CHECKED OUT AND RETURNED ALL MY BOOKS. ONE DAY, I HOPE TO EXPLAIN __________ MORE ____________.

I HOPE ONE DAY WE'LL MEET AGAIN. I HAVE SO MUCH TO TELL YOU. —RJ

He *knew* their mother.

Where had her father gotten this letter? Had it been in the mailbox? Or maybe RJ had delivered it a while ago and returned to check if their mother had received it? There was no date on it, no stamp.

"How did Mom *save* RJ?" Ronald asked. "And what did he come here for? What did he need to tell her?"

"He clearly didn't know that she's been gone." The letter trembled in Ana's hands, and despite how hard she tried to suppress them, tears spilled out of her eyes.

They needed their mother to translate these words, fill in the spaces that were meant for her.

If only their mother had been here to save RJ again.

Ana picked up the torn photocopied images. Where had Coleman gotten these photos from? Did RJ have them on him when he died? In one snapshot, RJ was at the Griffith Observatory with the LA skyline in the background. Ana's pulse quickened with recognition, followed by the memory of shame, the secret she had kept. She and Ronald had been there with their mother, yes—but without her father. Ana had been maybe six or seven. It had been the first time she had ever been trusted with a camera. She had closed her right eye and pressed the other to a viewfinder and focused it on him.

RJ.

Ana had taken this photograph herself.

But prior to this moment, she couldn't remember his face or his name. She'd never seen him again.

How had RJ known her mother? Had they been lovers? Imagining her mother as romantic or sexual disturbed her. Ana had never seen any affection between her parents, who kept their interactions short and businesslike. She believed that after Ronald had been born, they fell out of love, bound together simply by the obligations of a family, splitting the duties of raising two children in a foreign country that had often been inhospitable. No matter that she had been born here, no matter how well she spoke English, Ana had still been barraged with fake Chinese words yelled at her as she walked down the street, or mistaken for the only other East Asian woman at work, despite stark differences in their appearances and personalities. And yet in this unit they had created to get by, this family, could it have been possible for her mother to live without love for nearly two decades?

Seeing her face, Ronald asked, "You recognize him?"

Her brother was old enough, had a girlfriend of his own. Would he be able to handle that his mother might have desires outside the family, the routines that protected them?

"You wouldn't remember this," Ana said, "but when you were really young, like maybe two years old, Mom took us to the Observatory. With a man."

"A relative?"

"No, I'm pretty sure he wasn't," she said with the photograph of RJ in her hand. "She never explained who he was. But she called him a friend."

"Do you remember anything else from that day?" her brother asked.

Ana drew a blank.

How and when could their mother and RJ have met? Under what circumstances? None of it made sense. Their mother spent every day in Koreatown, which had become more and more Latino. She spoke very little English and had consumed herself with tending their house, cooking, cleaning, and only recently, art and gardening. She lived a sheltered existence. Ana knew so little about what her mother wanted, who her mother had been outside of being their caretaker.

"And his name," Ronald said.

"I know." It couldn't have been just a coincidence that her brother shared a name with RJ, could it? Their father always said they had named him after the president at the time.

"Should we tell Dad?" Ronald cringed. "About the Observatory."

"No, I don't think so. I'm not sure why that would matter to him now, right? I mean, Mom is gone, and RJ is . . . dead. It would just upset him in a way that . . . we couldn't help him understand. We don't have any answers yet," Ana said.

"But don't you think we should at least ask him about the letter? Why he ripped it up?"

"I am sure he saw her name on the envelope and it upset him," Ana said. "Maybe it's the first time he's seen her name on anything in a while. It could've been in the mailbox. Maybe RJ dropped it there before he went into the backyard to hide and look for Mom, or even . . . spend the night. He could've done all this while Dad was watching TV." Her heart quickened as she imagined RJ's desperation. "Maybe he heard Dad approach, tried to climb back over the fence, and fell down."

"Why would he do that?" Ronald asked.

"Because he was an intruder. He must've known that if Dad caught him . . . he'd call the police, or worse."

"Do you think the police . . . should know about this?" He held the letter in his hands. "And your memory of the Observatory. Does someone need to know about this? What if there's a lot more to his death than anyone realizes? And there's this Janet too. Maybe they'll need to question her. Maybe—"

"I'm not sure we want to do that yet. If anything, this letter is something between RJ and Mom, don't you think?" Ana wondered if it would be helpful or harmful to let the police know about RJ's connection to their mother. It wouldn't bring RJ back from the dead, and they hadn't been particularly interested in the fact that she was missing. "I mean, what do you think RJ would've wanted?"

"We'll never know," Ronald said.

"He wanted Mom to have this letter. She had something of his, and until we can figure out what, it might be best to leave the police out of it. Besides, that Coleman was . . . something was off about him, don't you think?"

With his long and narrow face, Ronald didn't look like Ana at all. Not a single one of their features resembled the other's. She always thought of her brother as handsome from their mother's side, and herself plain like their father. But then again, she had seen photos of her father in the sixties and seventies when he had still smiled, when his leanness was athletic, even glamorous. And yet all she could think about was how he appeared to her now—frail and spotted, his hair graying rapidly at the temples, his mouth always tightly closed, pressed into a frown, his bitterness written all over him like paintings in a dark cave.

"Since he wrote this letter, RJ didn't know Mom was missing." He adjusted the position of his legs beneath him on the floor.

"Right, but that doesn't mean the two aren't connected somehow," Ana said. "His death, her disappearance. Maybe Janet knows something."

If they could figure out more about RJ and how he was connected to their mother, perhaps they would learn something about her that could provide clues to her whereabouts, or what had really happened to her.

A knock on the door. "Dinner's ready," their father said. "I make jjigae, okay? Sorry, nothing nice, okay? Sorry. Tomorrow." His footsteps shuffled away on the carpet. Ana imagined that he had already set the table for three—two pairs of chopsticks for her brother and father, a fork for her.

"Let's go." Ana squeezed Ronald's knee before she heaved herself off the floor. "We can talk about this later."

"Nah. I can't eat." He lay on his bed and covered his face with his arms.

"Do you want the light on?"

"No, turn it off. Thanks." The defeat in his voice. What she would give to lighten the load of their lives. How she had believed that going to college and getting a decent day job would propel her and maybe even her entire family into an easier existence. Following the path of least resistance did work for many people, but others, like herself, only got lost along the way. She had been torn between doing good for the world and taking care of the family who loved her, who needed her most. She should just go to law school even if her heart wasn't in it. And her father wouldn't have to work so hard and maybe he could finally relax. She could pay off his house, and he could live here for the rest of his life.

In the breakfast nook, her father waited, head lowered. He picked up his metal chopsticks, not because he was hungry, but to signal that it was okay for Ana to start. It was his way of saying, *Go ahead. Please eat. I tried my best to make you something so that you stay healthy, so that you stay strong.* It was his silent form of love, which had felt at times inadequate, but ultimately truthful.

Tears filled her eyes. She touched her fork. She couldn't look at him. She wanted to ask him about the letter, where he had gotten it, why he had ripped it up, but she also knew that a confrontation with him now, after such a heavy twenty-four hours, wouldn't result in anything but more anguish and disappointment on his part. Of course, he tore up the letter because their mother's name upset him in a way that he couldn't handle or process. She should wait a couple days at least before she mentioned it.

With a loud sigh, he tapped his chopsticks on the table, evening them out. "Mommy wants you, your brother to be happy. Happy together."

As they ate in silence, she smiled at him every now and then, but he never seemed to notice, too preoccupied with his own self. She needed him to see her, tell her she was fine the way she was, that all the pain and sadness would pass, that they would be okay in the end, if they could just make it through, make it through one more day, one more year without *her.*

"Lot of work, today, tomorrow." He blew his nose on his napkin. "Sleep early."

It was all that he could take, all that he could think about, because any more than this would break him. And yet because he concealed himself so much, she never felt like she got to know him. All she knew is that he loved to hike. That he had lost his mother and siblings in the war—a brother, a sister, a home. That he hated his stepmother and didn't get along with his stepbrothers. That his father had died and that it hurt him. She knew how much he hurt by how little he could speak of the past, as if the words themselves might shatter him. He was bound by the routines that kept him safe, like one of the nursery plants in a container. And she supposed that was fine for him. That's how he survived—bunched together, knotted, and dried out. But the roots needed air. They needed water.

What if she said the thing she could never take back?

The phone rang, the sound releasing the pressure in the room like a kettle that had come to a boil, and Ana rushed toward the sound. "Hello?"

"Sunny Kim?" said a woman's voice, groggy and tired.

Her name. To hear her mother's name in a stranger's mouth.

"This is her daughter, Ana."

"Can I speak to Sunny Kim?" She cleared her throat. "My name is Rhonda. My father died in your yard."

Ana's hands shook. She pressed the receiver against her cheek. It would leave a mark.

For a few seconds, she could hear only both of their breathing. The disembodied voice on the other side. *My father died in your yard.*

"I went to the coroner's office today to . . . to pick up his belongings," Rhonda continued.

Ana held her breath. The dread. Her family would be accountable for this death, wouldn't they? In some way or another. They would pay.

"I'm sorry," Ana said.

"There was a library card on him. And . . .your mother's name, your address and number . . . in this notebook. Do any of you know him?"

"No, I don't think so," Ana said. Should she tell her about the letter? RJ had mentioned that he had used their addresss for his library card. But

Ana couldn't answer the questions that were sure to follow of how her father had gotten hold of the letter or where it had come from, or when.

"Can I speak to Sunny? It's urgent."

"She's not here anymore."

"She died?"

"She's been missing for almost a year." How uncanny for her mother to come back this way. In the script of a dead stranger's hands. This morbid delivery. It was almost worse than if her body had arrived itself. They only had more questions than ever.

"Could I come by tomorrow? I'd like to speak with you or . . . your dad? Is he there?"

"Yes." She closed her eyes, preparing herself.

"He used to live near where you live now." Rhonda's voice broke. "He owned a house, too. I found out about that. I didn't know until recently, and I find it to be so strange that—" She stopped herself. "They took the house away. The bank. They took away everything when he lost his job. It was our family's house. His family's house since the forties. It was the first thing they owned."

How to respond? There was no language for this.

"He was a veteran. And they did him like that. He was even a janitor for the fuckin' LAPD. He did everything right. Everything." Her voice rose. The scratchy sound of a handkerchief against the phone.

"How did he end up . . ."

"He lost his job and things sort of . . . spiraled from there."

"I'm sorry," Ana said. No matter how many times she said it, she could not bring Rhonda's father back, nor could she erase the injustices of his life, the legacy of those crimes on Rhonda's life as well.

"Is there anything we can do to help you, your family?" Ana asked.

In the silence that followed, Ana wondered if Rhonda had hung up, and of course, maybe Ana's question had been inadequate, and useless, in what had sounded like a lifetime of grief.

Finally, Rhonda said, "A detective showed up at my house . . . by himself this morning."

Ana gripped the phone. Her fingers cramped.

"He came by to notify me of my father's death, yet I have no idea how he figured out where I live, or who I am. I haven't spoken to my father since I was a little kid. And I live all the way in Lancaster now."

Ana held her breath.

"He was asking a lot of questions, wanted photographs of my father if I had them."

Was it Coleman? She and her brother had been uneasy about him as well.

"Something is going on here," Rhonda said. "And if your mother is missing, I'd like to speak with your dad. I also find it very . . . unusual that my father had fallen in your yard at the same address in his notebook."

Was Rhonda suspicious of them, their family too? Even if their mother had been friends with RJ, she couldn't have had anything to do with the tragedies of his life, or his death. He could've hurt himself anywhere.

It was a terrible coincidence that he had died in their yard.

For now, Rhonda did not need to know about RJ's letter until Ana could understand what Rhonda believed about RJ—who he was, and if her parents had anything to do with him. She wanted to help Rhonda but couldn't involve her father, because what would be the point of opening up old wounds that he clearly could not handle? She had to protect him as best she could. What would be the point of two fathers gone?

The next day, John inched the Eldorado up the driveway after he noticed a forest-green Camaro parked outside the house. A Black woman, wearing a burgundy sweatshirt with jeans and sneakers, stood from the driver's-side door, glanced at her cell phone, and dropped it inside a leather tote. This must be Rhonda, who Ana said would be coming today. She wanted to see where her father had died.

In front of this stranger, John could feel the layers of himself peel away like the skin of garlic. And the thought of baring his accent, his foreignness, which he never reflected on day-to-day, because the majority of his neighbors and customers were now working- to middle-class immigrant families, made his heart race.

Rhonda extended her hand. Her grip was loose and soft, surprisingly tender. She must've been in her thirties or forties with short hair, not quite as short as his daughter's, but close on the sides and dyed blonde on top.

Ana and Ronald emerged from the front door. Instead of joining him at the nursery, they had stayed home all day by themselves to rest.

"I just want to say—" Ana paused, and John could see her blinking back tears. "I'm sorry for your loss." Rhonda lowered her eyes. "I wasn't here on Friday. I live up in Berkeley. We're all . . . we wish we could help somehow."

For those few seconds, Sunny appeared in Ana's face, her soft brown eyes, how they glistened, how her brow strained. Even though Ana mostly resembled him with her square jaw, low nose, and wide cheekbones, her eyes were undeniably her mother's, so much that at times it felt like a trick when he faced her, as if Sunny had been hiding inside Ana this whole time.

"I'm just . . . gonna do some things inside. But I'll be back in a bit." Ana wiped her face with the sleeve of her sweater as she crossed the lawn and then disappeared through their front door.

"Can I go to the supermarket now?" Ronald whispered. Even though they were outside, the grief was everywhere, like stacks of smoke rising. You could cough on the thickness of it. "Can I take the car?"

"Sure, sure, okay," John said, unclipping the car key from the clump he kept in his pocket. He couldn't remember what some of the keys had been for, but he was frightened of getting rid of the wrong one, so he accumulated them on rings, dirty and blackened from his work at the gas station and then the nursery, with a bright blue plastic dolphin, red ball balanced on its nose, that had been his daughter's—a souvenir from a trip to SeaWorld when they were kids. John slipped two twenty-dollar bills out of his wallet and into his son's hand.

Studying Ronald as he backed out, John recognized that it was like watching a younger version of himself drive away. He had the impulse to say, *Come back.*

"Is that where he—?" Rhonda gestured toward the gate that separated the driveway from the backyard.

Darkness encroached. His arms tingled as the nerve itched down the back of his left leg.

His feet crunched on the gravel of the old unused driveway along the side of the house. Rhonda followed behind him. He stepped down from the concrete pad and around the garage toward its rear where the loquat tree, dull from soot and smog, hungry, stood a few feet from the fence between his and Rodriguez's yard. Passionflower vines scrambled along the property line.

As he pointed to where he'd found RJ's body, his arm trembled.

"It was very dark," John said. "I think he was sleeping."

Rhonda raised her hand to cover her face, mouth twisted. She crouched down and pressed her palms against the soil as if she could absorb him, as if she could pull him from the earth into her arms. John had the sudden urge to reach out to her, offer some support, but he didn't. He could feel, strangely, her heart, heavy, breaking. Or maybe that was his own.

"Do you happen to know why your wife's name was in his notebook?" she asked as she settled into a seat on the ground. She must've been cold too. "I told your daughter over the phone . . . his notebook listed her name, and this address, the same place that he happened to die accidentally." There was a hint of accusation in her voice. Why hadn't his daughter warned him about this? Who was she trying to protect now?

"Your wife must've known my father somehow. There was a library card, too. Maybe they had met at the library."

John shook his head.

"Did the police question you?"

"A little. Not much."

"I don't understand why that detective—or *how* that detective even got my address. He treated me like I was guilty of something. I am just a daughter who lost a father twice." Her eyes filled with tears. "The first time was when he left me and my mother. And the second time was in your backyard."

"Maybe your father . . ."

"How many times can a person die?" She met his gaze, her eyes amber and catlike. "But I *will* find out what happened."

Ronald pulled up to the small Korean shopping mall and grabbed a ticket, which swung up the red-and-white-striped barrier arm of the parking lot. His mother had frequented all the nearby markets, but this was his favorite one, about ten to twenty minutes from where they lived, for its proximity to the glossy French-inspired bakery that sold fresh korokke. He loved the flaky fried exterior filled with curried potato, meat, and vegetable. Before leaving the mall, he'd grab a few tonight for his family to have for breakfast in the morning, as well as some cream-filled puffs, which his sister with her sweet tooth loved. Tomorrow after school, he'd make japchae for their dinner, though he had only a vague sense of what ingredients he'd need (some kind of lean beef, vegetables, egg?). He'd attempt to re-create his mother's mak kimchi. He'd also promised to pick up banchan from the prepared foods section for Peggy, who would be volunteering at the VA hospital where her parents worked this week.

Although they technically lived outside Koreatown in a nondescript, residential neighborhood of LA, he'd always felt as if he lived here because most of their shopping, their post office, and his father's business were located amid the jumble of Korean-language signs. Although his father, who spoke English fluently, didn't need Koreatown like some of its residents, especially the elderly who might never learn English, they still remained in the area. Who knew what would've happened if their mother had stayed? Maybe they would've found a smaller home in the suburbs. But it would be impossible to know. They had to remain here now, waiting for her of course. They could never move away even if their father pretended she was dead. Ronald knew the truth.

She would return one day.

And while their father had been at the nursery, he and Ana had spent the afternoon searching through every dresser, drawer, desk, shelf, and closet in the house, the cabinets in the kitchen, behind all their unused plates and bowls, beneath trays of cutlery for any clues, anything unusual that might link their mother to RJ.

I'VE BEEN WORK____ ON ___________ AND HAVE COME BY YOUR HOUSE FOR _______________.

But all they found was the sadness and the sense of emptiness they had expected in their encounters with the remains of their mother—her clothing, shoes, and makeup, the scrunchies she used to tie back her hair while she cooked. Their father had the keys to the garage, which was in a sense a relief, because he knew that there they would find her art supplies, their father's college coursework, and the mementos their mother had kept for them—the class reports and science projects from school, the awards and certificates they had acquired through the years. She had so much hope for him, and yet now he believed that he, with his mediocre grades and lack of college prospects, was failing not only himself, but her.

By himself, he felt foreign in the supermarket because his knowledge of the Korean language had always been poor, worse than his sister's, and the interactions with the Korean-speaking employees could be somewhat awkward and tense. Of course, everyone looked at his face and wondered why his parents didn't send him to Korean school, or they simply found it odd that a teenager would be running errands by himself. Where was this boy's mother? Who sends a boy out for groceries? He should be at home studying.

Alone in the shopping center parking lot for the first time in his life, Ronald felt a sense of panic rise as he realized that he had always counted on his parents to know exactly what to buy. Why didn't he pay more attention? Now all he had was his memory. He should get a cookbook or find one at the library. But how many Korean cookbooks would there be in English? Most people relied upon their families for this kind of information to be passed down. What made Ronald think that he could re-create his mother's dishes on his own? He pushed open his door, nearly hitting the elderly woman who'd climbed into the car beside him.

"Sorry," he said involuntarily in English, bowing his head.

She waved at him; she was fine.

He had visited his grandmother only once in Korea before she died. He must've been nine or ten years old at the time. She had short gray permed hair and a long, brusque face. But something about the way she'd stand beside his mother and lecture her as they prepared their meals together made Ronald understand how much his grandmother loved his mother, her youngest daughter, and how much her hardness had been about the life she had lived, its tragedies and disappointments. She hugged him firmly. He remembered her smell—garlic and chives, briny as the sea. He wondered what his grandmother thought of his parents moving to a country where in a sense their lives had been financially and socially downgraded. Both his college-educated mother and father had, from what he could tell, come from middle- to upper-class backgrounds, and yet here in America they toiled without adequate healthcare and insurance, drove ragged cars, and couldn't even afford cable television. Ronald had never been to a dentist in his life. His sister attended UC Berkeley because she'd received boatloads of scholarships and grants.

He pushed a rickety shopping cart into the dried foods aisle for the noodles that he'd need. Easy enough, because the packaging of dangmyeon, which he could slowly read in Korean, had a picture of japchae printed on it. He backtracked to the refrigerated aisle, where he nabbed Peggy's favorite banchan—kkakdugi, seasoned spinach, and jangjorim—before he forgot. The only two white people in the market, a young artistic-looking couple wearing eyeglasses, stood analyzing the clear plastic packages like two scientists. They glanced at him, perhaps considering whether they should ask him for help, but decided against it and instead deposited the shredded dried squid in their basket.

Peggy would come by their house sometime this week after her volunteer work downtown. Was it downtown where her father worked or near UCLA? Without his own car, Ronald mostly relied on the bus and his feet; everything outside of Koreatown had seemed distant and remote, like separate planets. She had never actually been inside his house; he had been ashamed of the '80s furniture, dirty walls, and outdated bathrooms and kitchen. And she never pushed him about it, as if she understood his embarrassment.

Now he imagined her sitting in the dark belly of a VA administrative building. The other night, Peggy groaned over the mountain of paper files that she was helping to organize and transfer into some new system.

With a jolt, Ronald recalled Rhonda mentioning to his sister that RJ was a veteran.

"New system," Ronald said out loud to himself. If Peggy had access to these files, perhaps she could look RJ up? They knew his full name and could get a rough idea of his birth date from Rhonda. Maybe Peggy might find some clues about his life in those records. Was it possible they could even learn something about their mother, and how RJ knew her? It couldn't simply be a coincidence that she had disappeared almost one year before RJ's death. Their lives, if not their fates, had been intertwined.

Also, what war had he been a veteran of? Korean, Vietnam?

Ronald should get home as soon as possible. Rhonda could answer some of these questions. Then he'd call Peggy afterward.

But the vegetables. Did he have enough garlic and onion at home? He'd grab some extra, just in case. His father had been surprisingly generous when he handed him forty dollars.

He always remembered his mother saying that food should be colorful, that it should delight the eyes before you tasted it. The saturated dark green of the spinach contrasted against the bright orange carrots chopped into matchsticks. The thinly sliced mushrooms were brown, soft and chewy, the color of soil, dirt itself. Were they fresh?

As he stood in front of the shiitake mushrooms, confused, an ahjumma peered at the contents of his cart. She tapped him on the shoulder and shook her head.

"No?" he asked. His cheeks burned.

She pointed to a bag of dried mushrooms in her basket. "You need this one," she said in Korean.

"Ahhh." He nodded. "Gamsahabnida."

Back in the dried foods aisle, he snagged a package of roasted seaweed for snacking and shriveled shiitakes among the vegetables and roots which he couldn't name—earthy and vaguely medicinal-looking. Closer to the truth of this dish, he found himself unexpectedly alone again in the aisles of the market. Nothing could save him from the fact that he missed his mother and every day felt like fighting to get back to her somehow. He didn't know if he'd ever see her again. If she could see him, would she be proud of him? The plastic bag of dried mushrooms crinkled in his hand and his eyes filled with tears, but he stopped himself before they could fall and call more attention to him. If only he was as invisible as he always felt.

Ana pulled her pashmina over her head as she walked out the back door, passing her father, who didn't look at her. In the yard, Rhonda still sat beside the site of her father's death. The sky had purpled into the bruise of night. The loquat tree's gray trunk supported the heavy round crown of thick leathery leaves with sawtooth edges. Ana remembered how as a child her father had hoisted her up on his shoulders to twist and pluck the small yellow globes, honey-sweet fruit with large brown seeds. Despite their neglect, the tree grew, no matter how dusty, dehydrated, and cobweb-filled it had become.

Ana handed Rhonda the box of tissues that she had brought from the house.

"Can I get you anything else? Would you like some water?"

"No, no, that's okay." Rhonda wiped the tip of her nose. "I honestly wasn't expecting to come here and—" She stood up and brushed the dust off her legs. "I'm just surprised, I guess. I hardly knew him."

What would it be like to have a father, hungry and cold, dead so suddenly? Every person had been somebody's child at some point. If we thought about life that way, we might realize how much we all have in common, that someone had provided enough for us to survive, to be here now.

"Would you like to stay for dinner?" Ana asked. "We can order some food? It's a long drive back."

A strange invitation. To her knowledge, there had been no guests inside the house since her mother's disappearance, not even her mother's friends who had visited and dropped off food, reusable containers full of jjigaes and pajeon and kimchi. Her father had always made it seem so impenetrable, their front door. But Rhonda lived in Lancaster. It was far, and there'd be traffic, of course. Her mother would've invited her inside, fed her everything they had in the refrigerator, a humble and spontaneous feast, a gesture that proclaimed, *In our house, we are responsible for you.*

"Oh, no, that's okay," Rhonda finally said. "I'd rather wait till I get home."

"Would you like something before you leave at least? Some tea? It's pretty cold."

"That sounds good. I could use the restroom."

Illuminated by the amber of an old streetlight, they walked across the dead grass, up the concrete staircase to the back door, through the narrow kitchen into the dark and unused dining room where Ana gestured toward the bathroom. She sensed her father's nervousness, but she ignored him and steeped a bag of green tea, which her father drank all day long instead of coffee. She busied herself in the kitchen, washing and slicing two of the Gala apples her father kept in the fridge. She couldn't peel the fruit like her mother could, unwinding the skin with a paring knife, that single coiled ribbon. Uneven wedges would have to do.

Ana took the plate into the living room, where Rhonda sat on the couch. She raised her brows and smiled, ever so slightly. Perhaps, even though the gesture seemed silly, too formal, she recognized Ana's efforts. She lifted the dainty Corelle mug with its mustard-colored flowers and butterflies near the rim, the sight of which made Ana feel at home. Dishes clattered in the sink as her father tidied up the kitchen, busying himself.

"It's like the second time he's died," Rhonda said, long and narrow fingers wrapped around the cup. "He left me and my mother when I was young. My grandparents raised me. And I never really got to know him. Now . . . I'm stuck dealing with all this shit." She sipped the tea, then placed the mug down on top of its matching saucer. "I moved back here to Los Angeles. A few years ago. I thought I'd find him. Kind of silly, I guess."

"Where did you live before?"

"My mom and I moved to Alabama where her family is. After I graduated, I joined the army. Then I went to college, settled in Oakland for a while after that."

"In the Bay?"

"Yup."

"And once you moved back, you never found him? Your father?"

"No—my cousins knew him, or knew about him living in a motel." She sighed. "After a while, I kind of gave up, figured it wasn't meant to be. I'd lost track of him. I don't know. Maybe I could've . . ." She shook her head.

Ana herself had spent months worried frantically about her mother, unable to study or attend class. She drank and partied, which hadn't been part of her temperament at all, but she hadn't wanted to think about or feel anything.

"I imagine he spent a lot of time at the library." Rhonda looked at Ana. "He had a bunch of bookmarks. Titles, authors, written down in his notebook."

A jostling of the front door startled them.

"Who is it?" Ana asked.

"It's me." Her brother's voice. Ronald stood in the entry with several plastic bags of groceries in his hands, and removed his shoes.

"Did you get anything for us tonight?" Ana asked. "Rhonda might join us."

"Oh, no, I should be leaving soon," Rhonda said. Her eyes darted toward their father, who had entered the living room to help Ronald. "Your mother, Sunny. I'm sorry. I know she's missing. But do you have any idea where she is?" There was a hint of accusation in her voice. Ronald dropped the bags of groceries by his feet. "His notebook had her name in it," she continued. "This address."

Her father frowned in the most dramatic way that broke Ana's heart. She could sense the heaviness in his chest now. The weight of all he carried in this one life. How he shouldered everyone he had lost.

"Could they have been involved, you know . . . romantically?"

Ana's face burned. Rhonda had said it. She had said it out loud. Her poor father.

Rhonda stared at him, waiting for a response. Did she believe that their father had something to do with RJ's death, that their father of all people could harm someone like that?

"I'm sorry, but I really don't think my father would know," Ana said. She was so used to speaking on his behalf, on behalf of both her parents. The translator. The spokesperson.

"Have you gotten any updates from the police?" Ronald asked. Their father stood beside him still. How much Ana wanted to hold him. What was the chance of this happening behind their house, this house that had betrayed him in so many ways, this house that he had dreamed would be a place for all of them.

"Not since yesterday when the detective showed up at my house," Rhonda said. "He asked if I had seen anything unusual lately, if my father had tried to contact me, if he had sent me money or anything. I agreed to give the detective a couple photographs if he returned them, ones that I had found in my mother's house when she died." Rhonda shook her head. "But I never spoke to or even once heard from my father since I was a child. Shit. If it was an accident, why do the police care so much?"

"Wasn't he a vet?" Ronald asked.

"Doesn't matter if he was a vet or what," Rhonda snapped. "He was Black and homeless." She paused to take a deep breath, then said quietly, "Sunny's name was the only one in that notebook. I don't even know where to start looking to find out more about him."

Janet, the librarian. Derbyshire branch.

Ana couldn't mention any of this now since her father believed that he had destroyed the letter, and Ana had no idea how it ended up with him at all. Maybe Ana could say she found the note in the trash can—anyone could've thrown it out by accident—but why had it been torn apart?

Maybe she could still help Rhonda without showing her the letter.

"We can go to the shelters," Ana said. "The library. Maybe someone knows him, has some information."

"And my girlfriend is volunteering this week at the VA," Ronald said. "Her parents work there. Maybe I could ask her to do some digging . . . if you could give me some more information. His birth date and place."

Rhonda crossed her arms. "Why would you want to help?"

A question Ana had been asked in some shape or form many times. During her first year in college, Ana had been alone in her dorm room, sitting on her flimsy mattress, the phone cord wrapped around her finger as she spoke with her mother. Instead of studying, she had spent most of that fall semester organizing protests against Proposition 187, which would prohibit the use of public benefits—schools, healthcare, social services—by undocumented immigrants in California. And despite all their hard work, all the slammed doors they faced, the fliers discarded, the blank stares from strangers, the proposition, the "Save Our State" initiative, passed in the November election, 59 to 41 percent. Ana didn't understand how anyone could regard her and her friends, the children of immigrants, and sometimes undocumented themselves, as vermin, as a burden to this country in which they not only still paid taxes but worked and lived and raised families.

One day, she had tried to explain this to her mother, who replied in Korean, "Ana, you worry too much. Are you going to class?"

Ana maintained a C average by still reading the books and writing essays, but she was no longer pushing herself like she normally would. As much as she loved her classes, what was the point of working hard in a system that wouldn't allow you to live? But it was finals week and she was suffering. "Yes, of course, Mom. But—"

Her mother sighed, deflated. "Focus on class, okay? When you graduate, you can help other people. The most important thing is to work hard. You have to prove to the world why you are here, okay? You have to prove that you're good and smart. I know that you are. It's harder for us. We're immigrants."

The entire time Ana had been thinking in response: *But why do we have to prove ourselves to them? Why do we have to put our heads down? Why must we not rage and burn things down? Why do we have to prove our humanity, Mother? Why? Why isn't being alive good enough for them? Why must we work so hard all the time?*

But instead, Ana replied, "Okay."

Then her mother said, in English, word by word with such care, such tenderness: "You have a big heart."

Tears filled Ana's eyes as she recalled the strain and effort in her mother's mouth, on her tongue as she said those words as if she were saying, *If you remember anything, remember this now.*

Ana didn't know how to answer Rhonda's question. Not now. "How about tomorrow?" she asked.

Rhonda pinched the space between her brows. "Tomorrow what?"

"The library. Someone could know him there. I can do all the work," Ana continued. "Maybe you can bring some more pictures of him, if you have any?"

"Yeah. And I'll ask my girlfriend about the records tonight," Ronald said.

Ana could feel the tenseness of her father's body, his face, his mouth, as he reached for Ronald's bags of groceries on the floor. Her father wouldn't want any of them, including Peggy, involved. Wouldn't it be illegal for Peggy to snoop for RJ's records?

After a beat of silence, Rhonda nodded. "How do you know which library?"

Derbyshire was the closest branch to their house. Walking distance.

"I was just planning on going to the one near us," Ana said. "They could look up his account. They would know where he borrowed his books. But I guess I'm not sure if that's confidential or if I'll need proof of why—"

"I'll go with you," Rhonda said, her eyes steely.

"Of course," Ana said, unsure of what this meant. She had intended to find Janet right away, ask her about anything she might've been expecting from RJ, if he had dropped any clues in the past. Her father still stood with the groceries in his hands and his sad eyes.

Something had upset him enough to tear up the letter. Was it simply the sight of their mother's name?

Had he gotten the letter from the mailbox? Or from RJ himself?

"And no police," Rhonda said. "I can't trust them. They already got rid of my father once when they fired him."

1982

Stepping out the door of the dark apartment building, Sunny lifted her face to a bright cloudless sky. Mrs. Lee was watching Ana while Sunny ran errands. Breathless, she ambled down the sidewalk toward the bus stop. A soft breeze wagged the threads that hung from the bottom hem of her favorite skirt, which she'd had for years but now barely fit her. Its elastic waistband hugged the bottom of her cumbrous belly, like a moon jar itself, but stretched to its limit. With this pregnancy, unlike her first, she had gained so much more weight, not only in her stomach but throughout her body and face. She hated to see herself in the mirror, the brown splotches and the fine wrinkles. Her family, whom she hadn't seen in almost six years, wouldn't even recognize her. Her father, who had passed away soon after Ana was born, wouldn't have painted her.

She had planned to visit her family and friends in Seoul, but continued instability back home made her mother and sister wary of her traveling to

Korea, especially while pregnant and with a small child in tow. There were constant protests, violence in the streets, bloody demands for democracy under the current military regime. There was still so much uncertainty and fear in her country divided and brutalized, a nation, despite an armistice, at war with itself. Professor Cho had even penned a false address and name (Frida Kahlo) on the envelope when she alluded to an uprising in Gwangju in her last letter, a protest of tens of thousands that resulted in the murder of at least hundreds by the military. Anyone who spoke of the event could be considered a dissident. Professor Cho and her husband, whom she referred to as Diego, had contemplated a move to France or Canada. But they first wanted to have children before they uprooted themselves, which Sunny agreed with. How much easier life would've been to raise babies in a place where at least one's family would be there for support, helping hands.

Professor Cho as always signed the letter at the end with the two fingerprints made from peach paint. She remembered the moon jar. It wasn't only Sunny who could not forget. The reminder of that impression, and how it could travel through time within two separate people, with separate lives and families, instilled her with hope that they would meet again someday. And Sunny dreamed she could go back to not just Seoul, but to the North where she was born, to see all her friends and family laughing in one place over a boiling-hot jjigae on an unforgivingly cold night, or an icy bowl of naengmyeon on a humid evening when they opened all the windows and sweated through their light summer outfits. In Korea, each season had such a distinct personality and demanded adaptations and change, even in what they ate. In LA, the climate was so monotonous, sometimes onerous because the heat made it difficult to clean and cook. One day, one day, she prayed she would return to the North. If all the men who made decisions about war stopped to listen only to women and children, there'd be no option but peace. Children everywhere deserved to laugh and cry and storm, to call the entirety of the planet their home. The borders that divided us meant nothing to them at all.

America had been an answer to so many people who ran from all kinds of poverty, from all kinds of war. She had told herself that she had moved to America because she yearned for more freedom, an adventure, but in reality, she needed to get away from an entire country, torn and wounded, maybe even to get away from herself. When Professor Cho's fingers tucked Sunny's hair behind her ears, every inch of her skin tingled, her entire body flickered like a match that had been struck and dangerously lit. The stamps on the stomach of a jar. The impossible.

When Sunny finally reached the bus stop, she leaned on the back of the bench, gathering her breath. She settled down on the seat, leaving space between her and a Black man dressed in a charcoal gray shirt and matching Dickies pants, a work uniform, a notebook and a half-eaten apple in his hand.

The evening had grown uncomfortable, smelly and hot, as the fumes of the cars that rushed past gassed the air. She panted as her mind sloshed. Her body became a dark ocean, an ominous, white-crested wave rising.

The crash.

Her water broke, spilling down her legs and onto the ground. She screamed.

"Are you alright, lady? Shit." Beside her, the man dropped his apple, which rolled, almost comically, into the street. "Oh my God, lady. You're having a baby."

"Oh!" That's all she could say, until she uttered in fear and desperation, "'Welcome to [insert franchise here]. How may I help you?'"

He gave a surprised laugh, then said, "Listen, you need to try to relax. Do you have a husband or someone I can call?" He had a long face balanced by wide-set eyes, warm and bright, beneath a pronounced brow. A touch of gray speckled his short beard and hair, cut closely to his head.

She nodded, incredulous at the possibility of giving birth at a bus stop. Her first child had required almost five hours of pushing, but who knew about this one? She couldn't help but imagine her neighbor Mrs. Lee in a field of tall sugar cane, squatting over a hole in the dirt. That's how she had done it, and all her children had turned out perfectly healthy and strong.

"Do you have his number?" the man asked.

She reached inside her purse for her address book and placed the tip of her finger on the first page. He ran toward a pay phone at the gas station behind them. The wetness of her skirt cooled the skin between her legs. She shivered, teeth chattering, vulnerable on the side of a road on which cars zoomed by and honked, while she was covered in her own fluid. The embarrassment. The chill. The humiliation.

Breathing deeply through her mouth, she closed her eyes and reminded herself that she had plenty of time to go home, call the doctor, gather her overnight bag for the hospital. And how much she had loved Ana immediately when the nurse placed her on her chest, Ana's tiny head at the top of Sunny's breast over her own heart. Also how terrified she had been of being responsible for this new, tender life.

The stranger returned with a bottle of water. Sweat glided down the sides of his face, beaded his nose. He took her hand, tried to help her relax. She hadn't held a man's hand in a long time, not even her husband's.

But then all she could think about was the pain, the pushing, the baby, oh, another baby, the waves.

"Breathe, lady, breathe," he said. "You're gonna be alright. Your husband? He's coming for you now."

The rush of her heart. A wild animal's. The contractions gripped her. She nodded at the stranger, and as a bus approached them from down the street, she wanted to say in English, *Please don't leave me now.* She couldn't stand the idea of being at the bus stop alone, having wetted herself. Where could she go on her own? The stranger waved for the driver to pass. *Please don't leave me now.*

"Don't worry about it," he said. "I'll catch the next one." He laughed. "Not every day a lady gives birth at a bus stop." He wiped his brow with a handkerchief from his shirt pocket. "Whew."

His notebook fell to the ground. As he reached toward it, she glanced at his name tag and read out loud, "Ronald."

"Yeah, like the president," he said. "But everyone calls me RJ."

"RJ," she repeated. She couldn't understand what kind of name that would be: *Ar-jeh-ee? Arjay.*

"What's your name?"

"Sunny."

"That's a good one," he said. "Are you . . . Korean? GAHM-sahm-NEE-dah."

Despite the pain, she laughed at his pronunciation, the stress on the wrong syllables.

"I used to know some Koreans, in the war. I was in Vietnam though." He cleared his throat. "Yes, I did know Koreans there. Filipinos. Australians." His eyebrows twisted with a pang of something. "Your husband will be here soon, Sunny. Just hang on, okay?"

Tears leaked out of her eyes as she realized that her son would be born early. *Please God,* she thought to herself, *let him be healthy.* She swore that she'd never be unhappy again if God could ensure that they'd both live.

The contractions gripped her as she lay down on the bench. She cried out, "Umma." But who was she calling for—her mother or herself? RJ lifted and placed his jacket beneath her head. He rested his hand on her shoulder and she could feel some of her sadness melt away as she closed her eyes.

"Thank you," she said in English as a tear slid out of her eye. "Gamsahabnida."

She reached up and touched his fingers briefly before her husband pulled up beside them in their Oldsmobile sedan. The two men eased her off the bench and helped her plop down into the front seat. The car reeked of gasoline and cigarettes. Her husband paused before he slammed her door shut, caught his breath as he sweated through his tan work shirt. While they pulled away, Sunny laughed as RJ saluted her like a soldier.

1999

In the morning, Ana yawned as she waited outside the local library, a brick Tudor that resembled a cozy countryside house. She had driven her father in the Eldorado to the nursery at six a.m., still dark out, and then dropped Ronald off at school, his final week before the winter break. She had the car for the day. Tonight, her father would drive home in his work van that he used for picking up stock and local deliveries, a free service he offered that might've been responsible for keeping his business alive.

Somewhat embarrassingly, Ana disliked waking up early and had usually been late to her housing nonprofit job, which she'd quit a couple weeks ago. She hated—not its mission or its purpose, but the tediousness that seemed constant. Victories were few and far between. She needed more validation on a regular basis, or at least better dental insurance. But maybe her father had been right about something: she gave up too easily.

Not this time, with RJ. Or her own mother.

Last night after Rhonda's visit, her father disappeared into his bedroom and Ana grabbed his set of keys to open the side door of the garage. The smell of her mother's painting supplies and the dust and mold that grew on the windowsills made her ill. Cobwebs draped over her head, tickled her nose. A mouse caught in the glare of Ana's flashlight skittered across the floor. One day, they'd have to reckon with all the unused furniture, broken lamps, her mother's art, her father's books from graduate school, but not now. Too many emotions, abandoned selves, and memories emerged like ghosts without a story or sense of logic to guide her. She had to try again another day.

So, what did RJ want to pick up from her mother and what had he been "working on"? And why would her mother need to find Janet, the librarian? What did books have to do with anything? She hoped that something or someone here, inside the library she had frequented as a child, could shed light on RJ's—and maybe even her mother's—life.

A few minutes later, Ana spotted Rhonda as she approached, wide awake with a tall thermal mug in her hand. Ana couldn't help but feel guilty that she had kept RJ's letter secret, that Rhonda didn't know they were even looking for Janet. They exchanged stiff hellos and went inside the building where particles of dust floated in light filtered through stately windows that framed slanted gray limbs outside.

As a child, Ana would walk to this branch almost every Sunday, a museum of old wood and paper and floor wax, and would check out as many books as she could. With her backpack and arms full, she traipsed down the sidewalk, unbothered by the constant flow of cars that zoomed down the wide lanes. Back then and still now, stories organized the world. Their possibilities offered relief from the perpetual sense of being trapped in the chaos of her own home, the dynamics of her own family, this country, this difficulty of her own heart.

She thought of the first book that she cried while reading: Willa Cather's *My Ántonia.*

At the front desk, a young man in his early twenties was scanning the barcodes on a stack of returned books. Gone were the days of the card, the stamp, and the catalog, the gentle scrape of easing out the long wooden drawers to thumb through the soft, typewritten paper, like an apothecary in training who searched for the medicine that would cure or ease a loved one's ailments. As a child, Ana would find rolls of unused receipt paper on her father's desk at home and date-stamp them in tidy columns like a librarian.

She loved books still, but when did she forget that she found such great solace in the place where they could be read, borrowed, and shared, where they could be passed and circulated by touch inside an entire city or school or county? The quiet beauty of the library might be that even at the end of the world, it would be the last structure where you didn't need money to experience a sense of welcome, a broadness, this calm ocean of humanity.

The young man looked up from the stack of books. "Yes?"

"Do you happen to know this man?" Rhonda asked him. She slid two images of her father RJ in front of him on the large circulation desk, stained and marked by pens. One picture was taken outside the Observatory and the other was a copy from RJ's passport, his face unsmiling. "He was a homeless guy," she said. "He probably sat around and read—"

"Sorry," he said.

"He's dead now," Rhonda said.

He paused for a few seconds and held the photo up, studied RJ's face. How valuable a person became when they ceased to exist, as if they belonged to us all now.

"Could I help you, ladies?" An Asian American woman with salt-and-pepper hair in a low ponytail pushed an empty cart behind the desk, a variety of large ornate silver rings on her rough, unmanicured fingers, a tiger's-eye signet gleaming on her pinkie. She had the specific presence of a person who belonged exactly at this place and time, with a hard-earned sense of self-possession. It was like looking at Ana's future self, or a self she wanted to be.

"We were just wondering if you might know this man?" Rhonda asked.

The librarian slipped on her red-framed reading glasses from around her neck and held the image at a low angle. "Yes, of course, I do." Her eyes softened. "He's so young in this picture. So handsome." She smiled to herself. "Is everything alright?"

Rhonda shook her head. The librarian opened her mouth as if to say something, but she did not.

"He was found dead," Ana said. And at the end of that sentence, she understood what she had done there. She had eliminated her father from the scene. *He was found dead.* "Friday night."

The librarian leaned forward, her mouth a tight line. "Please. My office, could you . . . ?"

Ana and Rhonda followed her past the magazine displays, through a dark wooden door, and down a short hallway with shiny waxed floors. "Excuse the mess," she said. "We've got this huge fundraiser soon. I didn't properly introduce myself." She placed her hand over her heart. "I'm Janet."

They had found her.

Rhonda and Ana seated themselves on two folding chairs as the librarian plopped down in front of them behind her desk, which was covered in boxes and books and flyers for upcoming events. She adjusted the waist of her pants as she slumped a little to the side, removed her glasses from her face, and rubbed between her eyes.

"I'm his daughter, Rhonda."

"Oh, Rhonda, I'm so sorry." Her eyes glistened like the gemstone on her hand. "He'd sit in a corner and read the newspaper or a book. Or . . . scribbled in a notepad. He used the computers too. And the printer. But every now and then, we'd chat, kind of . . . kind of like colleagues." She smiled. "There was a period of time when he came in almost every day? Back in October, maybe November."

Rhonda nodded as she drank in the details of her father, his life.

"When I first met him—a few years ago—I didn't even realize he was homeless. I couldn't tell the difference between him and, you know, some of my teachers back in college. He had this one blazer, or jacket or whatever, with the elbow patches." She laughed a little to herself. "I called him 'The Professor,' and he loved that. He did. He absolutely did."

Rhonda grabbed a tissue from a box on the crowded desk. Janet got up to shut the door behind them with a jangle of copper desert bells that hung on the knob. On the wall was a poster of the human rights activist Yuri Kochiyama, her hair covered in a handkerchief, wearing clear cat's-eye glasses, a loudspeaker microphone in hand. Again, Ana glanced at Janet's tiger's-eye signet. A hanging mobile of delicate and colorful paper cranes, screened with patterns of gold, hovered in the room's corner.

"For the first couple years, he was here a few times a week, at least." Janet sat down again in her chair, which creaked, and she caught herself, moving to sit as upright as possible to balance herself in the seat. "But then he disappeared for a while. That must've been this past spring—March, April? Maybe as early as February. And then he came back in the fall. He was writing intensely then."

The letter. Ana remembered that his work had been related to whatever he wanted to pick up from her mother. "Any idea what he was working on?"

"I never asked. But . . . one day, I found one of his printouts."

Ana could feel Rhonda hold her breath.

Janet continued, "It was a memoir. Or a letter of some sort. I probably shouldn't have read it but I couldn't help myself."

"Do you remember anything specific about it?"

"It was about the house that he grew up in. He described the house and what it had been like to share a room with his siblings, how much he longed for those days, despite how cramped their lives had been." She furrowed her brow. "I remember the writing itself was beautiful."

"When was this?" Rhonda asked.

"Oh, it must've been weeks ago," Janet said. "I'm sorry. I wish . . . of course, I didn't know what would happen to him, but what I would give to have a copy of that book now. For you."

"Maybe it's still out there," Ana said.

Rhonda closed her eyes. Janet handed her another tissue.

"Any idea where he went?" Ana asked. "When he disappeared this year?"

"Vietnam," Janet said. "He had come back and he appeared . . . I don't know. I remember joking that the food must've been good for him. He said it was his heart that was full."

"Vietnam?" Rhonda asked.

"Yes, and I remember, beforehand, he had borrowed books on the language, traveling there. So it had to have been part of some plan."

"Anywhere specific?"

"Not that I know of. Even though I was curious, I always tried to respect his privacy. I could sense that . . . he needed that."

"And when was the last time you actually saw him?" Ana asked.

"Maybe just a couple weeks ago?" Janet's voice broke. "Honestly, now I wish . . . I had done more." She covered her face with her hand. "At times . . . he seemed particularly paranoid. Every now and then, he'd mention things about the police, and the government." She tightened her lips. "A good number of people say those things . . . that 'the government is after them,' 'the government is watching them' . . . because, you know." She shrugged. "Sometimes they *are*."

"Did he ever say why?" Ana asked.

"I figured he was just getting older, maybe a bit senile, but . . ." Janet leaned back in her chair, which tilted dangerously, but she balanced herself again by placing her foot on a drawer.

"Did you ever see him interacting with anyone else?" Rhonda asked. "Did he have any friends here?"

"Yes, a few. Sort of. I mean, we have many regulars."

"Any of them here now?"

"I don't know his name off the top of my head," Janet said. "An older gentleman. White guy. He wears the Vietnam hat? I can look out for him. They seemed . . . close in a way. Like coworkers, or partners, I guess. Maybe they had been in the war together. But it's been a while since I've actually seen him? Maybe months, or possibly longer than that. I just remember him as distinctly close to RJ. That could've been last year, even."

"Have the police come by yet?" Ana asked.

"Not that I know of. I can ask around." Janet blew her nose, wiped its pink tip with a tissue.

"Does the name Sunny Kim ring a bell?" Ana had to ask. She remembered two summers ago, she had noticed that her mother had carried home large art books from the library for inspiration one afternoon. But Ana hadn't bothered to note who the painters were.

"Vaguely. I mean, it's hard to forget a name like that," Janet said. "It's so . . . cheerful. But I can't put a face to it."

"She's my mother."

"She was a friend of RJ's, or knew him somehow," Rhonda said. "But it's a connection that doesn't really make sense to us."

"He died in our yard," Ana said like a confession, guilt consuming her like a fire she had somehow swallowed.

Janet covered her mouth, eyes wide. "And your mother? Where is she?"

"Missing. It's been a year now," Ana said. "It's possible she came to this branch. It's the closest. I remember she had borrowed art books. She might've come here." She glanced at Rhonda. "I wonder if . . . could they have met here somehow? RJ and my mother? We all love books in my family," Ana said to herself, realizing her father too had once studied them. "Well, not my brother. Maybe we can look up her account? Would that be possible?"

"Of course. And his too." Janet bit the top of her black pen. "I have a feeling we could . . . piece quite a bit together that way. I'll let you know what I find."

John gazed at the dinner plates, awestruck. The japchae glistened with tender strips of filet mignon, julienned and sautéed carrots and red bell pepper, blanched spinach, onion and slices of shiitake mushroom seasoned with soy sauce, sesame, garlic, and black pepper. John couldn't believe the attention to detail from his son, of all people, who always forgot to shut the windows when he left the house, who sometimes wore his shoes on the wrong foot, and who didn't wash his pimply face. Ronald had brought to life this dish that reminded them all so much of their mother, Sunny, his wife. She always made japchae, one of Ana's favorites, as a side dish on special occasions, or whenever the kids had a potluck at school and she didn't want to send them with something "too Korean" or inedible for the other students, who were mostly Latino, and sometimes Korean, Chinese, Filipino, or Black, but rarely white. Japchae could be enjoyed by almost everyone with its delicate savoriness, its mild versatility that managed to not be boring because of the liveliness of its colors, its layered ingredients.

"This is really good, Ronald." Ana devoured her noodles, rolling them onto her fork as if she were eating spaghetti.

"I think it's missing something?" Ronald asked.

"Maybe sugar?" She covered her mouth as she spoke. "But it's delicious. Not too salty."

"That's right," Ronald said. "Totally forgot. I could add some now but I think it might be too much. Or not really worth it."

Biting into the perfectly rubbery noodles, slick from vegetable and sesame oils, John realized he hadn't experienced anything this vibrant on their table in such a long time. His wife said that since we ate first with our eyes, it was important to always make meals pretty—multihued like the rainbow sleeves of a jeogori—but he never could hassle himself with creating a variety from oranges to greens and yellows. Everything he cooked had a mundane, monochromatic appearance. The only red on the table was from the small bowl of store-bought kimchi they had at every meal.

"What happened at the library?" Ronald asked. "And the shelters?"

"The shelters were really crowded, and they were so busy that no one recognized RJ," she said. "At the library, there was . . . Janet." She lowered her eyes.

"Oh?" Ronald glanced at John.

"She recognized him in the photo right away." Ana sipped from her bowl of sigeumchi doenjang guk with its threads of bean sprouts and boiled spinach. "She printed out a list of books, his records. Rhonda took them with her."

"Did you take a look?"

"There were collections of poetry. Octavia Butler. *Parable of the Sower*. Los Angeles classics like *Devil in a Blue Dress, If He Hollers Let Him Go*. A catalog of Carrie Mae Weems. *The Jungle* by Upton Sinclair. *The Autobiography of Ida B. Wells*. And several Vietnamese texts."

"So nothing new yet?" Ronald asked.

Ana shook her head. "He had a friend that he spoke with often, another vet." She dabbed her forehead with her napkin. Like himself, she often sweated when she ate. "Janet's going to try to contact him and let him know."

"Did you get a name?"

"She didn't have it off the top of her head. But she thinks she could figure it out."

As they ate, plates and bowls clinked on the crowded table, filled with banchan, their water glasses, and utensils. Outside, a mockingbird chirped like a car alarm, pathetic. John begged that they would change the subject. His kids had already wasted too much time helping Rhonda, a stranger, and her father. They had so much to do before the end of the world. John had to figure out a way to secure the backyard. Who knew what could happen to them next?

"I asked about Mom," Ana said. "At the library."

"What about her?" Ronald asked.

"Janet couldn't find an account for her. Her records could've been on paper, never converted to data . . ."

Lifting the bowl with two hands to conceal his face, John tasted his soup, which was the way that he liked it, a few days old. A fermented bean from the doenjang disintegrated in his mouth. A bit of spinach lodged itself in his dentures. He poked around with his tongue. "And . . . Rhonda. I spoke with her outside the library afterward," Ana said as she squeezed her napkin into a ball. "She still thinks . . . that the only person who could want to kill RJ would be . . ."

He wasn't stupid. How awkward, how painful.

First, everyone had blamed the disappearance of his wife on him, and now the death of a stranger in his backyard. What else could he be responsible for? He was a man—not a punching bag. He had worked hard enough already, raised Ronald by himself this past year, cooked and cleaned, toiled for long, mundane hours six days per week so that his son might have a better childhood than his at least. And now this woman, and her father, dared to upend their family again, right before the world might end. The apocalypse was here, right now.

He stood from the table, clearing his side, his bowl of rice, unfinished. How dare she—

"But if Dad killed RJ, wouldn't that have been super easy to figure out?" Ronald said. "The police. They had a bunch of people here analyzing and—"

"Not necessarily. I mean—look, Dad, I know that you had nothing to do with this, but . . . the police probably did a sloppy job. He was homeless. They don't care."

John lowered his bowls into the sink, overcome with an impossible sadness at the sight of this wasted meal, the bites of japchae on top of his half-eaten rice. He salvaged the food by moving the bowls to the counter instead. He'd cover them in Saran Wrap for later or tomorrow. He couldn't let this woman and her father do this to them, his family, what was left of it now.

Take care of your own business. Take care of your own house.

"How long are you here?" John yelled to Ana from the sink behind a tall freestanding cabinet that separated the nook from him. "Two weeks?" No response. "Huh?" The volume of his own voice terrified him. How dare this woman, this man, ruin what might be the last two weeks he and his children would have together. How dare they?

"Dad, we can't just . . . we *should* help her."

"Help *her*? If *her* father work, he not homeless. A bum. Stupid bum."

"Dad, that's not the point."

"She focus on her own job so she don't live like him. On the street, huh?"

"Dad."

"That's so fucked up," Ronald said.

"What did you say?" Strangled by a flash of heat, John stomped toward his son, shaking a fist in the air. Burn this all down. The ash in his mouth. The feet exposed. The shoes. The blood on the socks. The scream of bombs as they fell. The scream of babies lit on fire. This was hell. That was hell. These children didn't know anything.

"Dad, forget about it," Ana said.

"Did you get where he used to work?" Ronald asked. "What police station?"

"No, I didn't," she said. "Maybe we could figure out where he worked and see if anyone remembers him from back then."

"Police station?" John laughed, remembering what Detective Coleman had said: *Vista Park*. He cleared the plates and bowls in front of them and returned to the kitchen. "Forget about it, okay?" he yelled from the sink. "You do your homework. Police do their job, okay? Everybody do their job, okay? Do your homework."

"First of all, I don't have homework. Second of all, like I said, the police don't care about him. Why would they bother? He was old and homeless. Do you think they care? It's not their job to care about *every*one." Ana paused as if waiting for a response, then said, "Haven't you figured that out? They didn't care about you when your business was destroyed. Did they care about Rodney King? He had a family too. He meant something to someone."

"You think too much. You think police bad, huh?" John wrapped what remained of the japchae. Of course no one would finish their food. The entire meal had been ruined now.

"*I think too much*? And no, that's not what I said. But they don't care about him or you. They don't care about Mom, either. Give me a break." She scooted from the bench. He stepped back to give her room. "*I* think too much? *You* keep your head down. *You* do whatever they say," she screamed at him, before she grabbed her water and threw it across the room. And in that gesture, they both recognized him. They stared at each other as he remembered the fight, the fight that John and Sunny had when he had purchased the gas station. His cup thrown. The glass shattered. Ana crying in a corner.

She rushed to pluck the pieces from the floor and blot the liquid with a rag as if it had never happened.

"Maybe if you were more thoughtful, we wouldn't be in this situation in the first place," she said. "Mom might— Mom might still be—" Her face cracked. All the sadness inside her spilling out.

John bolted for his bedroom. He crumpled onto the bed, which creaked beneath his weight. His daughter was right, wasn't she? She was right, and he hated himself because she was right. Of course she was. What could he do now to fix everything? He wished the world would end so that he wouldn't have to make any more choices or decisions. He wouldn't have to make any more mistakes that he couldn't take back. He wouldn't have to keep waiting, waiting for her to come home.

He clicked on the lamp beside his bed, the lamp with a wooden and glass base, a rectangular box with a center that held a fake candle and a lightbulb shaped like a flame. A lantern. He remembered how much his wife hated the false gimmick of that fire. Grabbing the shade, he threw the lamp against the floor. If the windows didn't have security bars, he would've shoved it outside. But instead he lay down in the darkness, finding himself for the first time—possibly since they had married each other over twenty years ago—directly in the bed's center, an equidistant expanse on both sides of his body.

He'd go himself to the police station where RJ worked. He'd prove to his children that RJ, accident or not, deserved his lot in life, the plot he would be buried inside. *RJ* was the bad man. Lazy and reckless. He couldn't keep his job, pay his bills, take care of his own wife and child. He had to meddle in John's life, didn't he? He had to take Sunny away from him.

Yes, John remembered, it was *him*, wasn't it? He was the one with her on the bench, his hand on her shoulder. He was why she was now gone. But his children didn't need to know about that.

John was the hero. This was his story, after all.

1983

At least once per week, six p.m. had been a time of relief, when Sunny no longer felt her body running. A stillness—what precedes the beating, the rapturous rhythm of a flock of wings, the silhouettes of cranes breaking the last of the light—overcame, overwhelmed her. Despite the smell of gasoline, the ripeness of discontent, the burning, always something burning in the air, she'd run errands, buy groceries, stock up on diapers and baby food in tiny jars while her neighbor Mrs. Lee watched both Ana and Ronald, now one year old and standing proud on his own. And when Mrs. Lee asked her why she chose to leave the house so late in the day, at such an uncomfortable and ragged hour, Sunny replied, "I like to walk back home as the sun sets. It's my favorite time," which was only partially true, and Mrs. Lee, with her quick-wittedness, that charming smile, suspected, Sunny knew, something false, askew.

Yes, Sunny loved the streaks of clouds, fuchsia and bright, lit from below by an orange fire, with the amethyst of the evening getting closer to the horizon, sealing the day shut until the morning. But she also chose this inconvenient time because she knew he would be there at the bus stop. RJ. And ever since she had gone into labor on that bench, through the months of exhaustion, feeding and diapering and putting Ronald to bed, she had thought of, if only for a few seconds, the way RJ's hand felt on her shoulder as she lay down. How, when she reached out to touch him in acknowledgment, he didn't pull away, as if they were two deer in the woods, simply resting next to each other. His final salute as she drove away toward the hospital. The chuckle she couldn't contain despite the pain of the contractions through her body.

When did her husband stop laughing, anyways? Sometime in the past year after Ronald's birth and after his father died. Something about his father's death had changed him, broken him down like a cardboard box, and she could see perhaps his original shape, the hard folds, as if he had been designed that way from the beginning. Maybe it had been the abruptness of the loss? Or the way that his stepmother didn't even bother to tell him until after the funeral; a few weeks had passed. Maybe unbeknownst to Sunny he had been holding on to a potential life in Korea, and now there was no one to receive him if he ever returned, even if just to visit. He had in a sense deserted everyone and paid the price of this life, this immigration.

But there were so many other disappointments and tragedies in their lives cumulatively, how could you delineate one from the other when they overlapped like watercolors? This past year, she had even received an oddly confessional letter from Professor Cho, who still used her pen name Frida; she had been struggling in her marriage too. She had yet to have a child, and she and her husband had begun to disagree about her continuing political activity against the "president," who had assumed power through another military coup under which there had been concentration camps and the massacre at Gwangju.

Traffic choked the roads. At the sight of RJ from a distance, she quickened her steps, smoothing down the hair around her face. Her body had changed so much after her second child, thickening around the waist and the hips, but she was also stronger than she had ever been before, like the trunk of a tree. Besides, what did it matter now that she and her husband hardly touched each other? She was only another mother. She might as well eat to her heart's content, find some morsel of joy in the meals that she shared with her children or Mrs. Lee. Food had become the escape, the fantasy of being somewhere else.

This had been the fourth or fifth time that Sunny and RJ had "run into each other," and she considered each reunion to be a kind of event, a homecoming. She had so much to learn from him. Even though they took separate buses, they'd be at the same stop for five, once forty minutes, enough time to glean more information, but short enough to be unthreatening. There'd always be a bus to swoop one of them away before she couldn't figure out what to say or do next.

Relieved that she had caught him in time, she pressed her hand on the back of the bench. He turned his head to the side, smiling in response with a half-eaten red apple in his hand, always the red apple, although she didn't understand why because those were her least favorite. She never found them to be crisp or flavorful enough like the fuji or honeygolds, which had a bit more tartness and bite. And there were so many more lovely fruits that shined in their trees, like the persimmon that sang *pick me* in the autumn, *pick me before the squirrels and birds eat me.* She remembered how her mother hung the fruit on twine to dehydrate and enjoy like chewy candy over the winter. They'd spin and spin when you'd touch them. She would bring him one when the season changed from summer to fall.

"How's it going, Sunny?" RJ asked as she planted herself a couple feet away and rested her heavy purse on her lap. She noticed again a notebook with a pen on top of it close to his side. Each time they met, she sat a little closer, inch by inch, but of course, she'd always maintain some distance. It would never be the same as when she had gone into labor, a strange and beautiful occurrence, dreamlike in the fuzziness of its edges. But that feeling of his hand on her shoulder had been unmistakable, the warmth of it resting against her.

"How are you?" she asked with an awkward brightness, as if that was the first time she had said those words out loud in her life. She suddenly felt self-conscious, heart beating in her throat. Parched. Did he at least find her charming?

"I'm alright. Shopping tonight?"

"Yes, shopping. More milk. Make dinner."

"How's that baby of yours?" he asked.

"Good, very good. Everything . . . nice."

He bit into his apple, which had already browned. "You know, I never noticed until today, but they officially started calling this area Koreatown. They put a sign up down there. I've been so busy I don't even notice things like that anymore."

Usually they waited in silence and he would talk about himself, his life, in almost a monologue, asking her questions along the way, but she never knew how to maintain the back-and-forth of an actual conversation. Their interactions, somewhat strained, also managed to be easeful, as if they both respected the limits of what they could or could not say, could or could not understand about each other. Unlike with her husband, who didn't have as much of an excuse except there was never enough time for them simply to *be*, to be with one another.

She pointed to the notebook by his side. "Writing?"

"Oh, this?" His face glowed. "Ha, I just take notes, that's all. It's kind of like a . . . journal of sorts."

She shook her head, scratched the wood surface beneath her. The entire city seemed to perspire in the August heat, hot tailpipes panting exhaust.

"It's where I write down my thoughts, things I notice, observe what I like or . . . have questions about," RJ said. "I was never good with words out loud." He cleared his throat. "I stuttered when I was young. So I enjoy just . . . jotting them down. When I was growing up, I wanted to work for the newspaper, be a reporter, a journalist of some kind." He flipped through the pages absentmindedly, which fanned open to reveal ripples of blue ink. "I always liked the idea of leaving some kind of record, you know?"

"*Record*?" She pictured the small collection of vinyl her husband kept at home. The scratch of the delicate needle on them.

"Yeah, like a testament of sorts. Evidence. Uh, you know, *proof* that you were here. It's hard to know who you are, or to feel like you belong, unless there's some kind of proof, you know?"

"*Proof?*"

"It's uh . . . ha, now you're making me sweat." He rubbed the skin on his neck. "Well, it's kind of what you carry with you until you leave it behind. It's that thing that tells people what you did. It's a document or an item that tells a story of . . . like when my parents, you see, when I was just a kid, my parents moved to LA from Mississippi and they left everything behind with nothing but the clothes on their backs. There were jobs out here from the war and they had a lot to run from. Jim Crow. Do you know what that is? Before I was born, my uncle Marcus was killed. And that wasn't the first time things like that happened in my family, but because Marcus was so young . . . he was my father's younger brother. He was only twelve years old, and that tortured him, my father. When my parents came to LA, they started out everything fresh, and in a way, yes, they did find a better life. They did give us a better life." Tears filled his eyes. "In a way, none of us became Marcus." He nodded to himself. "So sometimes a *record* is written, and other times a *record* is . . . carried on through other people, children, I guess."

She had the impulse to hold his hand but did not. She hadn't heard him speak of his past before. Usually he shared thoughts about the news, details about his favorite places in LA, including the Griffith Observatory and the Santa Monica Pier. Once, he showed her a point-and-shoot camera, a Canon Sure Shot, that he sometimes carried in his bag. But today, for whatever reason, had been different, heavier with the past, almost confessional.

She remembered the fight she had with her husband a couple years ago, what she had said about him buying a business in a Black area, and a great sense of shame burned as her own racist words pierced her: *They destroy their own neighborhood.* It was so much easier to be angry at, to blame people we didn't know, wasn't it? Because being angry at people whom we knew intimately was like being angry at ourselves. We had some great stake in it.

And despite their financial tenuousness, the continued political instability in Korea, and the legacy of the traumas of the war, her family at least, because of their backgrounds, college educated and middle- to upper-class, had more of an escape route, which RJ probably didn't have. There was always the potential for future inheritances that could serve as forms of down payment, collateral. (They had even been waiting for almost a year to receive a distribution from her father-in-law's estate.) In fact, she and her husband had been able to immigrate to this country because of what they *brought* with them, their "skilled labor," their "professionalism," which was not a reflection of their culture at large, but the specific class they happened to be born into.

They destroy their own neighborhood. Maybe they never felt like it was theirs in the first place.

"Did you say your husband works at a gas station down there?"

"Yes, gas station."

"I moved, well, we moved to this area so that my, uh, ex-wife would be closer to work downtown." He finished his apple and threw out the core with a gentle thud in the trash.

The first mention of a wife.

Did he have children too? He used the word "ex." What did it mean? She'd have to ask Mrs. Lee later.

Sitting down, RJ continued, "I do miss the old neighborhood though. Back then, when I was growing up, there were four of us kids, and we had a two-bedroom house. All four kids in one bedroom. Two bunk beds. Do you know what a bunk bed is?"

She shook her head.

"Two beds, one on top of the other." He crossed his legs, revealing the bottom of his black work shoes, clean as if they were new. "I mean, not that things were easy, but we all seemed so much closer together. Now everyone is so far apart, don't you think? We used to be able to just knock on a neighbor's door back then, share meals, bring food over when someone was sick. We took care of each other." He furrowed his brow. "There was a woman who ran a daycare in her house. She was so cool, a photographer. Mrs. Roberts." His face glowed. "She introduced us to our first camera, a pinhole. And she had her own little darkroom and printed us a picture of ourselves that was blurry because none of us could stand still for long enough. That was magic."

"Magic?" Sunny asked.

"Yes, like something you can't really explain but that is wonderful."

"Magic." Sunny imagined the two peachy fingerprints at the end of Professor Cho's letters.

"People were so close back then without even having to explain themselves. It was like each block was one big yard full of rooms, houses that connected to each other. Now everyone's too scared. Serial killers and shit."

"Yes," she said. It felt like he had been speaking for them both, in a way. What was a *serial killer*? She pictured the red box of Lucky Charms with the cartoon man in his green outfit that her daughter loved so much, the hard marshmallows of different shapes and colors. *Cereal.* "To kill" was to take a life. Someone who killed "cereal"?

"You must feel that way too, I guess. I bet you were all so much closer in Korea, right? Your family?"

"Yes. Mother, father, sister."

"I mean, even the military was less lonely for me. I hated the lack of privacy, but at least it was its own family."

Military. Army?

"I was in Vietnam. I worked on helicopters." He pointed to the sky, spun his finger like a propeller. And she heard the vicious *chop, chop, chop,* the buzz and the horror of the sounds, traffic in the air, the tanks, powerful and frightening. Even after the armistice, she and her friends had found the remains of vehicles, dead and abandoned in a field or in a ditch, and they would climb them like children's structures, the playgrounds of war. How ugly and unnatural all of it had been, how much her country had been destroyed by bombs, the combustion of chemicals, gunshots and fire and smoke. How she had longed for clean air, the frost, the snow as it melted, dripping off branches into her mouth. Wasn't there enough death, enough harm, enough sadness in each life already? And as her family fled when she had just been a baby herself, the last thing her parents must've thought about was the beloved photographs and art, the books on the shelves that could not be carried. But for people like her husband, who had been thirteen years old during the war, and she guessed had experienced some of its worst, much worse than herself, it was always the worst kind of dawn. The sun was not a sun but a ball of fire, a bomb frozen in explosion. It was hell. But how could she ever explain this to anyone out loud.

RJ sighed. "America sure keeps the world busy."

She didn't understand what he meant. By war? There would be war without America, but war looked different because of this country, its power to spread its stories, war would always be framed differently. For Sunny, war between the North and South was like siblings fighting, siblings who had too much in common, too much history, too much love for them to not figure out a way to be together under the same roof, the same language and culture. Yet outsiders like America pointed out our differences so that we'd hate each other.

Self-hatred made us easier to control.

A bus pulled in front of the stop, kicking up the dust and detritus in the gutters, warming her face with the heat from its exhaust. RJ glanced at his watch. "That's mine. Late today." He stood with a hint of difficulty, brows scrunched as he grabbed the back of the bench. "Ha, I should skip work and we should do something fun. Could you imagine? Someone else could clean up for those cops. God, those bathrooms are the worst." He shook his head.

He had never mentioned his actual job before, but she figured from his work clothes that he was some kind of repairman or janitor.

"We should go to the beach or the Observatory like two kids." He brushed off the front of his pants, slipped his notebook in his backpack. "Have a good night, Sunny. Say hello to that baby and husband. What's your baby's name, anyways?"

She pretended that she didn't understand him and smiled as she waved goodbye.

When her son had been born a year ago, John had been surprisingly satisfied with her sudden choice of the name Ronald. He had assumed the moniker had been in honor of the current president. "Ronald Kim," her husband said out loud as she held the soft and squishy newborn against her heart.

Once again she thought that next time she'd bring RJ some fruit, something different from the apple he always ate. She could offer him a pear or an orange to have at work, some bit of relief in what she imagined to be a long and lonesome evening by himself. She'd repay him for the ways he kindly gave her so much, probably without even knowing the effect that he, his words, had on her little enormous life.

America sure keeps the world busy.

That had been true, but America also made these encounters between her and RJ—two very different people from different worlds—possible, even desirable. In his presence, the universe expanded. Forbidden and bold.

1999

Even though it wasn't lunch yet, Ana was hungry. She reheated some of the leftover japchae. She always preferred hers warm enough so that the noodles remained soft and slippery. How long had it been since she had last had japchae? Months at least, maybe even a year. Throughout college, she had always expected her mother to cook for her when she returned home for the holidays, or to send her some dry goods from the Korean supermarket. But then her mother—and everything she held for them, every banchan that she had made by memory and taste, the names of all their relatives in Korea, the names of all their homes, whether accessible or cut off by borders—had disappeared along with her, evaporated into a kind of ether. She had held all of that knowledge for her children.

Even though she couldn't say it out loud, Ana was certain their mother was dead. She suspected that perhaps she had planned to return but lost her life unexpectedly. She couldn't fathom that her mother would just run away from their life, unhappy or dissatisfied as she might've been. She loved them too much. She would've wanted to be there to support them, especially her brother as he transitioned to adulthood. So for the past year, Ana had replayed in her head how her mother could have died—a car accident; murdered, even. Who knew? It was a dark fantasy that her mind indulged in on some nights—that she could one day have an answer, that her mother's death was not senseless or meaningless, that there was justice, order somewhere in this world for her too. She had finally attained the peace that her own country of origin, still at war with itself, couldn't achieve yet. She deserved that at the very least. Rest and relief.

Even if her father claimed that she had most likely died, there had been signs that he believed, or at least hoped, otherwise. He had not only continued to sleep on his side of the bed, but he had also kept her clothes in their drawers, her toothbrush in its cup, her towel on the bar next to their shower, as if she had never left. He probably believed she would come home someday, and to his great relief, they would maintain the status quo of their family, even after her lapse in judgment.

But by holding on to the hope that she would return, both her brother and father would never move on.

Yesterday, outside the library, as if in response to the odd sight of them—two women not going anywhere, two women that should be *doing* something—Rhonda had pulled a pack of cigarettes out of her back pocket. She'd cupped the flame of the lighter with her hand and inhaled, scrunching her face as if the sting of the smoke hurt her lungs. "I really shouldn't be smoking," she said as she closed her eyes in relief. The tobacco smelled dark and bitter but sweet. Ana hadn't had one herself in years.

"I'm still not sure why you want to help," Rhonda said. She turned her head to the side. The smoke rushed out. "Why does any of this matter to you so much?"

A leaf scratched as it circled the ground.

"Your father died in our yard," Ana said. "He was homeless." Guilt and shame flooded her face. Now was the time to mention the letter that her father had torn apart. But she was also afraid of what Rhonda would assume that meant. "It's clear that your father and my mother were close." Fortunately, this detail from the letter had emerged when Janet had gone into RJ's account: "Close enough for him to use her address for a library card."

"That was . . . interesting," Rhonda said.

"And this is all . . . a part of her life that I didn't know about. Ever since she disappeared, there have been so many questions that I've had and . . ."

Rhonda took another drag of the cigarette before she flicked away the ash. "Are you trying to prove that your father didn't do it?"

"No." Ana shook her head. "Honestly, it doesn't—"

"Imagine this: What if your dad had gone outside and my dad had confronted him?"

"About?"

"Your mother," Rhonda said.

"What do you mean?"

"What if he had asked, 'Is Sunny here? Can I talk to Sunny?' Would your dad have been pissed?"

"He— He would've been thrown off, I guess."

"And?"

"He doesn't like to talk about it, my mother, at all."

"Do you think he's capable of hurting someone like that?"

"I . . . don't think he'd be strong enough. I guess I don't know."

A silence fell. Ana imagined her father during the war, hungry and displaced, thirteen years old, still a child, leaving his home with his father and nothing on him but what was in their pockets, what had been sewn into the linings of their clothes. And *his* mother, who remained faceless to Ana, holding down the fort of their house. She'd always imagined her father as waiting for his mother, that she was forever separated from him by a border, the border between the North and South, but for the first time, Ana realized that it was *him* that disappeared. It was him and his father who left, who abandoned *her.* It was them that never made it home. It was them, like her own mother, running as fast as they could.

"Did you see how skinny my dad had become?" Rhonda finally asked.

Ana shuddered. "I wasn't there."

"You didn't have to," Rhonda said. "You know, that's the first time I've seen him, as an adult. At the coroner's office. On a table. I asked to see him." The smoke trailed out of her mouth as she continued. "The last time I saw a dead person like that was my grandmother. But at least she was in a casket. She looked comfortable. She *was* comfortable, thank God." A group of teenagers, who appeared to have skipped school, passed them on their way to the library. One of them stopped and paused to stare before he continued on with his friends. Rhonda slipped on her sunglasses, gold and frameless with gradient brown lenses. "I couldn't ask him anything. He never had to answer for himself."

"I am so sorry," Ana said.

"And now he's gone."

"I mean, my dad may be a bit rough, but to kill someone is too much. He would've— Honestly, he would've just called the cops." Ana gulped the bile in her mouth. That wasn't the right thing to say, but it was the truth, and she needed to acknowledge this out loud, even if she could feel the humiliation, the shame of it rising from her gut. People like her father, homeowners—yes, an immigrant and person of color, but not one who physically threatened others, given his age and the color of his skin—would've called the police, would've assigned the handling of the "trespasser" in his backyard to someone of a more official capacity, someone with a badge and gun. That was a privilege he had, even if they might've been jaded about the lack of protection they received from the police during the riots. On an everyday basis, he could reach someone for help. They might belittle him with racist comments, but most likely they would take his claim seriously and—at the very least—would not kill him.

And they would've taken RJ's life easily. No one would have paid for it.

She hated the truth, but it wasn't worth dancing around, not with Rhonda, not now.

"Maybe that's just the way you want to think of him," Rhonda said. "Maybe you don't know him." She paused. "Just like I didn't know mine."

Rhonda was right. Ana knew her father only as a man, often quiet—in front of the television, cooking dinner, preparing a vegetable juice for himself—or angry, short tempered with both his children and himself, angry at the world, at circumstances outside his control. How many times had she heard him say, "Goddamnit," when something went awry—a late delivery of inventory at the nursery, an unhappy customer who wouldn't budge, a stain on his shirt or pants? Anything could set him off. She was right. But no, he couldn't have *killed* anyone.

"What if my father had confronted yours? Has anyone ever confronted your father about your mother leaving?"

She did not leave; she disappeared. She's dead.

"Don't you think after— What has it been? How long has it been?"

"A year."

"Don't you think your father would've been upset to hear a stranger say his wife's name? What if my father blamed him?"

"I don't know if I can answer that. I mean, he's always been . . ." She couldn't finish the sentence.

"Exactly."

"But he's not physically violent." At least, he had never been violent with her. But had he ever hit Ronald? Not to her knowledge. If he had, would that change her perception of him? Maybe he would treat a stranger differently. For many years, he did own a gun—she had seen it herself—to protect his stores, to protect them whenever he picked up day laborers to work on the house. But had he ever gotten rid of it? And what about during the war? She had assumed that he never hurt anyone, but who knew how desperate one could become under the worst circumstances imaginable? Who knew how far anyone could be pushed?

"Could I have a cigarette?" Ana asked.

Rhonda reached in her purse.

Ana's hand shook as she lowered her head to the flame of Rhonda's lighter. She couldn't hide it. She inhaled and coughed, light-headed.

Remembering this buzz now, Ana scrubbed the Tupperware for the japchae in the sink with lemon-scented dish soap, bright and sharp. Rhonda had every reason to suspect her father of killing RJ. He was a property owner. RJ, an intruder. But Rhonda also didn't know her father the way Ana did. That despite his flaws, something always stopped him from being his worst.

The phone in the living room rang.

It was Janet, the librarian. "I tried calling Rhonda but no one picked up."

Ana's heart pounded inside her throat, her face.

"RJ's friend was Jacob Hendricks, another vet." Janet sounded concerned. "He came by today."

"Were you able to ask him anything?"

"He was in a hurry. I told him about RJ."

"What did he—"

"I ran into him by the computers. Maybe he was looking for a printout or something. He was searching. He looked . . . scared, kind of angry rather than sad. He asked me how I knew. He was in such a rush that he left his wallet behind. That's how I got his name. There's an old driver's license in it, but it expired in '87."

"Shit. Could you make a copy before you return it, the driver's license? Or if there's any other way you might have to reach him?"

"Sure," Janet said. "I'll see if there's a number. Try to contact him. If not, it'll be here in the lost and found."

Perhaps Peggy, who was still looking for information about RJ at the VA, could look up Jacob Hendricks too. Anything that could help her and Rhonda get in contact with him. Even if he had nothing to do with RJ's death, he might at least be able to help them piece together RJ's life.

"Why would he have been scared?" Ana asked herself out loud. "RJ's death was an accident." She thought uneasily of the detective who had come by their house, and Rhonda's too. Should she tell Janet about RJ's letter? But how could she explain why she hadn't told Rhonda earlier about it except that she had witnessed her father tear it apart? She could leave that part out. But then why wouldn't she have turned over the letter to the police? "Do you know what Jacob might have been searching for?"

"The memoir, the one I mentioned before," Janet said. "Maybe it was more than that?"

Ana thought back to RJ's list of recently returned books. *Crusade for Justice: The Autobiography of Ida B. Wells.* What had RJ been writing?

"Did he tell you he was a janitor for the LAPD in the eighties, maybe seventies?" Ana asked.

"No, he did not," Janet said. "He must've seen a lot."

The camera. Ana had closed one eye to look out the viewfinder as RJ stood on the observation deck. It had been the first time she had been allowed to use a camera aside from her father's Polaroid once or twice. *Hold it steady, Ana,* she heard him say out loud with a clarity that startled her. Was her mind making up his voice, or was this an actual memory, one that she had submerged because it didn't make sense within the story of what she knew of her mother? *Take one more just in case.*

"I wonder how he ended up on the street," Janet said.

"The only person who knew him was Hendricks, *possibly* my mother, and of course, you."

"And . . . your mother is gone," Janet said.

Gone. That word stung. It was as if, for this past year, her mother's disappearance were a private matter that they had discussed only among themselves, their family. But Ana realized now, with RJ's death, how much her mother had been part of the world at large.

"I'm positive that my mom borrowed those books from the library. I know you couldn't find a record the other day, but what if . . . it's under a different name, like 'Sunhee Kim'? S-U-N-H-E-E?"

"I can look. I can look now." Ana heard Janet typing in the background.

"Or what about . . . I wonder if she used someone else's account?" Ana asked. "Like under my dad's name, or maybe even mine? John Kim, which I'm sure there are a million of. Anastasia Kim. Same address as RJ's."

Ana waited in silence for a minute, listening to Janet's breath, steady but shallow, as if her heart had been beating fast.

"When was the last time you used your library card?" Janet asked.

"Oh, it's been years. Not since I was in high school, so . . . maybe 1994? I'm not sure. I've lived in Berkeley since—"

"Last year. You checked out several books . . . Gauguin, Magritte, Frida Kahlo, *Surrealism and Women*, photographs of Vietnam, a Vietnamese cookbook."

"What?"

"This was in the summer and the fall: October, November, even December."

Why would her mother have used her card? She supposed her mother could've found it and figured it wouldn't matter. And why was she also researching Vietnam? "Could you print out a list?" Ana asked Janet. "I'll come by. I can walk. If you don't see Hendricks again or reach him somehow today, maybe I'll drop it off. His license. At the address. I bet it's old. But who knows?" She could borrow her father's car tomorrow.

"Hmm, I don't know if I can just give you his wallet," Janet said. "Plus, the address is in Anaheim."

"Shit, that's far," Ana said. But she had this hunch that he would be the only one left with answers now.

"I wonder why he was coming all the way over here," Janet said. "I actually looked, and he doesn't even have an account. So he wasn't here for books."

"How long has he been coming to your library?"

"I'm not sure, but it's been years now. I guess it's where he would meet RJ. But he didn't seem surprised or particularly upset when I told him RJ had died."

"You said he was scared?" Ana asked.

"Yes. As if for his life. And angry too."

"What did he need that RJ had?" Ana said.

And when would Ana tell Rhonda about her memory of RJ at the Observatory? Why had she not mentioned it earlier? Was she afraid that it would link her mother too closely with RJ, supporting Rhonda's belief that her father could've killed RJ in their yard in an act of revenge? Who exactly was Ana helping?

"Whatever it was, he was looking for it like his life depended on it," Janet said.

"I really think . . . if I could only return the wallet to him, we might get some answers, don't you think? If he was scared, I doubt he'd come back."

Janet sighed. "You're probably right." She took a deep breath. "But I hope you know what you're getting into."

"Unfortunately, I don't," Ana said, realizing now that she might have to confront Hendricks herself. "But I have to try."

"Just be careful, okay?" Janet lowered her voice. "Don't go alone."

1983

In the morning, Sunny and John lay in the dark beside each other, with him on his back and her on her side. Both their children, like a miracle, were asleep. Ronald in a crib in their room, and Ana on a bed near the dining table.

How cruel the light could be sometimes. Some nights or early mornings, she yearned to stretch the darkness just one more hour. There was never enough time to rest anymore. How she longed for a day off, just her and her husband, to be adults. Her brain had become saturated in the sounds of children's speech, the cries and laughter of babies, and yet she wanted something else too besides this exhausted sweetness.

"I received the money yesterday," John whispered. "My stepmother. The money finally came through."

Three weeks after the birth of their son last summer, Sunny, harried and sleep deprived, had been home alone and opened an airmail package, shoebox sized, that had arrived for John. The box held photographs of an adolescent John and his father, as well as a pair of very thick eyeglasses alongside a note that indicated that his father had died weeks ago from a stroke, but that John's stepmother didn't have the heart to tell him before the birth of his son. She wrote that she knew that John, as a child, always liked trying on his father's glasses, so she thought he would want to have this sacred piece of him around.

"It's about fifty thousand dollars," he said.

"Oh my." She turned onto her back. She couldn't quite wrap her head around what they could do with all that money. Maybe they could start a new business, one that would allow the whole family to work together, or take an extra day off every now and then so that he could spend more time with the children. Her heart quickened. This amount could change their life. But she could feel his somberness, this heaviness he had since his father died, holding them back.

"You seem so sad," she said.

"It should've been more."

A fly buzzed overhead. She waved it away with her hand.

"After I left for America, my father cut me mostly out of the will." He sighed, closing his eyes. Was this regret? She wondered what he regretted most—leaving Korea or coming to America? Maybe, despite their love for their children, *that* was the only thing that bound them together these days: they both hated decisions they had made in the past. And to acknowledge this would be a way of insulting each other, wouldn't it? How could they ever get over or forgive one another for what each might be ultimately saying, that *choosing this life together has destroyed some part of me, some part of me that I desperately need to survive*?

"Most of the money went to my stepmother and stepbrothers."

It made sense to Sunny that his stepmother would inherit the majority of his father's wealth. She had taken care of his father during his old age, during the most difficult years of his life, and supported him, with his son off in America. But Sunny suspected that in reality, the money, although much needed by them, was more important to John in that it symbolized a final severance from his life in Korea. Now that his father had passed and he had received this sum, he no longer had any reason to have a relationship with his stepfamily, who were cordial at best, but never took any interest in him, outside the fact that he was technically his father's eldest child. And because the inheritance had not helped to equalize their socioeconomic conditions, it would be even more difficult to cultivate a relationship with them.

His father, now dead, was also the only person in his life with any connection to his mother and siblings in North Korea. Even if John never spoke to his father about them, they shared memories, some knowledge of them, which didn't need words and somehow kept the missing alive.

Yet for John, Sunny knew, it would always be easier to talk about money, to make this about money in the end. What happened to the man whom she had married—the literature major, the dreamer, the storyteller?

"Maybe now you won't need to take the bus anymore," he said.

Sunny couldn't understand the connection to what they were talking about at all. That's what infuriated her: that he never pushed the conversation to where it wanted to lead, somewhere meaningful, somewhere that would bind them together, and instead gravitated toward the practical, the everyday, as if life were only about solving its little nuisances, its tiny hindrances toward living the most "productively." Who cared about productivity when they were all so lonely and quietly miserable? Riding the bus, timing her errands so that she could speak with RJ, even if only for a few minutes, meant the world to her now, provided the only relief she had in the week, except for when Mrs. Lee came over and made banchan alongside her in their kitchen.

"It's dangerous, don't you think? Carrying all those bags by yourself, having to coordinate the bus schedule with Mrs. Lee."

"I don't mind." She kept her voice as low as possible.

"Have you been taking it at night?"

"Not when it's dark." She almost said, *I don't feel alone when I'm on the bus. I like the bus. I'm fine.*

"There are murderers, bad people out there," John said. "I think you should learn how to drive."

"I don't want to drive," she said. "I've been living in America . . . how long? Seven years already and I never needed to learn. I like the bus. It's easy and I don't have to worry about much, parking or gas. I'm in no hurry. Murderers? Where?" She laughed.

"That one they wrote about in the newspaper. The one who killed all the people at night."

"The newspaper is just trying to make us all scared. They caught him, didn't they?"

"Yeah, but who knows who else is out there? And now with the kids . . ."

"I feel safe on the bus. There are other people. It's safer when there's more people. We look out for each other."

Ronald sucked on his pacifier in a loud rhythm that made them suddenly aware of his proximity.

"We should buy a new car anyways," John whispered. "And then you can learn on the Oldsmobile. You could bring the kids with you when you run errands. You don't have to depend on Mrs. Lee so much. She has her own family, her own worries. She is also getting very old."

"I don't think it's too much of a burden. I make her banchan, give her fruit all the time. We keep each other young."

In the dim light, he turned to look at her almost long enough for her to remember how much she once admired and loved him. Before they had had their children, before he became overwhelmed by work, the persistence of stress and anxiety on his face, the hunch of his back. He had been so handsome and hopeful and brave, but the hours, the lack of sleep, had aged him. Sure, they'd never starve, but the dullness could kill her.

Aside from her husband and kids, she had church, Mrs. Lee, RJ, the annual letter or two from Professor Cho (a.k.a. Frida Kahlo). Yet what had caused such intense dissatisfaction in her everyday life, a melancholy she could not shake? Sometimes she felt trapped in her regret, longing for the past. Other times, she was haunted by the gruesome images and sounds, projected on the walls within her head. There were the everyday objects and people who constantly needed her, and then there was the intensity of the war, inside of her still, which she never spoke about. Would her husband understand? If only she could figure out a way to put into language exactly what she thought and felt, but she was never good with words. She once had painting and art, everyday friendship and laughter.

She had believed that immigrating to America would make her worldly, iconoclastic compared with her peers who chose quieter, more conventional lives as the wives of professionals—lawyers, businessmen, doctors, engineers. But instead in America, she had simply become lonely and invisible. A sense of novelty and adventure had worn thin and threadbare through the years as she grasped exactly how difficult life would be for people who sounded and looked like her, foreigners, and for those whose inheritance would be outweighed by trauma.

Sunny touched the side of John's face, which she hadn't done in a long while, and he closed his eyes as if asking her for some kind of forgiveness. He placed his hand over hers to hold her there for a little while longer so that he'd know they were still real, in the flesh. And she could feel the thrum inside her chest. She could see him, for a few seconds, as he was, and she had the impulse, despite her exhaustion, to take care of him.

It was the children, wasn't it? Their presence, their newness, had changed John.

Perhaps they were reminders of people, maybe even the siblings—his sister, his brother—he had lost in the war. Actually, they were about that age, weren't they, when he had seen them last? His sister was five or six and his little brother, a baby. Maybe she had become like his mother, too, someone he could lose all over again. He and his father had left them behind because they were weak, because they could not survive the journey. His father had said they would return for them once they settled in the South, but the war and the border had kept them apart forever.

"And the rest of the money we could use on a down payment for a house," John said, breaking the silence between them.

"A house?" Yes, they needed more space, but she had so many other pressing concerns. "Have you ever considered that maybe we could start a new business instead? A business where we could both work. I could bring the kids. There must be something we can do in Koreatown, like a laundromat, or a corner store, something like that. We could all work together that way."

"I don't want you to have to work with Ronald at his age."

"But if you chose something we could do together, we could trade off some days. You could stay home with Ronald and I could—"

"It's best for him to be with his mother, don't you think? It's better for you to have more space at home."

What about his father? She wanted to say but didn't. She couldn't.

"Then when Ronald is old enough, when he's in school, we could revisit the idea of a business for both of us."

"But there are ways—"

"You don't want the kids to be at work when they are so young, do you? It can be dangerous. You even said that yourself, remember? Remember?" He turned his head and she could smell his morning breath with his recent loss of teeth. He never took care of his health.

"Yes, but—"

"I have a gun. At work."

She hated to hear that word. She knew he kept one behind the counter at the gas station to protect himself. What kind of world was this?

"I don't want you—"

Ronald cried like the sweetest bird. How her heart broke a little whenever he stirred. He groped for his pacifier, which he found and inserted into his mouth and sucked to appease himself. All with his eyes closed.

"Maybe we should move into a bigger apartment instead? Do we really want to buy a house now?" There was a time, prior to Ronald's birth, that Sunny had yearned for more space, a home, but these past couple years, she cherished her relationship with Mrs. Lee, their proximity to Ana's school, the supermarket, the bus stop. RJ, of course. "Maybe we could find one in the building. That way we won't have to move too far."

A house would solidify them too much in this country, where even after seven years, still she didn't feel as if she belonged. What rooted oneself in a place? A family should be enough—her two children, beautiful and bright and troublesome, and a husband who worked all the time but, yes, loved her. Perhaps she had been the one holding herself back, refusing to thread herself into this life.

"If we buy a house, we'll have a bigger kitchen, a yard. You could play with the kids. You could plant what you want—fruit trees, vegetables, roses. Wouldn't that be nice? We could have barbecues in the summer. A Christmas tree in the living room. Birthday parties for Ana and Ronald. Maybe we could be on a better street. The kids could learn to roller skate and ride bikes. When they both go to school, we can revisit you working, or maybe you can paint again. We could make a studio for you. We'd have a garage where we could keep everything. You could paint. You used to paint so well. Just think about everything we can do with more space."

You used to paint so well. But she was certain that she had forgotten it all, that she'd have to learn from scratch. She doubted she could even reproduce those stupid peonies and Mandarin ducks. She doubted she could paint anything at all. *What are you painting these days?* Professor Cho had asked. *Besides your lips.*

Two fingerprints, pads wet with the color of skin.

As the light crept in through their single window, she had stirring within her the life she could share on canvas or paper. Art always had a point of view. It's what made them human, the most human act, the opposite of war. She caught a flicker of joy in her husband's face as he glanced at their son in their crib. From the rumpled bed, she sat up and could see in the mirror that, despite her age and the new aches in her body, she still had time to be that person, the woman she had always wanted, or wanted to become.

1999

As Ronald and Ana approached Jacob Hendricks's khaki-colored two- story house, Ronald absorbed the foreign scent of freshly mowed grass tinged with the vague sulfurousness of explosives from nearby Disneyland. He had never spent much time down in Orange County, only once every few years when their father would treat them to a trip to the theme parks. He had always associated the county with predominantly white suburbs and large pockets of Asian immigrants and refugees and Latinos who could afford life with better public schools and clean new playgrounds for kids, like the ones near Peggy's house in La Cañada.

On the phone last night, Peggy had said, "There were three Ronald Jones, or possible RJs. Two of them are Black. One of them was a helicopter mechanic. He was discharged early after a leg injury. He also had seizures. TBI. PTSD. I mean, both Ronalds had them."

"What's that?"

"Traumatic brain injury. Post-traumatic stress. He had been in for psychiatric help. There were huge lists of medications. But to be honest, there isn't much that's . . . unique about him. I looked at other files too, and they all seemed to have the same things. Some of them were living on the street. Drug addiction. Suicide. I don't know how my parents do this. It's really depressing."

"Ugh. Imagine how many people died. Like, innocent people. Children. Those kids, they never get help," Ronald said. "Or the families that get split up. My mom's family stayed together. But my dad lost, I think, a brother and a sister . . . and his mom."

"Do you know what happened?"

"Nope. He was thirteen at the time, I think, and he never saw her again." Chills ran down his spine. "I think he saw a lot of people killed, a lot of bodies. He had to ride on top of a train. He saw people falling to their deaths. Some people even pushed each other to make room for themselves. My mother was only a baby so she didn't remember anything. But I'm sure it affected her too. How could it not? There was so little to eat back then."

"Oh my God." She paused, collecting herself. "Do you think your dad feels guilty? That he survived and maybe his mom and his brother and his sister didn't? Honestly, I think I would for the rest of my life. Wouldn't you?"

Of course Ronald would. He even felt guilty about his mother's disappearance. He should've appreciated her more while she was still around. He wanted to share this, but instead tears leaked out of his eyes as if to quench the flames of his face. He couldn't help himself. There was so much he longed to say, but if he opened himself up too much, what would happen when Peggy inevitably left him because their lives were too different to stay together?

"Oh, and Jacob Hendricks? His friend. He flew helicopters in Vietnam," Peggy said. "The only thing that really stood out was 'Agent Orange Exposure.'"

"Ugh. Maybe that's how they met? RJ and Hendricks. RJ was a helicopter mechanic, right?"

In front of Hendricks's door, Ana rang the bell, which chimed, friendly but loud, somewhere deep inside the house. She had borrowed the car, lied to their father that she had planned lunch with a friend to discuss leads for a job. Ronald had skipped school so that he could be with her now. His sister had been surprisingly okay with that.

"Who is it?" a woman asked through the frosted oval glass.

"Good afternoon," Ana said. "We're looking for Jacob Hendricks. Is he there?"

"No, he's not. Anything I can help you with?"

"We have something of his? A wallet that we found."

"A wallet?" The door swung open, startling Ronald and Ana, as it revealed a white woman with large eyes, aggressively mascaraed.

"He left this in a library in LA," Ana said.

"LA?" She cracked the billfold open, its leather sticky and stiff, as if it had been submerged in water. "Which one?" Her glossy fingernails had been painted plum.

"Near Koreatown."

"Koreatown?" the woman asked. "He hasn't been here . . . for weeks."

"Any way we could reach him?"

"Not that I know of. He prefers a different lifestyle." She shook her head.

"A friend of his died suddenly and we want to make sure—"

"Who is it, Beth?" a gruff voice behind her asked. He nudged his wife aside, revealing the Confederate flag on his chest, emblazoned with the words SAVE OUR STATE. Ronald couldn't believe the man wore this shirt in broad daylight. "We're not buying anything." He placed his hand on the edge of the door. "I'm so sick of solicitors. Did you see the sign?" He pointed to the side of the doorway.

"We're here for Jacob Hendricks," Ana said. Her voice was stiff.

"Your dad knew these people?" The man guffawed.

"Mitch." Beth looked at Ana. "Was he police?" she asked. "The man who died?"

Ana looked confused. "No, he was a janitor."

"What was his name?"

"Ronald Jones. He went by RJ. He was also a vet."

Ronald couldn't take his eyes off the Confederate flag. He struggled with the fact that so many could despise him and the people he knew, the people he had grown up with, who had all been so ordinary to him and necessary to the life and the illusions created to maintain the status quo. Mitch and his ilk blamed immigrants, "outsiders," for everything, for the problems we had all helped create or at least collectively ignored. But if they wanted to be upset at anyone, why not people with actual resources and wealth who didn't pay their taxes and stole from everyone? Not some guy selling paletas out of a cart on the street or a woman who took your blood pressure at the hospital.

"You could leave me your number? And I'll have him call you if he comes by," Beth said.

Mitch disappeared as Beth stood, partially obscured by the door. Her eyes had a flat look of dull terror, and Ronald realized that she probably always looked that way and it wasn't just him and Ana, two outsiders, that had caused her agitation. It was perhaps her husband too. Yet she wasn't exactly a spectacle of sadness living in this pleasant house with this beautiful green lawn.

"When was the last time you saw him?" Ana pressed.

"Thanksgiving weekend," Beth said.

"And he lives on the street?"

"Yes, by choice, sort of. He's difficult to pin down."

"Any reason why he would be in LA?"

"He was . . . a police officer for the LAPD. That's why I asked earlier about the man who died." Beth turned her head to a sound in the kitchen.

Did Jacob work at the same station as RJ when he was a janitor? Was *that* how they knew each other?

"I think you should leave," Beth whispered before closing the door. "Thank you for returning this. I'll make sure he gets it."

Outside Beth's house, Ana and Ronald each lit a cigarette in their dad's parked car with the windows down. It had been the first time they shared one together, and he enjoyed watching his sister, the straight-A student, the Berkeley graduate, break some rules. Their dad forbade smoking in general, and in his car especially. His sister was more fun than Ronald had realized.

"He was a police officer," Ana said. "Which means he and RJ could've known each other from work."

"Or maybe from the war. Peggy did say that they both worked with helicopters."

"Does Peggy happen to have any relatives at the police department?" Ana smirked before she blew out a long trail of smoke.

"I mean, probably." Ronald laughed. "She does have a big family."

"Maybe she needs another place to volunteer." Ana smiled. "Someone should be able to figure out the exact connection between RJ and Hendricks. But who?"

Ronald caught sight of Mitch adjusting the blinds, probably uncomfortable with their presence, ruining their property value just by existing out front. All he could think about now was getting back home. He longed for their neighborhood, its chain-link fences and barking dogs, the silhouette of a dying palm tree against the ombre of a citrus sky. There was a kind of beauty to that fight of being alive. He used to hate that hunger, but he could see now how it had shaped him and who he was.

He started the engine and blasted Tupac, loud as he could in his father's beat-up blue Cadillac Eldorado, with pride.

The day before, when his sister had picked up Jacob's wallet at the library, Janet had given her a printout of the books that their mother had borrowed with Ana's card. Her mother had clearly been interested in Vietnam, possibly because RJ had served there.

"What if Mom and RJ ran away together?" Ronald asked as he merged onto 5 North, already a wall of traffic, gray and dull. "What if it was just her that stayed in Vietnam, and RJ believed that she had made it back to LA?"

"Wouldn't he have mentioned that in the letter?" Ana asked.

"True."

She took a final drag of her cigarette, stubbed it out in the ashtray. "We have to stay focused on what we can control. The facts that we have. I think it's all buried somewhere," Ana said, her arms folded. "There's still the Observatory. The picture. The photograph, I remember. We should go there next. There's the garage, too. Mom's art. There're more places we could look. We're not done yet."

"I can't go in there." He felt nauseous even thinking about the garage.

"You can't?"

"No, not since she left," he said. "It makes me sick. The smell too. Everything about it. I've tried, but I can't. I don't think Dad has either. It brings back too much."

"I know," Ana said. "I feel the same, but . . . I don't think we have a choice. I can do it again myself. I wasn't very thorough last time."

Why was it so difficult to get rid of things you couldn't even look at? When would he ever be able to think about the past without such a crushing sense of sadness?

"Saturday . . . I think it's one year after she left, right?" Ana asked. She closed the window on her side, leaned back. "We should go to the Observatory. I haven't been in years. Something might come up. And if nothing does, it's still beautiful, right? We can remember her there." She closed her eyes. "I'm not sure grief ever goes away, but it gets easier, I think. Maybe the more experiences you have, the layers of your life, like washes of color, watercolors, transform the loss or how you perceive it at least. So the grief is still there. But it has a different tint to it."

"That's deep," he said, not really joking, but of course it came out that way.

He agreed with her. He imagined himself as a toddler in his mother's arms. The four of them, including RJ and Ana, getting out of her car, the beige Oldsmobile Cutlass sedan, which had been missing this past year as well.

1983

"Alright, Mrs. Kim." In the passenger seat, John jerked the steering wheel in front of her as they remained, engine off, perpendicular to the painted stripes of an empty bank parking lot. "Prepare for your untimely demise."

"Oh, shut up and start instructing, Mr. Kim. Remember who's in the driver's seat."

The crisp autumn sun softened the landscape with its honey-colored light. On Sunday mornings like this, with generally less traffic, the city could smell sweet and musky with the last of the summer blooms that faded in the waning daylight hours. She loved this season, always her favorite, with the fire of its foliage, dazzling maple and gingko back in Korea. Even in Los Angeles, she appreciated the relief from the summer's scorching heat, which allowed her and the children to spend more time outdoors on walks down the street, when she'd admire the bizarre junglelike leaves and the alien cacti and succulents in every shade from chartreuse to burgundy that reminded her of images of coral reefs. A city block could be a kind of public gallery with its gardens and sidewalk strips as expressions of pasts and futures—hauntings, hopes, and dreams.

They had decided to skip that morning's church service and ask Mrs. Lee to watch the kids in order to begin Sunny's lessons as soon as possible. And even just this slight disturbance in their routines invigorated her with a secret giddiness that had substituted her anxieties about driving.

Perhaps part of what she had feared all along might be her own personal agency. What would she pursue if she could get away with it, what wildness, what breaking of rules?

"Left pedal is the brake and right is the gas. You gas it when you want to go and you brake it when you want to stop," John said. "Remember, you want to be very gentle, very smooth about it all. It's like you're touching a woman, or in your case, a baby."

"Ha, I've touched more woman than you ever will."

He opened his eyes wide and whistled.

"Oh, get your mind out of the gutter."

John kissed her on the lips with a dramatic sound, her face in a cage of his fingers. It had been the first time in a few months that she had felt the heat of him like that, desired again just from that one simple act. After the birth of her son, she had become self-conscious about her body, and her husband's lack of advances confirmed her bias against herself. But now his hand slid up her thigh and squeezed. His breath, heavy on her neck, closed into a bite that made her laugh. She wriggled away from him despite the temptation, the glint in his eyes, the possibility of danger, and he smiled devilishly before he retreated to the passenger seat. She touched the part of her skin that had felt his teeth, glanced in the mirror at four tiny red marks, which she rubbed with her palm as if to spread the ink, erase the evidence.

John reached over and turned the engine on with a twist. The Oldsmobile roared and vibrated beneath them. Sunny gripped the steering wheel with both hands like the reins of a horse. A living thing. Not simply a machine. An animal that needed to be fed.

Why couldn't she have it all? The children and family that she loved. The art. RJ too. The adventures he proposed. *We should go to the beach or the Observatory like two kids.* His friendship, maybe more. She didn't want whatever they had, the conversations once or twice per week, to stop. She realized now that he had been the first English-speaking person who took her seriously, bothered to get to know her at all. He welcomed her to this country in a way that no one else had before.

Although the car itself, a bulky beige sedan, had not been seductive, she could feel both the responsibility and the power of this car, where it might take her whenever she wanted with a full tank.

But that night, hours after her first driving lesson, the phone rang, which it rarely did past eight p.m. Sunny rushed to pick it up; she didn't want the children to wake. She knew that a phone call at night could possibly be from Korea, where it would be the early afternoon now.

"Sunhee." Her sister Sunmi's voice. "I'm sorry to call you so late."

They had been close once, but after Sunny immigrated to the United States, the distance, the responsibilities toward their families, their disparate experiences, had driven them apart as if their relationship could exist only suspended in the amber of their childhood. Sunmi had been four years old, while Sunny had been a baby when they had fled their home in the North. Thus, their general temperaments differed remarkably. Sunmi had always been much more serious, dedicated, and studious, a star student, unlike charismatic Sunny who couldn't sit still and faltered in every subject except art. She had even been described as lazy at times, but the racing of her mind, its collision of images, her sensitivities to sounds and bright lights, her anxieties about public speaking and large crowds, exhausted her.

Of course, it could only be bad news. Sunny braced herself, gripping the phone's receiver.

"They found Professor Cho, her body near Bukhan River," Sunmi said. "She had been missing for weeks."

"No, no, no," Sunny said, like fingers plugging holes in the bottom of a sinking boat. She covered her mouth, bit down on the flesh at the base of her thumb to keep herself from screaming. She imagined Professor Cho slumped on a riverbank in a pool of Cadmium Red that seeped into the dark mud. The stain of a life. Wide-angled cheekbones broken, a moon jar smashed. How cruel and unnecessary. How alone she must've been in those final moments without grace, like an animal hunted for sport. If only Sunny could run to her now, cover her body with her own, and hold the soft pieces of her tight. How much her letters meant to her. How much she needed her in her life. "No," she said one last time. If only she could simply rewind their lives, if only she could've been there, to press down into blood. What would she have said if she could? Every word she could think of that really mattered: *I'm grateful. I'm sorry. I love you.*

"It appeared that she had been mugged, beaten, and abandoned there." A car zoomed by in the background, a motorcycle puttered. Her sister must've called from a pay phone. An expensive phone call, but she must've not wanted anyone to overhear or trace her. "Several months ago, the police had taken her in because of her . . . political activity. She was gone from campus. When one of her students— Do you remember Chung Jiwon? The ceramicist? When she ran into her in Insadong, her face was . . . her mouth cut open, her eye, swollen and black. She barely recognized her except for the leather bag that she always carried. The large brown one with her supplies." She sighed in condolence as if she knew that Sunny wept on the other side.

Sunny remembered the first time she had met Professor Cho, and how she lifted the cross-body strap over her head. Her ponytail had gotten caught and slipped out of its elastic, which she then held between her lips before she retied it. She had two large sweat stains under her arms in the gray linen dress shirt she wore, and Sunny couldn't help but imagine the dark hair there, the shape of her breasts when the arms flexed above. For whatever reason, it had been easy to imagine her naked. Her father painted many nudes, and much of her life had been surrounded by the bodies, the curves of women hanging on the walls of their home.

"She was always involved in the protests," her sister said. "So many people had warned her. I think her husband even left her."

Tears dripped off Sunny's chin onto her chest. She didn't bother to wipe her face.

How could something like this happen to a person, regardless of their political beliefs, or what they might represent? If the police could commit such violence in the life of a citizen, how could anyone trust the government, the entire system? You could be murdered for having ideas, passions, different conceptions of what it meant to be alive, and there would be no repercussions. Who paid the price when the state itself robbed us of life? Who decided which ideas would be the most dangerous, which should be eliminated?

Those two fingers tucked Sunny's hair behind her ear.

Those two fingers pressed peach into the end of her letters. The signal, a sign that only they would understand. A common language. How to reach that color again? The swirl of white, yellow, and red. How to touch that color again?

And as a student seeking Professor Cho's approval, the thrill and the terror of becoming a woman grew manageable. She had a singular focus, an edge on which to sharpen the roundness of childhood. Instead of worrying about her body and comparing herself endlessly with her peers, the nervousness she still experienced while on her period, the fear and shame of bleeding through her clothes, she could pinpoint her efforts into pleasing *her*.

And one day, she did—enough for Professor Cho to write her those letters all these years since she had left. The stamp of two peach fingers on the page. The perfect imperfection of that moon jar, shaped with such godlike precision, yet graced by those two reminders of its humanity, the humanity behind the craft of this porcelain. How Sunny wished now that she had never left her, never left herself, behind there in that gallery. What had she been running from? What was the point of a life concealed like the man and woman beneath Magritte's sheet?

"I bet you're glad you moved to America," her sister said.

For most of her life, even before immigrating to America, Sunny hated how trapped she felt in history all the time. But love could force you into the present moment, plunge you into a future that seemed hopeful and bright. Of course, she could never explain that to Sunmi, not to anyone. She wiped her nose with the back of her hand, unable to move from where she stood in the dim kitchen. She squeezed the receiver so hard that her fingers hurt.

Her son cried out, just once, in their bedroom, where John now rested too. Her daughter had been fast asleep.

"Please let me know if you learn anything new," Sunny whispered. "Take care of yourself. Thank you, thank you for taking such good care of Mother." She hung up the phone before she said too much, and retreated to the small bathroom redolent of the bright green soap that her husband preferred to her own creamy-white floral one. She rested on the dark-gray tiled floor with her back against the tub, wads of toilet paper in her hands. Not only did she mourn for Professor Cho, but she grieved for her country, for home.

Her beautiful teacher, bloody, another casualty on the ground. She had seen the dead before and they were like dolls, lifeless and strewn about, toys that had been forgotten. That was an entire life, that was someone's sister or best friend or lover, that was someone's baby, or someone's baby once.

Each time Sunny thought of those two fingers pressed on the side of the jar, she couldn't help but imagine Professor Cho's hands impressing themselves on her. Had Professor Cho felt the same? Sunny would never know. What other opportunities might she miss if she always made decisions guided by fear in this one life? What if instead she chose calmness, courage? Would she choose danger? Would she choose herself?

1999

John caught his reflection in the police station's doors and hiked his navy Dickies over his slim waist. He adjusted the tuck of his long-sleeve shirt beneath the burgundy windbreaker he always wore. The waiting area smelled of an artificial pine cleaner, a familiar, almost comforting scent he had used to scrub his own floors.

At the front desk, a woman with auburn hair hunched over a series of black-and-white forms with a highlighter in hand. Bangles jingled on her wrists. She popped her bubble gum and, without looking up, asked, "Can I help you?"

His sneakers squeaked. "I was, uh, looking for information about Ronald Jones."

"Who?"

"Work here. 1970s, '80s. Ronald Jones? RJ?"

"Doesn't ring a bell," she said.

What did that mean? *Doesn't ring a bell.* Despite how long he had been in America, he still couldn't understand its idioms, a currency of language which revealed perhaps how integrated you were within the larger culture.

"I haven't been here that long, but maybe—" She twisted herself toward the back. "Priscilla," she called to another woman in front of a screen filled with magnified letters. "Hey, Priscilla."

"Yeah, what is it?"

"Did you know a Ronald Jones? RJ?"

Priscilla leaned back and paused. "Of course."

"This man has some questions about him. I gotta take a break in fifteen minutes."

Priscilla turned off the screen she had been looking at before carefully feeling her way past chairs and desks. She appeared to be Latina and in her fifties or sixties with her wavy brown hair pulled into a short ponytail, penciled crescents for brows, and powdery skin that gave a general impression of softness, or fuzziness like the flesh of a peach. She frowned, deep creases appearing on her forehead. She squinted because of some difficulty with her vision. Her eyes, grayish blue, struck him as strangely tender, stunning too—pale as the underside of a rabbit.

"Can I help you with something?" she asked. Phone lines rang, lighting up the desk in a sad disco of red.

"RJ worked here?"

She nodded, wringing her hands. Her lips parted. "What about him?"

John wanted to ask how he lost his job, but instead he said, "He . . . died last weekend. His daughter looking for, uh, information."

She covered her mouth. How he hated to deliver bad news. When his wife had disappeared, at least he had been able to tell his daughter over the phone. But with his son, he remembered how he had touched his bedroom door after Ronald had slammed it behind him. He had been desperate for his son to know that he had always tried his best and that he would do everything he could to bring his mother back.

"Oh my God." Tears spilled from Priscilla's eyes, clung to her long eyelashes. The receptionist handed her a tissue. "Did they ever . . . meet? Did he ever find *her*? His daughter. Her name is Rhonda, isn't it?"

John shook his head. RJ clearly wasn't just anyone to Priscilla.

"How did—"

"I help her find out about her father." It wasn't exactly a lie, but he needed to know why RJ had left or lost his job, why he had been homeless and behind John's house with a letter to his wife. His well-meaning children needed to know who was the real villain. *Not* him—an immigrant who had worked hard his whole life, paid taxes, followed the laws—and survived based on his tenacity and merit. It was RJ who had doomed himself.

"And are you . . . a family friend?" the receptionist asked.

"He died in my yard, at my house. My children want to help her, his daughter." He grabbed a pen on the counter and thumbed the end, its cap. He could almost break it. He could almost make it snap.

"I actually have to get these files put away, but if you wait about an hour, I'll be on lunch break. Do you have time to wait?"

John studied his watch. He needed to be sure that Ana would be okay at the nursery a while longer. He expected another delivery. "Sure, okay. But can I use your phone?"

After checking in with Ana, John retired to the waiting room where he observed a teenager about Ronald's age who fidgeted in his seat, chewed his nails, and glanced at his pager often. A woman with shiny slicked-back hair leaned her head on a shoulder, a man who closed his eyes to make up for lost sleep last night. Why were these young people here and not at work or school? They could've found a job anywhere, like himself at a gas station or a convenience store back when he had first come to America. If they stayed busy, they would not get in trouble.

The tap of a thin white cane. Priscilla appeared refreshed, a rosy glow from her face and lips. He had an urge to lower his face and smell her like a flower. "I was gonna grab lunch at the sandwich shop a few blocks away. Do you want to get lunch together?"

The thin white cane. What did it mean? How did she work?

"Sure. Uh, okay. Can I help you?" Nervous, John extended his hand in an offer to guide her somehow, but then he realized she probably couldn't even see his gesture.

She laughed. "Oh, no, no, I'm fine."

How had he not noticed earlier that she was blind? Or was she blind? She had been staring at a screen. Maybe she was only partially blind, but he panicked as he watched her a couple feet in front of him, guiding the way for *him*. Following her down the street, he did everything in his might to contain his urge to yell, *Please be careful!* But she didn't seem to notice or care about his concern at all.

"What was your name again?" she asked.

"John."

They stopped at a wide intersection, waiting for the light to change. But how did she know when to cross? Two cars honked at each other as they sped by, spewing noxious fumes into the air.

"I mean, things would be easier if they were designed a little differently."

"Can you see anything?"

She laughed. "I see everything, but blurry. I'm legally blind. I used to have a guide dog until I realized that I didn't have to feed a cane. Canes don't need kibble *and* they don't need to take a shit." She led him across the street when the light changed. He could barely resist grabbing her arm as if to shield her from traffic, yet nothing about her step or her posture suggested she needed aid.

At the counter, they ordered sandwiches. Priscilla folded her cane and settled into a booth against a large floor-to-ceiling plate glass greasy with fingerprints. "I always like to sit by the window. You know, I spend so much time indoors and we don't have any natural light . . . I always feel so much better in the sun, even though my eyes and skin are so sensitive. I'm like a plant of some sort. A vegetable."

John couldn't help but laugh. What kind of vegetable would he be? He hadn't worked in an office environment since college. He had never been confined to that kind of job, day in and day out. Perhaps that was what he hated so much about studying, and why he eventually dropped out of graduate school in America. He always needed something to look at, people to watch, otherwise he grew bored and fidgety, impatient and angry. In America, he wanted to take in the world, as if looking away might mean he'd miss something, something vital, some clue that could change his life. Things had been so different in Korea, where a book offered a kind of dependable salvation from a life he hated, destroyed by war, governed by autocrats and the threat of death.

"RJ and I were friends," Priscilla said, reminding John of why he had come there in the first place. "I missed him so much when he left, but—"

"Tuna! Salami." The deli man belted behind the counter before he yelled in Cantonese at his son who played video games in the back. John could feel the father's pain. The son picked up their orders, hefty like two bricks of food in his hands, and brought them to their table.

She unwrapped her sandwich. Her face grew red. "I knew he was homeless."

The delicious bread, mayonnaise, shredded lettuce, and deli meat reminded him of when he had first moved to Los Angeles and everything had still been an adventure, a novelty. He had even worked at a white bread factory in Beverly Hills. The mildness of the flavors soothed him, unlike the brashness of Korean dishes. He had been in America long enough that this food had become a part of his memory, his template for longing. And how ironic that a Chinese American man, between bouts of yelling at his son, had created this very American moment for them.

"Do they even know how he died or . . ." Priscilla hesitated. "Did someone . . . was he murdered?"

"It was accident. He fell down."

The smell, the shoes, the foulness of him. Urine and sweat. The stench.

Priscilla rested her sandwich on the table. She rubbed her forehead with the tips of her fingers. Her nails had been unpainted and broken. Her fingers wrinkled. She didn't wear any rings at all. Simply a gold necklace with a cross. He couldn't help but wonder if she and RJ had ever dated or been romantically involved. Whether her feelings for him overwhelmed her, brought back memories she chose to forget.

"I tried to . . . I shouldn't be talking about this. But I know . . ." Her lips trembled as her eyes filled with tears. "We'd been out of touch, but I know that he lost his job, his house too. This was in the early eighties. It all happened so suddenly." She shook her head. "I ran into him once, a year or so ago, and I couldn't believe it." She wiped her cheeks. "He looked so helpless. He read so many books. He cared so much about the world, other people too. He was a vet, you know?"

Shame burned John's neck and face. He had no idea what to do, how to help this woman in front of him, crying. He felt responsible for her, her well-being. He didn't want anyone to hurt. He would take all the pain in the world if it would relieve them. But it never did. So he had to keep working and maybe one day his children, someone would finally see him. They would hold the entire truth of him.

"He was climbing my fence," John said.

Priscilla wiped the tears off her face, dabbed the corners of her eyes with a folded napkin. "I have two kids. Well, I guess they're not kids anymore, but . . . one's in college. I can't take any risks."

He nodded, even though he didn't know exactly what she was referring to.

"How's his daughter? How'd you find her?"

"The police find her. I don't know. She live in, uh, Lancaster?"

"Lancaster? Wow." Priscilla picked up her sandwich again. "That's really not too far. He talked about her a lot. I could tell how much it hurt him, you know? His ex." She nodded before taking a bite. Her eyes appeared to be searching for something inside herself as she gazed out the dirty window.

"Ex-wife?"

"Yeah. She took his daughter. Down South, back home or something, in Alabama, I think. She practically kidnapped her."

John didn't understand.

"He was devastated. They were both young when they had her. He must've been sixteen or seventeen. And then I guess at some point he served in Vietnam after that." Priscilla continued, "He was disabled and worked for us as a custodian at night. After he lost his job, he went to look for his daughter in the South. But she was already an adult. Gone."

At least now, Rhonda would know that her father didn't simply abandon her. There had been more to the story. But no, John had to prove that RJ had been terrible, didn't he? He had to prove that he had been a bad man, that he deserved to die and be forgotten so that they would all move on, and when Sunny returned she would know the truth of him, a villain. John was the hero here. He'd forgive her for anything if she came back.

"Why, uh, why did he . . . lose job?"

"I can't talk about that. It's confidential." She shook her head. "When I ran into him about a year ago, he was back behind the station in the dumpsters, I don't know, probably collecting food or some stuff, and I said something and he turned around and acted like he wanted to hug me, but of course, I didn't recognize him or his voice. I don't see well and he just seemed like a homeless person. He said my name, and I could tell by his voice how much had happened." She crinkled the paper for her sandwich in her hand. "Some people always want to do what's right."

"Yes," he said. She understood him.

"Unfortunately . . . we live in a world that'll punish them. I've accepted that."

He winced. He didn't want to believe that was true, but he couldn't argue against her either. Again, he had failed; not even at RJ's former workplace could John prove that RJ had deserved the unfortunate life he had, his death.

"I might be large in size"—she laughed a little to herself—"but I am . . . very small. We all are." She swept the crumbs off the table with her hand. "But RJ, he deserved to live more than anyone I know. I promise you that. I wish I could say more, but—" She cut herself off.

And in that moment, her face and neck flushed red.

John knew Priscilla had been hiding something the whole time.

1983

Sunny reclined on the living room couch as Ronald banged every pot and pan in the universe. With great showmanship, wooden spoons gonged metal lids. The determination of a toddler rooting through every drawer and cupboard went unmatched. Repairing Ana's T-shirts and pants, Sunny pressed and pulled the thread taut, a meditation which kept her sane through the clanging. She focused on the textures, the soft cotton in her hands, the sense of accomplishment when she tied each knot twice. How incredible to think that the world, even at its most mundane, could be magnificent and sublime within a child's gaze. Perhaps the greatest accomplishment might be a return to that former self, the open expression, a wonder like the fullest breath. An expansion of soul and spirit. A defiance of death.

The month had passed in a daze since Professor Cho's body had been found. Routines, including Sunny's rides on the bus, had ceased. She barely found the energy to feed or bathe herself. When her husband had finally taken notice, she had confessed that someone very close to her from college had been killed.

"Did she ride the train by herself?" he asked. "Once we buy a new car next week, you'll be able to drive the Oldsmobile as much as you'd like. It's too dangerous to be a woman alone in the dark."

Of course, he couldn't imagine that she not only mourned a life and a friendship, but also a relationship cut short, a different future for herself. And she didn't bother to mention any of Professor Cho's political activity or the possibility that she had been murdered by the police.

At a knock on the front door, Sunny returned her needles and thread to the Royal Dansk cookie tin where she kept her sewing kit and rushed to meet Mrs. Lee who, back hunched, leaned on the wall and removed her outdoor slippers. Her skin and clothes smelled of sesame oil and ginger like the comforts of home. "Grandma's here," she said, making herself comfortable on the couch. Ronald sprung from the kitchen floor and hung on to her knees between her legs as he begged, "Up, up." Mrs. Lee lifted him, thin arms shaking, onto her lap and rocked side to side as she squeezed his torso with birdlike pecks on the top of the head. "Big boy," she said in English.

"I don't have anything prepared." Sunny wrung her hands, glanced at her watch. She had only about thirty more minutes to catch RJ at the stop. And since she hadn't seen him in weeks, she couldn't lose any more time. She had something for him tonight. "There's some kimchi jjigae from last night in the fridge," she said.

"I haven't heard from you in a while." Mrs. Lee brushed Ronald's hair away from his eyes.

"I've been . . . not well," Sunny said. "I'm better now." She poured Mrs. Lee a glass of orange juice. She almost dropped it with the shaking of her hand.

"Oh, thank you, dear." Mrs. Lee sipped, pinching her lips. She had been one of those women who grew into herself with age, as if she had achieved her final form as grandmother, kind and wise, mottled branches wide, an empress. Eyes glittering.

Without any warning, Ronald jumped off Mrs. Lee's lap and scampered around the kitchen, where he banged a lid onto the ground. Sunny cringed. Her head pounded from hearing the sound all day long.

"I've just been feeling very tired lately." Tears filled her eyes. How could Professor Cho be gone from this world? But now was not the time. She sniffled like she had a cold.

"It's a difficult age," Mrs. Lee said. "One day, your son will be on his own and you won't even know what he's doing, or where he is." She beamed as the memories and feelings for her own children pooled in the complicated expression of her face, a mix of love, disbelief, and heartache. "Believe it or not, you'll miss this. I do. All things pass."

"I keep trying to remind myself of that." She glanced toward Ronald, who crushed an empty milk carton that he had gotten ahold of from who knows where.

"I know it seems like an eternity, but this is the one thing I can guarantee. When you are old like me, no one ever says life went by too slowly."

From the bedroom door, she said goodbye to Ana, who had been reading on the floor, her favorite activity, with her back against their two pillows. Sunny gathered her jacket and purse and rushed down the stairs into the building's dark and damp ground floor with the list of things she needed etched into her mind: doenjang, two heads of napa cabbage, dried anchovies, milk, cereal, cookies, eggs.

In the sudden darkness of November, she raced down the sidewalk as if no time had passed, although it had been weeks since she had left the house and run errands by herself. On the bench at the bus stop, RJ sat waiting, to her relief. He bit into his red apple under the amber glow from a streetlight above. She deposited her hand into her pocket and squeezed the gift she had brought. He caught sight of her, folded his newspaper, and waved. A fog of breath rushed out of her mouth as she calmed herself and presented the persimmon in both hands like a nest cradling a small bird.

RJ lifted his brows. The surprise on his face.

"Knife?" She made a motion with her hand, pantomiming the peeling of its skin. "Very good. Delicious."

"Oh, thank you, Sunny." When he picked up the fruit, his fingertips grazed her hand. "I was . . . worried about you." His eyes sparkled despite some change in his face that had aged him since they last met. Had he experienced some fresh tragedy or wound from which he had still been healing too? "I don't know how, but it seems like we managed to miss each other?"

"Driver's license," she said, pointing to herself.

"You? You're driving?" He smiled. "Congratulations, Sunny."

She wanted to say that she preferred taking the bus, that although she did not speak to anyone, she loved the familiar faces each time she boarded, found a seat beside one. The people's voices, their noises—from a long sigh to the zip of a jacket—sounded some days like music, a lullaby of the city in a vehicle that rocked.

"So, you're not taking the bus anymore?" he asked. "No more bus?"

"My husband buy new car. I drive old car."

"Ha, that makes sense. Maybe one day you'll graduate to something nice. A Mercedes-Benz."

"You drive?"

"I used to but I injured myself. I'm not allowed to drive anymore." He grimaced. "In a way, it's good I guess. I have more time on the bus to think and write. I've been so busy these days." He gazed into the street in front of them. Cars sped by, or slammed on brakes when the light changed to red. "I won't get to see you as much, but maybe, I don't know, maybe we could finally go to the Observatory, or the Pier together. Ha, we could even take the kids now that you drive, don't you think? Does your husband ever take you anywhere?"

She didn't quite understand what he meant.

"Do you take day trips . . . the beach, the mountains, the park? It's important to get away, to recharge."

"Husband too busy. Work every day."

"I get it." He sighed. "Everything costs a lot." She observed his fingers gripping the persimmon she had given him.

"Are you . . . okay?" she asked finally.

"Me?"

What else could she offer him but an ear, the silence of her listening without judgment. She wanted to say, *You can tell me anything, and I'd care about you the same way. You wouldn't judge me either. I know it. There are things that I never talk about as well, things that weigh heavily on me. But I've always believed it was my fate to carry them by myself because no one would understand me, or maybe I am simply ashamed.*

"Sunny, can you keep something between the two of us?" He lifted his brows. "Can you keep a secret?" He gazed into the distance, as if gauging the space between him and a bus that was nowhere in sight.

"Yes," she said. "Yes."

"I don't know how much you'll know what I'm talking about, but some days it feels like I can't keep myself out of trouble. Or maybe . . . that's not it." He exhaled with a loud puff. "I feel— I feel on the outside of life."

Yes, she nodded.

"I've always been hungry for the truth." Tears filled his eyes. She had the urge to hold his hand but she didn't. She remembered the comfort of his on her shoulder now, the warmth of her body softening in that spot. "When I was in Vietnam, I saw things that I never spoke about, and I realize how much those things ate away at me. Ate away at my friends. All those things we kept to ourselves, in the dark, they fester." He tightened his lips and cleared his throat. "And so when I see something, I have to write it down. There's been . . ." He shook his head. "Where I work, I've witnessed things and I realize in a way, that this is what I was meant for all along."

"*Witness?*"

"Remember when I said I wanted to be a journalist? Work for the newspaper? Well, it's like a story just landed in my hands." For a few seconds, she lost track of where they sat. She didn't even know whether or not either of their buses had passed. All she could focus on were his words, and collecting them somewhere inside her mind so that one day she might understand them. "There are things I have overheard at my work the past few weeks, things I've seen. Then I've been—remember my camera? I've been taking pictures, collecting . . . evidence. No one really notices me. It's surprising sometimes. When I'm in certain places, I disappear entirely. I'm just some random guy, a janitor, quiet."

Of course, she related to this.

"I decided that I can't let people keep hurting people with less—less power—no one to listen to them. I can't live in a world like that. And I have to wait until I have enough proof, enough to . . ."

She could tell he had been tortured. She felt as if she knew in a strange way exactly what he had been trying to communicate.

"Ironically enough, never in my life have I had a friend like you, someone I could speak so easily with." He beamed. "Maybe it's because I know you can't understand everything I say, but yet, I also feel like you *know* me."

Yes, in a strange way, she did.

"The only person who I've told is Priscilla, this nice lady I work with. She and I have overheard a lot of things. But unlike me, she's smart and she stays out of trouble. I've been working on this by myself. It's lonely, sure, but even if the world wasn't made for me, I know my parents, all my family survived the shit they did so that I could do this honestly, so that I could live honestly, you see? It's all I ever wanted."

The bus pulled forward in front of them, and to her surprise, he stood with his backpack on his shoulder. For whatever reason, she had believed that he would continue regardless of where he had to go. "Hope to see you soon? I appreciate the fruit." He tossed the persimmon into the air like a baseball. "I appreciate you."

Stunned, she remained on the bench, despite a few minutes later her own bus passing by.

My parents, all my family survived the shit they did so that I could do this honestly, so that I could live honestly, you see?

His bravery reminded her of Professor Cho. Both had been unable to look the other way. What risks had he been taking of late? What had he been recording and taking pictures of? She couldn't lose anyone else anymore.

And who exactly was Priscilla?

She never had the chance to ask him these questions, nor ask him what he thought about the persimmon with its honeyish flavor and slippery texture. Or to bring him another and another.

After that final encounter, her husband had purchased his own car, a Cadillac Eldorado, which seemed ridiculous for their frugal lives, and she now had full access to the Oldsmobile. And since Mrs. Lee had suddenly been engrossed helping her son with his new restaurant, Sunny didn't have the ability to leave her kids at home. Unseen, for weeks, she simply drove by RJ on the bench, with the children, rambunctious, legs and arms everywhere behind her, despite her shouts, her pleas for them to *please stop*.

For now, she settled for the satisfaction of observing RJ from a distance, where she could experience a morsel of him but still be safe from both the world and herself. There was something about watching—the ability to hold another in one's gaze, to observe and notice. If Professor Cho had taught her anything it would be to understand the value of an appraising eye, its power like a sharp pin that kept a butterfly under glass. She couldn't describe why or what her actual aim had been but simply to not let go of him. She dreamed of all the places they could go. They could drive to the ocean or to Griffith Park with its exuberant, almost psychedelic merry-go-round, grand observatory, and dusty rides on adorable ponies. The clock was ticking.

But one December night, cigarette in her hand like a stick of incense on this altar of an American life, she passed the bus stop, only to see it was empty. Trash flittered by in the breeze, and pigeons pecked at concrete for edible debris. She circled the block several times, but she had missed him.

She returned again the following week after she had found an hour that worked with Mrs. Lee to watch the children. Alone in the car, Sunny parked a block away where she could wait and keep an eye on the bench. But something had changed. Instead, a different person—a teenager with his headphones over his head, an elderly woman with a foldable cart—waited in RJ's place. A homeless man, his back curled, slept where once her water had broken. Weeks and months passed this way through winter, into a new year, when the heady scent of jasmine offered some relief from the smog.

Maybe he had moved, or changed jobs. How much did she really know about him?

Maybe someone had hurt him. *I decided that I can't let people keep hurting people with less—less power—no one to listen to them. I can't live in a world like that. And I have to wait until I have enough proof.* She drove and drove, sometimes in circles around blocks, even with her children in the back seat, burning through gas, which her husband for whatever reason never questioned. Gas prices had been steadily dropping since the oil crisis in 1979. There was so much of it after all, and since he had insisted that she should drive, he couldn't hold her accountable for how much she spent when he himself filled up the car at his own business.

Maybe one night she should visit the police station where he worked? She could use the phone book to find each one in the area. Maybe if he had left, the person named Priscilla would know his whereabouts? Who was she anyways? Maybe they had run off together.

But then when her husband had finally purchased a house, west of Koreatown, in a residential neighborhood with mostly single-family homes where people of different races and economic backgrounds, from working- to middle-class, lived, John filled their apartment over the weeks with a dizzying array of discarded boxes and newspaper to wrap everything fragile. She spent hours wrestling with her children, who seemed hell-bent on undoing all of her work as she organized and sealed boxes. And she no longer had time to worry about RJ, at least while they packed their lives up, which had been traumatic for her. She had a nervous breakdown when she had found the letters from Professor Cho, hidden after she had died. John, unable to leave his gas station untended, brought the kids to work for three days while Sunny slept like a dead person, without even rising to eat or drink once. Only then did she finally accept the truth: Professor Cho was dead, and RJ was gone.

1999

The soondubu restaurant glowed like a pristine crystal box with its clean glass and glossy tables. Ahjummas in black aprons rushed from customer to customer, carrying stone bowls of piping-hot soup that roiled like volcanoes. John was reminded of how little he treated himself to a dinner out these days with only Ronald. It was a luxury to pay someone to cook and serve you. After Sunny disappeared from their lives, food became exclusively about survival until the next meal. How trapped he had felt in this cycle, and now through the plate glass, as he waited in line on a bustling Friday night, he marveled as if watching people in a fish tank.

The tip of a cane tapped his shoe. Priscilla.

After he had left the police station yesterday, John returned to the nursery and spent the afternoon thinking about Priscilla. Her name and number burned in his billfold, which he kept in his right back pocket at all times. There was something about her—her easy smile, the warmth of her eyes, her confidence as she crossed the street with the white cane—that buoyed him in a way that had been different from anyone he had met in his life. Even before Sunny disappeared, after he lost his mother in the war, he had learned to avoid the riptide of his emotional life. His father and other boys and men shamed each other for what they felt. They should go through life only affected briefly, momentarily, before it was time to soldier on, reaching their destinies as individuals with duties and responsibilities. No one could afford to listen to their heart. Its beating and its blood would never write a check, pay the bills, keep the lights on at night.

But all day long he couldn't ignore the palpitations in his throat, in his cheeks, and behind his eyes, which he hadn't experienced since they had first purchased the house almost fifteen years ago. He couldn't deny when this happened, when his brain had been seized by thoughts, by dreams of being with someone, sharing their breath. And a curiosity, too, of what she might be hiding. He extinguished any flash or flicker of guilt with the reminder: Sunny *left* him.

That night, the same day they had lunch, he called her. Priscilla had been working late. He asked if he could see her again, and she said yes. Tomorrow, Friday night. She loved Korean food. She could meet him at a soondubu restaurant. And here they were. The tip of her cane had touched his foot.

Customers cleared the area for Priscilla as soon as they noticed her; a few dramatically jumped out of the way. John had to admit that he himself didn't know what to do, and that his inability to speak this language of interaction with someone who navigated the world in such a different way caused a paralysis of fear and shame. Did she need his help or was she fine? He didn't want to push or scare her away. Why would she want to spend time with him, this lonely old man who had grown awkward and clumsy through the years, anyways? It was all about RJ. She wanted to help his daughter. And he was okay with that, as long as he could observe and be close to her.

"I haven't been here in forever," she said. "Mind if I use your arm? As a guide."

He extended his right arm like a wooden toy soldier. With a smile on her face, she reached for his hand, lowered it, and held his tricep, which tingled beneath her grip. A place he hadn't been touched in a long time.

"You could relax your arm," she said. Her black mascara covered half the length of her eyelashes. The roots revealed that her hair was almost white. He enjoyed the details of her face, her skin with its snowlike softness, a fuzziness.

"Just down by your side. Your arm. I'll follow behind once we go in. It's pretty narrow in there, right?" She squinted through the window and pursed her lips. "I haven't had a soondubu in such a long time." Her face beamed. "Ooh, the seafood one. I love that one so much. I can smell it." She inhaled through her nose, eyes closed, face relaxed. For a few seconds, he imagined holding her between his arms, her downy hair under his chin. But then a pang of guilt. Haemul soondubu was his wife's favorite too. How happily she'd pull the shrimps' heads and legs off with her fingers and pile their translucent skins in an empty banchan bowl, a banchan that she didn't like much and didn't need refills for, such as the kongjang, the braised black beans too sweet for her taste. She preferred the salty and the savory—earthy namuls, such as kongnamul and sigeumchi and doraji—nutty with sesame oil.

Tomorrow, Saturday, would be the one-year anniversary of the day that she left and never came home. In the decades he had worked under this American sun, inside the fumes, the exhaust from cars, and then the compost in his lungs, he had never imagined that Sunny would be gone.

The skin of his face burned with the memory of the smoke and the last fire that he lit. *Coward.* He was supposed to light candles for her, prepare a special meal. But RJ had distracted them all, turned their lives upside down again.

"I've been blind since I was a teenager. It's been a long time. So nothing is new to me. It's the world that is behind." Priscilla laughed. "The world is *behind* me. It needs to catch up." Did she just squeeze his arm a little? "All this technology and computers and they can't figure out basic stuff, you know, like how to teach people about *other* people who are different from them. Who ever knew being different should be such a pain in the ass?"

"Yes." The affirmation felt like a wood block tumbling out of his mouth. How rarely he used that word, "yes," except when he was speaking to customers. And even then, he usually said "okay" instead. *Okay, sure, okay.* As if to shoo them away. "Yes" was strange. "Yes" was full of possibility.

"Why exclude anyone? I think we'd be less lonely." She sighed.

"Thirty-eight," a waitress called. The number on the deli ticket in his hands. "That's us," he said. That number. The irony of it. The thirty-eighth parallel. He could never get away from it.

He kept his right arm by his side as Priscilla followed from behind. He had the urge to protect her, even though he knew she didn't need it. She simply wanted an arm because of the unpredictability of a restaurant with so many people, so many bowls boiling hot. Even though he led her, he could feel her guide him as well. Her hand pushed him.

"Our table is here," he said.

She reached forward until she touched the edge of the lacquered surface. When she sat down, a wave of relief washed over him. They had made it. Nothing awful had happened. They were safe.

"I'm not an egg," Priscilla said.

"An egg?"

"Everyone thinks that if you're blind you're more fragile than everyone else. People's comments are this weird mix of 'You must be so terrified all the time' and 'You are so brave and strong!'" John couldn't help but laugh at the theater of her movements, her expression. "Look, I'm just a person who does stuff differently. I never go around to sighted people and say, 'Congratulations! You woke up today! I bet you didn't feel like waking up!'" She shook her head.

He smiled, the widest he had in a while, unselfconscious about his teeth, his mouth, the dentures he'd had for decades now. He knew she couldn't see and that it wouldn't matter to her anyways.

Her fingers touched the edge of the menu. "Usually, I might ask you to read this, but it's haemul soondubu for me all the way."

"Your Korean is good. Accent good." He felt like a different person, someone who was curious and open. How strange, this lightness. He could die and float away right now. Was it the laughter?

"I've been living in Koreatown and the area, for what, thirty years now? I've been here forever. I probably know just as much Korean as you know Spanish, right? Maybe even more." Was that a wink?

As the waitress spread their banchan in front of them, John ordered for them both. He always chose the beef soondubu, satisfyingly rich and simpler to eat since you didn't have to use your hands, efficient and practical, while his wife enjoyed a slower life, the experience of every moment. He only wanted to shovel food into his mouth so he could have the energy to work. Work and work and work so that he didn't have to feel anything, he realized now. But he still did. He still felt everything.

"What do I have in front of me?" Priscilla asked.

"Uh, in front—"

"You could describe it like the hands of a clock? Like, 'At twelve o'clock, there's this.' Or, 'At three o'clock, there's that.' "

He appreciated the instructions. "At twelve o'clock, there's the fish. Do you know this fish? It's called gulbi." He could smell the saltiness of its flesh like the sea itself.

"Oh, I love that. That's perfect with rice."

"And then at two o'clock, there's kimchi. The kimchi here is good." As he described the other banchan, he realized this was the first time he had ever eaten at a restaurant with someone who wasn't Korean. And yet everything had already been familiar to her. She didn't judge or wince at the smells or ingredients. Because of all his early experiences in America, he had always assumed that non-Koreans would be disgusted by their meals, the way they knew how to nourish themselves.

With her chopsticks, she dangled a long strip of kimchi into her mouth, which amused him. "Do you make kimchi at home?"

"I buy it." He cleared his throat, crossing his arms in front of his chest. "My son wants to cook. My daughter, she is visiting, you know. He wants to cook for her, kind of like their mommy used to cook."

"Is she . . . ?" A look of concern crossed Priscilla's face.

"One year ago." He knew that he misled through omission. But he couldn't explain any further than that, not here, not now.

"I'm sorry, John."

He bit into the kkakdugi kimchi that he loved. The freshness of the mu bled through the dominant flavors of red pepper, garlic, onion, and salt. The contrasts in his mouth. The perfect bite, the balance of light and dark.

"My husband passed away almost ten years ago," she said. "It's been hard being a single mom, of course. I haven't had much choice. I needed my job. It's one of the few places that would hire me with my vision.

They couldn't get rid of me, even if they wanted to." She sighed. "I don't always agree with things there, but it's kind of a family now."

The waitress gently lowered their two heavy bowls of soondubu in front of them.

"Oh my, this smells so good. Where's the egg?" Priscilla asked.

John handed her one from a bowl. "Here it is. It is . . . nothing like you," he said, and quickly regretted those words. But she laughed. For a second, he felt the soft skin of her palm as his fingers dropped the egg inside it. His chest inflated and fell. His heart beat through his mouth. She moved her fingers across the table for her small steel bowl of white rice, sticky and moist.

John shoveled his jjigae with his spoon, turning over the beef and soondubu as he waited for it to cool. How comforting life could be. How lonely it didn't have to be.

"I wanted to ask, did you talk to RJ's daughter yet? About his wife leaving him?"

"No, not yet."

"I've been thinking about this a lot, about what I told you at lunch. Maybe you could keep me out of this entirely?" Priscilla blew into a bite of soondubu before she touched it to her mouth. Too hot. "I would love to help Rhonda. I really would, but . . . you know, he overheard a lot. So did I. He saw a lot. That was his nature." Her nostrils flared. "But he took things to another level. And he got caught. They fired him."

John had the urge to reach out his hand and touch her. But, no, that wouldn't be appropriate. Instead, he stared at the soondubu and zucchini boiled and broken down.

"As awful as I feel, I know that I did the right thing at the time. I never said anything to anyone. And that's why I'm still here. Why I'm here at this table now." Her eyes glistened. After a minute, she continued. "John, I have children. I take care of them by myself. I've been doing this for almost ten years now. My oldest, she's at CSUN. She wants to be a teacher. The first in my family to go to college. In Mexico, my parents only finished elementary school. They came to this country and did everything so that me and my kids and *their* kids wouldn't have to struggle like them. If it wasn't for them . . . I wish I could help RJ's daughter, but I don't think I can. I hope you . . . can you keep all of this between us?"

"Yes," he said. Of course he understood. He felt the same way too. They should distance themselves from RJ and his death. Whatever the circumstances, they each had too many of their own cares and worries to tend to now, their own families. As the daughter of immigrants, Priscilla understood the depth of their sacrifices.

"I've worked very hard, John. I deserve some time for myself, don't you think? With my pension. I could retire one day. A dream. I would focus on my garden. I would plant things in my yard."

"Your yard?"

"Yes, I have a small one and I've never had time to do anything with it."

He had plants. He could help. "I can bring you something," John said. "Some plants. Flowers, too."

She laughed, as if she knew that would never happen, as if the world might end tonight. Enjoying her soup, she remained silent for a few minutes, until she said, "I really wish— I really wish I could help RJ's daughter more." Her eyes filled with tears. "As bad as I feel, nothing can bring him back now. He's gone. But I will say this." She took a sip of her water, which had gone untouched, and stared right at him. "I think his death was a warning of some sort."

"Accident."

"Yes, but . . ." She shook her head.

John gulped down the saliva in his mouth. He hadn't intended for the conversation to go this way. He simply wanted to know why RJ had lost his job. He didn't want his children to waste any more time on this, on helping Rhonda too. They should move on, focus on themselves. Stay out of trouble. No good could come out of the truth. No good could come from RJ either.

"Unfortunately, I can think of a number of people who might've wanted him dead," Priscilla said. "The same guys who had him fired, of course." Her eyes hardened as she stared off into some distance inside herself. "Isn't it strange that . . . they knew how to find his daughter?" She wiped the corners of her mouth, squeezed her napkin into a ball. "She probably knows this, but I hope Rhonda is very careful. You too."

1984

The stucco house had been built in the 1910s—three bedrooms, a dining room, a den, and a galley kitchen with a rear exit that faced the backyard, dry and barren with straw-like grass and weeds scorched by neglect and sun. A concrete driveway out front transitioned to loose gravel along the structure's side toward a detached garage, where they'd store all their belongings, items which they couldn't let go of but didn't have any space to ponder in their everyday lives. Ana and Ronald would have rooms of their own, a luxury previously unimaginable, while Sunny and John shared the master at the front with its own standing shower. The children commandeered the tub in the main bath with their colorful toys, plastic buckets, and wash mitts hung to dry on little metal hooks.

As a family, they had been like a tree root-bound in a planter, suddenly let loose into the ground. There was air. There was water. Space to project and protect themselves. The dream, a dream for people like Sunny and

John who had spent such formative periods of their lives with nothing, running, unable to imagine where they might land out of fear that it could be bombed or destroyed or raided at any moment. They could close their eyes now and fall asleep, living inside this house, which was in essence, an account, both literal and metaphorical, a dwelling of story and stock.

The house itself had been owned by only one white family before, and their block outside the western edge of Koreatown was the most diverse place that Sunny had ever lived with its Black, Latino, and Filipino neighbors, who waved from a distance and were for the most part friendly but not too friendly, because something about this city made it difficult to get to know anyone. Perhaps it had been that everyone worked so hard there wasn't any time for the kind of casual conversations that might build into actual relationships. Isolation and labor weighed down the spirit. Extravagant signs of life appeared a few times a year for graduation and birthday parties—helium balloons in Disney and animal shapes, piñatas, quinceañeras and debuts, large, fanciful dresses that transformed families into royalty, the sulfurous odor of fireworks that terrified her with their booms, and sparklers held in tiny hands. Sunny laughed when she thought about how Koreans only really had large celebrations for two years out of an entire lifetime—ages one and sixty—like bookends. *Congratulations, you lived.*

As she filled the white-painted cabinets of the kitchen, narrow but twice as large as the one in their former apartment, Sunny listened to her husband chase the kids, their high-pitched squeals outside in the backyard, which had more square footage than the house itself. She felt herself unfurl, petal by petal, into this life. A calm sense of domesticity quelled some of the uncertainty, the general anxiety heightened since Professor Cho's death and RJ's disappearance. Although she knew that her husband would have to work harder to keep up with the mortgage payments and the increase in bills, at least here she had space to plant and raise trees, maybe even fruits and vegetables, which she hadn't had the chance to do in years. With the kids, she could walk fifteen minutes to a playground, a jungle gym, slides, and swing set, in the sand. If she wanted, she could carve a space for herself in the garage for art. She could tilt open the large car door for air, set up an easel, and when the children went off to school, she could find an hour or two to explore all those ideas she had years ago like seeds that had been saved in an envelope. The man and woman who kissed beneath a sheet in Magritte's *The Lovers* . . . who were they? She could practice reproducing a fabric's drape and fold, shadows and light, with paint. In plain sight, would the man and woman still desire each other? Or did the veil allow them to be more free somehow, to be themselves?

She would need to try oils again. The irony that the hideous fumes produced by the cleanup of the brushes and thinning of the colors, that distinctive ether-like scent of combustibility, had been replaced in her life of late with the stench of her husband's clothes after a long day of work at the gas station.

And after having achieved, with the help of his inheritance, his dream of owning a home, John had been much more ebullient, less mysterious these days. Even on the first night in the house, exhausted from tending to the kids and moving boxes, they had made love for the first time in a year. He almost tackled her with an *oomph* as she brushed her hair, before they crashed down onto the mattress laughing, confident that the children had fallen asleep in their own rooms. What a luxury to have walls that separated them now. How many lives could they each have, how many separate people could they be with doors that closed, voices hushed? Perhaps freedom hadn't been wide-open spaces, endless umber and ochre, a manganese sky and stars like pinpoints of light in Spinel Black, but instead this—a private room. The silence of the heart. A quiet mind.

"What do you think about the house, Mrs. Kim?" John said. He rested on top of her now. The tips of his fingers traced the dent of her collarbone.

"It's okay." She smirked, barely able to contain her laugh.

"Can I fix anything for you?" He nibbled on her ear, his breath hot against her skin.

She grabbed his head, smiling beneath him as she pushed his gray strands out of his eyes, warm and soft, made of candlelight. The glow of him was still somewhere, somewhere inside. He hadn't been snuffed out. She merely had to blow a little to give him air. He kissed her on the mouth with a loud smack, and she lightly slapped him on the cheek. They could still play. Adult life, its hardness and edges, had buried the children they once were inside them, those children who had managed to laugh even after bombs fell. How powerful, how wise youth was. That smile.

"My husband will be back any minute," she whispered.

"You said he works all the time, Mrs. Kim," John deepened his voice.

"He's so boring these days. Complains about his back."

"He sounds terrible and dull."

"Maybe we can have a little fun before he comes home?"

She hadn't laughed that hard in a long time as they settled into the heaviness of their lips and bodies pressed against each other. His hand on her breast, alongside her thigh before he pulled off her underwear beneath her nightgown. He ran his tongue along the side of her neck. She gripped his hair and gasped for breath. The fire was still there.

And the next day after they all had breakfast, rice and runny eggs, within the nook that looked out into a corner of the backyard, her husband unpacked while she watched over the kids. Ana rode her little scooter on top of the large pad of concrete in front of the garage, and Ronald stacked brown leaves that had fallen from the loquat tree, heavy with globes of yellow and green. She imagined what she could plant and where, bathed in light for most of the day. Ana and Ronald poked their arms through the shared fence, covered in dusty passionflower vines that separated their yard from the neighbor's.

While Ronald and Ana napped after lunch, Sunny leaned on the handrail of the landing outside their back door. A tabby cat, who appeared curious about the home's new occupants, crouched on the roof of the garage. Sunny meowed, and as a cat should, he didn't care for her affection at all. John wrapped his sweaty arm around her shoulder. He had been carrying boxes all morning. He wiped away the streaks on the side of his face with a handkerchief he kept in his pocket.

"Once we get everything fixed up, we could do something back here." He caught his breath, admiring the yard, the blank canvas with only a loquat and palm tree at the far corners, dirt and weeds, dry and yellow. The previous owners had been too elderly to do much with the space by themselves.

"I'd love to try growing some vegetables," she said. "It's so bare. All you see are those telephone wires."

"What would you plant?"

"A persimmon. I'd bet it'd be so happy there." She pointed at the empty space between the two existing trees. She couldn't help but think of the fruit she had given RJ that last time she had waited at the bus stop with him, five months ago in November.

"What about you?" he asked.

"What about me?"

"Where do we plant you?"

She laughed. "I'm always in the kitchen or doing laundry anyways, but at least I could look outside at something."

"I bet there is a nice little spot for you in the garage for your stinky paints."

"It's not the paints that stink. It's the turpentine. It's cleaning the brushes. But that's for oils. I only have watercolors—"

"I bet there's a nice little spot for you in the garage and your stinky brushes."

He kissed her on the top of the head and they swayed a little as his chin pressed down gently upon her. She—*they*—could feel something again, couldn't they? The opportunities these days seemed scarcer than ever, but still somewhere inside her she carried some bulb, her needs, ripening at the first shocks of warm weather. She imagined on this blank canvas the branches from the trunk reaching into the light, the chartreuse of the new leaves vibrating as they colored the air, which beckoned, *Grow something here.*

On a July day, oppressively arid and hot, Sunny started the car with Ana and Ronald in the back seat, then rolled down the windows for the relief of a single cigarette on their way to the local swap meet. The children needed furniture for their rooms, dressers and beds. They had been sleeping for the past couple months on floor mats, ironically much like they did in Korea, which Sunny (and her aching back) preferred. But John wouldn't have them live for long that way, shameful, as if they were "barnyard animals." Comments like those, jokes that dug at their culture, rattled Sunny, but she didn't have the energy to respond. She hated the suggestion that they had been primitive or uncivilized like on that show *M*A*S*H*, which she accidentally watched once. The only Koreans on-screen were dusty servants and prostitutes with high cheekbones. She was tired of this image of them as lowly creatures who needed to be saved, a myth that perpetuated their erasure, their destruction, their separation from themselves through borders.

She nearly missed the sight of RJ as he made his way down the sidewalk in the opposite direction. She jerked the car to the side of the road, where she could park in an empty spot. Ana screamed from the unexpected swerve, while Ronald squealed in delight. Sunny's heart thumped as if she had seen a ghost, which in a way RJ had become, an apparition of what had once been possible for her, a series of alternatives that she could've never imagined before he had entered her life. Instead of his usual uniform, he wore a pair of jeans despite the deadening heat, and a teal-and-white striped shirt, sporty and casual. He carried a mostly empty backpack slung over one shoulder. However, she recognized him right away by the shape of his face, his wide-set eyes, although his posture seemed different, more confident perhaps, lighter. She honked her horn and through the passenger-side window yelled out his name.

The children had fallen silent in the back. At almost seven years of age, Ana was precocious and observant, but Sunny had also been confident that when bribed with one of her favorite desserts (cream puffs), Ana could keep a harmless secret. Sunny tilted the rearview mirror and caught a glimpse of Ronald in the back, who waved to her like a pageant queen from his car seat. "Hi," he said in his high-pitched voice. "Hi." How difficult but adorable this age had been.

Sweat streaming down the sides of his face, RJ stooped to peer inside the car. She couldn't believe that in this city of over three million, she had finally found him. It was like winning a lottery. He flicked his cigarette to the ground. She had never noticed him smoking before, or detected any smell of tobacco on him. A new habit? Or perhaps he had been dabbling like herself. His eyes darted toward her ashtray, which he must've noticed was nearly full.

"Go to work?" Sunny asked. She didn't know how to ask him where he had been without revealing to her daughter too many details about their relationship. She should keep this interaction as simple as possible.

"Not tonight," he said. "I only work during the day now, at my friend's car stereo shop on Pico. It's so close to my place, I can walk." He smiled. His eyes, tender and soft. "And who do you got there in the car?"

With a calm and serious face, Ana waved. Ronald chuckled and said, "Ba-ba."

"Bye bye?" RJ leaned inside. She detected the tobacco from his mouth, his skin. Or was it hers? "What are you and the kids up to?"

She had no plans but to take her children to the swap meet before dinner while there was still light. The heat in the house had been unbearable, and her husband wouldn't be home until ten or eleven o'clock. Rather than sit in front of the fans at home that oscillated back and forth, or the television full of depressing news and boring shows, she preferred to move with the air rushing inside the car despite the exhaust of summer, the fumes, the burned rubber of tires.

"Have you ever been to the Griffith Observatory?" RJ asked.

She had only seen the outside of the Observatory, striking and imposing, on drives with her family through Griffith Park, where her children could ride the train, the ponies, or the merry-go-round. She always assumed the Observatory didn't contain much for a person who didn't speak English and didn't understand a thing about science or the stars, as much as they interested her with their poetry and movement. She had been curious, yes, but not enough to pay an entrance fee to a museum where she'd feel out of place and confused.

"Do you want to go to the Observatory?" he asked. "That's where I'm heading." He asked Ronald and Ana, "You kids want to go to the Observatory?"

"Ob-ba. Ob-ba. Ob-ba. Ob-ba."

"Observatory," RJ repeated as clearly as possible. He creaked open the door and settled inside the car, which immediately felt cramped. She had never had a person other than Mrs. Lee and her kids as passengers. Her husband always drove when they were together, frustrated by her cautiousness and hesitation, her glacial pace on the road. And here, a man whom she once knew, RJ, a man whom she had spent months searching for, now resurfaced again and rode beside her, as if no time had passed, and they belonged together as naturally as any other family.

"We're going there at school," Ana said.

"You're going there at school? Do you mean your class is going on a field trip?"

"Yes, I think, next year," Ana said.

"How about we get a preview tonight? That way, when you go with your friends, you'll be able to show them everything you already know. You could be a tour guide. Sound good?"

In the rearview mirror, Ana possessed a brightness in her eyes, as if she had won something.

Of course, Sunny would've preferred to keep her children separate from her relationship with RJ, to avoid confusion, but she had no choice. She had pulled over and said something to RJ. What would be the likelihood of them running into each other again? And with him beside her now, she felt like an entirely different person, as though she had a confidant, someone whom she could trust with what kept her up at night. She'd have to learn English as soon as possible. She could explain herself to RJ. She knew he might understand her. Her loneliness, her grief over Professor Cho, the fear that she would never be able to reverse the decisions of her life without saying goodbye to the children she loved so much, that she had spent so many hours trapped in what seemed to be another person's dream. A nightmare for her.

"Do you mind?" he asked, and held up a packet of cigarettes.

"Yes, yes." She had been trying to say *go ahead*. He misunderstood.

"Yes, I can?"

"Yes, you can." He passed her one too as he gestured toward Vermont Avenue, which had been as familiar as the back of her hand until she reached the city college and the intersection with Santa Monica Boulevard, where the demographics eventually changed from immigrant and working class to tree-lined and fancy. In Koreatown, she had been terrified that someone might see her, but at the same time, who cared? Her husband had been too busy at work to even go to church these days. RJ was simply a friend by her side. They were two adults who were escorting her kids somewhere new. She deserved a bit of novelty and joy as much as anyone else. That was what Professor Cho would've wanted most for her. Not just safety, but the safety to indulge herself.

"How's driving for you?" RJ asked.

With one hand hanging on the bottom of the steering wheel and a cigarette in the other, she wanted to say that she missed taking the bus, the familiar faces, the sounds of people's voices, the cacophony of their noises, which sounded some days like music, kaleidoscopic and wondrous. She loved the expression of the eyes, the flatness of a mouth without any awareness of being observed. But at the same time, she knew that she now had different opportunities, a wider range of places to explore in this city that had once, in its endless stretches of concrete toward mountains, oceans, and deserts, overwhelmed her. She had such limited time away from home, and she could make the most of every minute, every hour with a car.

"I miss it. One day I'll drive again," RJ said. "What's your name, little one?"

Had she never mentioned their names? She must've always referred to them as "my daughter" or "my son."

"Ana."

"And yours, little man?"

"His name is Ronald," Ana answered for him.

"Good name." RJ glanced at Sunny. "Both of you. Good names." Of course he had recognized his own, but he didn't mention it. He beamed with the compliment, turned himself to better face them in the back. "Are you excited to go to the Observatory? It's beautiful at all times of the day. You can really see the city from up there." He waited but hadn't gathered a response. "At night, the world lights up into this dazzling grid. All that electricity. And there's a big telescope too. Do you know what that is, a telescope? It's what the Observatory is built around. It's this device that lets you see things that are far, far away. It's got lenses. They're curved. Do you know what lenses are? Kind of like in a person's eyeglasses. They curve and gather light. You could see things like planets and stars with them. Does your daddy wear glasses?"

Sunny had the impulse to answer his question for Ana. Instead she drove in silence in order to appease everyone for now. She didn't know how to dull this sudden awkwardness. But on Los Feliz Boulevard, after they passed the spectacle of a vandalized water fountain, like a broken sprinkler that spewed near an infamously hellish intersection, at the entrance of Griffith Park, Ana finally said, "Yes, he wears glasses sometimes," as if no time had passed.

"To see near or far?" RJ asked. "Have you asked him?"

"I think *far*? He wears them when he drives. Sometimes he takes them off at home. He rubs his nose between his eyes. I don't know why. Maybe it hurts."

"Eyeglasses leave little marks on your face. They're kind of heavy. But they let him see things clearly. Have you ever picked them up?"

"Yes. I get in trouble."

"That's probably because they are expensive. But if you're gentle you can see that those pieces of glass are curved. It's gonna be blurry to you, but they are curved just right so that he can see crystal clear."

As she followed the claustrophobic procession of cars that coughed and climbed toward the top of the hill, the reality of their actions, RJ in the car with her kids, finally hit her. Now that she saw other people in the parking lot, the giant slate-gray dome, the magnificence of the building in the still bright late-afternoon summer light, she worried about whether Ana would tell her father about this excursion, RJ in the car. How would she explain to Ana that we could keep this to ourselves, that some things didn't need to be shared with everyone, even those whom we loved?

The cream puffs. She would need to stop at a bakery tonight.

"Great job, Sunny. We did it." Outside the car, with his backpack on his shoulder, RJ raised his fists in the air, cartoonishly victorious. Ronald laughed and copied him with a battle cry as saliva dripped down his chin, which RJ wiped with a clean handkerchief from his pocket. Ronald had been teething forever. "They've got snacks here. How about Uncle RJ buys everyone a hot dog?"

Ronald clapped the palms of his little hands. For whatever reason, he hadn't been speaking much, in English or Korean, despite how Sunny tried to encourage him, narrated the world for him so that he'd learn more sounds. She wondered which language he dreamed in. It must've been English for her daughter, who rarely spoke Korean these days, especially since she had started school and her husband never used it with the children, only with her, like a secret language between the two of them.

"Hot dogs for everyone," RJ said.

RJ pushed Ronald's stroller in front of him, lifted it onto a curb, as Sunny squeezed Ana's hand, pulsing her fingers. She noticed Ana's pink shoelaces had become loose, so she stooped to tighten them, and when she looked up, she caught tears, globs in her daughter's eyes. Sunny hugged her as tight as she could and said in Korean, "I'm sorry." About fifteen feet away already, RJ circled and zigzagged on the sidewalk, while Ronald giggled and squealed in delight. They were so natural with each other. Would her son ever know the truth of how he got his name?

"I'm sorry," Sunny said again to Ana. "Everything is okay. We are safe."

"Where's appa?" Ana asked.

"Appa is at work. We will see him tomorrow morning. Uncle RJ is here. Let's have a good time, okay?"

"But appa . . ."

"I miss appa too. But we have to make the most of our time, right? Appa wants us to be happy."

She wiped her daughter's cheeks with her thumbs. How much Ana resembled her father then. Her nose with its low bridge, a button. The squarish jaw. The eyebrows thick as if they had been painted on by a large calligraphy brush.

"Let's have a hot dog. I will buy you two. You can keep the extra one in your pocket." She tickled her little belly. Ana laughed and grabbed her hand as they waited in line.

Afterward, they ambled toward the outside staircase that led to the roof deck with its panoramic view of the city. Sunny didn't generally like American food, but something about the portability of a hot dog delighted her as she watched Ronald in his stroller, bobbing his head back and forth, a piece of bun smashed in his tiny hands. At the bottom of the stairs, RJ unclasped Ronald's buckle and hoisted him up on his hip. Sunny couldn't help but smile, even though she had been terrified of RJ holding her child in public. What if someone from church saw them? Would they even recognize her? Or would she appear too carefree and happy? Honestly, no one could stop the ecstasy from the freedom she felt now with her two beautiful children and a friend with whom she could share this world. Not even those judgmental ahjummas.

"This was my daughter's favorite spot," RJ said, as he absorbed the beauty of the city and the surrounding hills, golden with dried grass and grayish green with scrub.

A *daughter*. He'd never mention one before. Sunny imagined a little girl that looked just like her father. Where was she?

"This is why I come here," RJ continued. "Not for the stars, but for the memory of . . . experiencing what she felt, the purity of that joy of seeing the world as if for the first time." He cleared his throat. "If you ever get tired of this city, you could come here and fall in love again." His eyes grew misty. "I'd hold her on top of my shoulders like this." He lifted Ronald above his now, where he rested like a tiny king, surveying his country. "Kids are tough, but they are so perfect, aren't they?"

"Yes," Sunny said. No matter how tired she always was, her children, having them around, reminded her of how miraculous, how surprising, life could still be. As they discovered the world, as they discovered their own selves, she remembered where and how she had begun. The passage of time, which always gave us so much fear, so much anxiety, collapsed, ceased to exist momentarily.

"Thank you," she said without explaining to RJ why. She had a sense that he understood she had not just been responding to his compliment about her children, but that he had brought her here, that he had shared this place, its meaning, with her. She could feel him close to her, their arms inches away from each other's. The Lovers. If only they had a big sheet to obscure them, under which they could hide. There had always been menace and death in that painting, but what if, what if it was possibility too, the possibility that only disappearing could provide.

Ronald reached for her as if he wanted her to carry him instead. His timing had been impeccable. RJ carefully lowered him into her arms.

From inside his backpack, he slipped out a small black rectangle, a film camera.

She had been wondering what he had been carrying that he didn't want to leave inside the car.

"Could you do me a favor and take a picture of me, young lady? I'd like to send a photo to someone special."

Ana's eyes lit up, endowed with this sense of great responsibility. Her father never let her touch their camera, afraid that she might waste film or scratch the lens. She peered with one eye into the viewfinder as RJ posed, leaning toward an arch. Los Angeles. Unmistakable.

"Hold it steady, Ana," RJ said.

Click. Sunny remembered the last time she had seen RJ at the bus stop in November and what he had said: *There are things I have overheard at my work the past few weeks, things I've seen. Then I've been—remember my camera? I've been taking pictures, collecting . . . evidence. No one really notices me.*

Had he quit or been fired from his job at the police station?

"Take one more just in case." He smiled as the sweat glided down his neck. She wondered who the photo was for, the audience or recipient of the image. He appeared relaxed in a way that she had never seen before, and she realized that a change of scenery had transformed and awakened them both, holding space for the previously implausible.

Back inside the car, they shut the door, and Sunny glanced at her watch. Almost eight o'clock. The sun still hadn't quite set yet. She wished they could stay longer to take in the city lights, but they couldn't be any later for Ronald's bedtime. He needed to sleep early or would be cranky all night. She had made that mistake only once. She inserted her key into the ignition.

"I'm thinking of trying to find my daughter," RJ said. "In Alabama, where my wife's family is. Far away from here."

"Alabama?" She wondered how old his daughter was. Did she run away? Where was her mother?

"I could take the bus or train, probably. I've been going through a lot these days, and I've been thinking about her a lot. How she is still young, and maybe I'd have a shot."

Sunny imagined the two of them, her and RJ, driving this car on a nameless highway through desert and mountains to get to wherever he wanted. She would take him. It would only be temporary, of course. A couple weeks. She could leave behind the kids with Mrs. Lee. It was nothing but a fantasy, she knew, but nonetheless, Sunny couldn't help but wonder what would happen if she disappeared like that. Her family would survive because they wouldn't have any other choice.

"Your job?" she asked.

"Oh, at the stereo shop? My friend doesn't care if I—"

"Police station." She wanted to mention what he had said about the evidence he had been collecting. "Priscilla." The name she couldn't forget.

His eyes opened wide, shocked that she'd remembered.

"I lost my job a while back . . . in December." He inhaled deeply through his nose. His leg trembled. "It's been, well—part of why I want to leave, actually, is that. It hasn't been good for me. The things I observed, noticed. Remember I was always writing? It got me in some trouble, and they found a way to get rid of me. I was fired, and now I'm a little lost, to be honest."

That was why he had been missing for so long.

"I was convinced that what I was doing was right. But now I just gotta keep my head low and focus on myself, you see? My own family. I gotta fix things for myself before I take any more risks. When I think about my daughter, I'm reminded that I have too much to lose. I have to be alive in order to find her. You see?"

Of course she understood.

"Anyways, we should probably go now, don't you think?" he asked. "I bet Ronald Junior . . . I mean, *Ronald*, is tired back there." He beamed, trying not to laugh.

She had the urge to grab his hand, but she couldn't. Not in front of the kids. No, never in front of them. And she would need to put together the words, somehow, to let him know her thoughts. That they could have a plan. It sounded wild, unattainable, but still . . . why couldn't she get some relief from herself, her life, as if she were young again, as if she could, for a couple weeks, take everything back. Of course, she never regretted having Ana and Ronald, but deep down, she wished she had known beforehand what life would really be like as an immigrant, dependent on her husband in so many ways, her husband who worked so many hours. She never realized how much she needed her own dreams and art until they had all been taken away and she clawed to have them and her sanity back.

"Have to figure out the logistics, put my stuff in storage." RJ lit another cigarette and blew smoke from the side of his mouth.

"Storage?" The word was familiar, but foreign still.

"Yeah, a place to keep my stuff, you know. I'd be gone for months at least." He shook his head.

"Garage?"

"Yeah, a garage. Possibly."

"Garage, my house," she said. Her heart pounded. *Yes.* Their garage was almost entirely hers anyways. And his belongings would only bind them together in another way, concrete and palpable. An arrangement. An opening and a closure.

"Your house? You got a garage? Congratulations. I didn't know you bought a house."

"Yes, big. Empty." She couldn't actually leave Ronald at this age anyways. So much happened in a child's life, even if she would be gone for only two weeks. An escape would have to wait until her children were much older. But if she stored RJ's belongings, he would return one day. He couldn't simply disappear again.

"You think I could keep my stuff there? Not furniture. But personal stuff, like photos, some records, books."

"Yes." She glanced in the rearview mirror. How much would Ana remember? She needed to stop at the bakery before it closed.

"For a few months? Maybe even a year. I don't want to inconvenience you. Your husband. Ha. I bet he wouldn't like that."

"Big. Empty. Temporary. Okay."

She turned on the engine of the car. The headlights flashed in the dusky light, purpling into black. Her husband wouldn't even know. And now he wouldn't be the only one in their family who made large decisions on his own. She smiled to herself as she pulled out of the parking lot. The mischief of this harmless secret was the kind of rebellion that she needed.

1999

Vermont Avenue bustled with cars, a mix of people and placards in Korean and Spanish, through Little Armenia and Los Feliz, toward Griffith Park, which included the zoo, the Autry Museum, and the Hollywood sign. Today was the anniversary of their mother's disappearance, and the first time Ana and Ronald had gone to the Observatory together since they had been there with her and RJ fifteen years ago. Ronald would've been too young, a toddler, to remember that. However, Ana still hoped a visit might help spark something, coax memories out of herself, since she had been older, six or seven at the time. She remembered vaguely the feeling of the camera in her hands, its magic and power, and how he had trusted her with something so valuable, not only the device itself but the taking of a picture: *Hold it steady, Ana.*

After they had gone to Jacob's house on Wednesday, three days ago, they had realized they would need help from the police to figure out the connection, if any, between Jacob Hendricks and RJ. This might lead to an understanding of what both of them had been trying to find—at the library and with their mother. Ana and Ronald had debated reaching out to Detective Coleman but they didn't trust him, and they knew that Rhonda was suspicious of him as well. They also didn't want to risk revealing the existence of RJ's letter, which their father, of all people, had torn up and failed to report. Without knowing it, their family had dug themselves into this hole, where they had no one to really rely on but themselves, Rhonda, and Janet the librarian. Ana couldn't shake the idea that her mother's disappearance had something to do with RJ's death. How could it simply be a coincidence that RJ had surfaced seeking their mother, only to end up dead?

And who could be next?

She couldn't sleep at all, her mind raced with clues, reached for facts, as she clung to all the details she could remember about RJ and the Observatory. Fifteen years ago, her mother had driven them with RJ in the passenger seat, and the most significant detail she remembered were the stares, the silent interrogation of eyes that lingered too long on their bodies, their presence. Only now did Ana realize it must've been because RJ was Black, walking with them—Sunny, Ana, and Ronald—three Korean Americans. Their mixed company offended some, since RJ was obviously not their biological father. What had everyone assumed? That their mother had been a woman up to no good, a woman who should be ashamed of herself? Or did they see something else?

Maybe they hadn't been lovers, but something perhaps even more profound than that. A friend. A brother.

"How long have you and Peggy been dating?" Ana rolled down her window in her father's Eldorado, which they had borrowed again. She inhaled the dirt and dust, the smell of exhaust, buttered corn, and bacon, street vendors who cooked and sold snacks and meals beside the road at all hours.

"Three years?" He scratched his head. "We were just friends before I guess. So maybe two years."

"Does she know where she wants to go to college?"

"She's open. But she went on some field trips to visit, you know, those fancy schools. I bet that's what her parents want."

"Do you know what *she* wants?"

"I suppose the same," he said. "But I never ask directly, to be honest."

As they passed the Greek Theatre, the outdoor amphitheater, on the left, the temperature cooled even more under the shade of anonymous trees. She had become interested in them only once she had moved to Berkeley and could then appreciate the vast differences between the redwood, eucalyptus, oak, cherry, elder, and beech. In Los Angeles for the most part, she either thought palm tree or *not* palm tree, shade or no shade, and never had the time to look up much, or bother to study what had been at her father's nursery. They entered the Mt. Hollywood Tunnel, the cold, dark tube that had been so rare in this city of open air and freeway underpasses. As they wound their way up Observatory Road, they passed cars parked to the side at the various lookout points into the haze and cloud of the city and the low golden hills dotted with brush. There had been many trails in the park, but their father always preferred the less touristy Mt. Wilson and Topanga Canyon for his Sunday-morning hikes. As a child, she'd gather acorns and speckled rocks that sparkled on those walks. In his own way, her father encouraged this appreciation of nature, even though she hadn't admitted it until she had moved and found herself as an adult in botanical gardens, fascinated by the birds of Lake Merritt, on a hike in the hills of Oakland and Berkeley, where she'd gasp for breath in front of serene undulations of earth and plant, or the glitter of the bay dotted by sailboats and bound by bridges.

In the Observatory's lot, they wandered through the open area to the roundabout. Ana marveled at the grandeur and symmetry of the Observatory, with its three dark domes atop the low facade with tall windows like the keys of a piano, sharp against the murky backdrop of the sky. She could understand why her mother and RJ would come here on a day off; the views had been astronomical, and the building itself suggested a formal sense of importance that had been missing in their everyday lives. *Something special happens here. Something that matters.*

"What about you?" Ana asked. "What are you thinking, after high school?" They climbed the steps toward the viewing deck. She had avoided this conversation, didn't want to apply any pressure on Ronald after all they had been through the past year. But still of course she worried. She was her father's daughter, after all.

Ronald stopped at the top of the stairs. "I'm gonna start at Santa Monica College, spend a year or two there."

"You've been through . . . a lot," she said. "Don't rush yourself." She caught her breath. "I rushed myself."

"And you did fine."

"I don't think so. I don't feel that way," she said in a low voice. After her mother disappeared, she'd returned to school right away. She had been a senior still, one semester away from graduating, and of course she couldn't lose any momentum then. She also couldn't afford to take time off since she had a four-year scholarship and couldn't shoulder any additional debt.

She had always believed that in the past year, if she worked hard enough, her mother might return. She might earn her mother again. But instead she graduated with almost straight As and an aching emptiness.

Although she loved the books she read, as well as her professors, she couldn't understand how to apply any of her studies to a world that disappointed her, or didn't seem to assign any value to a woman who simply loved books. Could she go back and get a PhD? But how would she survive the brutalities of an academic job market? Eventually, she needed to make a home near her father and brother, or at least a reasonable driving distance from them.

She wanted her brother to do something different from her, to travel and explore. She wanted to tell him that eventually she would take care of everything here, in this place that she had been ambivalent about her entire life, yet nonetheless, had been, yes, a place where she could begin to see herself now as an adult. He didn't need to wait for anyone.

As they stood together in about the same spot as RJ in the photograph, they stared out at the city, the haze of gray past the hillside, the sky shaped like a perfect dome atop the grid of streets and boulevards they had called home. *Hold it steady, Ana.*

"I don't think she's ever coming back," Ana said.

Ronald closed his eyes as if to protect himself from the harsh light of her words.

She knew it. She was never supposed to ever say that out loud. Regardless of what she thought or felt, that was the one thing she was never supposed to share, as if saying it out loud was like making a wish, when it was simply the truth, her truth.

"I just don't want you to wait." Her voice cracked. "I just don't want you to think . . ."

No, it was a mistake. She had to fix this. She shouldn't have said it.

"I'm sorry, Ronald." She wanted to hold him.

She could see her brother trying with all his might not to cry. Anger rose in his face. But to not share what she really thought didn't help or heal them. The opposite was true. Pain was not a fire they could smother. They had to give it air and let it burn until it died out.

"I just don't want you to think . . . you should stay here and wait for her," she whispered. They had been turned toward the city, the view, so they didn't have to look at each other. But none of it could touch or impress her now. All she could feel was her heart breaking, for Ronald, for herself, for her father. "Dad can take care of himself." She wiped the streaks of tears from her cheeks. "If you wanted to move to the East Coast, or try somewhere new—"

"I don't want to do that." He closed his eyes. "There'll be other . . . there'll be other guys. Guys she'll have more in common with."

"Oh, don't say that. What you have seems really special."

"It's not worth it," he said. "For either of us. I'm fine here. I'll be fine."

Had she underestimated him? Even if on the exterior she had appeared more successful with her straight As and college degree, maybe in reality he had figured his life out more than she had. It could be hard to admit that your little brother might not *need* you. Or maybe he needed her differently now? But how could she ever be closer to him if she didn't show who she was, if she never shared what she thought?

"You don't have to worry about me anymore," he said.

But how? If anything, what her mother would've wanted the most was for them to look after each other, forever and ever. She always emphasized that they had only one sister and one brother, and that they were responsible for one another, that Ana was responsible for making sure her brother would be okay, that he did his homework, that he got home from school every day. That was her job, and who was she outside of this role? No one. Just an idealistic woman in her twenties who still believed in the world's ability to change, but could no longer feel or see herself. She had slipped out of her own skin, like a shell, after she had lost her mother. And now she went through life, nerves exposed. It was all too much.

"So you really believe she's not coming back?" he asked.

The tightness in her throat. The dryness of her tongue.

"I think she would've come back already by now, if she was."

"Do you think . . . do you think she's dead?"

"Yes."

He blinked tears from his eyes, downcast. She could feel the burn of them on her own face.

Their father's mother, their grandmother, had been lost too like their own. And yet all these years, almost fifty now, their father had continued on, not knowing what had happened to his family, because there was no other choice. They had to keep going. They had to see this life out to its very end. They had to witness this world. They had to take in all of its sound, and find the song that carries. That's how they survive this broken, beautiful heart.

"It's not your fault, you know," Ronald said. "I always thought maybe you felt responsible for how Dad and me . . . don't get along. Like maybe you should've been here after Mom disappeared. I don't know."

"Oh, Ronald," she said. A boulder inside her chest. "I could've taken time off school." She hadn't realized until now that indeed she did feel responsible for the way her brother and father lived, the barrenness of their relationship, the closed doors, the silences, yet how could she be blamed for being a college student and wanting to escape a little, live her own life too? Sure, she could've taken a semester off, but why interrupt her studies and return to a place that only reminded her of why, why she needed to get away, to disappear? The books gave her an escape. The campus and its handsome buildings surrounded by trees, shielded by the softness of foliage. She had fallen in love with ideas. The romance of an education. Was that what happened to her father when he had moved to America, when he had left his family behind?

How much she had been like him in the end.

"I hope you also know that none of this is your fault." Tears streamed down her cheeks. "That's why I think she's dead. She couldn't have just left us. She couldn't have done that. She would've wanted to be there for you."

She folded her arms across her chest as they leaned on the railing. She closed her eyes, wishing she could evaporate like water, drops of dew before they fell to the ground. The height at which they stood. Her head spun. The sun on her face. She reached for his arm and squeezed, grounding herself. *At least we have each other,* she thought. *At least, she had* him.

"I'm not sure why I never come here," she said.

"Probably the same reason why it's a pain in the ass to go anywhere in LA. This city fucking sucks." He laughed. "The parking, the traffic. Shit, there's so much to do, but we're all stuck. I bet you miss the Bay already."

"Eh, it's not that much better there. Well, there's BART at least."

"I love BART, how it goes underwater."

"It's so crowded all the time."

"Yeah, but it's cool, you get to kind of just read, or look at people."

"You can do that on the bus here, you know."

"But it takes forever," he said. "Maybe I'll visit soon."

As they descended the steps, tourists and families beside them climbed into the heavens of this city of strangers. Millions of strangers. A tiny girl with dark-brown pigtails and a pink Peter Pan collar bounced in her father's arms. A boy in a black superhero shirt dashed by and drummed his hands on the banister like a conga drum. A gray-haired grandmother in white orthopedic shoes counted each step, proud of how she took care of herself.

"I wish I could remember more about her and RJ," Ana said. "I don't remember shit from back then."

"Do you remember how you felt?"

"It's hard to describe. It was weird. It was like being in another country of some sort. Or inside a dream." She stopped on the stairs to take in the sight of the city one last time. "I guess, that's what happens when you have a view like this. You see things differently. You see things as if for the first time. You feel huge, but also very small. You realize how small we all are." A lump in her throat. "What do you miss most about her?" she asked.

"I felt like I could be anyone around her," he said. "She'd love me no matter what. I didn't have to be a specific person, or do anything to impress her."

"I think that we live in this world . . . where you have to work so hard to prove you matter. But it shouldn't be that way, I don't think. It doesn't make sense that some of us have to exist more than others, right? It's too much to ask of each other." Before they reached the car, she said, "I'm proud of you, Ronald. I don't say this enough, but . . . I love you. We all do." She couldn't help but smile. "You matter to me a lot."

"Likewise? This is awkward." He reached forward and hugged her for the first time in years. She couldn't even remember the last instance they had been this close. And finally, finally she felt home.

As they left the parking lot, Ana noticed a car back out of a spot and silently pull up behind them. She didn't think much of it, focusing instead on the conversation she'd just had with her brother about their mother being gone. Together, they realized they had never gotten any clear details from their father about what had happened the day their mother disappeared. They never really talked about it. What did he remember? But then she noticed the same blue Ford Explorer had tailed them the whole route back to their house.

"Someone's following us. Don't look back." She tried to make out the face in the rearview mirror but couldn't. The man wore a hoodie over his head, sunglasses like the Unabomber. He could've been anyone.

"Are you sure?" Ronald asked.

She circled around the block, and from the corner they watched as the car slowed down in front of Rodriguez's and paused before speeding off.

Someone was watching them, but why? RJ's death was an accident. They had stayed away from the police and had simply been finding out more about RJ and their mother—except perhaps when they had gone to Jacob Hendricks's house. Maybe that had been too much of a leap. Maybe Jacob had found out somehow, and they had overstepped some boundary, gotten too close to him for whatever reason. But why did it matter? It was their mother who was the big mystery, the aching unanswered question.

She shooed the thought away from her mind as she remembered they'd still need to go to the grocery store to make dinner tonight. Their mother's favorite fish, grilled mackerel, which Ana hadn't had in a very long time, because it reminded her of Sunny.

"I'm probably just imagining it," Ana said. "I mean, what have we done wrong anyways?"

But even she didn't believe herself.

A young fuyu persimmon tree, gray and twiggy and wan, slumped in the back of the van.

Guilt had consumed John after his dinner with Priscilla yesterday. His desire for another, while his wife was missing. He needed to drown her out. Drown the words *I think his death was a warning.*

John didn't care. He had wanted only to prove that RJ was flawed, like him.

At the nursery, he had found this tree, which he would plant, no matter its meek appearance, this weekend in Sunny's honor. He would take care of it forever—at least until his wife came home, where she belonged, and took over.

His wife always loved the fruit in the fall and winter, savored its delicate and honeyish flavor, the charm of its glossy orange skin and its calyx toupee. She adored the tree itself because it dared to be beautiful in every season with its bright chartreuse foliage of spring and summer, its red flames of fall, and the elegance of its bare branches, which would hang with any fruit that remained like sweet lanterns in winter.

Two cats, a tortoiseshell and a tuxedo, lounged on the sidewalk in front of the driveway where his children had returned the Eldorado. John inched his car forward but they didn't budge. A standoff.

"Fuck," he yelled to himself before he shifted into park. He ran out of his van and waved his arms, stomping. The cats sauntered off to their next warm patch. John gritted his dentures as he pulled up his gray Dickies pants. He'd get those cats one day.

"You okay there?" Rodriguez asked.

"The cats," John said. "They shit all over."

"Like I said, you need a dog, man."

Another mouth to feed. John wanted to snap, *Maybe YOU need a dog.* But instead he sat in his van, buckled his seat belt, pulled up the driveway, finally, and parked inches from the rear of his Eldorado.

"Did they find anything else?" Rodriguez asked. His hand rested on the low chain-link fence that separated their yards. He tossed a trowel to the ground. "About the dead guy?"

"No." John heaved the sad, leafless tree out of the back. He would pretend with his children that he honored the anniversary of her death, but in reality, he knew she would return. Death was always easier to explain, and he would wait here for her and her letters forever, or at least until the end of this stupid world.

A paletero jingled the bells of his cart. In his straw hat, long-sleeve button-down shirt and jeans, he pushed his cart covered in colorful stickers for ice cream bars shaped like deformed ninja turtles or red, white, and blue rockets. Sunny had often treated the kids to one of the more natural flavors like coconut, strawberry, or mango. John had stopped eating sweets himself years ago to protect his few remaining teeth and his blood sugar, but he could feel the stickiness of their hands as they licked the bars that melted in the summer, his wife's pink tongue that flitted in and out of her mouth. His lips over hers. The last time they had sex, afterward her hair had clung to his neck, tickling him. When was the last time he had really laughed?

"Cops don't give a shit." Rodriguez spat into the dirt beside one of his aloe plants. "Too bad."

In all the years they had lived beside each other, John had never spoken with Rodriguez beyond a casual hello. His wife had often waved and complimented him on his colorful dry garden up front with its variegated succulents, from the purple echeveria to the reddish-magenta fruit of the prickly pears. Sometimes she would even drop food off at his house since she knew he lived alone. John hated these gestures, wished she'd mind her own business. She had said, "Oh, stop being so stingy. We might need him one day. We might need each other. Who knows? We should be friendly with our neighbors. We have plenty to give."

And he hated to admit this but she was right. It wasn't just a fence, or a property line, that they shared, but something to maintain and protect, a common set of values, despite how different Rodriguez was from them with his faded blue-green tattoos that reached up to his neck. The Virgin Mary on his leg. He had probably spent some time in prison himself. Who knew? He had a teardrop under his eye. Did that mean he had killed someone once?

"You still thinking of getting a taller fence?" Rodriguez asked.

"Yeah, yeah. Next year."

"Oh, right . . . *after* the end of the world." He grinned and revealed a missing tooth on one side. "Shit, I just wish the apocalypse would wipe out my bills and my taxes. Am I right?" He crossed his arms in front of him, narrowed his eyes as he took in the splendor of his yard, the years of hard work he had put into this small plot of land, his pride.

As John lugged the young persimmon toward the rear of his house, his sneakers crunched down on the gravel driveway. He then shuffled over the mostly dead weeds, pale and yellow like straw. The pain in his left knee twinged as he rested the tree that he would plant with his kids this weekend. Opposite the loquat, the spot had once been occupied by a date palm that some hotel developers purchased from them for one hundred dollars after they had first moved in. At that time, the amount of money had seemed like a lot until John himself owned a nursery and realized the true cost of raising something so large, the years of water and patience and light. Never in his lifetime would he be able to raise a tree that mature in his own space.

After brushing the dirt off his pants and hands, he unlocked the front door, greeted by the distinctive oily smell of mackerel being grilled. His wife loved seafood so much. The ocean in general. He rarely cooked fish, forgetting that his son might enjoy it sometimes too. His children laughed as they stood by the stove—the greatest, kindest sound in the world. They had borrowed the car this morning, but neither of them wanted to be at work afterward, so instead here they were, cooking as a way of bringing their mother back. Had they finally accepted that she might be dead? He had never explained to them any of the anniversary rites, which he had failed to perform for his own ancestors in Korea, yet he assumed they had come up with their own version, their own way of remembering Sunny and honoring her, even if it had been only a year since she had disappeared from their lives.

He removed his work clothes, which stank of soil and compost, and stepped into the hottest shower he could endure.

He blasted the water to drown out the sound of his cries as he held his face in his hands and the tears and snot ran down.

He hadn't anticipated the one-year anniversary of her disappearance to be this difficult, this emotional.

Coward. How right she had been when she said that word.

But once, he had been brave—when he had fled the North during the war, hungry and bloody and lice covered, and when he had first immigrated to this country on his own as a foreigner, a student, who had been spit on, made fun of, and then demoted to work difficult and menial jobs despite having grown up as a golden child, the first son of a lawyer and an academic. After many years, the experience of this country made him terrified and weak, whittled him down to his most vulnerable and angriest form. Was it this nation and its endless amounts of work, or was it his family, a family that he could give and give to but still lose and fail, that frightened him into a fearful rigidness that made him bland and unlovable like the sad jjigaes he threw together? Was he unlovable?

A war taught you how to be useful or useless.

Maybe his children might forgive him one day. Maybe Priscilla or some other woman might see him for who he was—finally. He was simply a ghost now who kept the lights on, the refrigerator full, and the heat running.

He dried off with a towel as best he could and buttoned his light blue pajama shirt over his chest. In front of his two children, who sat beside each other in the breakfast nook, the mackerel shined, its skin striped and iridescent beneath the pendant light that hung over their heads. There were two types of kimchi and store-bought kongnamul muchim, hobak bokkeum, and gamja jorim. A feast.

He tapped his metal chopsticks on the table to even them out.

They ate in silence for a few minutes until his daughter unexpectedly whimpered despite how hard she tried to contain herself.

"We've been spending all this time this past week trying . . . to figure out what happened to RJ," she said. John didn't want to hear RJ's name anymore, ever again. "We never talked about what happened to Mom, what everyone thinks happened to Mom. We never talked about it, did we?"

Ronald lowered his head. John's heart thumped, his breath rushed in and out of his mouth. They would never understand shame the way he understood it. He had been a good man—a good American—worked hard, paid his taxes, followed the laws, and yet he had failed spectacularly as a son, a husband, a father. He was in too deep now. He had gone too far. They would never ever understand.

John stared at the bones of Sunny's favorite fish in front of him. Thick and defined, milky white.

"Did you suspect *anything*? The day before she left. Was anything off?"

"I don't remember," he said. "She was cooking, uh, making, uh, lots of banchan, food because you coming home," John said. "She was, you know, getting ready for you. Very busy."

"They got into a fight," Ronald said. "Before she disappeared. I don't remember exactly when. Outside. They were yelling."

John wiped his mouth. The fish bones glistened.

"Do you remember what it was about?" Ana asked.

"It was about me, I think," Ronald said.

"Do you remember this? Dad?" Ana's voice shook.

Of course he did.

"I couldn't hear everything but—" Ronald's voice cracked. A sob escaped his mouth. Ana placed her hand on his shoulder. "It had something to do with her . . . spending too much time on her art, in the garage." He cleared his throat. "He . . . he blamed her because I wasn't doing well in school." His son cried like he used to as a little boy. John hadn't seen him this way in so long.

Any deficits in their lives, he blamed on their mother, because he couldn't handle the idea of never being enough.

He felt a shift in Ana then.

"When I was young, I remember RJ." Ana's eyes flashed. They were her mother's eyes, full of rage. "He went with us once to the Observatory, while you were at work."

I'll never forgive you, Sunny screamed. *Coward.* Her words stung like smoke.

"Ana," Ronald said.

"Ronald was there, but he was too young to remember."

John crinkled his napkin in his hand. A fist.

"Maybe she never wanted any of this, but she didn't have a choice." Tears dripped onto her shirt. "All those years she was just doing the best she could. It was hard for you. But it was always hardest for her."

He needed to get out of this room before he hurt someone, before he hurt himself.

"Maybe RJ appreciated her. Maybe she liked her feelings. Maybe she wanted to feel something. Unlike you."

His fist slammed down on the table, frightening them all. He could throw every plate and bowl in front of him to the ground. He was tired. He didn't care about RJ. All he wanted was his wife back. All he wanted was for his daughter to return to LA so the four of them could start all over again. He clung to the idea that they could be a family in America, they could have everything he didn't have growing up, but instead, he found himself here, alone, just as he had felt when he was thirteen and had stolen a man's shoes, a dead man's shoes, off his feet so he could cover his own. He couldn't get out of the war. It was eating him. It had eaten his family. He wished Sunny were dead now. He was glad she was gone like his mother. A burden. Weak.

"Did you even love her?" she asked. "Why did you bring her here? It seemed like the two of you had a better life in Korea. Both of your parents had money. You had gone to college. Why would you even bother to come here?"

"You don't know what it was like back then. It was not like now," he said.

"Like what? Could it really have been worse? It's hell here. It's absolutely fuckin' hell. All you do is work. Your children— Your children hate you. What could be worse than that?"

He laughed. He wanted to say, *Do you know what hell is like? Hell is having your home bombed and burned. Hell is not only leaving the dead behind but stealing from them. Hell is hunger, a hunger so bright and sharp, you'd kill someone to stop it. You'd kill someone. You'd run in the opposite direction of your mother, your brother and sister, the graves, their graves, people and places you were built to protect your whole life. You'd destroy anything that meant something to you. You'd see babies tossed like trash in the road, run over by tanks. You'd find little baby torsos. That was fucking hell.* Yes, perhaps he and Sunny had fled to a country that had fed this war and their suffering, but everyone knew that if there was a gun in the room, you'd rather be, even if you repulsed yourself, the one holding it, pointed away from you. *That is who we are. That is human. That is who we are.*

"At least she had *him*," she said.

He grabbed the bowl, chopsticks, and spoon in front of him. He leaned on the counter.

"The least we could do is help his daughter. Maybe he— Maybe RJ actually loved Mom. Maybe that's all she wanted."

He breathed through his mouth. Curled his fingers into fists, his nails digging into his palms.

"His wife left him," John said. He couldn't help but laugh at the irony of it all.

"Who?"

"His wife left him, too. Ha." He wasn't supposed to say it. He had promised Priscilla. But there was no turning back now.

"What do you mean?"

"Yesterday, Priscilla tell me his wife took his daughter. She left him." RJ's wife had disappeared like his own. How strange lives could mirror one another. Neither of them could keep a woman by their side.

"Who the hell is Priscilla? And how does this change anything for us? It changes nothing. Mom is still . . . he was around for her. He was still around for her, Dad. Unlike you. *You* left her. You brought her to this country and abandoned her."

The wooden bench in the breakfast nook creaked. Ana now stood a few feet away from him. He loosened his fists. His fingers, their joints, ached from the tightness of his grip.

"You tried to stop her from doing anything for herself. You never saw her as a person, did you? You couldn't."

Coward.

He stomped away through the narrow kitchen to the rear of the house, where he slammed the door behind him. Standing at the top of the stairs outside, he yelled through his teeth, "God damn you. God damn you." How much he hated this place but couldn't admit it to anyone. How trapped he had become here. The whole backyard had been overgrown with weeds, yellow and dry. The persimmon tree. His wife loved them. She always wanted one in their yard and yet he never bothered to bring one home. Why enjoy a life that he hated so much?

He rolled up his sleeves.

He needed his shovel. The grip of it in his hands, how smooth the wood had become through the years, the metal handle, the coldness of the handle. But that shovel was gone.

He found the spot where he might dig, and dug and dug and dug with his hands, clawing into the earth with his nails, cutting open his skin. The blood burned.

"Sunny," he called out. But his voice didn't sound like his own. He fell onto the ground, grabbed at his heart as if trying to tear it out of his chest. The dirt in his mouth. "Sunny. Sunny. Sunny. Sunny." He shouted as if she might hear him on the other side of the earth. Rocks and pebbles pressed into his face. He belonged here. He could rest.

Let me die, he thought. He stared at the scurrying of feet in slippers. Hands pulled him onto his back. He closed his eyes into the softness of a lap beneath his head, which felt like it had been split in half. Pain ripped through him and his vision went dark. Dimly, he heard his daughter cry out.

Let me die, he thought again. *Let me die. Please, please, Sunny. You were right. I'll never forgive myself. Let me die.*

1992

In the sixteen years since Sunny had left Seoul, both everything and nothing had changed.

More roads had been built, and cars, despite their compact size, bullied the air with their stench. And regardless of the allure of glossy department stores, which smelled of cleaning chemicals and floral French perfumes, she preferred dark and damp Namdaemun market, where she feasted on crispy bindaetteok and warm soondae—soft and earthy and gelatinous—dipped in a delicate mix of salt, chili pepper, and sesame seeds. She delighted in the narrow paths, survivors of industry that wound through quiet neighborhoods with their surprising nooks and crannies beneath doorways and windows, the curves and alleys, places to hide like the inside of a mind. This old construction, the veining of these passages, was like a portrait of a self, its branching, its perpetual mystery.

When she first glimpsed her mother at the doorstep of her Gunpo apartment building, Sunny shed tears of joy and great relief. Her mother hadn't been well these days. She'd suffered a heart attack at the beginning of the year, and Sunny had feared her children might never meet her.

Her mother had grown her hair out white. She possessed the same mix of geniality and toughness that she'd always had, a toughness that made the tenderness of her smile and the sparkle in her eyes shine like the iridescent interior of an abalone. Sunny couldn't help but abandon all formality and embrace her mother like a child, body rocking from side to side. Her mother laughed, eyes wet. She then hugged Ronald, nine years old, and Ana at this vulnerable age of fourteen. She had started her period, and her posture, the forward curve of her shoulders, suggested she was ashamed of her breasts. An awkward, difficult time.

"Have the kids eaten yet? They are so big already. So tall," her mother said.

"No, not yet. The food on the plane was terrible. They're starving."

"They're at just the right place for that." She grinned and revealed a missing tooth at the side of her mouth.

They climbed to the third floor of the apartment building in Gunpo, a smaller city about twenty kilometers south of Seoul. The building itself appeared to be in good shape, and Sunny could feel some of her anxiety lessen as she realized that her sister Sunmi had been taking such great care of her mother, checking in on her at least once per week. Sunny had been concerned about her taking on so many duties by herself. Sunmi had a life of her own too, a husband and a son, whom they'd meet for the first time that night.

The scent of grilled mackerel, her favorite fish, distinctively oily and rich, welcomed them inside the apartment where her father's artwork, his framed paintings, hung on every wall, reminding Sunny of his absence, the silence of his being gone. She couldn't have imagined what a life in Korea would be without him. And his work was what he had left behind for them to remember him by—the portraits and the pastoral scenes in the North where they had been born, the women carrying baskets of fish on their heads, the children riding an ox, the nude women bathing in a river. She had always wondered who the women were. She had never asked. There were some things she knew never to talk about, but she imagined they were his older sisters whom he had been split from and lost during the war. The colors he often chose were muted and dull—earth tones like Sienna and Ochre—but she imagined the women as if they were alive. She stopped in front of one painting, a matriarch, geometrically drawn, carrying a wide, shallow bowl with a large fish on her head as if she had just come back from the market.

"I have some artwork if you'd like to take it home with you," her mother said in a low voice, as if not to disturb the dead. "Some of your father's paintings."

The walls of Sunny's house were so empty. How lonely she had been without any art in her life. Even if you didn't stop to look at the paintings, she always felt that somehow they were watching her, the way ancestors never left you behind. She realized just then that although they had been different in so many ways, both her husband and her father had been separated from family in the war. They never spoke about the missing. The paintings were one way her father shared his stories, the greatest gift he could ever pass on to her. An inheritance that was more than a down payment. An image of the self on which to build a present life. If she ever died suddenly, what would she leave for her children to remind them of her, to remind them they were loved still, that as long as they walked this earth, she would watch over them as best she could?

Ana planted herself, elbows on the dining table adjacent to the kitchen, which smelled of history and home—sesame, garlic, onion, and chive, fermented vegetables, oysters, and shrimp, the salt, the sourness of it all. Ronald tugged her hair. She batted away his hand.

"Umma, do you happen to have a fork?" Sunny asked.

"A fork?"

"Ana never uses chopsticks," Sunny said.

"Ha. Have your kids become that American? We can give her a spoon for now. I don't know if I have a fork. Only the tiny ones for fruit."

Sunny's face burned. Ana was a daddy's girl, even forgoing the Korean language with him as well. They chatted in English and her husband preferred things that way, as if Korean had become useless, because why? Because that was the language Sunny clung to? Because to him, it was a language of the past—a language dead to him.

"What about the other one?" her mother asked. "What can he eat?"

"We can give him our food. Let's sit down, umma." *I missed you. I want to look at your face. I want to drink up your face. I want to hold you with my eyes.*

Her mother set down a plate of mackerel, salted and grilled to a perfect crisp. Then one by one she brought forth a stack of kimchi pajeon, bowls of doenjang jjigae, and the banchan—sigeumchi namul, kongnamul muchim, mak and mu kimchi—all magnificently and perfectly assembled in dark earthen bowls, a symphony of familiar colors and smells. Her mother may not have been an artist by formal standards, but she understood texture and tone for every sense—the eyes, the nose, the tongue. How effortless she made it all appear. Sunny knew that preparing so much banchan required hours over sometimes days to soak the dehydrated roots and vegetables, salt the cabbage and mu.

"I want chicken," Ronald said in English.

"There is no chicken," Sunny spat. The jet lag had worn them all down. "Look at all the beautiful dishes your grandmother has made for you. Aren't you happy to be here?"

"Chicken," he said again.

"What's 'chicken?'" her umma asked.

"Dak."

"Oh, we don't have that now but I can make that for dinner?"

Ronald didn't seem to understand her Korean at all.

How ungrateful. The shame. To be a guest at their grandmother's house and to be fed so impressively, only to reject the bounty that had been gifted them. Who raised them to be this way?

"Oh, umma, don't worry about them. Whatever you'd like to eat tonight is fine."

"Chicken!" Ronald cried. "Chicken, chicken, chicken, chicken."

"Please, not in front of your grandmother." She nudged a piece of the mackerel off the bone and placed it on top of his rice. "This is so delicious, umma. How I've missed your food so much." She cracked a smile, but her mother could tell how difficult her daughter's life had become. She furrowed her brow as she spooned a bit of jjigae with a bite of softened zucchini into her mouth.

"Here, let me take him so that you can eat," her umma said. "You've had a long journey with these two kids all by yourself. Your mother must be starving." She nuzzled her face into Ronald's hair. At that instant, Sunny, despite how hard she tried, burst into tears.

She couldn't hide any of it from her mother. That was partially why perhaps both she and her husband had lost touch with their families. With them, they couldn't deny the truth of what they'd become—outsiders both here and there, outsiders to even themselves. They could attempt to obscure who they were, but it would take too much work and she was already exhausted. She had lugged two children around the world by herself. She was practically a single mother with her husband at work all the time. She could sense her daughter observing her as she wiped the tears away from her face and blew her nose. Her daughter who had become so withdrawn lately, so emotional as well.

I love you very much, Sunny. Those words which comforted her. That voice. On the airplane ride there, she had worked with every ounce of her body to quell thoughts of RJ and the last time she had seen him eight years earlier, after he had placed his boxes in the garage. *You're my sister. I love you very much, Sunny.* The first time she had heard those words in English in her life. The fire of those words. The strangeness. *I love you very much, Sunny.* In her family, no one ever said that out loud, and to hear her name at the end of that sentence. How sentimental. There was no space in their everyday lives for this kind of feeling. Was it culture or had the war simply wiped these words from their mouths, had war made it too difficult to expose yourself this way? And he did it. He said it. But then he left her.

How she had humiliated herself into thinking there might be something else, that she could leave her family, temporarily, that she could drive him down south. *You're my sister.*

He wanted to be alone. He said that he'd take the bus.

She had waited eight years, but he never returned. Instead she came here with her children. She needed to see her mother before she died, she told her husband. And he agreed. This way, perhaps while she and the children would be out of the house for two weeks, he would have a break himself. He could do anything he wanted. She needed air, an escape, and yet she came here and the burning was everywhere, the gasoline, the fuel. The smell of progress was ugly and never had an end, did it? When would we say enough was enough? Would we wait until the end of the world to feel our greatest regret? Why did we allow ourselves to feel so powerless in the face of a progress we didn't want?

Ana ate in silence, raising her face to smile at her grandmother.

"You must be so tired, dear," her umma said.

"I am," Sunny replied. "Yes, I am so tired. It's a long flight."

"Why don't you go and lay down in the room over there. I will stay with the children and feed them."

"Yes, umma. I should. Thank you for this lovely meal."

As she tucked her chair beneath the table, her eyes, dry and blurry, rested on a portrait of two women who bathed nude in a river, baskets of fish improbably balanced on both their hands, pine trees and an ox in the background. Were they sisters or friends? They appeared complete with each other.

"I forgot to mention," her mother said. "I was in Insadong the other day. There's a gallerist there who had been interested in putting together a show, a retrospective of your father's work."

"Oh, that's nice." A mix of jet lag and general exhaustion made her head light, but she couldn't move. She had surrendered to the soothing shades, the angles and curves in her father's painting.

"She said she was your teacher at the university, that you had so much promise. But she lost touch with you after she moved to France. Things had become difficult for her, I guess."

Sunny's mind flooded with light, as if the curtains had been pulled apart inside it.

"I have her business card." Her mother retrieved a piece of paper from her handbag. She squinted as she read the words, " 'Cho Myunghwa.' A painter herself. Sound familiar?"

On a park bench with the sharp light of spring nearly white on her face, Sunny waited, eyes fixed on a single cloud, fluffy and cartoonishly defined. The nude trees twitched as birds flitted about, bending and strengthening branches that would soon hold the weight of their leaves, full-blown. An image of RJ a few feet away from her sprang into her mind, and then his fingers on her shoulder. Tears filled her eyes. How different life was in LA, how much more complicated things had seemed. *You're my sister. I love you very much, Sunny.*

After sightseeing with the kids for a few days—trips to parks and palaces and the most charming of neighborhoods like the Hanok Village with its exposed wood, delicacy, and decorum—Sunny secured a few hours to meet up with none other than Professor Cho. Her mother had offered to take Ana and Ronald to the local market in Gunpo with its wet floors from the ice that melted as it chilled the fresh-caught fish and mounds of dried peppers in every shade of red, deep vermillion to bright scarlet. How much her mother knew and understood her with so little said.

Sunny had never envisioned that so much time could pass without seeing her family, but it did. In America, they had been busy, seemingly always behind, and there was hardly enough money to pay for their living expenses. When she had first immigrated, she imagined going back home every couple years at least, but that had never happened, and the next thing she knew all the bills had stacked up, and the minutes and hours, the days and weeks had flown by. Her son was nearly ten years old. Ana would be fifteen.

Her sister too had changed. When she reunited with her, met for the first time her husband and son, she embraced her, laughing like children again. But something about Sunmi had hardened also. Lines of worry had been carved into the space between her brows. Her sister, who had once been so pretty and charming with her round face and squarish jaw, wide eyes rimmed in a gray catlike shape, appeared downtrodden, weathered, a fallen log. Her son and husband had been the moss, dewy and bright, growing on the bark. Was her sister lonely too? Or maybe a little resentful about her younger sister "abandoning" them for a new life, another country, a different kind of family, much smaller and with fewer obligations abroad?

It was hard to say and could've been easily all those things at once.

"Lee Sunhee."

She heard her name like a student at roll call.

"Professor Cho," she said as she stood. She couldn't believe her eyes. She hadn't believed Professor Cho would actually arrive until now.

"Just call me unnie." Myunghwa embraced Sunny, and for a few seconds they held each other's forearms, pressing their hands into each other as if they couldn't believe that the two of them existed here, now, eyes locked. Clearly the rumor of her death had been incorrect. Or the body of the woman found had been misidentified. So many had gone missing or had been murdered—students, teachers, activists—during that time. Now Sunny and Myunghwa resembled two schoolgirls in a dance, grinning and giddy.

"It's been too long." Elegantly dressed in a cream silk shirt and tawny pants that flowed down her legs, Myunghwa sat beside Sunny on the bench, their thighs ever so slightly touching. Gray hair sprouted around her temples, and the high bridge of her nose had been bent as if it had been broken, evidence of what she had endured.

Nonetheless, to Sunny, she was still the most beautiful woman in the world.

"Everything has changed so much. But you . . . you look wonderful."

"Ha, that's because I don't have a husband," Myunghwa said.

Sunny laughed. "What are you doing these days, then?"

"I'm busy with the gallery, and my own art. After I was fired from the university, I moved to France. I decided that teaching wasn't for me."

"Fired?"

"Yes, after . . . after I had been arrested."

"I'm sorry to hear that." She remembered hearing that one of her classmates had run into Professor Cho, who had told her she'd been beaten during her interrogation. Apparently, she had then lost her job and fled the country.

"And you? I wish you had brought your two kids."

"I thought it would be a bit too much. I wanted to try riding the subway." Sunny smiled.

"What do you think?"

"A miracle. It's so much better than the buses in Los Angeles. I drive now though. A big American car." Sunny laughed. "We have two cars now."

"Fancy. How is it? Do you think I should move too? I'm so tired of everything here."

"To America? By yourself?" She could feel the flush of pink on her face.

"Sure, why not? Maybe I could open a gallery. There are still protests all the time. The government. I thought things had changed after they had elected—" She pressed her lips together as if she shouldn't say too much more. "And what about in America?"

"We are so busy with the kids. My husband has his business. He works all the time." She nodded. "We have problems there too. A lot. It's different though, I guess."

"But it's so much easier for you as a woman, isn't it?"

"It's hard to be a woman anywhere." Sunny smirked to cut through the sadness ripening between them. It was true, wasn't it? Even if men too—especially of certain races and classes and sexualities—could be oppressed, women still earned less generally, and had been socially held more responsible for taking care of others, as if it were always their "nature." And if they didn't have their own money or income, like Sunny herself, the hours of her life had been assigned to someone else, children or husbands or the community.

"But I don't feel like I'd be bothered so much about my divorce in America," Myunghwa said. "Or not marrying again. People would just assume I killed my rich husband and I got away with it. I'd be . . . okay with that?" She laughed.

Couples and families and the elderly passed by, enjoying their day in the sunshine, hats covering heads, far away from any social upheaval, but Sunny knew how tumultuous and brutal this century had been for her country, her people—from the Japanese occupation to the war to the omnipresence of America and its military and the oppressive dictators who ruled. Still, people everywhere, regardless of the conditions of their lives, found moments of joy and bliss, comfort on a quiet afternoon in the grass, holding hands. The heart could find a home in even the most difficult conditions, and as long as it did, there was no reason to give up on this one life, this world.

"Maybe I could disappear for a little while. Here, everyone seems to know everyone." Myunghwa smiled to herself. "I guess I just don't like the rules. And I can't pretend like everyone else. I'm terrible at it."

Sunny understood her more than Myunghwa might ever know.

On the grass around them, finches with yellow beaks flitted about, searching for seed.

"All those poor students killed," Myunghwa said. "Students. I'll never get over it."

Sunny closed her eyes. The uprising, the massacre in 1980. The dead and the missing.

Imagine what it was like to die before ever falling in love.

It was the children, those students, fearless and young, who inspired us to preserve our humanity the most. And Sunny realized what made people human was not how well they behaved or followed the rules, because even ants in colonies could be tremendously organized and productive, but how much we could contemplate and create beauty for its own sake. A bee might land upon a flower because it had been attracted to its shape and color, but a human could pluck the bud and arrange it in a million ways simply to please the spirit. In this sense, art didn't save lives, but it asserted what made us unique and soulful, worth saving at all.

"We are so tired of bad news here. The news is so awful, America is even starting to look good." Myunghwa laughed. "I never thought I'd say that, you know. But we all have our limits. I'll eat hamburger if I have to."

"Ha. We are tired too. And please don't eat hamburgers. My husband is addicted."

"How is he?"

"My husband? Fine. Fine."

"He likes his business?"

"I honestly don't know." Sunny had no idea what he liked anymore. Hiking? Did he like hiking or did he need it? And was there even a difference between the two? "He works all the time. I hardly see him. I'm a single girl like you." She cracked a smile as a tear slid down her cheek. "Honestly, I could run off and he wouldn't even know as long as the kids were clothed and fed."

Myunghwa pressed a handkerchief from her purse onto Sunny's lap. "At least you have a family. I honestly don't need a husband, ha, but I do love kids."

"You were always so good with them. Us students were very lucky."

Myunghwa smiled tightly as if withholding something that might burst from her mouth. Sunny was silent, waiting. Patient.

After a few minutes, Myunghwa said, "When the police had taken me in, I was raped." She relayed the facts, one by one, as if she had detached herself from the words somehow. "I found out I was pregnant and had to get an abortion. I didn't have a job either. I had already been fired by the university."

Sunny clutched Myunghwa's hand.

"One of my friends recommended a doctor, but he wasn't even a doctor. It was a scam. I bled and bled for months. I got a divorce and left for France. I disappeared. Everyone, except my family, thought I was dead." Myunghwa sighed. "After that, when I wanted to . . . have a child with my second husband, I couldn't get pregnant. We divorced, and that's when I came back to Korea."

Sunny's entire body wouldn't stop shaking.

"Here, take my scarf. I have another one in my bag." Myunghwa draped the soft silk, hand-dyed a gorgeous ochre, over Sunny's head.

For a second the fabric slipped over her eyes like a sheet. As Myunghwa tied the bow, the back of her hands touched Sunny's chin. "I never told anyone this." She squeezed her arm. "Really, being a mother suits you. And I'm so proud of all that you've done, all the adventures you've had. I've always wanted the best for you."

Her ears rang beneath the silk. High-pitched. Her head, her head could explode. A siren for air raids.

"My husband blamed me for not being able to have a child," Myunghwa said. "The French one. He was also an asshole."

"If the world ended, they'd blame us for that too, I suppose," Sunny said. She wiped away the strands of hair that had been clinging to the tears on Myunghwa's face.

"Definitely," Myunghwa said with a bit of a laugh.

"Oh, is it raining today? I'm sorry, that's *my* fault."

"I'm so glad you're here." She grabbed Sunny's two hands and held them to keep them warm. "Do you remember the moon jar?" She poked Sunny's cheek with the tips of two fingers. She tucked Sunny's hair behind her ear. Her body tingled, her arms, legs, the distance between them. She imagined the folds and the drape of the fabric over their heads. "I'm your sister now. *Unnie*. Not your professor," she said. "In America, I hope you make your life beautiful. I promise to visit you one day." She whispered, "Will you have space for me if I come?"

1999

After the stroke, the evening had passed in the emergency room with his daughter and son by his side in a blur of conversations overheard between patients, doctors, and nurses.

John listened to the genteel voice of a young man with an eye injury who had been assaulted on the street. He didn't have insurance and would wait until he returned to India in a few days for treatment.

John himself was four years away from Medicare. He had never been to the emergency room in his life and had learned to deny treatment because he had heard so many horror stories of the bills that had been received, the houses that needed to be sold, the life savings depleted. Grateful that the stroke had been minor, he was likely to be discharged from the hospital before sunrise. As he lay in his bed, which crinkled around him with every movement, he attempted a calculation of how many years he would still need to work (forever and ever). If he had to sell the nursery to pay the hospital bill, where could he get a job now? His children didn't understand that after a certain age, he didn't have a choice but to hold on to the business that they viewed as a dead end. Only as a small business owner could he continue to work without having an employer discriminate against him, his accent, his health. His customers had been mostly forgiving, realizing that he very much needed them to get by, that although sometimes grumpy and curt, he wasn't a bad man. Yes, he had made terrible choices to survive. But all his actions had stemmed from the aching fact that one day he had to leave his children, and he'd have to prepare them as best he could, provide a shelter, teach them to feed and protect themselves. He had failed spectacularly in so many ways.

Now, back at the house under his blanket and the spell of the chirping birds at dawn, John wept by himself. He didn't even believe in the Lord, and had attended church all those years because his wife argued they needed a sense of community to survive, but he found himself in this moment, eyes closed, praying.

Please keep them safe.

His daughter was right. In a way, he had left Sunny behind. He had abandoned her by ignoring her needs all those years, because he was overwhelmed with the fear of loss. That was what the war had done to him. America had not only bombed his country, destroyed entire villages and towns, but it had made him terrified of his own heart. Maybe he had become invested in the apocalypse as a diversion from what was really lost. Like a toddler, he clung to repetition, the end, the end, the end, to impose a false sense of control over his emotions.

Because John did not have the courage to face what had happened between him and Sunny.

Last night, his own daughter had attempted to wrest the truth from him with her questions about the night that his wife disappeared. He had learned that once RJ had taken them all to the Observatory. Even his own son, his son named Ronald, had been there. *Maybe RJ appreciated her. Maybe she liked her feelings. Maybe she wanted to feel something. Unlike you.* In a fit of rage, before he could destroy something in the house, John had fled. Outside, he dug, clawed into the hard soil with his bare hands, fingernails bleeding, so that he could finally plant his wife's persimmon tree, which might survive them all—and it nearly killed him.

He never told his wife this, but after he had found out about his father's death over fifteen years ago, he had reached out to his stepmother one last time in a desperate attempt to figure out the whereabouts of his family in North Korea. His stepmother could apply her money and resources, his father's status and influence, to launch a search that could at least determine if his mother and his siblings had survived the violence, the hunger.

"You know there's nothing we can do about that," his stepmother had told him. He imagined her perched on an ornately upholstered chair in his parents' salon, her delicate hands manicured and moist from never having to cook or work around the house. "Why not just enjoy your own life, the one life you have, Jung Ho. It's not your fault that they didn't make it across the border. Who knows? They might even be fine. They might even have forgotten about you already."

She had been notorious for her callousness, especially toward him. He had been a reminder of a life that his father had fought so long to leave behind, not just physically but in his mind, his heart. Who knew what kind of nightmares his father had when he slept? Only his stepmother, perhaps.

John could never forget the last time he had seen his mother, right before they had fled under the cover of night. Rumor abounded that his father would be captured soon for his anti-Communist work, which had been a secret to Jung Ho himself. His father needed to escape as far south as they could, to Busan if possible, with only his eldest son, a few books, and the bulk of his writings in tow.

"You take care of yourself and your father, okay?" Even though they had been about the same height, his mother brought his head down to her chest and spoke into his hair because she couldn't stand to look into his eyes. Her shirt smelled of comfort, of toasted sesame seeds, and barley tea. "We will be fine here and eventually we will meet up again. Your father has to leave now."

"What about you? Who will take care of umma?" Jung Ho asked.

"We have each other. I have my parents. I have to take care of them. Your brother and sister will be okay. You have to leave now. We will see each other again."

As he followed his father, he burst into tears as quietly as possible. He hated the moon and the stars, any source of light that might reveal who they were, his weakness, that he should abandon tonight, right now. He was only thirteen years old, but he needed to be a man to survive. His father had plans to reach a friend's house, where they'd sleep and hide, twenty-five kilometers away by morning. He would have ten to twelve hours to reckon with himself as they dashed with a canteen of water, jumeokbap, an entire boiled chicken, a variety of currency, including won and yen, and gold sewed into the linings of their coats. And for the rest of his life, he'd resent his father for *not* leaving him behind.

His father probably believed that he had salvaged John that night. But what kind of life did John have that was worth saving? A life haunted by both the living and the dead on the other side of a brutal border. A life in which he erased himself in order to survive. A life in which he learned to run away, come to this country, America, in order to start all over again, only to lose his wife and have his own children hate him, the way that he hated his father.

Now he wished only that he had told Sunny more. Would it have changed how she had felt about him, the life they had built together? Or would she have considered him a coward for not dealing with the fact that he had used his dream as a diversion from what hurt him, the pain like a prison, or a country, he could never escape. No wonder why so many of his friends growing up drank and smoked; they lived in a perpetual state of combustion.

"Sunny," he said to himself now, still in their bed. "I was wrong."

How foreign those words sounded from his mouth. In what language might she hear him?

She had become the story that no one could tell. Until a dead man, a stranger appeared in their yard.

Tears leaked out of his eyes. He itched to get out of their bed now, but his body resisted, his limbs heavy like sacks of rice. He shuddered at the thought that he might not even make it to the end of this world. He might never die his children's hero. He didn't have a will or any clear explanation of all his property and accounts. Who knew if and when he might have another stroke? He needed to find a lawyer as soon as possible. He needed to make it, his final words, official.

The sun had cracked open like a psychedelic egg, a runny yolk that bled magenta and orange into the indigo that encroached, second by second, until the stars, muted and dull, flickered behind smog.

On this Sunday, less than two weeks before the apocalypse, Ronald flipped on the brash floodlight that they'd keep on all night—a practice his father enforced since he had discovered RJ in the backyard. He was now off from school for the winter break, and he couldn't help but laugh a little as he recalled the romantic green light at the end of the dock in *The Great Gatsby*, a book that he had actually enjoyed in English class, for its dark swiftness, hopeless longing, and violent demises. (It was also short and easy to read.) A stranger from a distance would regard their house with the opposite of enchantment. They might experience repulsion, even fear. The ugly reach of tense white shouted, *Do not even think of getting close! I am watching you!*

After he spent the day with his sister tending their father, all soups and teas and water, he needed to be outside where he could smoke a cigarette and finish his father's job of planting his mother's persimmon tree. He scanned the yard for the shovel that they never used but always lay around like some archaeological tool caked with ancient mud. There had to be another way to dig a hole.

Cigarette still in his mouth, he turned when a figure scurried from the shadows in the corner of his eye. He jumped out of his skin and the butt slipped from his lips onto the ground.

"What the fuck," Ronald shouted.

A man climbed the fence that separated their yard from Rodriguez's. Ronald collected himself enough to stamp out the red glow of the lit tobacco, as the intruder lost his grip and fell down. He hoisted himself up, squinting into the light. "Shit. My ankle." He winced.

Ronald recognized him from his driver's license. "What the fuck are you doing here?"

Startled, Jacob Hendricks raised his hand, shielding his eyes. "Who the fuck are you?" He wiped the sweat off his brow, rubbed his mouth. "Is that your Eldorado out front?"

"I live here," Ronald said. "It's . . . my dad's."

Jacob patted himself down as if looking for something he might've dropped. He wore plain clothes, a pair of blue jeans and a gray sweatshirt. His salt-and-pepper hair had been slicked down onto his sweaty forehead as if he had been caught in a thunderstorm, but there hadn't been any rain for weeks. He picked up his cap and slapped it back onto his head and groaned.

"How long have you been back here?" Ronald asked. "Fuck."

Did Jacob know about their visit to Anaheim? The wallet they returned. The driver's license.

"I wanted to see where he died," Jacob said as he limped. "Shit."

"Why didn't you just try the fucking doorbell like a normal person?" Ronald asked.

"You think you would've opened it?"

"Maybe." Ronald rested his hands on his hips. What would he have done if he hadn't recognized him? An encounter with a stranger in your backyard was terrifying. Fight or flight.

"He died . . . there." Ronald pointed to the loquat tree, a shaggy outline in a dark corner behind the garage.

"Jesus Christ." Jacob shook his head.

A siren howled in the distance. The night air was frigid, breath clouded their faces. Ronald wiped his nose on his sleeve.

"And Sunny? Where is she?" Jacob asked.

Her name again. In a stranger's mouth. The pang in Ronald's chest like a bullet.

"How do you know her name?"

"He talked about her." Jacob smirked, sucked his teeth a little.

Son of a bitch, Ronald curled his fingers into a fist. "She's gone," he said.

"Yeah? She coming back or what?"

"She's *gone*. Leave her the fuck alone."

"RJ told me . . . he told me a friend of his held on to some of his stuff." Jacob jerked his head toward the crushed cigarette on the ground. "You got another one of those?"

Careful not to let his guard down or get too close, Ronald handed him his packet with his lighter. He had been standing with his back to the floodlight.

Hands trembling, Jacob lit his cigarette and his face glowed with an orange cast that softened his appearance. He blew out a stream of smoke and coughed, clearing his throat. He returned the cigarette packet to Ronald.

"I warned him," Jacob said through the cigarette he pinched between his lips. "I told him he'd get killed if . . ."

"*Killed—?*"

"We became friends again. Last year. He told me things . . . he shouldn't have."

"How did you even know him?" Ronald asked.

"From the war and . . . and I got him his job. At the police station."

The connection between the two.

"What did he tell you?" Ronald asked.

"That he was writing a book." Jacob took another drag of his cigarette, and coughed until he spat on the ground. Ronald couldn't tell how old Jacob was, but the years had clearly not been kind to him.

"Sounds innocent enough," Ronald said. Was his sister still in the house? Where was she? He wanted to warn her to stay away, but he couldn't without losing sight of Jacob.

"Innocent? Ha. He thought he was some kind of journalist." He snickered to himself. "Ever heard of a *janitor* journalist? He was so fuckin' proud too." He wiped tears from the corners of his eyes with his thumb, the cigarette still burning. "He shoulda known he could get killed for that shit. Nobody wants the fuckin' truth."

"I do," Ronald said.

"You're just a kid, that's why. You know what people *really* want?"

The question terrified him.

"You know what all those advertisements are for . . . drugs to smile, to feel good, to sleep. That's what people want. They want a story that makes them feel safe so they can sleep at night. They'll take any story they can, even if it's a total lie. Do you think they want a story about the good guys being bad? Fuck that. No." He took another drag and stomped his cigarette out.

"You turned against him?" Ronald asked.

"He wasn't family."

"But—"

"Family are the ones who keep you alive."

"But you're dead in other ways." The volume of Ronald's voice surprised him. Was he speaking to a stranger still? "You backstabbed someone who wanted—"

"The only shit that matters is that I'm *not* dead. That it's him and *not* me." He pointed to the center of his own chest. "It's only kids, idiots like you who think there's a point in all that . . . 'do what's right' bullshit." He spat into the dirt. "Right and wrong . . . it's all relative anyways. War teaches you that. The only thing that makes sense is *dead* or *alive*. And I win."

But there were gray areas like his mother. There were different levels of death and different levels of life. And there were ways to be alive and dead at the same time. But Jacob was already lost. Even Ronald, a *kid*, an *idiot*, knew that.

"So is it the book you're looking for?" Ronald asked.

"Ha, it's more concrete than that. Nobody would believe a homeless vet. Probably fucked in the head. It was what your mother had. It was what he left with your mother. And now she's fuckin' gone."

"Did he tell you my mother had it?"

"Everything points to her," Jacob said.

"How do you—"

"We became friends again, me and RJ, and would spend time at the library together. Like some boring old-ass couple. Then one day . . . I found pages from the book he was working on, at the printer, no less. And of course I had no choice but to—could I get another one of those? Shit."

Ronald handed him his pack. "Take them all," he said.

"Like I said . . . he told me a friend kept his stuff." Jacob gestured toward the loquat tree. His eyes filled with a sudden sadness. "And look where he ended up."

But how did Jacob know where their house was, unless he'd followed Ronald and Ana back from Anaheim somehow. Only the police and Rhonda knew where they lived, and Ronald was sure that Rhonda would have told them if she had spoken with Jacob.

Had they mentioned to Jacob's daughter that RJ had died in their backyard? Ronald could no longer remember exactly what they had said. He'd have to ask his sister.

Tears spilled from Ronald's eyes. The helplessness. He couldn't take it anymore. He had to put an end to all of this. He just wanted everyone to leave his family alone. RJ was a kind of curse now. He could understand how his father felt, how his father despised him, because RJ's death revealed all the aspects of their lives they had been ashamed to share with anyone. And now everyone knew who they were—struggling, exhausted, hopeless Americans. Failures.

"I bet she's dead too," Jacob said.

"What are you talking about?"

Jacob shrugged, and seized by a sudden sense of rage he didn't even know he had, Ronald grabbed him by the collar. He tackled him to the ground with an *oomph*, reared back, and punched him in the mouth. Pain shot through Ronald's arm, but he would break every bone in his hands if it meant getting rid of the agony inside him. Jacob tried to fight him off, but Ronald jostled him by his shirt, which had torn with the weight of his body falling down.

"You might as well tell me what it was, then. What did RJ leave with my mother?" Ronald smeared blood all over his face as he wiped his tears and snot away. He had never beaten anyone in his life. And for a few seconds, it felt good, until now, until he saw the horror in this man's eyes. "If it's all over, give us some peace." His voice broke. He didn't care if anyone could hear him. "Give us some fuckin' peace."

"Are you fuckin' done now? Feel better?"

Ronald shook his head. "Fuck." He caught his breath, reached out to help Jacob, who refused his hand and held his nose to stanch the bleeding.

"Peace? The world is fuckin' over," Jacob said. "Delete."

"How can you walk away right now, then? Knowing how wrong everything is. How could you—"

"If I don't find what I need—" Jacob stopped himself, shaking his head. He picked up the cigarette that had flown out of his hand and flicked the ash into a spark that didn't catch. "Not only will I pay, but you will too, you hear?" He spat blood onto the ground. "I'll come back in a couple days and you better fuckin' have some more answers for me. I want to know where your mom went. Search through every fucking bit of this place," he sneered as he wiped his nose on his sleeve. "And stay away from my fuckin' house. I've been watching you, too."

1992

As the plane touched and bounced twice on the tarmac, Sunny released the loudest, the least self-conscious sigh, like a belt unbuckling, exhausted yet relieved to hit the familiar ground of what had become her home, *our* home. Here in Los Angeles, she could insert herself and disappear inside the cadence, the rhythms of day-to-day life, even if she didn't feel as if she belonged. Here she had no understanding of history, outside of what was required for her citizenship test, the legacy and weight of responsibility beyond her immediate family. She could be free even from politics because she knew that all she had to do was focus on her own survival, which hinged on the success of her American-born children. That was the promise.

There was no place quite yet for her in Seoul. She longed to see her mother and sister more often, but life had been difficult there too, especially for women, even college-educated ones like Myunghwa, a former professor who could be punished for choosing to remain unwed but who possessed the luxury of self-employment in the arts simply because her family had been wealthy. Otherwise, she would've earned less and often endured the scrutiny of a society that prodded, directly or at a slant, *Where are your children? What is the point of life without them? How old are your children? What will you do when you get old? Aren't you lonely by yourself?*

Was there anywhere people could go to be free? Or were we all inevitably trapped in the circumstances of our lives, our own mistakes and those of others, their desires and choices?

As the plane rolled down the runway, she seethed in her seat, touching the window, marking it with her fingers as she remembered Myunghwa's words: *In America, I hope you make your life beautiful. I promise to visit you one day. Will you have space for me if I come?*

The cacophony as everyone gathered their belongings. The metal unclasping. The groans of bodies heaving bags and luggage from above. The fever of excitement. The relief of being on the ground. The money she kept on her body at all times, even when she had relieved herself in the tiny airplane bathroom. The money her mother had given her weighed heavily in her purse. She didn't even have time to count it before she departed for the airport. Her mother handed it to her and told her that she should hide it as soon as she got home, in case something were to happen to her husband, who worked in such a dangerous part of the city, in case of an emergency. Her husband didn't need to know, did he? She had to protect herself in America, where she had no family. She didn't even have time to argue with her mother as she attempted to shove the money back, but she took it, because she knew her mother was always right. Her mother hadn't survived the atrocities of colonization and war twice without knowing anything. She had a kind of predictive quality about her, almost psychic.

Ronald and Ana sat in the row behind her. She glimpsed herself in Ana, quietly staring out the window, streaking the glass. Even though Ana resembled her father with her squarish jaw and low nose, the flicker of sadness in her sleepy eyes reminded Sunny of herself at that age.

John was waiting for them at the airport gate. He appeared as if he hadn't showered in days, his hair greasy, and his eyes wild and hungry, like a man stranded on an island finally reconvening with humanity again. He hugged Ana and Ronald and kissed Sunny on the cheek with dry lips. She yearned to grab hold of him, but she couldn't in public. Even if she didn't often agree with her husband, she trusted him and would trust him with their lives forever. She hoped he felt the same about her. Sure, he worked hard and was often missing from their lives, but he hadn't been cruel or selfish. He provided for them all. He did his best, and she trusted that he would never abandon them.

As they walked through the airport with him holding Ronald's hand and wheeling their suitcase, and Ana following behind them, Sunny clutched her purse, basking in a new lightness, an unburdening.

After she returned from Korea in the spring, Sunny embraced the poten-tial of their dull and barren backyard, which she now imagined as a canvas, fresh and full of possibility, roamed by feral cats that she befriended much to her husband's chagrin. She could replace all the weeds with low-water plants, an edible garden, and more trees to offer shade in addition to the loquat behind the garage. There was never such a thing as too many trees where birds would live and thrive and fill the mornings with song. A sanctuary that would be their own. She'd have to be resourceful and find ways to water the new plants, given all the restrictions of late. Because who would rather see an empty sky, gray and burning with gas and smog? But she could collect the soapy water after the children bathed or when she rinsed the vegetables from the market.

The television and the city simmered in anticipation of the verdict of the Rodney King trial, which had been moved to Simi Valley, a controversial relocation to a suburb with a majority-white population and jury. She prayed that Mr. King might receive some justice for the horrific crime he had endured. It had been obvious to her from the footage repeated on television who the victim was. The men who assaulted him wore uniforms, possessed guns. There were so many of them. The power had been completely disproportionate.

A couple of the women at church had argued that Mr. King was a criminal, that if he didn't want to be attacked, he should've not broken any laws, that if he stayed out of trouble the way *they* stayed out of trouble, he wouldn't have suffered so much.

"But it wasn't up to the police to punish him," Sunny said one Sunday during after-service lunch. "That isn't their job. How would they know what he had been guilty of without an investigation, without a trial, without anything." She couldn't help but think of the cruelty that activists like Professor Cho endured at the hands of the state, all the students who had been murdered, beaten, raped in Gwangju. No one wanted to talk about them. No one could talk about them. But they had been killed because they had wanted democracy, killed by men with guns and power. Many of them even went missing. History had made so many of us nameless.

Mrs. Chung, who owned a beauty supply store, laughed. "*She* doesn't have to go to work like the rest of us. So she doesn't understand."

Sunny could've slapped her in the face. Her teeth clenched. "When people say that we are weak, and all we do is work and work, like animals too, when they make fun of our faces and accents, do you believe them? When they call us Chinese, do we believe them? Are we suddenly Chinese?"

"At least we work hard. That is true," Mrs. Yoon, whose family managed swap meets, said. "For some of us, at least."

She knew she was not alone, and yet the women who might agree with her remained silent lest they fall victim to Mrs. Yoon's and Mrs. Chung's sharpness of tongue. They were the kind of women who were so "generous" with their time and money, traveling the world on missionary trips and organizing the church's social functions, that they could get away with anything. Everyone admired them and their fancy cars and their children with high SAT scores.

But Sunny did not. These symbols of status they acquired simply justified and obscured their bullying. And the bullying reinforced their power, but also their loneliness.

"Just because you interact with people that you don't like on a daily basis, doesn't mean you've learned or know anything about them," Sunny said. "You can have an education, a degree, and still refuse to think outside of what you want to think. It can go both ways."

"If it goes both ways, then what happened to Rodney King goes both ways too. Maybe if he acted different—"

"But the power between the police and Mr. King is not equal." She fought back the tears in her eyes. She couldn't believe she allowed these two women to rile her up so much. "The police had more resources than him in that moment, and in life. They have more power, so the violence was unnecessary. Why can't you see that?"

"Don't you think the police worry about their lives too? What about their families?"

"They were supposed to protect the man they harmed." Sunny's volume alarmed everyone. "That's what they are paid to do."

Mrs. Yoon and Mrs. Chung glanced at each other, communicating what they knew about Sunny. Even though she had gone to a prestigious university, she was an outsider, ignorant. Of course her children would fail with a mother like that. How dare she?

Sunny pulled her purse higher up on her shoulder, and glared at the other women, who did not speak up despite knowing that she was right. Without having touched her plate of food, she departed to find her daughter and son.

Now Sunny stood in the garage and touched the cardboard boxes that RJ had carried inside. This was before the drought. She remembered the air had smelled wet and clean early in the morning after her husband had left for work. RJ had marveled at her home; she and her husband had so much to be proud of. She held Ronald, who clung to her, his weight against her hip. The downy hair of his head brushed her cheek. How strong he was clasping to her side. He was no longer a baby, *her* baby, but a boy.

RJ touched the loquat tree behind the garage. "These trees will always remind me of my house. We had two in my backyard." He shook his head. "The things I've lost."

After he had finished setting down the three boxes from his friend's truck, he wiped the sweat from his brow with a handkerchief. "I'll be back . . . in a few months? Is that okay? I don't want to be too much of an inconvenience."

"No, no. Okay." But she didn't want him to leave.

They walked down the gravel path toward the front where his friend had parked his car on the street. He stopped as if about to tell her one last thing, but before he could, she blurted, "I want to go with you." She had rehearsed these words, this sentence, for days. She placed Ronald down on his feet and he reached up to cling to the bottom of her shirt, stretching it down like a tent over his head.

"I want to go with you," she said again as if RJ hadn't heard her the first time. She thought to her son, *Let go of me now.*

"Sunny." His eyes softened, afraid to blink.

"I drive. I can drive." She loved how the word "can" sounded out of her mouth. It was a word she hardly used.

"You want to come with me?" He laughed. A perfect tear slipped down the side of his cheek. "What about this little one?" He rubbed the back of Ronald's head, ruffling his soft black hair to distract him.

"He come. We go together." She bit down on her tongue.

His face dropped, as if for whatever reason, horrified. She had said the wrong thing, hadn't she? She had been foolish, but there was no stopping her now. "I go temporary. One week." Her voice cracked.

"I can't let you do that. I can't let you leave . . . your husband like that."

"I can."

"I'll take the bus. I like the bus. You don't even know if . . . I bet Ronald wants to stay with his father." RJ's eyes filled as if a dam had cracked inside him. "I don't think you can split them apart like that, Sunny. I don't . . . that's not right."

She had misread him.

"To be honest, I would rather be alone," he said.

She picked Ronald up and held him close, smelled his powdery scent.

"I'm sorry," RJ said as he cried, unashamed. His friend waited silently in his truck.

Her face burned. She wanted to disappear behind Ronald now. She could use him as an excuse, run inside the house. A diaper change. A feeding. The shame. The humiliation. What an idiot she had been.

"You . . . you are like a sister to me," he said, blowing his nose on a handkerchief from his pocket. "I'm grateful for you. I am."

She held her breath. The word "sister" was so beautiful to hear.

"You're my sister."

She didn't know how to respond.

"I love you very much, Sunny." He wiped his face. "Shit." He laughed a little to himself. "I just want to find my daughter. Eventually she'll understand me too." He tried to smile. "I never . . . I still love my wife. I'm still in love with her." His voice broke as the words crashed over her.

Of course Sunny understood him. Some feelings couldn't be erased. Life would be too easy if they could just end. They'd no longer be human.

"I'll be back as soon as I can." His hand squeezed her bare shoulder.

Eight years had passed since then.

Sunny had no idea what was in those boxes and for how long she should keep his belongings. Did he ever make it back south? Did he find his daughter? She hoped so.

In the living room, she had hung up her father's two small paintings, oil on canvas, that she had brought with her from Seoul, which included the two nude women who bathed themselves in a river. She herself had mostly focused on watercolors in school, but now wanted to create something bold, foreign, and substantial. Thus she would need to set up a studio here in the garage, where she would still have plenty of room despite all they kept, all they carried in this dark, cobweb-filled space. She would buy herself a new set of brushes, acrylics, which would be easier to use than oils, to start, an easel, and make herself a home.

She sliced open the tape on one of his boxes, which had been stacked in the corner farthest from the door. She found journals scribbled full with words she couldn't read or understand. Books in English. Novels and poems. A recorder. Rolls of undeveloped film and cassettes in a blue zippered pouch like the one her husband used to deposit cash at the bank. VHS. Photographs of him, his daughter, and a wife. She had been stunning, and it was easy to understand how he could never get over her. The heart could be so plain and stubborn.

But what would she do now with all that he had left behind?

A sense of calmness overcame her as she imagined the ways she could—despite the questions unanswered, the half translations, the great absence and silences—preserve what they had, and what it had meant to her. She held one of the notebooks close to her face and smelled him, the apple in his hand, his touch on her shoulder.

1999

Who knew an American could own so much?

With his son off from school, working for him at the nursery this Monday afternoon, John lay on the couch, his head heavy with the worries that had sprouted, sinuous as a vine, after his visit to the office of a local attorney that morning. He had told his daughter he needed to run an errand despite her opposition that he should remain in bed. The attorney's assistant had provided John a long-winded questionnaire to pen with his assets, preparation for his last will. He had only the house, his beloved Cadillac Eldorado, his Ford work van, a checking and savings account, which included their emergency funds, and his business's inventory and supplies since he leased the property itself.

But what made things complicated was if, after he died, his wife were to return.

She would be entitled to at least half of everything. He could disinherit her in his will, but that would be suspicious to his children, and she might still have some workarounds since California was a "community property state."

Technically the house was *theirs*, not simply his. Even though she had been absent for a year, she still had a say in everything he had purchased while they had been married the past twenty-three years. He couldn't free himself from her even if he tried, unless she remained gone for longer than five years; then he could file a petition to the court. She could be presumed dead.

Who knew if and when she might return? Maybe never. Maybe tomorrow. And should he tell the lawyer this? No.

The phone rang, jolted him off the couch. What *now*?

He could hear breathing. Then the soft static of a palm on the receiver released.

Priscilla.

He imagined her fingers. The downiness of her being. How many days had it been from when he had seen her last? Two, three? Yet so much had happened since. The anniversary of his wife's disappearance. The fight with his children. The stroke. The hospital and the attorney's office. It was all like a curse that ran its dreadful course.

"I've been thinking about you," Priscilla said. "I had such a good time on Friday night. It's been a long time . . . since I've gone out like that."

"Me too," he said as he remembered the way she laughed without obscuring her mouth, the tremble of her pale blue eyes, the hand he wanted to hold.

"Can I bring you and your kids some tamales for Christmas? Maybe some for Rhonda too? I've been thinking about—"

"Oh, no, that is okay. Very busy. Lots of work." His heart broke as he betrayed himself again.

Everyone around me only gets hurt. I only know how to hurt people. Stay away from me, Priscilla.

"I could drop them off there. Or at your nursery? You can show me some plants, for my yard. I wanted to speak with you about—"

"I don't think . . . I don't think we talk anymore. I had a nice time at the restaurant—"

"I've been thinking about RJ and what . . . he would've wanted and what had happened to him. I'm taking the next week off at work for the holidays. I'd like—"

"Thank you for, uh . . . we are okay." He didn't deserve Priscilla's kindness or friendship or whatever it was at all. He was tired. His life had become complicated enough. He had to end all of this. Forget RJ. Forget his wife. Forget them all. It was the only way he could get through the final task—to take care of his children, make sure they would be okay. He had already failed at everything else. He couldn't lose them too. He had to get in the final word.

"John, something happened that I've never talked about. About one of the officers. Only me and RJ know," Priscilla said. "Back in the eighties . . . RJ lost his job because they figured out that he had been . . . investigating things himself." Her voice broke. "When I ran into him last . . . remember when I told you, I ran into him about a year ago? He was by the police station, the dumpsters. I didn't . . . it's been bothering me because he asked . . . he told me he needed help. That he had become friends again with someone who had betrayed him, a former officer. Jacob Hendricks."

He had never heard of this Jacob Hendricks, and couldn't understand what he had to do with John, his house, his family.

"RJ was writing a book about all of this, and he had the evidence to prove it," Priscilla said. "A year ago . . . Jacob . . . ratted him out. And so RJ had to go into hiding. He had to leave the country or . . ." She wept.

"He was begging me for help so he could leave, but . . . I pretended I didn't know him. I was so terrified to see him like that. And I couldn't get involved. I am sure that broke his heart. To be treated like that when he needed me most."

John wished he could reach through the wires and hold her now.

But apocalypse or not, he had to protect Ronald and Ana, keep them out of danger. He wanted nothing to do with this anymore, nothing to do with Priscilla—or what sounded like another crime that involved a police officer and had nothing to do with them. He had already gone too far. None of this was *his* business. She even said RJ's death was a warning.

"John, are you still there?"

"Yes," he said.

"I've been hiding at my sister's house ever since . . . my son said someone had been following me home. On Saturday, that's when he saw him outside our house. There was a car, and then the next day too. Last night, I packed my stuff and I'm here now. But I have to talk to Rhonda. Before it's too late. Could you arrange for us . . . I could get a ride on—"

With a single finger, he hung up the phone. He had to rest and heal himself now. Who knew what kind of chaos and carnage the end of the world could create? What would be the point of getting close, of developing feelings for anyone?

The thing about war was that it never ended. Treaties signed, borders carved. But the people left behind like him, that thirteen-year-old boy, didn't know how to stop hurting. Without pain, he would be nothing, another casualty, a piece of evidence to burn and destroy.

In her father's bedroom, Ana lowered the receiver as gently as possible. She had been pretending to tidy up as she frantically searched for whatever it was that Jacob needed. Last night, her brother had told her everything about his encounter with Jacob in the backyard, and she knew their lives were at risk. They could no longer delay the inevitable; the truth needed to come out.

But after his stroke, she couldn't confront her father again.

And then the phone rang. She picked up the receiver at the same time as him, and almost said something before she heard an unknown woman's voice. Priscilla.

The woman he had mentioned during the fight before his stroke.

Priscilla tell me his wife took his daughter. She left him.

She covered the mouthpiece with her palm and listened.

"He was by the police station, the dumpsters. I didn't . . . it's been bothering me because he asked . . . he told me he needed help. That he had become friends again with someone who had betrayed him, a former officer. Jacob Hendricks."

Ana trembled as she perched on the edge of his mattress.

"He had to leave the country or . . ."

He had gone to Vietnam, hadn't he? Ana almost interrupted the conversation on her end of the line, but she kept her mouth shut. She wanted to add that Jacob had gotten so desperate that he had showed up in their backyard last night. Her brother had shared that, at the library, Jacob had found pages of RJ's book, which somehow incriminated either him or someone he knew, and that Ronald was convinced that their mother had hid some kind of evidence that Jacob was looking for now. But she was gone.

"I've been hiding at my sister's house ever since . . . my son said someone had been following me home . . . But I have to talk to Rhonda. Before it's too late. Could you arrange for us . . . I could get a ride on—"

A beat of silence. Her father must've hung up.

"John, John?" Priscilla asked. She sighed with an intense sadness and slammed the receiver down.

What was wrong with him? Couldn't he tell this woman needed help and that she had been put in the same position as them? Maybe someone had been following them too. Ana couldn't get the blue Ford Explorer from the Observatory out of her head. She needed to get ahold of Priscilla, whoever she was, because she understood the connection between what RJ knew and a crime that had been committed by the police. Perhaps she knew exactly what Jacob Hendricks had been after, which could help Ana locate the evidence if it was indeed at their house. She could actually make a difference in this world.

She tiptoed out of her father's bedroom to check on his whereabouts, and after she confirmed that he was resting on the couch, remote control in hand, she returned to the phone and dialed *69, her heart beating in her throat. Her mouth dry. They needed as much information as they could get.

Priscilla, please pick up the phone.

"Hello?"

"Priscilla? Hi, this is Ana. I'm . . . I'm John's daughter, Ana. I've been working with . . . RJ's daughter to find out more about him."

"How did you—"

"I overheard you. I called star sixty-nine. I'm sorry—"

"I . . . we should talk in person. Is your dad okay?"

"Yes, I think so. I'm sorry about my dad. He's . . . he's been going through a lot."

"We should talk about this in person. I can come to your house." Priscilla asked Ana for their address. "How about Christmas Eve?"

Four days later. "What about sooner than that?"

"I can't. I'm at my sister's. And I won't have a ride until she is off from work on Friday."

"Maybe we can go there? I can bring Rhonda."

"No, I would rather not. It's hard to tell who is being followed where. I don't think it's safe."

There was a pause, then Priscilla said in a lowered voice, "RJ knew too much. Me too, I guess."

"Did you work at the police station?" Ana asked.

"I still do. At the front desk."

She was the connection they needed. But Priscilla had also gone out on a date with their father? What had he gotten himself into? Rhonda had asked them to stay away from the police, and of course he didn't listen. He must've figured out where RJ worked somehow.

"We can talk more about it on Friday, okay? I'll still bring you the tamales. Can you . . . see if RJ's daughter can meet us? At your house. Unless you don't think it's safe?"

"It's probably not," Ana said. "But I'm not sure where would be at this point." She remembered the vehicle that followed them home from the Observatory. Was it the same person watching Priscilla? "The person . . . you said someone has been outside your house. What kind of car was it? Was it an Explorer?"

"My son said it was white. Like an SUV. It was at my house both on Saturday . . . and Sunday morning. So I left last night. My house is empty now."

"Do you happen to *know* Jacob Hendricks?" Ana asked.

"Yes," Priscilla said.

"He came by here last night, our house. Looking for something. And he left the impression that if he didn't find it, and if we didn't help him—"

"You can't trust him, Ana. Wait until Friday, okay? We can talk about it. Please make sure RJ's daughter is there."

"But can you tell me what I'm looking for? Why does everyone care so much about this now? All of a sudden."

"After they got him fired, I bet they thought RJ wouldn't, or couldn't be a problem anymore. This was back in the early eighties. But when . . . when they found him dead in your backyard, it brought up everything again."

"Jacob said he had found pages of a book, a book that RJ was writing. This must've been last year," Ana said. "I think RJ told him about the evidence too. They had become friends, hung out at the library, and I guess RJ confessed what he had been working on. Maybe Jacob then went to whoever was involved—"

"Yes, that makes sense," Priscilla said.

"And then RJ fled to Vietnam."

"How do you know that?"

"There's a librarian who was friends with him. She knew he was in Vietnam this year and returned just this fall, in October or November."

Ana remembered he had spent the past couple months working intensely on his book. He must've finished it and then felt ready to retrieve the evidence from her mom, which led to his death in their backyard.

"Maybe they knew he was in Vietnam so didn't think he was a threat anymore," Priscilla said. "And then when he showed up again, dead . . . they realized that he might've still been working on the book, and that the evidence was still out there. Somewhere near."

But who was Jacob working with, or for, then?

"We need to be very careful, Ana."

"Is he working with someone? He made it seem like . . . we're dead if we don't find whatever it was that RJ gave my mom." Ana felt sick to her stomach. Never before had she been this terrified for her life, for their lives. She couldn't imagine the trouble they had managed to get in, despite being "good immigrants." She had done everything "right"—worked hard, studied for every test—and yet there she was, there her family was, tied into some intricate plot, a series of crimes. Unbelievable.

"I don't think you want to find anything, Ana. It's too dangerous," Priscilla said. "Honestly, with him, you could be dead either way."

"Who can we call, then?" Ana asked. "Are you saying . . . we can't even call the police, right? What if I find the evidence? Then I can take it to them. How could they turn me away?"

"If the evidence even still exists, and it might not, it's better off hidden . . . for now," Priscilla said. "I'll be there on Friday. I promise, okay?"

Priscilla hung up the phone. Ana closed her eyes, catching her breath. While she had been speaking with Priscilla, the realization—that Ana, too, was a beneficiary of this specific system under which so many like RJ had been harmed—crept throughout her body. She had worked hard, yes, and up until high school, displayed excellence in all the subjects that centered the perspectives and accomplishments of gatekeepers (mostly, straight white men). In turn, she received affirmation in the form of good grades, high test scores, scholarships, and grants. She—no, *they*, including her parents—played by the rules, and although her family struggled in so many ways, they still had this house, this roof over their heads, this sense of place where they could build a future.

Ana had options. (She almost had too many and often felt crushed by the weight of them.) She had always thought of herself as an activist, but how had she also been an accomplice, complicit in a society that actively harmed, erased, killed those who challenged its mythologies of fairness, meritocracy, exceptionalism? This included RJ and Black people, who had generations stolen from them through forced migration, slavery, Jim Crow, and Native Americans, through theft of their land, genocide.

The crime scene wasn't simply their backyard but an entire country.

Her brother was still at the nursery. Once her father fell asleep on the couch, Ana grabbed his keys for the garage while there was at least an hour of light outside. Even though Priscilla had warned her away from the truth, she'd tear this home apart until she got to the very bottom of it.

1995

Three years after the riots that had destroyed the gas station, after they had finally received their loans from the private bank via the federal Small Business Administration, and less than a week before Ana would begin her first semester at Berkeley, Sunny's husband answered a classified ad for the sale of a plant nursery in Koreatown that had survived—because who wanted to steal or destroy plants? Seven days per week, he had been working at a local video store combined with a stockroom job at a glitzy new supermarket with a bakery that sold the Korean-French cream puffs, fluffy and indulgent, which Ana loved so much.

Of course, her husband had zero experience with plants, yet had been compelled to attempt something new, a business much closer to their home, where Sunny could help as he continued his part-time jobs until he built up enough inventory and clientele. The previous owner had passed away months ago, and the site had been neglected with its sorry, untended plants in their black plastic pots and the muddy cracks in the uneven concrete pathways.

"We should name it Sunny Nursery," John said as they surveyed the site. "*Sunny* Nursery. Get it?"

Sunny pretended not to hear him. A wasp's nest buzzed under the eaves of the tiny gray office with its shiny brass dead bolt and knob. The door had been dirtied by hands over many years. Before she entered the building, she stepped in a puddle, deeper than she had expected, from a hose that leaked. "More like Soggy Nursery," she said to herself.

Her husband switched on the light of the bathroom, too bright and level with the eyes. Next to the counter, two carousels of seed packets creaked with the sadness of being untouched, but the section of Korean vegetables, which included kkaennip, gochu, buchu, and mu, delighted her. She had so much to grow in this space and at home with only a little water and care.

Afterward, she beamed; they had finally found a business that they could work on and develop together. It was close enough, only fifteen minutes away from their home, and would provide access to the materials necessary to work on their yards, which for the last several years had served as battlegrounds for squirrels and litter boxes for the neighborhood cats. Here people would buy plants to feed themselves and their eyes, rather than gasoline for guzzling cars. She'd been feeling for the first time in so long hopeful, full of excitement for the future, their home. She never even had to tap into her emergency savings, the ten thousand dollars her mother had given her on her trip to Korea. Sunny could create a refuge out of the backyard with a persimmon tree, a vegetable patch, a bench where she could sit with one of the feral kittens on her lap. She could pretend that she didn't hear the traffic roaring on nearby Pico and

Olympic Boulevards as she listened to the chirps of birds impersonating car alarms. She'd have an art studio in the garage, a place to relax and invite the neighbors, including Rodriguez, who had two surprisingly gorgeous gardens, one dry out front and the other tropical in the back. If only they were not so busy, trying to remain afloat, they could get to know and understand, learn from one another. He must've been extremely skilled to have kept such a beautiful place by himself. And his tattoos did not intimidate her.

Although they had spent most of the past two years skimping and scrounging, her husband had managed the crisis well, because of his knowledge of English, their credit, and the resources available to them as owners of a home and small business—their safety nets. Recovery had been slow, but ultimately everyone had seemed eager to help those who had been victims of riots that they had nothing to do with, who were innocent bystanders, hardworking immigrants. Of course, she despised the violence, what had happened to Rodney King, but ultimately, she and her husband had been separate from the individuals who had committed the crime against him.

"See what happens when you follow the rules," her husband said as he signed the paperwork the next day finalizing the purchase of the plant nursery that they would call their own, a victory. "America has been wonderful, don't you think?"

She didn't want to admit it, but he had been right: opportunity was everywhere, if they'd focus on themselves. Forgiveness might even be possible. He stood from the breakfast nook and she pressed her face against his chest and she heard a new calmness in the beat of his heart, a relief, as if to have her in his arms he would carry less. She raised her face to his, afraid he might not kiss her back, but he did. He pulled her to their bedroom, and without even taking off their clothes, they made love. It had been years since they had last had sex—when she had just returned from Seoul—and despite her age at forty-five, she still felt young. She didn't care about how she looked, no matter how self-conscious she had become of her body. Desire burned away their worries, and they became, even if only temporarily, one.

There had never been family vacations because staying in hotels would be an extravagance for a family who worked six days a week, sometimes more than twelve hours per day.

But for the first time, all four members of the Kim family boarded a plane together. Since Ana would be moving to Berkeley, Sunny insisted that they all go at once. They should ensure that she had been set up in her dormitory room with everything she needed. They should have a nice meal out and walk around the campus so that she could imagine where her daughter would now spend her days. They should all be there for her to know how much they supported and loved her, how proud they were of their little girl who, starting off in their cramped one-bedroom apartment, was no longer *only* the daughter of immigrants—a father who owned a plant nursery but dropped out of grad school and a mother of small stature who couldn't speak English and never left Koreatown.

Ana was now an American woman, a university student, an important person.

On the airplane, Sunny asked the flight crew if she could view the cockpit. She had always been so curious about the different lights and switches and knobs that made them fly, even though she knew her bravado humiliated the rest of her family, who wanted her to stop calling so much attention to herself among these foreigners, the white people. As she approached the door that separated the pilots from the cabin, Sunny glanced behind her and caught Ana staring out the window as if she didn't know her. Ronald smiled in approval and gave a thumbs-up. Her husband fumed, already buckled up and quietly, diligently following procedure.

"Hello, young lady." The pilot's American voice startled her. "This is an altimeter, which indicates the plane's altitude above the sea. Very important. Do you know what altitude is?"

"AR-ti . . . ?"

"*Altitude.*"

"AR-ti-tude. Arti-tude," she repeated to herself as she strutted back down the aisle, victorious. Ronald laughed. Ana tightened her lips. Her husband's leg shook. She realized just then that since her trip to America had been alone, she had never actually flown with him before. She stuck her tongue out in jest before she squeezed past his legs into her seat and buckled up with a satisfying click of metal. Her childishness, they might realize one day, was a kind of saving grace. She had distracted them from their worries—John missing work for the first time in his life over a weekend, and Ana living on her own and outside Los Angeles. She created distractions, smoke and mirrors, to amuse and charm her family, when oftentimes deep down inside she simply wanted to stare out her own window or quietly draw. Because a woman's role was to step up wherever she was needed. Because why would a woman need her own silence? Why would she need time for her own mind, her own spirit? What dangerous things would she come up with?

But Ana was different, would be different. And when she had received an acceptance letter from every university she had applied to, Sunny thought to herself, *Run. I want to see you go as far as you can, away from here, from me. I want more for you. I love you and your brother more than I had ever imagined loving anyone, more than even my mother and father who had been the world to me for most of my life. I'm grateful. And I'm sorry. And now that you are leaving, I will be better. I will have to be better so that you will return sometimes.*

Ana had done it all by herself. Unlike kids with private tutors or SAT classes, she had only books they had gotten from the library. She worked at the mall on the weekends and during summer and winter breaks too. She was naturally bookish, introverted, observant, and polite, which would be and had been rewarded at school.

Perhaps Sunny's husband, who had been an English literature major, would've led a more scholarly life, but sometimes the demands of this country pushed you to other extremes, ones that were foreign to the self. So instead, John had owned small businesses, the only type of work in which he could prosper with his South Korean degree and accent, where his customers wouldn't suspend their ability to purchase simply because of his lack of credentials, his only credential being that he had enough cash and credit to own something from which he could sell things. His job forced him into the company of others, into false extroversion, odd jokes, which betrayed who he was. It should've been Sunny, who could at least muster some bit of theater, showmanship, who could be friendly behind the counter of their stores. But convention forced her to remain at home where she'd be safe with the children.

And in many ways, she punished them, the children, didn't she? She had loved them dearly, sacrificed every hour of herself for them, but at times, she had been prodding and cruel. She made snide remarks about

Ana's eating, in particular, her weight. She had said to Ana that she needed to take better care of her skin, that her neglect was showing, and that it was important to keep up her appearances, to at least look neat and tidy, in addition to being a good student. But this wasn't who Sunny even was. She didn't really care how her daughter looked as long as she was healthy, but the expectations of this adult life didn't allow her and her husband to be themselves. As perpetual foreigners, concerned with how they were or might be perceived, they had to posture at all times in order to survive. It was exhausting.

Of course, she humiliated her husband when she had gone up to the flight crew for permission to view the cockpit. Her voice revealed who they were—outsiders. She should quiet herself and disappear, lest they become targets of ridicule or even violence. When she was prodding her daughter, she was asking her to fit in because she didn't want her daughter to ever be alone, the way Sunny had been so lonely all these years.

Now on campus with its brick buildings laced with trees, serene walkways that wound through the greenest grass where young people rested and laughed on blankets, Sunny perceived the abundance of her daughter's freedom. As John and Ronald unloaded the rental car downstairs, she surveyed Ana's dorm room, utilitarian and bare, which she'd share with another student she had yet to meet. Sunny closed the door shut.

"Ana. I've been wanting to tell you this for a long time now," she said in Korean.

Ana looked frightened. She didn't want to hear any of this. She had been so busy, nervous to meet new people. It was her first time living outside Los Angeles. But Sunny needed to say it anyway. In case . . . in case they might not see each other again. Who knew?

"I'm sorry," Sunny said.

Ana sighed as she unpacked an overnight bag full of clothes and toiletries.

"I want you to know how much I love you," Sunny said.

"Mom, I know." Ana laughed nervously. Sunny held her daughter's hand to stop her from unpacking.

"I want you to know that I'm hard on you because I wanted to protect you," she said. "I know you think I'm only hard on you. I'm only hard on you and not your brother."

"Mom, I get it. It's okay." Ana looked at the door. Her father and brother were still unloading the car.

"It's different for us. For me and you. You know? We are women. It's . . . it's more difficult." Sunny wanted to say, as if it would be the last time she'd see her: *I'm hard on myself the most. I'm sorry. I want you to know how much I love you. I'm afraid you won't love me if I tell you the things I've seen. The things I've endured, and dreamed about for myself. I'm afraid you'll think I'm weak and that you won't love me anymore.* Tears sprang from her eyes. It was probably only the second time her daughter had seen her cry. The first had been when her father had died years ago.

"I do better," Sunny said in English.

"Mom. It's okay." Ana lined the inside of her drawers with the pages of an abandoned calendar, the way they did at home. "You did a good job. I know it was hard for you. I know you . . . wanted more. You deserved more." Her eyes grew red and wet. "I'm going to work hard and make it easier for you. I'm going to make it easier for you and Dad one day. I want you to be—"

Sunny brushed Ana's hair away from her face. She could see how self-conscious and withdrawn her daughter had become. She had been too hard on her because the idea of someone hurting Ana would destroy

Sunny, and she needed her to be tough. But in reality, there was nothing she could do to shield Ana from the world. She could only encourage her to believe that she was strong enough to not only endure but make her own way.

"I'm so proud, you," she said in English, fighting back more tears. Saying those words, *I'm sorry. I'm so proud of you,* felt like a release into the wild of herself. It was a way of letting go of all the habits that harmed, the habits she had formed in an attempt to protect them all. Those habits were like addictions, much like that of her husband's. He needed to work because he had convinced himself that if he stopped, they would all become vulnerable, and with vulnerability came harm, came violence, just as it had during the war. How powerful those words were. *I'm sorry. I'm sorry. I will do better,* she had said in English. Doing better also meant taking care of herself, didn't it? How else would she teach her children to nourish themselves when she would inevitably be gone forever? How would they stand up on their own? Could they do it? Of course. But she had to show them how.

1999

After she had hung up the phone with Priscilla yesterday afternoon, Ana had waited for her father to fall asleep on the couch that night before she went into the garage, flashlight in hand to compensate for the single meager fluorescent fixture above. Priscilla had warned her; she couldn't trust Jacob. But now that their lives and Priscilla's might be at risk, Ana couldn't stall anymore, despite how painful it was to revisit so intimately their mother's life—or the parts of their mother's life they never bothered to think about or know.

About a week ago, the same night they met Rhonda at their house, Ana had entered the garage but was overwhelmed by the dankness and the odors, the painting supplies, the mold, the cobwebs that dangled and clung to her skin and clothes. She had quickly given up. She hadn't been able to handle the claustrophobia, the seeming endlessness of the task at hand, which would require her to consider all the mundane details of what mattered to her parents enough to hold on to in the dark—her father's books from graduate school, the certificates the children had earned, report cards, poster boards from precious history and science projects.

While her father slept, Ana dug alone in the garage, covering her mouth and nose with the collar of her shirt, until she discovered, hidden beneath a pile of dining chairs haphazardly turned over into what resembled a shelter or pyre—three identical bankers boxes, pristine as if untouched by air or light. Ana sneezed as she carefully lifted the lids to uncover the artifacts of RJ's life—journals, recollections of his family, his old home, his neighborhood and daughter, photographs in albums with pages that stuck together. How many of the people who fled, whether from wars or violence and poverty in the South, lost everything? Her parents had abandoned their possessions, their lives as children, with only the clothes on their backs and their bodies full of hunger. And there was no way to trace their histories now, because an impenetrable and unnatural border separated them from their families.

In one of RJ's spiral notebooks, alongside a black-and-white photograph labeled with the handwritten words, "Marcus, age 7" on the back, she read:

MARCUS WAS MY FATHER'S YOUNGEST BROTHER. HE WAS IN MANY WAYS THE REASON WHY WE LEFT, WHY MY FATHER COULDN'T EVER RETURN TO THE SOUTH. HIS VIOLENT DEATH (AT AGE 12) HAUNTED MY FATHER FOR THE REST OF HIS LIFE. HE DIDN'T WANT ANY OF HIS CHILDREN TO BECOME MARCUS, AND WHEN I HAD BEGUN TO RESEMBLE MARCUS, BOTH PHYSICALLY AND IN MY LOVE FOR BOOKS AND WORDS, MY FATHER TREATED ME WITH SPITE. HOW MANY NIGHTS HAD I SPENT TERRIFIED OF HIM? MY MOTHER WORKED HARD TO PROTECT ME. AND IT TOOK ME MANY

YEARS TO MAKE THAT CONNECTION: THAT MY FATHER DESPISED ME BECAUSE I HAD BEEN A REMINDER OF THE LITTLE BROTHER HE COULD NOT SAVE FROM THIS WORLD. I HAD BECOME HIS GHOST.

Tears spilled out of Ana's eyes, and she wiped them on the sleeve of her shirt, fearful that she might tarnish the words. To encounter this now, and the rarity of what RJ had entrusted their mother with, spoke to not only the singularity of who he and his family were, but the extraordinary nature of the relationship that he had with her, despite the different languages they spoke.

She had to call Rhonda now. She carried the three boxes inside the house where her brother met her at the back door as if he had been waiting there the entire time she was in the garage.

"I came home and he was just passed out on the couch," Ronald said as he helped her. "Maybe he'll sleep through the night. Who knows?"

Right away, Ana snuck into her father's bedroom and dialed Rhonda's number. But no one answered the phone, so she left a message on the answering machine. She'd try again in an hour. Maybe Rhonda was still at work or out to dinner.

Together, Ana and Ronald hid in his bedroom, sitting on the floor with RJ's most cherished belongings, which smelled dusty but were organized and clean like the inside of a library. The paper, although delicate, carried the weight of words unsaid, histories that had been hidden in order to escape destruction. A hush fell over them as they considered the materials with as much care as possible.

"Are you hungry?" Ana asked.

"No, I'm fine. You?"

Ana shook her head. "Besides I couldn't eat anything now."

"I don't understand why Jacob or anyone would care about this," Ronald said. "Nothing here has anything to do with him or the police directly."

"What we're looking for would be much more specific, relevant to his time in either the war or the police department." Ana wiped her nose on the back of her hand. "I'm just glad we found this. I'm honored."

Ana spent most of the night with her brother, reading RJ's words, learning of his parents' jobs in munitions and various wartime industries. His mother was a riveter.

At the age of sixteen, he fell head over heels for an older girl named Lavonne who lived in his neighborhood. Not only was she beautiful, but she had a rambunctious sense of humor. When their daughter Rhonda was born in 1958, he dropped out of school and found a full-time job at an aviation plant.

I DIDN'T UNDERSTAND THE GRAVITY OF HER MENTAL HEALTH, WHICH DECLINED AFTER THE BIRTH OF OUR DAUGHTER. SHE WAS UNABLE TO LEAVE THE BED SOME DAYS. I OFTEN FOUND HER CRYING BY HERSELF. I HAD BEEN HELPLESS IN THE DEPTH OF HER SUFFERING. SOME DAYS, I AM ASHAMED TO ADMIT, I COULD NOT STAND HOW PESSIMISTIC AND DEPRESSED SHE COULD BE. BUT I LOVED HER STILL. EVEN THOUGH I HAD BEEN CONCERNED FOR THE SAFETY OF OUR DAUGHTER, I COULDN'T THINK OF A LIFE WITHOUT LAVONNE. AND I WANTED TO TAKE CARE OF HER.

WHEN THEY DISAPPEARED, I WAS LOST. I DID EVERYTHING I COULD TO FIND THEM, BUT NO ONE IN HER FAMILY WOULD HELP OR ANSWER ANY OF MY CALLS. I HAVE NO IDEA WHAT SHE TOLD THEM ABOUT ME, OR EVEN WHY SHE HAD GONE EXACTLY. SHE AND MY DAUGHTER COULD'VE BEEN DEAD, FOR ALL I KNEW. I NEARLY KILLED MYSELF. INSTEAD, I ENLISTED IN VIETNAM.

Then it was the next morning, Tuesday. The living room couch creaked beneath Ana as she, without any sleep, reached for the receiver on the side table. Both her brother and father had gone to the nursery because her father refused to stay home any longer, despite his need for rest. He had been convinced that the nursery would go under without him. Only he knew how to take care of the plants, which wholesale businesses to call, which customers would be serious about actually buying anything. He hated people who simply browsed.

To Ana's relief, Rhonda picked up the phone. "I fell asleep early last night," she said.

Ana described to her the three boxes they had found in the garage, their contents, as well as her brother's encounter with Jacob in their backyard.

"Shit," Rhonda said. "I honestly don't feel ready for any of this." She broke down into tears.

"We can keep the boxes longer . . . if you'd like." Ana had been at a loss for how to console anyone at this point. Certainly Rhonda and her father had endured too much for any family. "Whenever you're ready. I just wanted you to know they're here." Ana promised herself to be as transparent with Rhonda as possible from then on, regardless of how she or her family might look. And at this point, she didn't know how to backtrack and tell her about the letter without completely losing her trust.

"I can come by tonight," Rhonda said. "Take the boxes home. Open a bottle of wine, I guess. What a year this is."

"Have you ever heard of someone named Priscilla?" Ana coiled the phone cord around her fingers.

"No, never."

"She was . . . a coworker of your father's," Ana said. "I don't know how or why exactly, but she has been in touch with . . . my dad."

"What?"

"She has more information about what everyone is looking for that she only wants to share in person. She'll come by this Friday," Ana said. "She's in hiding."

"Hiding?" Rhonda asked.

"Yes. It's bad. Someone's been . . . watching her. She mentioned a crime that your father knew about, had evidence regarding. It involves the police, at least one of the officers."

"Ha. It just keeps getting better, doesn't it?" Rhonda said. "I'll be there Friday. And I'll also come by tonight . . . for the boxes. After I get off work. I have some things to do at the office."

Ana realized she had no idea what Rhonda even did for a living. "Where do you work again?"

"I'm an attorney. Criminal defense. Mostly DUIs and shit, but sometimes something more interesting," Rhonda said. "Busy time of year, unfortunately."

For whatever reason, Ana had assumed that since Rhonda had been in the military, she might've worked in the government. But that she was an attorney seemed fitting.

"I guess Dad couldn't stay out of trouble," Rhonda said. "He was practically a kid when he had me. I always imagined he just didn't want to settle down. But seems like trouble followed him instead."

Ana wasn't sure if she should say this now, but she did. "Priscilla mentioned . . . that your . . . it was your mother who left him. It wasn't your father who left. It was your mom who ran away with you. No one knows why exactly, but . . . Rhonda, are you still there?"

"My mother is dead," she said.

The words pierced like a knife in Ana's chest. "I wasn't sure if I should tell you, but I just thought . . . you should know. How much he loved you."

Tears filled her eyes. Maybe Rhonda's mother didn't feel like she had a choice; she had to leave him. But based on what Ana knew, RJ loved his daughter. He loved her more than Rhonda ever knew, whether or not he had the means or the chance to demonstrate this. He wanted to provide for her. He wanted to give her a home.

But this world had stripped one thing after another away from him.

And then he was dead in their yard.

"My grandparents practically raised me." Rhonda wept as Ana wondered what she should or could say, if anything at all. "It's really strange, but now . . . certain things make sense. My mother, she was so . . . sad at times. I figured she was heartbroken because of my dad leaving her, how difficult it was to be single, poor, to not have enough." She cleared her throat. "But the only person who saw her sadness was me. She was so charming and hilarious with everyone else. And so I blamed myself for what I think was her depression. It took me years to realize that maybe I was the only one she was able to be herself around. It's hard to be a woman. Maybe it's just hard to be human at all."

Ana remembered her mother's words in her dorm room when she had dropped her off for her first year of college: *I want you to know that I'm hard on you because I wanted to protect you . . . It's different for us. For me and you. You know? We are women. It's . . . it's more difficult.*

"No matter how much I've always wanted children . . . I never wanted myself to end up like her. I even broke up with my last boyfriend because he wanted to have kids and I didn't, or I was too afraid that . . . I don't know, I'd end up alone, depressed."

"I'm so sorry," Ana said. Strangely enough, Rhonda's words sounded achingly familiar. She herself had never desired children, partially because it seemed that in order for her mother to be the mother she was, she had to become separated from herself, her own dreams and desires, while her father had been relentless in the pursuit of his. It was only after Ana had gone to college, and Ronald had become a teenager, that her mother had begun committing time to her art, expressing herself as more than just an extension of her husband's wants and children's needs.

"Shit. I should go. I'll see you around five?" Rhonda asked.

Ana could hear her gathering her belongings.

"Is it okay that I read his writing?"

"Of course," Rhonda said. "Honestly, it's not really mine anyways, you know?"

"I think in a way I'm fascinated because nothing like this exists in my family."

"Your parents . . . your mother didn't leave anything for you? To help you understand her? Or why she disappeared?" Rhonda asked.

"No, not really. I mean, yes, only her art, I guess. But we've been avoiding the garage, where she kept all her stuff. My brother especially." Across from the couch where she sat, her grandfather's paintings hung on the wall. One of them with two nude women in a river bathing themselves. Ana realized that she had always assumed that her mother's style had never evolved, that like her paintings from college, her art in recent years would've been traditionally feminine and naturalistic—cranes and peonies and plum trees. But what if Ana was wrong? She would know only if she could find some of her mother's work, even simply sketches. She had to keep looking in the garage. This time for her mother.

1998

One warm evening in early October, Sunny journeyed to her usual art supplies store in Koreatown, the only one she had been able to find, dusty and crowded and delightful as an antiques shop. She loved its smell of mineral and chalk, the plastic of erasers, and the wood dust from pencils being sharpened, which reminded her of her father, his silence in front of the easel as he mixed and smeared colors on the palette. This level of intimacy had been surpassed only by when she had fed her babies in the middle of the night as they slept in her arms and received a warm bottle like a dream, or when she stood in the kitchen preparing meals for her children, and Ronald would hang on her legs and beg for a bite of the chewy noodles that she had just rinsed in the sink. She coiled them around the tips of her fingers before placing them between his tiny teeth, his dark brown eyes lifted in approval. She missed their giant littleness, their grand eagerness.

And with Ana out of the house, the yearning to create had filled Sunny's life, as her existence for the past twenty years—the harried trips to schools for drop-offs and pickups, to the doctor's office, to the supermarket—slipped like sand between her fingers, despite how hard she squeezed them. In the sweep of time, which included her daughter's acceptance letter, her prom and graduation, Sunny realized that soon enough Ronald would be next. Who knew where he would go? And could she blame him for wanting to leave this place, this home, which had few comforts except for the food that she provided, and simply from the outside world's perspective, Koreatown, a springboard for bigger and better? If Ronald moved away, she and her husband would be left with themselves and the business, which they needed to help the children until they were on their own financially, and to pay off all the loans and maintain the mortgage.

In a shadowy aisle of the art supplies store, she lingered near the expensive tubes of oil paints, the names of the hues that always sounded otherworldly, from Cadmium Red to Burnt Umber to Yellow Ochre. She decided to splurge on a small set for herself, carrying the colors like fine gems, along with a few hog bristle brushes and a bottle of turpentine. Although it had been years since she dabbled in the medium—she had been much more confident with watercolors and less-expensive acrylics—she craved the opacity, the range and brilliance of the pigments that could be smeared and mixed on a palette, much like her father had. She would be in a way speaking to him through the brush.

After her spree at the art supplies store, Sunny drove several blocks, the sky above her Indanthrone Blue, to the supermarket for haemul pajeon ingredients to supplement tonight's leftover kimchi jjigae. She needed the frozen seafood mix with squid, mussels, and clam, more green onions, and a jar of minced garlic so that she could prepare mak and mu kimchi, which her family ate almost every night.

She parked her car in the already busy lot full of vehicles from all over the Los Angeles area, from fancy German sedans and giant military-style SUVs to her own hulking and dilapidated Oldsmobile, which they had had since the early 1980s. She herself wished she had a more fuel-efficient car like a Honda or a Toyota, but her husband insisted on buying only American, including his Ford E-150 work van, which her son joked was a "serial killer car," despite its primary use for hauling plants, soil amendments, and mulch. She never understood the reference.

Outside the Korean market, the sky had deepened and the yellow lights flooded the hustle and bustle of grocery shoppers with their carts and bags. She had spent too much time at the art supplies store, and now in a rush, she barely noticed the gray-haired man who stood in long pants that trailed the floor, bottom hems torn, and an old military jacket over his gaunt frame. Customers steered clear of him like a wild animal. She had noticed more homeless people these days, their tents or cardboard boxes on street corners and under covered doorways and stairwells.

She had been startled at a gas station a week ago when someone approached her in Korean, asking for change. She had never seen a Korean man unhoused in America. Most of them had been Black or white, English-speaking, and it was easy to wave them off because she didn't speak their language. And since she had been shocked, she simply shook her head in response. But the image of him rattled her the entire night. He reminded her of war, the hungry; she had been one of them too, her entire family had. The ripped clothes and the broken feet, the way the cold, even in Los Angeles, could pierce through to the bone, especially when one slept on the ground. But where was the war here? Who waged it? Why had there been so much cruelty toward the most vulnerable? And why did we do so little to stop it?

Was it because of the constant distraction of worshipping, aspiring to be one of the exceptional ones who had "earned their riches" through genius and hard work? Yes, her husband, the homeowner, diligently followed the rules, always juggled jobs to make ends meet, but he, like herself, had come from a privileged background in Korea that allowed for an inheritance to secure them a down payment. They would not have recovered so quickly from the riots, if at all, otherwise. They would not have sent their daughter to UC Berkeley, most likely, if they hadn't gone to the finest schools themselves in Korea. Why in a nation so large did we have to carry on the illusion that only the special few should reap the rewards? She hated this mentality. There had been so much to go around, so much already stolen, land from Native Americans or labor from Black and brown people. Even she, who did not study much of US history, knew this, although it had been couched in softer language on television or in the movies back when she had time to watch.

A private security guard approached the man outside the supermarket, gesturing for him to leave.

She turned away. She had to stay focused since she was already running late for dinner, but then she heard her name: "Sunny. Sunny!"

She froze as if caught in the floodlight like amber. That voice.

Her knees weakened, almost buckled under her weight.

She met his brown eyes, which sparkled as they did years ago. How they reminded her of two gentle lakes, beckoning in the summer. But his breath smelled foul. His skin had been dirtied with grease, and his hair had turned the whitest of snow alongside his ears and temples. How someone could change so much in a single decade.

She held back tears. His face. The cheekbones. The feeling of his hand on her shoulder as she lay on the bus bench as they waited, waited, the wetness of her broken water between her legs. The humiliation. He didn't allow her to be alone. He called her his sister. He said that he loved her in a way that she had never heard before. What was love but a ripeness of unexpected feeling, a rush to dedicate oneself, to kneel at the altar of another's well-being without losing, but in the process, gaining another self? She was his sister, just as she had become a wife and a mother, accruing more lives, each with its own spectacular and private truths. She was an artist too, and a student. And a teacher. This was the kind of richness for which she had always aspired.

Sister.

"RJ?" she asked, breathless.

He smiled. A few of his teeth were missing.

"Daughter? Your daughter."

"She was gone already," RJ said. "I stayed there for about a year, then traveled some." He scrunched his brow. "But now . . . I'm back. It's been hard for me, as you can see."

Sunny wished she had more clothing to give him. The side of his pants had been torn, revealing his bare leg, which had lost muscle and weight. Just looking at him made her feel the pain of his hunger, the kind she hadn't seen since the war. He, too, appeared destroyed, like a house that had been bombed, ripped to shreds.

"Ahjumma." The security guard gestured to take her arm, but she waved him off.

"I *know* him," she said in Korean.

"He has to go," the security guard said. "Tell him to wait at the corner."

"I bring something, eat," she said to RJ. "Food. Okay? Stay, stay, okay, wait, okay? Corner."

Sunny ran inside and bought what she could in the prepared foods aisle, knowing he could carry only so much—kimbap, jeon, and tteok. She picked through the produce for fruit—apples, his favorite. She remembered when she had handed him the persimmon that she had cradled in her pocket until she had reached their bus stop. The glimmer of his eyes. How many details she had noticed about him back then. Yet how little she had done to help preserve him. She imagined his hand on her shoulder now. The kindness of a stranger was always unexpected.

Should she invite him over? For a bath, a spare bed.

How would she explain him to her husband? RJ could stay in Ana's room. He needed a roof over his head tonight. He needed clothes. A hot meal. He could die on the street like this. She had assumed she would never see him again, but she hadn't imagined that if she did, he would be living like this.

Sunny rushed to pay for the items and found RJ leaning against the fence on the corner, cold and exhausted. "You come . . . you come my house?" she asked. "Stay." She realized that if he were uncomfortable with that, he could retire in the garage.

"No, no, I can't do that. I've got a place tonight. Don't worry. Thank you."

"Where sleep?"

"A mix of places. Sometimes the shelter. Sometimes under the freeway. Sometimes in a friend's backyard. Or when there's a house for sale? Ha. So much is for sale these days. I am fine."

She had so many questions. But they both stood shivering as the traffic passed. In the fall, the city cooled down dramatically each night. They could sit in her car, couldn't they? He could eat something, hydrate himself.

"Come, come," she said, beckoning with her hand. A man with a baseball cap frowned as he passed them, making their way to her car toward the rear of the parking lot. She opened the door for the passenger side and rolled down the windows from hers. He needed laundry, a new pair of pants that would at least cover his legs.

"I wash for you. I buy clothes," she said.

"Don't worry about me, Sunny." He sighed. "I should get going." He rubbed his forehead with the tips of his fingers. His nails, broken and uneven. He was clearly embarrassed about his appearance, how he smelled. "I've wondered about you. Your family, everyone okay?"

"Yes, yes." She wanted him to know that he was safe with her, that she didn't care about what anyone thought, and that she only wanted to help him stay alive.

"Ronald, the little one. How is he?"

"High school. Big. Tall boy."

He laughed. "I figured. And the other one. What was her name? Your daughter?"

"Ana. She go to college. Graduate next year. UC Berkeley."

"Wow. That's wonderful. I bet she's very smart like her mother."

They sat in silence, an eternity. She wanted to ask him more but she didn't know how. Where to begin? Where to find out about his life? How could she help him? Instead, she reached into the grocery bag and pulled out the package of kimbap, peeled off the plastic wrapper, and gestured for him to eat. The smell of the sesame oil and danmuji filled the air. He picked up a roll with his two fingers, and she placed the styrofoam plate on the armrest between them. Tears filled her eyes as she could tell he had been ashamed of his hunger, his neediness, even though he should never have to be. How desperate people could become within the circumstances of their lives, no matter who they were, no matter how hard one worked. Humans needed each other, and she believed it was a lie to think anyone created life on their own. No one was God.

"This is delicious," he said. "The best thing I've eaten in a long time. I'll try not to have too much."

"Eat, eat," she said, handing him a napkin.

"I don't want to upset my stomach. I will save it for later." He wiped his mouth. "Good Lord." He sipped from the bottle of water she had handed him. His legs shook. "Do you mind if I have a smoke?"

As RJ lit a cigarette, she wanted to ask if he had at least found his ex.

"When I got to Alabama after a week on the bus, I called up my ex's family and found out that my daughter had already left, joined the military. My ex, Lavonne, was working as a secretary of some sort, and she didn't want to speak with me at all, except one day, after enough begging, she agreed to talk." He inhaled his cigarette, which by the harsh expression on his face, seemed to burn his lungs. "She told me that she never loved me at all. That I had been an escape, and she never meant to get pregnant." He winced. "I asked why she didn't just leave Rhonda with me in LA, and she said that Rhonda would've had a better future with her family's help. In a way, she was right."

Sunny didn't understand everything he said, but she could get a sense of the depth of RJ's heartbreak, the bad luck he had suffered in so many ways. He had fallen in love with a woman who didn't love him back. Certainly, we all knew what that was like, but that she would take away their daughter created another layer of unimaginable grief.

"I mean, look at me. Maybe she was right to take her away. It's hard to know how my life would've been different if I had my daughter. Maybe I would've stayed out of trouble." He stubbed his cigarette out in the ashtray. "Yes, now that I think about it . . . I definitely would've stayed out of this shit I'm in now. It's like trouble keeps following me."

Sunny didn't know how to respond.

"The boxes. Do you still have them, Sunny? The boxes in the garage?"

"Yes," she said, of course. What else could she have done with them? Even if he had never returned, there was no way she would get rid of his belongings. He had trusted her.

"I was thinking of stopping by, reaching out . . . but things just kept . . . getting worse."

"You stay in Alabama?"

"Oh, no. After I finally spoke with Lavonne, I left. I was only there for maybe a year. I traveled, worked odd jobs, and I started to write more and more, about my family, my life. I figured that if I couldn't know my daughter, I wanted to leave her something, in case she ever wanted to know me. Do you mind if I have another one?" He showed her his packet of Marlboro Lights. "But what I wrote didn't feel particularly focused. I needed to organize the whole thing somehow. I started to read more too. And I realized that the themes of my life, so much of what I had experienced, had in some ways been tied to what had happened to me both at the police department, and in the war." He took another sip of water. "But I couldn't write about those experiences honestly without talking about what I had seen, what I had witnessed, regardless of how it made me look. Does that make sense? The work demanded the truth, and only through the truth could I finally move on."

"*Witness?*"

"Yes, what I witnessed, you know . . . what I saw, what I observed. The things that happened to me. The things I did. Like a court trial has a witness. When you see something, and you know it exists. I can't stay quiet. I've got nothing to lose anymore."

She understood him, finally.

"You know I was fired from the police department, right? I was framed for theft, and they fired me. But that wasn't the real reason why they wanted to get rid of me. I had overheard things, recorded them, taken pictures. I don't think they understood the full extent though, until—" He took another drag of his cigarette. "I came back to LA a couple years ago to finish my book. I've been writing at the library, and I ran into an old friend, a coworker, and one day he figured out what I had been working on, asked me about it. He said my words, my testimony couldn't prove anything, and I told him that I actually had evidence, that a friend of mine, *you*, kept some photos and audio that I had recorded." He blew a long stream of smoke out of his mouth. "But he turned against me. He went to one of the police officers involved who . . . cornered me as I was leaving the library. I told him that it was a joke, a lie, that I didn't have anything, but of course he didn't believe me." RJ shook his head. "That asshole. Hendricks. I'm an idiot for trusting him." He took another bite of kimbap and chewed slowly as if his teeth hurt. "I've got to get out of town anyways. And I guess the timing is right."

He had been speaking so quickly she couldn't quite register what he had been referring to when he said "you." Something to do with photo and audio. *Evidence*. The boxes in the garage?

"I'm going back to Vietnam for a few months. I have a friend who . . . who works with children. In orphanages and such. There are all these children. With issues. Birth defects." He wrapped the rest of the kimbap with plastic wrap as if he couldn't eat any more tonight. "All the chemicals. The ones we dropped. They stay in the earth."

"*Chemical*?"

"Yes, you know in the war? There were these chemicals and they stay in the earth, the water. They never go away. Some of these children are missing body parts. Even after the war ended, there are all these children, all these people. The war never ended for them. There are the chemicals. Agent Orange."

She hadn't heard of it before. It must've been called something else in Korean.

"I— I killed them." His voice trembled.

Those words. That word, "kill," terrified her.

"I killed children. I keep killing them, you see?" His eyes, bloodshot from exhaustion, glimmered in the lamplight. "I worked on the helicopters that sprayed them. The chemicals. I killed them. I've been killing them. There's still . . . fire. They're still burning."

"No," she said, understanding only the words "I killed children." He couldn't have done that. He couldn't have harmed anyone. The word "kill" jabbed at her like a knife. She hated that word. For a minute, she was terrified of what he would say next.

He covered his face with his hand. "War never ends. That's the thing. We go home. But everyone there is still fighting and dying for generations. I am fighting and dying too. It's unnatural. We're not meant to kill like this. People are not meant to hurt each other like this. There are children, you see? Children, like—" Tears slid down his face. "Children like yours and mine. I have to help. I feel so powerless sometimes. And that's why I write."

His pain frightened her. It could rip through the earth.

RJ hadn't known the full effects of his actions in the war. He, like so many others, had simply been doing what those in power had told him to do, what they believed was right, just as she, a civilian, a refugee, had done the same.

"When I . . . being around you and Ronald and Ana changed me. I never really cared . . . I didn't know to care until then, you see?"

How did they change him?

"I tried not to think about it," he said. "I knew what was happening, but it was easier to ignore, to pretend it didn't matter, that what we were doing was right and we'd all be rewarded." She reached into her purse for a handkerchief, which she handed to him. She wanted to wipe his eyes. She wanted to hold him. He dabbed at his face. "When I was growing up, we didn't have that kind of care. Things were too hard for my parents. The world was against them. So I never thought children were good because I had been so unhappy. Me, a child."

He flicked the cigarette out of the car and lit another one, hand shaking.

"I have to make it right now, you see? That's the only way I can move on. I have to go back."

"How . . . I help?" she asked.

"I don't need anything, Sunny. But please, my boxes. Could you . . . I hate to ask you this but . . . inside those boxes, the ones in your garage? I have this blue bank deposit bag. It's filled with rolls of film. Some cassettes. Could you go in and hide them somewhere else? Somewhere no one can find them, okay? The blue bag. It'll stand out from the rest."

She knew exactly what he was referring to.

"Yes, just a little while longer. I don't want to travel with any of that. And I need to disappear for a while. I'll be back though, I promise. We'll find each other, okay?"

RJ opened the passenger side door, and the memory of them driving up to the Observatory flashed in her mind. "I'll see you soon. Don't worry about me. Thank you." He glanced at the groceries she had given him. "I promise I'll take care of myself. I hope you do too."

Afterward, she sat immobile in the parking lot, shaken by the encounter. Would she ever see him again? He'd have to call her or come to her home. She should warn her husband first. But what would she tell him?

Sunny glanced at the clock. She had been gone for almost three hours and she hadn't even bought the groceries she needed. Her husband and son must be worried about her already. She should find a pay phone, let them know that she had run into an old friend, from Korea, that she had lost track of time. He would be upset that she hadn't called him earlier. But she would hide behind his perception of her as oblivious.

In reality, she knew what she would do. She would guard what RJ needed with her life. She had the perfect spot in mind.

1999

With his snub-nosed revolver on his belt, John crept down the stairs, scanning the backyard under the harsh floodlight.

Priscilla had mentioned a crime that RJ had either witnessed or kept evidence of, and she was afraid herself, hiding at her sister's house. No one was safe. If only he could protect her too—but he had to focus on his family, his house.

And the persimmon tree, still in its container. He couldn't let it die.

He'd have to water it now. Even if the end of the world was in less than two weeks.

Chaos. Pandemonium. Riots. Looting.

Lawlessness was hell.

He remembered that after the trial against four police officers who had brutally beaten Rodney King, which had been seared into the minds of

Americans through black-and-white video footage on the nightly news, the "not guilty" verdict had struck like an earthquake, rattling the city, their lives. And a few hours later, the fires started. The weather had been warm, in the seventies. All their windows had been open. And the roars, the screaming and shouts, the dragging, the violence, was like nothing he'd seen outside of war itself. Of course, the city knew that the four officers could be acquitted by a jury in Simi Valley, a distant, mostly white suburb northwest of LA. But the video had played day in and day out on television, as if to numb us, to condition us to suffering through repetition. Instead it stoked an already simmering sense of anger and desperation, exacerbated by economic stagnation and nearly six years of drought, one of California's longest.

Hence, the city exploded in an uprising, burned like a wildfire.

And they tasted ash in their mouths for weeks. An eye for an eye. Teeth for teeth.

John heaved the heavy hose, which always kinked in multiple places, and doused the bare persimmon tree in its container.

The night of April 29, 1992, the phone rang and rang like the most dreadful, unending alarm. John's gas station was only minutes from Florence and Normandie, where Reginald Denny, a white truck driver, had been pulled out of his car and beaten on live television by a group of Black men, and later saved by Black residents who had witnessed the attack and driven Denny to the hospital. In a blur, he slammed the receiver down and scrambled for his keys and wallet.

He had to get in his car. He had to save all his work, his sacrifices, what little he had that was his own. No more loss. No more death. No more abandonment. No more separation. No more questions. No second, third, or fifth chances. No.

"What are you doing?" His wife grabbed his arm, nearly tore his shirt.

"I have to get my gun," he said. The gas station was on fire. The revolver was inside.

"It's gone. It's too dangerous out there," she screamed. The children hid under the dining table. "Do you think this is a game? A movie?"

"You don't understand what it's like—"

"You don't need to prove anything," she said. "You're not a cowboy. You're the son of a law school professor. An English literature major. Stay home where you belong."

He had the urge to punch everything in sight. Break windows, glass. His wife ran to the children, huddled with fright. He darted through the kitchen, out the back door, and yelled, "God damn you," at no one. "God damn you."

Yes, that day she was right. But today he knew—between RJ's death and Priscilla's fear, the tremble of her voice—he would never again go into the backyard, or anywhere in this city, without his gun.

Those shoes gray from dirt. The ammonia scent. RJ was just another anybody, wasn't he?

Until he said her name, Sunny, and he became something else.

Her name in a stranger's mouth. How it pierced straight through John's heart.

Each syllable, a bullet.

It wasn't even the name that she desired for herself. He remembered the pride she had when she had first declared the one she actually wanted—*Anastasia*. He'd laughed at her impracticality, the quantity of syllables, that was foreign to the formula in his head—a husband, a wife, two children, a boy and a girl, a house. An honest job and two cars. A gun to protect them all. They might belong somewhere finally.

And then, after what he did, his wife fled. And she was gone.

A cat mewled. He dropped the hose on the ground and grabbed his gun. He pointed in the darkness beside the loquat tree. "Motherfucker," he said to scare it away. "Motherfucker!"

"What are you doing here, Dad?" His son emerged from the house, turned the hose bibb off.

"Just . . . water tree."

"What's that?" his son asked.

Immediately, John replaced the gun in the holster. "Nothing, nothing."

Would his children ever know that he had done his best? That he had made mistakes and that he would pay for them all? He would find a way to make things right. But despite how many languages he spoke and understood, he would never know how to explain exactly just what he felt, the fear and anguish of what he had experienced as a child while also being their father, a father, a man—strong, stoic, reliable.

Ronald broke the silence. "I know Mom's not coming back," he said.

John couldn't believe that his words, trying to convince his son of his mother's death all those months ago, had finally worked. Remorse filled him.

"You don't know where she is, do you?" Ronald asked. "I thought maybe you did, and for whatever reason, you kept her from us."

John wanted to respond, but no words came.

"She's dead," his son said. "I know that's what you want us to believe. And it's probably the truth." Tears streamed down Ronald's face. "Your mother gone. Ours too." He wiped his cheeks with a fist covered in his sleeve. "We must be cursed."

If only his son knew the depth of his guilt, how much he had hurt their mother, ignored, even reviled her, and how much he regretted that now. How much he carried. How much he wanted the world to end so that they'd all possess the same fate, inseparable, finally. It was about control, wasn't it?

Without another word, his son abandoned John in the backyard.

Only his wife could fix things now.

"Sunny, please come home," John said to himself, eyes filled.

Even if the child was not his, he'd take care of him or her too. An infant, tender and new. He'd do better, be better this time. If given one more chance.

Who could Ana turn to now? Yesterday, after her morning phone call with Rhonda, she had gone through her mother's sketchbooks and art supplies in the garage. She had been surprised, caught off guard by the startling number of self-portraits and still lifes, with bizarre, dreamlike elements, which included a depiction of their house, its shape and structure, made of glass like a greenhouse with a lawn of chives and a drawing of a large moon jar cracked in half with a woman's fingers emerging from it like a hermit crab. But what had been seared into Ana's mind was a single pencil image she had chanced upon: a pregnant woman lying down on a bus stop bench with her head on a man's lap, a loquat tree behind them, an apple in his hand. The street gutter resembled a river, or stream, from which mackerel leapt out of the water. Ana had been reminded of Frida Kahlo's *The Two Fridas* in its mix of poignancy, vulnerability, determination, and strength. She couldn't believe her mother had found this surrealism to express the mystery of herself in a way that had been both enigmatic and completely beautiful.

The image somewhat resembled RJ and her mother. But what did that mean?

Later that afternoon, Ana had given Rhonda the boxes with RJ's journals and photographs they had found in the garage. Rhonda had silently taken them home to pore over the contents by herself. She would need time, of course, but she planned to return on Friday, Christmas Eve, two days from now, when Priscilla would drop by to speak with them all.

A lot could happen in two days. Who knew if Priscilla, or they, were safe?

They had no idea yet what exactly they were looking for, but they had searched everywhere. Something to do with a crime, a police cover-up. She paced in the kitchen. Maybe she should call the library to check if Jacob had returned. They needed all the parts to come together, including whatever RJ had been working on. The book. If they couldn't find the evidence, they would at least have his words. Who knew what his writing could lead to? Maybe combined with Priscilla's testimony, they could reveal the truth finally, seek justice for any victims.

Ronald entered through the back door.

"The book that RJ was writing," Ana said. "We have to find it."

"The book could be anywhere, or destroyed."

"I know. But . . . where would you keep a book if you didn't have a place to stay?"

"Somewhere you could just walk in and store something. Maybe something portable, like a computer disk? I guess I'd always carry it on me that way. Or the train station, a locker there? But then we wouldn't be able to get inside of them. If I had something important . . . it would need to be somewhere safe but accessible to anyone—"

"The library," Ana breathed.

"Seems like the only place he could get to regularly and wouldn't get kicked out. He could write there easily. Use the computer. If he didn't have the disk on him, and if it hadn't been destroyed already, that's where I would keep it. In the aisles. There are some that no one ever goes to. Like certain kinds of history. Poetry. No one touches that."

"That's not true." She laughed. "I love poetry."

"Well, I would look there," Ronald said. "It's mostly kids and teenagers at that library. They're always reading magazines."

"Are they still open?"

"Yeah, for a bit longer."

On the living room couch, Ana slipped the business card out of her purse and dialed the number for the local branch. Maybe she could ask Janet if she could stop by tonight, after hours, so that she could search the shelves herself. She knew that RJ had to have left the book somewhere, or had even created multiple copies. He couldn't have written such an important document, over years, only to have it be destroyed.

She wouldn't accept that until she searched the entire city.

The phone rang and rang until she hung up and tried again.

A man answered, voice shaking. What was wrong now?

"Could I speak to Janet? This is Ana Kim."

He muffled the receiver with his hand as he spoke in another direction.

"Ana?" Janet said, catching her breath. "Ana, I've been . . . it's been . . . it's been quite a day. We closed. I meant to reach out earlier but . . . it's been . . . they found Jacob outside the library this morning." She sniffled as if she had been running outside in the cold. "Jacob Hendricks."

"What?" Ana's heart raced.

"I had come in early, couldn't sleep last night." Her words rushed out. "It was still dark. There was this shape at the door. His body— He was just at the door. I thought it was someone sleeping. But when I got . . . I got closer . . ." She broke into a sob. "I could see the blood. Blood leaking out of him. Footprints. Never in my life—"

"Oh my God."

"The color of his blood was . . ." She paused. "There's a video camera, some footage down the block, but who knows?"

"I'm so sorry." One by one they would be picked off, plucked before the fall.

"He was shot . . . and they left his body here like that."

This was it. Whatever Jacob had been afraid of had caught up with him. Were they next?

"It was a warning," Janet said.

"Are you okay? Do you feel safe?" Ana asked. She'd have to get ahold of Rhonda.

"I don't think anyone is," Janet said with a mix of fear, anger, and something else. "Not even me, a fucking librarian."

1998

On this November afternoon, perfectly cool and ripe, Sunny took a break from the fumes of her garage after she had cleaned her brushes and rested on the dead grass underneath the loquat tree. The fresh air alleviated the intensity of her nausea and the flashes of heat that struck her face and then spread to her neck and chest, the sudden sweat like warm summer rain.

After running into RJ at the grocery store last month, Sunny burned through her free time by painting in the garage, where she stood guard not only for herself, but also for RJ and his stacks of boxes. She hadn't run into him again, despite how hard she looked, and she assumed that he must've already fled: *I need to disappear for a while. I'll be back though, I promise. We'll find each other, okay?* She had to protect him as best she could until he returned from Vietnam, a country she admittedly knew so little about except for the terrible war that people around the world protested against because many of its atrocities, which included the killing of children, as RJ had referenced, had been so well documented and photographed.

Witnessed.

It was strange to think that wars happened everywhere all the time but the remoteness, the abstractness, made the violence feel foreign, when in reality, we too, like parasites, lived inside the body that committed those crimes. In what country on earth was it legal to torture and kill babies and children? We learned to look away because they were not "ours," but they could've been hers or *her*—a baby tied to her young mother's back, a mother who ran until her feet blistered and bled, and she nearly had them amputated.

And terrified of what great cruelties we might be capable of, we further distanced ourselves by distorting humans, their children even, as invasive, a plague, responsible for crimes and pandemics. But in the process of drifting farther from, building fences in front of *them*, we became severed from the expansiveness of our humanity. Fear made us too tiny and brittle to hold the magnificence of love in all its forms, mysterious and worth protection, worth living for.

She had to protect RJ and his belongings as much as she had to guard her own art. Without her paintings, life would be one falsehood after another. Only on paper and canvas could she exist enormously, as an entire self—without the constraints of time and location. The images she could create expressed who she was, purely, and her yearning to live beyond the limitations of this one body, this one life, this one deadly host.

At first, Sunny had sketched ideas in a pencil-smeared sketchpad where she began with objects from everyday life—a head of garlic, a small branch of the loquat tree's boatlike leaves, a fuyu persimmon with its calyx that resembled a flower-shaped hat, a kitchen knife that badly needed to be sharpened. She caught up on the phone every couple weeks with Myunghwa for practical ideas and tips. Large art books from the library, a ten-minute walk from their house, kept her inspired. In addition to the two small paintings she had brought home from Korea, she studied one of her father's exhibition catalogs, which she flipped through as if there might be some detail she hadn't noticed before that would push her, like the crash of white foam, forward.

"I wish I had brought more of his art with me," Sunny said one afternoon to Myunghwa on the phone. "What are you painting these days?"

"I don't have time." Myunghwa laughed. "I'm too busy with the gallery. Honestly, I'm a better businesswoman than an artist. My life is the only original." She said "original" in English as if she was making fun of the word itself, which reminded Sunny of when she ordered her son's favorite style of Kentucky Fried Chicken. "I'm like a performance artist," Myunghwa said. "An old woman who dares to live alone."

"You're doing well then, it seems. You're the best performance artist I know—personally." Sunny wrapped the spiral cord around her finger.

"Maybe you should look into women artists? They might see us, themselves, differently, don't you think? It seems like you only mention men—French men, the Russians. Spanish men. Picasso was a prick. They all were. Maybe Marc Chagall was nice?"

"Ha, does it matter?" Sunny asked.

"Kind of. I mean not personally, but I'm talking about the work. The cruelty of the work," Myunghwa said.

"Isn't beauty enough?"

"Beauty to who?" Myunghwa asked.

"The person at the museum, the person in front of a painting."

"But maybe it's beautiful because someone put it there, someone made you look. Did the woman yearn to be displayed on the flat white walls of a museum? For whom was she made?"

"But who else should we learn from, then? How else do we become great?" And when Sunny had said those words out loud, she realized how problematic that mentality had been. When only one group of people represented the best, and declared the rules, of course others would often have to betray the self to live up to someone else. And what if the goal of art wasn't exactly greatness as defined by the special few, the chosen ones. Maybe art with a broader appeal, that didn't feel forced or repeated, or chiseled to perfection, could actually move, move people toward their best, their most human self?

With Myunghwa's suggestion in mind, she became more and more interested in women artists, especially those who embraced and created different realities, from Frida Kahlo to Leonora Carrington. Magical realists. Surrealists beyond Magritte's *The Lovers*.

In her latest work, she sketched a portrait of herself, bulbously pregnant, lying down on the bus stop bench, her head on RJ's lap, an apple in one hand, the other on her shoulder. It was not even romantic, but simply a gesture, an acknowledgment of what she carried, what they carried differently, and what they carried together. One day, she wanted her children to see her like this, resting on this bench, her body part of the world, as opposed to just a mother at home.

She should paint this with her new set of oils.

She penciled behind the bus bench a loquat tree that shielded them from the sun, offered fruit when they were hungry. Instead of a street gutter, there would be a stream in which they could drink and wash themselves, their hands, and the water would be clean, filtered through sediment and rock. This art was not a fantasy but the reality of how things could be, her reality that she held on to whenever she lost faith in the world, her husband, or herself. This nation might've split their home abroad, might've given them so few options here, but yet she and RJ had both been brought together, their passions, their flaws, in a way that had never been possible in human history before.

Only a surrealist could have created the flawed, aching beauty of this place, America—its promise yet to be fulfilled.

"There you are," John said, startling Sunny. He never came back behind the garage. His feet crunched on the fallen twigs and dead grass of their yard as he approached her under the loquat tree. She wrapped her sweater around her body, self-conscious because of all the weight she had gained, which she supposed had something to do with her age and early menopause. At forty-eight she noticed the gray at her hairline, white which sprayed out like a cat's whiskers, and the brown spots, like droplets, on her face, growing in size. She had generally become more aware of how she appeared, but also understood that this might be part of the process of accepting who she was—finally. All those years of raising children, she avoided mirrors, only glanced at herself briefly in the morning, and on special occasions, when she applied makeup, eyeliner and lipstick. Now her art was the reflection she could bear, training her eyes to admire what she had done and what she had still to do.

"I looked inside the garage. I didn't see you," he said.

She stood, wiped the dirt off her hands. For a minute, their brown eyes held each other's. At sixty years old, her husband too had changed. His hair had grown entirely white at the temples while the horizontal lines on his forehead and at the corners of his eyes had deepened into permanent grooves.

Did men look in the mirror less? What did they see when they saw themselves? Were they kinder or did they simply ignore the details?

Or perhaps refrained from judgment since their heads had been full of "bigger questions" and decisions? How well did she really know her husband? Except that she had loved him and their children, but she never quite agreed with or understood him. Did he feel this ache, this loneliness, this foreignness too, which had grown only sharper in his presence? If he did, he must've decided to live with it, which she refused to do. Or maybe he simply had feelings and sensations in his body, but had no name for them.

How had he ever been a literature major? Somewhere buried inside John was a man who loved books. A man who needed air.

She reached toward the canopy of the loquat tree above her, the dark green leaves, with curves that reminded her of fishing boats that skimmed the surface of dark water, muddy with life. It was a mystery how a tree like this, bold and tropical in appearance, could survive with such little care somewhere as dry as Los Angeles.

"I wanted to talk to you about Ronald," John said.

His tone. She couldn't help but panic. "Is everything alright?"

"Maybe you're spending too much time out here, painting or whatever."

"What do you mean?" she asked.

John pulled a weed, twisting it at the base before he tried to yank it out of the ground, but the stem ripped off. "Maybe Ronald needs more of . . . your attention." He brushed his hands clean on his pants. "He needs his mother."

After the riots, after they lost their business, which sent their routines into disorder, their son would disappear for hours on his skateboard during the day and skip class altogether. She knew that he often took the bus to Santa Monica, where he'd meet up with friends and play games at the arcade on the pier, because he fished through her bag for quarters, his daily catch. Of course she noticed. But he was different from his sister—more sensitive perhaps, or sensitive in another way. He didn't enjoy books or sitting still, needed interaction, the company of friends. He was more social, and Sunny didn't see any harm in that if it helped him get away from this house. His father did nothing but work. Sunny and John didn't fight anymore, because for the past couple years they had simply stopped speaking with each other except to convey information. So it was hard for Ronald in many ways and maybe escaping the home offered him some relief, choices in a life that had often felt preordained, confined to a certain kind of fate.

Despite the war, Sunny herself had had a much easier life in Korea than her children had here. There had been years of hunger and hardship, but after her parents established themselves in the South, her father as an artist and teacher, they bought a home in the undeveloped Gangnam area of Seoul. They later sold that land to developers for profit and always took care of all her financial needs until she had married John at the age of twenty-six, essentially "passing her on" to someone else, someone they thought would offer her more opportunities, a chance at a life of even more privilege and fulfillment abroad. Freedom. She had been spoiled in many ways, had attended the best schools.

She worried about Ronald but also knew that he would find his own path. He needed time. Even if his life didn't look like his sister's. His differences didn't mean that he couldn't support or create a life for himself. She trusted him and his instincts. She *knew* him.

What did her husband know except for following the rules? He had never even been in the military for health reasons, including frequent earaches and partial deafness because of the explosions he had endured during the war. Hadn't they gotten away from the dictatorships in Korea for a reason? So that they could be *free*?

"Maybe you could help him with his homework more," John said. "Check on him, make sure—"

"I wake up early. I make him breakfast and lunch. I drive him to school. What else can I do? He's not a child anymore. He doesn't want to stay home all the time. He's not that kind of kid. He's *not* Ana."

Her husband pulled more weeds, which made her uneasy.

"Maybe you could spend more time cleaning, then?" he asked. "The bathroom—"

"What is wrong with you?" She raised her voice unexpectedly. "I'm exhausted. Maybe *you* should do those things. If you see something that needs to be cleaned, clean it yourself."

"A son needs his mother."

He was referring to himself, wasn't he? *A son needs his mother.* How much we each found ways to talk about ourselves, our unexpressed needs through our children. How much it was easier to talk about life, about history, through them. But it was too much for them, the children, to bear. They deserved better. What did he know about what Ronald needed? He wasn't even around enough to understand him despite the fact that they spoke the same language. Her English was still poor and Ronald's Korean even worse, but somehow they comprehended each other because they spent enough time caring, being careful together.

How had English even served her husband? What was the point of language without love?

"A son needs his father, too," she said. Tears spilled out of her eyes. How their hearts broke, how helpless they felt, and yet instead of holding each other, they lashed out, because when exhausted, they behaved like hungry animals. They couldn't fully hear the other.

"I'm trying—"

"I can start to help at the nursery." Sunny reached for his arm and rubbed it with her thumb. "That way you can—"

He shook his head.

"Have you ever thought that maybe I would prefer to go to work sometimes? What if you become sick one day and I have to take over? I could go twice per week. We could split—"

"I won't get sick."

"That's ridiculous." She crossed her arms in front of her. "Sometimes I want . . . I want—"

"I have to make some phone calls."

As he walked toward the house, she yelled at his back, "You don't know a thing about plants, about growing anything."

"The nursery is fine. I'm doing fine," he shouted. The door slammed behind him.

She reached into the loquat tree's dusty and cobweb-filled canopy, gritting her teeth while she yanked until a branch snapped, unexpectedly releasing a bunch of leaves and who knew what else on top of her head. She had cut open her hand, which now itched all over.

Was he right about Ronald? Was she not doing enough?

She often spoke to her son at the dinner table or before bed, asking him about his day. Sometimes he rested his head on her lap and she combed his hair with her fingers. His ear was a perfect seashell shape, and like a Dora Maar photograph, she had imagined fingers emerging from it like a hermit crab. She never shared this with anyone. She never asked about school or his grades, knowing that he felt like an outsider there, that he struggled to fit in with the Korean kids because his Korean was weak and he didn't like church, that his friends were all Mexican and Filipino. She knew a lot about him. She didn't think he needed any more pressure. There was enough of that already.

She washed the blood from her hand under the ice-cold water from the spigot outside. She splashed her face, and unexpectedly retched. Catching a sudden movement in the corner of her eye, she turned to see a Calico cat as it approached, its face half-orange and half-black, its green eyes glowing like two jade coins. She rubbed the soft space between its ears as the cat flexed its claws, and then turned over to reveal its belly, pregnant and round.

1999

Driving home with a bag of compost to supplement the unplanted persimmon tree, Ronald realized he still needed to buy Peggy a present for Christmas, which was in two days. He'd nearly forgotten, with everything that had been going on. Tomorrow, on Christmas Eve, he could trek to the mall, either Baldwin Hills (the closest) or the Beverly Center (the fanciest), and procure a few things from Bath & Body Works or perfume from Macy's. But that wouldn't seem special. Maybe new books, or a gift certificate to Borders where she could buy music too.

This would be their last holiday together before Peggy went off to some faraway college or university, manicured, draped in handsome foliage, buildings ivy-clad. He had already invited her over for dinner this weekend, which would be the first time she had actually been inside his house. Now, at nearly the end of the world, he had nothing to lose. He didn't care if the house or his father embarrassed him. He was running out of time. And if the weather held up, he could cook galbi by flame in the backyard. He'd have to purchase a small charcoal grill. With his sister, they could figure it out. A meal like that would be meaningful, and although it would be cold outside for LA, dropping possibly into the fifties, they could always eat at the dining table they hadn't used since their mother disappeared. It would be a way of taking care of everyone at once, and would give Peggy something to hold on to and remember.

Once home, he heaved the bag of compost out of the Eldorado's trunk, pungent with the odor of wet earth and manure. His father had stayed back at the nursery to finish up some end-of-year accounting, and would drive his work van home. His sister had remained at the house all day, poring over their mother's drawings that she had found in the garage.

He carried the stinky bag of compost on his shoulder and plopped it down next to the persimmon tree, realizing he couldn't remember when he had last seen their shovel. It must be somewhere in the backyard, or in the garage, which Ronald still hadn't worked up the courage to go inside of yet—fearful of what he might find of his mother's. Despite what he had said to his father, that he accepted that she might be dead, he wasn't ready to confront a version of his mother outside of what he knew.

He searched the dusty yard, corner to corner, for a shovel or any tool he might use to dig a hole. There must be something, even a trowel, lying around. He had to finish this, get the damn tree in the ground.

Behind the fence, Rodriguez, raspy and low, muttered something in Spanish, a complaint of some sort. Ronald peeked through the passionflower vines, careful not to make a sound. A white straw hat. A bottle clinked on the ground. A mandarin-colored Jarritos. Was he with the paletero who always jangled his friendly bells as he made his way down the street in his leather cowboy boots, paunch hanging over his belt? In the summer, Ronald loved the creamy white drip as the popsicle melted in his hands, the shred of the coconut toward the bottom like a reward. His sister preferred the sweet strawberry and tart mango flavors, which she dipped in the Tajín they always had in the cupboard. That single bottle of chili lime salt might've been five years old, but they had been grateful when they needed it. His stomach growled like a dog and he slipped on the roll of a fallen branch. Twisting his ankle, he said, "Shit, motherfucker" before he fell. He couldn't help himself.

Rodriguez's head popped over the fence as if he already had a ladder out. "You okay, man?" Did this guy ever wear clothes? Ronald couldn't understand how he could be standing in the frigid night air with only a white tank top and his tattoos to keep him warm.

"Yeah, yeah, I'm fine." He couldn't stand straight, so he brushed the dirt off his pants in an attempt to hide his face and the excruciating pain above his foot. He'd never get this persimmon tree planted at this rate.

"You need help?" Rodriguez asked.

"I'm alright." He motioned toward the black container. "It's basically a twig."

"It has potential." Rodriguez cocked his head to the side, which revealed the sinuous tattoos up the side of his neck. Ronald had always figured he had been a veterano with the blue-green teardrop underneath his eye. But now a gentle and kind veterano. His mother often pointed out not only his garden but also how he treated the neighborhood cats like his own. He never gave anyone the impression that he was still involved in any criminal activity, never had parties, or even friends or family over, except this one, the paletero now. How strange. Those two men seemed from such different backgrounds.

The paletero, a family man with a dad body. Rodriguez, a former gang member who had probably killed people.

"So, my friend"—he gestured with his chin toward the paletero—"he said he noticed a Ford Explorer parked over here next to my house." Rodriguez lived on the corner of their block and shared borders with two residential streets, mostly quiet except for the neighbors' cars that overflowed on the sides. Rodriguez rarely had guests, and neither did they. "Ey, Jesús, que color? Azul?" Standing on the ladder, he leaned with his hand, knobby and scarred at the knuckles, on the fence between them. He turned around again. "A blue one. Thought it was strange." He finished his Jarritos and dropped it with a soft thud onto the ground.

"What day was that?" Ronald asked. Jacob's body had been found yesterday morning, Wednesday, at the library. The security footage revealed that he had driven a Ford Explorer, the same make and model as the vehicle that had followed them home from the Observatory. Apparently, Jacob had attempted to break into the library, and at some point in the night, he had been shot, his body dragged to the front door like dead prey.

"He says Tuesday night," Rodriguez said.

Could Jacob have driven to their house again and gone to the library afterward, where he was killed?

"I haven't seen your dad in a while?" Rodriguez asked.

"He hasn't been well. He had a stroke last weekend. A minor one, but he's recovering."

"That man works too hard." He shook his head. "He'll kill himself if he keeps at it. End up dead like that guy." He pointed with his chin toward the loquat tree.

"What about you?" Ronald asked. "You seem to work all the time too." Ronald had often seen Rodriguez's large American truck loaded with construction equipment and materials like Sheetrock, tiles, and buckets of paint. He had been gone at odd hours, in the mornings, sometimes overnight, but of course, many people in the city had multiple jobs and worked on the weekends to make ends meet.

"I make sure to enjoy myself." He laughed. "I take improv once a week."

"Improv?"

"Yeah, you know—theatre, no script. It's fun."

"Oh." Ronald asked, "But . . . where do you work?"

Rodriguez paused as if he had never been asked that question before. How strange. Perhaps his tattoos, the toughness of his skin, marked as consistently as a reptile's, scared people away. Everyone assumed that he had been up to no good, but Ronald and his family knew he lived a quiet, almost gentle life, far from whatever trouble he might've once caused. "Jesús and I, we've got an events business. He does the food. His wife, the decorations. I do the entertainment." He mimed a DJ holding his headphones to his ear and scratching a record with his other hand. "Kids' parties, Christmas shit, quinces. I'm also a plant manager at the high school. I can do tile work. Landscaping. Roofs—"

"The high school?" Ronald asked. "Never seen you around."

"Mostly at night." He turned his head, and said, "Hey guey, otra." Then with a profound level of disgust on his face, he curled up his lip. "You kids are disgusting. Somebody gotta clean that shit up." Descending the ladder, he said, "If you need anything, let me know, okay?"

The sound of a lighter. A plume of smoke from behind the fence.

Ronald slipped his own pack of cigarettes from his back pocket. But he didn't have any matches. He must've left them in the car.

"Do you have a shovel I can borrow?" Ronald asked. "I can't seem to find ours."

"Sure, yeah, yeah. Hold on."

Ronald tapped his foot on the ground until the heavy blade had been hoisted above so that he could reach it.

"When you're done, just throw it over, okay? Make sure not to hit anyone though."

Ronald couldn't help but laugh. Of course, with their luck, he would.

"Do you have a lighter?" Ronald asked. Why not?

"And how old are you, young man?"

"Old enough to smoke." Almost, at least.

"You can keep this one." A red rectangle flew over the fence and landed in the dirt.

As he lit a cigarette for himself, Ronald cradled the flame and the heat in his hand. Footsteps receded into Rodriguez's house. What else did he have back there? Had the police searched his yard as well? Ronald assumed they had, but who knew how thorough they had been. A part of him wanted to ask but didn't want to keep getting his neighbors involved. Not now. He trusted Rodriguez, but at the same time, he didn't really *know* him.

The nicotine loosened his mind, which unraveled like a skein of twine.

As he dug into the earth, he couldn't get the image of the old shovel out of his head. Its wobbly blade caked in the years of dirt that had hardened into rock. Their shovel had to be here somewhere. But maybe his father had taken it to work for some reason. Ronald kicked down on the step of Rodriguez's and only chipped at the ground. He'd mash the soil with his weight no matter how long he might take. He touched what would be the trunk of the persimmon tree one day, now fragile and gray like a long stack of ash ready to fall down.

1998

Sunny hung up the phone with her index finger, as the hiss of the furnace kicked on. Her sister had sounded relieved, of course, not because she did not love their mother, but because it was *she* in Korea who had taken care of their mother, no longer able to leave her room, requiring a bedpan and sponge bath. Her sister also had a family to care for and feed since her husband, a computer engineer, worked long hours and commuted every day to Seoul.

Her mother's death had been inevitable, but after her sister's phone call, after her sister had mailed an entire box of their father's paintbrushes and family photographs that had survived each displacement, each attempt to shatter their lives, from colonialism to war, all forms of migration, catastrophic separations from the land and the self, Sunny woke up every day for about a week with a strange sense that someone had been watching her—a ghost or some higher power. For years she had held on to the naive notion that her mother's health would improve, that one day, after their finances had stabilized, Sunny would be able to visit her again, that life in Korea would remain the same, waiting for her return.

Art continued to distract Sunny—both from her mother's death and the absence of her daughter, who was still in Berkeley and had become consumed by her volunteer work and the election of Gray Davis as governor. She had lost her daughter physically to the move, and now emotionally, as Ana hardly had time to pick up the phone anymore. Sunny understood the depth of her daughter's outrage, but she had also through years of war and living under military dictatorships worried about the danger Ana might find herself in at protests, which could erupt into gunshots and riots.

Her husband never voted, but she knew he supported the current gubernatorial administration and its rhetoric. John believed that people didn't deserve "handouts," as he referred to social services, when they weren't willing to "obey the laws." He believed that if he could find a way to immigrate to this country by going to college, studying and working hard, anyone should be able to as well. Her husband argued that rules existed to protect everyone who followed them.

"Who is *everyone*?" she had asked. "Does everyone include the child that runs from his home because it is violent? Because the family is violent? Because the country is violent? When you were young and you left your mother, was it a crime when you picked weeds and berries to eat? Whose weeds and berries were they? Were you stealing from the earth? Whose property was it? Under the stars at night, did you and your father sleep on someone else's property? Did the stars belong to someone else?"

John snickered as if she had lost her mind. Once he called her a Communist.

But he knew she had made valid points. And the more she shared her thoughts, the more she had been despised by him.

After a couple more arguments that resulted in him stomping out of the room or finding any reason to pick on their son (the clothes he didn't fold, the dishes he didn't wash properly, the lights he forgot to turn off), she never brought up her political opinions again. She let him believe whatever he needed, to keep the peace of this house. Even if his line of thinking justified the unnecessary pain and hardship of others, the most vulnerable within our system, those who suffered like RJ.

She buried herself in her art, transferring her sketch of herself and RJ on the bus bench to a small canvas she had bought. Using a portion of the cash that John provided every week for groceries, she had even splurged on more colors to add to her kit, Viridian and Dioxazine Purple, which sounded like potions for revenge. She experimented, thinning the oils with solvent and binder to slow the drying times, and had been steadily underpainting the composition and structure of her newest work, *The Intimacy of Strangers, or The Seasons,* in Burnt Umber for weeks.

But one day in December, after Davis had won the general election, she had come home from the supermarket and found her husband unexpectedly in their living room, pacing like an animal. At four p.m., he must've left the nursery earlier than usual. Ana would be home in two days and she had spent the last week preparing all of their daughter's favorite banchan and foods.

She braced herself for what she knew would be one of his outbursts about his favorite subject, his "failure" of a son, the son he would've given the world to, and had sacrificed his own life, working hours that broke his humanity, so that Ronald could have a better, a freer future. Unlike his sister, the star student, who required little coaxing if any at all to be who she was, their son, lazy and stubborn, took everything for granted.

"I got a call from the school yesterday." He brushed his hair away from his face with his hand. "Ronald has been skipping class again. At this rate, Ronald won't even make it to college."

She steadied herself. It took so much out of her to remain calm, to keep the peace in this house. But she couldn't stand having this conversation, which resulted in nothing.

"He's going through a lot," she said. "It's hard at his age. There's so much pressure."

"*Going through a lot?* He has no bills to pay. He gets whatever he wants—"

"That's not true," Sunny said. "He compares himself to the other kids. He doesn't always feel . . . good about himself. He is under a lot of pressure. You're always comparing him to his sister—"

"He doesn't *feel* good. Oh, so now these American kids get to have their feelings. Do you think I got to have feelings?" He pointed to his sternum. "I still went to school. I still got my degrees. I studied hard. I never stopped working. I never will. I'll never rest because of these kids."

"It's not the same. It's not fair to compare yourself to him. He's a different person. He's more—"

"I told you that if you kept spending so much time on your art, ignoring him, he'd become this way."

She could feel her blood pressure rising. *Stay away from my art.*

"Is he in a gang?" John asked.

"That's ridiculous."

"Is that where sensitive boys go because they don't want to study? He should try prison."

"Give him a break. I'll talk to him—"

"I won't let him drive anymore. Or hang out with his stupid friends. Or his girlfriend, whatever her name."

"Peggy," she said. "And she's very nice."

"*Very nice*. Is that what they say about you too?"

"What?" What had he been referring to? What was he insinuating? Was he drunk?

"And you, ha . . . too much time outside in the garage." The veins in his neck looked like they could burst. "Why do I have to do everything around here, huh?"

She stepped closer and could smell the alcohol on him. The heat. The whiskey. For as long as she had known him, he never drank much. But earlier this week she noticed a bottle of Crown Royal stashed in the dining room hutch. She couldn't quite understand what its metallic blue box had been doing in the house, but it was there, and now apparently he had too much of it. What time was it? Four o'clock? What was happening to John?

"I'll talk to him about it." Sunny reached toward her husband, but he stepped away as if disgusted by her touch.

"No. I'll show him. I'll show him if he wants to be a man, do whatever he wants." He rolled up his sleeves, balled his fingers into fists.

"Stay away from him." She gritted her teeth. If he even tried to hurt her son, she'd kill him. "He's hanging out with his friends. He doesn't like to be in the house all the time. It's lonely."

"Lonely? Ha. Like you?" His smile, devilish and cruel.

She should leave. She should drive away somewhere far, anywhere away from this house, this man who had worked so hard yet had been reckless with their hearts, including his own. She couldn't believe that once he had been romantic, courted her with chocolates and flowers, read poetry for comfort. His bitterness had made him into an animal.

"What are you doing back there anyways?" he asked.

"What do you mean?"

"I noticed you're different. Gaining weight?"

His words sickened her. She could slap him in the face.

"You've been eating miyeok guk," he snickered. "What, almost every day?"

He noticed. He had been watching her too.

"I hate miyeok guk, you know that? I've always hated it," he said.

What had stunned her more: That he actually had been paying attention or that he managed to hide so much of what he knew? She stood in front of him as if she had suddenly encountered a stranger in her home, an intruder. She had the impulse to both run and fight. She had no idea who he was anymore, nor did she want to know.

Exactly when had she given up on them? It must've been before the cars, the house, RJ. Maybe since the beginning, even before she had gotten on the plane to America for the first time. Had it happened at the altar when she wore the tiny hat covered in pearls, and all she could think about was Professor Cho? Immigration, marriage, domestic life had been like theater, as if all the lines she memorized had been prewritten.

Her husband cursed to himself as he made his way through the house. She heard him slam the back door shut. After she put the groceries away in the refrigerator, the house had become eerily quiet. She had been expecting to hear him enter, assail their son again. But instead, she smelled fire. She knew something was wrong.

She ran outside. His face glowed red in the heat of the flames that spat trails of black, tainting the sky with its signals of smoke.

He had found the painting—her pregnant with Ronald, her stomach a bulb of garlic from which sprung scapes out of her naval, her head on RJ's lap, who was holding his red apple. The loquat tree shaded them from behind the bench. A clear stream of water flowed where fish jumped and tadpoles swam instead of a city gutter. Two persimmon trees framed the scene in the foreground—one in winter, leafless and gray and sculptural, and the other in summer with its shiny green canopy. Visible root systems nearly mirrored the branches, intertwined in a cross-sectional diagram of the earth full of worms, insects, and bones.

He had found a metal trash can and thrown her work inside of it, incinerated her painting.

She screamed in a way that terrified even her, as if she were giving birth.

Everyone could hear her.

And second by second, she now knew exactly what had been happening to her body.

She counted the weeks, the months since she and John had last had sex. September or October, two or three months ago, before she had run into RJ, before she had hidden the bank deposit bag, the evidence that threatened his life. Her periods had been irregular before then, spots in her underwear. She craved miyeok guk because of the change in weather, she told herself.

But now, after he burned her art, she and he could not exist in this same world, this same house, no matter how much she loved her children. They were old enough to at least temporarily fend for themselves.

Let him eat the world. Let him choke on what he made.

And she knew exactly what must be done.

1999

On the afternoon of Christmas Eve, Ronald slept until noon and emerged out of the back door to check on the tree he had planted last night. The leafless persimmon shockingly glinted at him with at least a dozen CDs hung onto its branches like holiday ornaments, spinning in the breeze. His heart pounded as if they had just been the victim of some sort of vandalism or prank, or that aliens or the ghost of Jacob Hendricks or RJ himself had emerged to threaten them with this menacing image of metallic rainbows. What did it all mean? Didn't they have enough reasons to be afraid?

Ronald slipped on his father's broken outdoor slides, approached the glittering iridescence, a radiant sea, an oasis of light in their dusty and barren yard. But as he, step-by-step, closed the distance between him and the tree, he realized the CDs were simply those for free trials of AOL. Only his father would've saved them. Only his father would've done this to the tree, but for what?

Were they a form of protection? An omen? Or did he simply have a momentary lapse in judgment after the stroke? Maybe it had been a type of holiday decoration. They didn't get to put up their Christmas tree this year. But his father never really did anything for appearances. He cared only about the practical, the usefulness of objects and actions.

Did he think the flashing would scare away people? He remembered once after their house had been burglarized in the 1980s, his father had made a tape recording of barking dogs, played on repeat every time they left the house. His mother joked that it would be more effective for her to stay home all day and "mung! mung!" every time she heard a sound.

Regardless, Ronald grabbed the heavy green hose, always knotted or kinked, and heaved it to the tree, which he watered with a sense of pride. He imagined his mother, her arm wrapped around his shoulders as she had done the day of his middle school graduation in that photo by his bed. His mother and her hands, which would've planted the world for him, the hands that rubbed flakes of red pepper into cabbage, boiled and drained the noodles, the fingers that fed him.

He burst into tears as water from the hose splashed onto the gray toes of his socks.

What would he plant for her next?

His sister had said that she had sketch pads, old watercolors in the garage. He remembered the photorealistic flowers she drew at times—on napkins, even on placemats at Chinese restaurants. If he could identify what kind they were, source their seeds, starters, he could raise them here. If only he could find an expert, a botanist, since his father owned a nursery but didn't know much about plants. He could go to the library, borrow books. Dig and dig and dig between pages, in the dirt until he didn't hurt. And what would be left of him without pain? Maybe love. Simply, by itself. He imagined earthworms through the cage of his ribs, what would grow there, what could grow there now but a tomato vine or a dahlia, top-heavy and divine, Peggy's favorite flower.

He turned off the water, checked the garage door, which must have been unlocked since his sister had been inside. He himself hadn't gone into the garage in years, fearful of all that his mother had abandoned, all the hopes she had for herself, all that she had been proud of once. And now where was she? What did any of it matter now? But it did. It still mattered. He'd prove that she still mattered, yes, because she inspired him more than anyone, and there was still so much to learn about her, if only he were less afraid, less afraid of the truth of who she was.

Inside, the musty and vile odor of mold and mouse feces and paint thinner suffocated him like a plastic bag over his head. Had the smell gotten worse since his sister had been in there? He held the collar of his sweatshirt over his nose and mouth. Wary of stepping on poop, he switched on the flickering light and navigated the narrow spaces in between boxes and furniture. Cobwebs dangled everywhere like streamers thick from the spin of spiders, undisturbed. Why did they even bother keeping so much? They should give everything broken or forgotten away. But they had all been avoiding this place, this place where she, their mother, had stored all the things, kept all the people she wanted to be one day.

A pale blue pillowcase between boxes caught his eye. The color was familiar, the same shade as his father's pajamas. It reminded him of police uniforms on television.

He bent forward and yanked the fabric. He knew.

The dragging sound, the weight. The dark stain of blood.

Despite the smell, the air rushed in and out of him. He could almost faint. He leaned on one of the cardboard boxes and gripped the handle at the end of which he found the dirt-caked blade, clotted with that unmistakable shade of once red. Who would've placed the shovel here besides his father, the only one with the keys to the garage? And why hadn't his sister noticed this pillowcase when she had been inside there on Monday? Jacob Hendricks was dead. By gunshot. Rodriguez did say that the Explorer had been parked beside his house on Tuesday night. Could Jacob Hendricks have planted this? But it was *their* shovel, so that seemed far-fetched. RJ's death was an accident. Or was this the weapon that—

He needed to get out of the garage. He needed air. He gripped the shovel through the blue pillowcase out of fear that he might've been leaving fingerprints on it. He had to get rid of it. It was *their* shovel covered in blood. It was *theirs.* It was *them.*

Outside, he inhaled the deepest he could, as if he had been holding his breath the entire time, and shut the door behind him. He leaned the shovel against the side of the garage, sat on the concrete step, and lit a cigarette, hand shaking, with the red lighter that Rodriguez had given him. He nearly burned his thumb.

He could throw the shovel in a dumpster or off the side of a bridge into the river. He had to speak with his sister. After only a couple drags, he stubbed out his cigarette, left the rest of the pack and the lighter on the ground. He ran into her room, but it was empty. What day was it? Christmas Eve. He remembered now that she and Rhonda were going to meet Janet at the library to search the aisles, and they would come over to the house to speak with Priscilla afterward. Fuck. Nobody he knew had a cell phone. Maybe Rhonda, but he didn't have the number. The library. He could call the library. He could even run over there if he needed to. He reached for the phone, but then he heard his father's Eldorado creak to a stop in their driveway. "Fuck," Ronald yelled as he slammed the receiver down. His father had come back early from the nursery.

Ronald ran outside, nearly tripping on the sandals as he put them on.

"Dad, can we talk?" he yelled through the open driver's-side window. "In the back. I want to show you something."

"Later." His father still had the engine running. "Car make funny sounds."

"I need you to come with me now," Ronald said. The firmness of his own voice surprised him. A reversal of roles. How he sounded like a man. He stomped down the gravel path and he could feel his own father following him.

"Stop." His father's voice cracked. "I have to—"

"I found this in the garage." Ronald lifted the shovel in the pillowcase from where he had left it leaning against the wall.

His father's face appeared frozen in fear, then disgust. Ronald had never seen this expression, its depth of devastation, on his father before. A man who masked so much of his heartbreak with rage. His father tightened his lips, but he couldn't suppress how much he shook, bracing himself for the tears that would spill down his face. His father had believed himself to be a hardworking and honest man, a follower of rules, valiant and noble, much like the country itself, but he hadn't been truthful, had he?

He lied by omission. The violence had been literal. How could he do this to them?

He killed RJ.

It was *him*.

"You should put it in your car and take it to work, okay?" Ronald couldn't contain his disgust. But they needed to act quickly. Who knew when his sister and Rhonda would come back home?

"What?" his father asked as if Ronald spoke a foreign language that didn't at all make sense.

"The fuckin' shovel. Go. Now. Take the shovel. Ana and Rhonda will be back soon. Priscilla is coming over." Ronald tossed it at his father as if he were a dog. He couldn't control his own anger now. He knew that his father had been responsible for his mother's disappearance, and now this? He ruined everything he touched.

"Priscilla?" His father was confused and stunned.

"Go back to the nursery," Ronald yelled. "Get rid of it now." Who knew what had happened to his mother? "You've done enough," he shouted. He couldn't believe what had been happening, and the words simply burst from his mouth. He gritted his teeth. "Unbelievable. Now all we can do is save what we have left, right? What good would it do to get caught?"

1998–99

In front of the round grill of a samgyeopsal restaurant near Hongik University, Myunghwa flipped the delicate meat which smelled of delicious dripping fat as Sunhee remembered the fire her husband had built, the glow of the inside of the metal can, the sizzle and errant pop, as he burned her art. As a woman who had been a child in war, she had never before witnessed such wasteful personal behavior. Ironic considering how judgmental her husband had been of the rioters in 1992, who destroyed, yes, perhaps their own neighborhoods too. Yet what had she *actually* done to warrant such a strong reaction, this final act of her erasure? Did he find her imagination to be so threatening he couldn't even endure its product? Or was he unable to accept that she had an imagination at all, because surely he must've seen the image and realized that its intent had been fantastical, surreal?

And so he had reduced Sunny to dust.

After the flames died down on their own, and she had said, "I'll never forgive you," he went straight through the backyard to the front, climbed inside his car, and pulled away for who knows how long.

She thrust her hands into the bin, covering them in the ash that she would never be able to scrub off. She wiped them all over her clothes, went into the house, and smeared her fingerprints everywhere like a crime scene.

"*You* can clean it up," she yelled at no one.

Her daughter was gone. Her son had been growing more and more independent as he spent less time at home.

Her mother had been right. In an emergency, she might need her own money.

Yes, both her parents had died, but still she could find some comfort now back with her sister, who might need assistance settling all of their mother's affairs; and, of course, there was Myunghwa too. So much unfinished business. *That smear, the peachiness of it. As if the jar itself is a face, painted white, and someone had taken two fingers and simply removed the makeup right there.* Her funny kissing sound into the air.

Sunhee couldn't think of anyone she would rather be with right now, even if only temporarily, to get away from this place. She would miss her children, but she also knew that they would be okay.

I promise to visit you one day, Myunghwa had whispered. *Will you have space for me if I come?*

She'd never forgive her husband for this final act, an affirmation that she had been unsafe around him. She rubbed her forehead with the pads of her fingers, darkening the skin into gray like clouds full of rain. It was the water they so desperately needed.

As she sat on their bed, which she had made perfectly this morning, Sunhee realized that her husband must've misinterpreted the image of herself and RJ. Maybe he had assumed there had been something sexual between them, but couldn't he have seen that the painting that she had titled *The Intimacy of Strangers, or The Seasons* had been an homage to the interconnectedness of life in its different stages, the arbitrariness of labels and language in nature? Maybe that might seem immature or obvious to some, but it was *her* painting, and not intended for him as an audience. Otherwise, he wouldn't have been so offended.

But then again, maybe his lack of inclusion is what pained him the most, that he couldn't see himself, her art didn't revolve around him, nor this country, like everything else.

She had to trust herself this time. Follow no one. Lead the way.

She had hidden her emergency savings, split into five plastic bags, in the bottom of the succulent planters she kept at the front of the house—a jade plant, elephant bush, hedgehog aloe, Christmas and Easter cacti. She had to turn over and plop each one out in order to find the wads of cash, which totaled approximately ten thousand dollars that her mother had converted herself from won. Her son would be out of the house all day at least, so she could go to the travel agent where she had purchased her last ticket and secure a one-way for herself to Seoul. She could decide later when she'd return.

Who knew where her husband had gone? Probably back to the nursery where he could seethe by himself, pretend to "work." He had definitely been drunk, but she didn't care. Let him have his Crown Royal to himself.

She'd leave as soon as possible. Today, tonight. Right now.

She would need to call her sister and Myunghwa, but she could also do that at the airport as soon as she arrived. Neither of them would turn her away. She'd then write a letter to Ronald, let him know that she'd return. She wouldn't need to pack much, simply her passport and some toiletries, since they would both have clothes she could borrow. What would she do with RJ's belongings? She had to trust that her husband would never enter the scene of his crime again; that was his nature. The boxes could remain. The bank deposit bag she had hidden separately would also be safe.

She was confident that no one would, or could ever find it. And wherever RJ had gone, whether Vietnam or somewhere else, she felt she would be closer to him, or at least to who he was; she too refused to settle for a world that didn't want or bother to understand her. She would take control of her own story.

And now in Seoul, Myunghwa devoured her samgyeopsal, which she wrapped with matchsticks of scallions, pa muchim, in leaves of lettuce still wet from being washed. Sunhee had first spent a week with her sister in Gunpo, where their mother had lived too. She then moved to Myunghwa's elegant and art-filled two-bedroom apartment in Seoul's Hongdae neighborhood with its dance clubs, graffiti murals, and vintage stores. They had spent the afternoon at a clinic, surrounded by a bunch of teenagers, where she had determined she was three to four months' pregnant.

The last time she and her husband had sex must've been in August.

If she wanted an abortion, she'd have to go back to America. She couldn't legally get one in Seoul.

"Do you want to keep the child at all?" Myunghwa asked.

Despite how much she loved samgyeopsal, Sunhee couldn't eat any of the meat in front of her. She wasn't hungry these days and she picked at the kimchi instead, which satisfied her cravings for pickles. They had come to this restaurant because it was Myunghwa's favorite. Sunhee wanted to treat her friend for taking such good care of her.

"I'm too old," Sunhee said.

"For what?" Myunghwa smiled. "You're younger than me." She took another giant bite of lettuce, filling her mouth, but still spoke. "Want to raise the kid together? I'll be Daddy."

Sunhee laughed, almost spit out her water. "Unnie, my back hurts." As much as she missd her daughter and son, as much as she longed to feed and hold them, she had also been relieved that they were old enough to mostly fend for themselves. "I'm tired of taking care of everyone else. Really, they're cute for only . . . eh, half the time you have them. When they cry, their faces look all screwed up like . . . those shaman masks for exorcisms."

Myunghwa grinned as she chewed her food. Sunhee had noticed her mannerisms had changed after all these years, much less polite, and perhaps more like a man's? She had become relaxed in a different way, had abandoned her fancy Bukchon hanok for a much more urban lifestyle now. She would almost describe her as *punk*, or "punk-uh sty-uhl."

"And once again, my back," Sunhee said, rubbing her kidney for dramatic effect. "My whole body is different now."

"Of course. I look pregnant too," Myunghwa joked. "But I tell myself the past looks good on me." She lightly tapped her cheeks. "I'm healthy," she said in English.

Sunhee couldn't help but smile as she took a bite of the pa muchim, still fresh and crisp despite the deep nuttiness of the sesame oil and seeds. "I had honestly thought it was too late to get pregnant," Sunhee said. "That I was going through menopause. My periods have been so irregular the past couple years anyways. Who knew a halmeoni like me could get knocked up?" She patted her belly. "Did you see all those teenagers at the clinic? Rabbits, all of them."

"You're not even fifty years old!"

"You know what I mean," Sunhee said. "Halmeoni in spirit. I'm proud. It took me all these years to make the art, and the life I wanted, but I did it."

"I know where you can go if you'd like to get an abortion, where it would still be legal for you. And you wouldn't have to go back to America,"

Myunghwa said. "It would be safe. My assistant had gone herself. She even came back with a tan and a tattoo."

"China?"

"Vietnam," she said. "There are other countries also, nearby. A quick flight. I'd go with you. What else do I have to do? The gallery runs itself. Well, kind of." She sipped her beer. "I mean the economy has been terrible, so when you have few customers . . . everything kind of runs itself into the ground . . . or into the sky." Myunghwa shrugged, then crossed herself. "Whatever your religion."

Vietnam. Could RJ be there still? Sunhee had suspected he had fled there, but didn't know when or where exactly. He had mentioned an orphanage of some kind, but there must've been many. Nonetheless, her curiosity had been piqued.

"We could make it a *vacation*, unnie." Myunghwa laughed. "BEH-KAY-shion," she said in English as if she had been making fun of the language. "Christmas in Vietnam." She opened her eyes wide.

"Do we need a visa of some sort? Is there a way to get there without anyone knowing?"

"We could pay our way through," Myunghwa said. "I've done it before. Not for an abortion but . . . long story."

"I should write the kids a letter." Sunhee picked up her chopsticks again. Her appetite bloomed and she dabbled in the pork that Myunghwa had set aside for her on the grill. *Christmas in Vietnam.* It sounded like a movie or a musical.

"Yes, of course. Let them know. Let someone know that you are fine. You are here. Interpol can rest. You don't even have to tell them about our trip, or why. Is it good?" Myunghwa gestured toward the remaining meat.

"Delicious. Hard to find samgyeopsal like this in America." Sunhee filled a leaf of red lettuce with the samgyeopsal that she dipped in sesame oil, salt, and pepper, ssamjang, and pa muchim for the perfect bite that combined so many opposites—crispy and meltingly soft, cold and hot, dark and nutty with acidic and bright. She had become ravenously hungry. *CHRISTMAS. IN. VIETNAM.*

"Don't forget to chew," Myunghwa said.

After a few minutes, Sunhee paused, licking her teeth for any pieces of lettuce that might be stuck. She sipped from the glass of cold beer in front of her, which Myunghwa then filled for her with two hands, and released the loudest "Ahhh," from the back of her throat. She hadn't had alcohol in years, and her mind swayed like a drunk twenty-year-old in heels despite consuming only half of a tiny glass.

"I have a friend who said he would be going, but I don't know if he made it," Sunhee said. "He was in the war there, and he was planning on some kind of volunteer effort." She never mentioned to Myunghwa anything about the evidence she had hidden, or the subject of his writing. His secret was safe from everyone. "The friend from the painting."

"The one your husband burned?" Myunghwa asked. "It's a big country. I doubt we could find him, if that's what you're thinking."

"No." Sunhee smiled, eyes clouded with sadness. "Not quite. But it would be nice to go anyways. Who knows? He might still be in America."

"Was it romantic?"

Sunhee refilled Myunghwa's glass with the last of the beer. "No, not quite. I mean, yes, but not sexual. Does that make sense?"

"Of course. So many friendships are that way. A building or a landscape could even be romantic, but you don't want to have sex with it."

"Exactly. More of a feeling."

Sunhee imagined holding her children now. Ana was already an adult, but she would still comb their hair, kiss the tops of their heads if she could.

She loved their smells, the downiness that tickled her nose. How quickly they had grown. "I miss my children," she said.

"Of course." Myunghwa grew serious.

"But I have to figure out a way to change things. I want a divorce. But I'm not sure how I'd make it on my own in America."

"You'd find a way. You're resourceful," Myunghwa said.

"I'd still be here, you know. I'd stay if it weren't for my kids."

Myunghwa squeezed the top of Sunhee's hand, which Sunhee turned over to grip her back, their fingers laced in a prayer. How fortunate she had been to have her in her life, someone who understood and accepted her with such fullness, without judgment. Someone who could also make her laugh in the most dire of circumstances.

"Do you want to call them?" Myunghwa asked.

"I don't think I can," Sunhee said, overcome with a sense of helplessness. "What if he picks up the phone?"

"Hang up?"

"I'm scared that if one of them . . ." Sunhee shook her head. "Honestly, if I hear one of their voices, I won't be able to . . ."

"I think you're stronger than you realize," Myunghwa said. "You're quite fearless actually." Myunghwa squeezed her hand once more, but this time the tips of her fingers pressed into the flesh between Sunhee's knuckles, and she felt herself flush a little from her feet to her face, everywhere in the middle.

"Now, finish up this samgyeopsal before it gets cold," Myunghwa said. "And let's go for a walk in the snow. Not sure if they have that in Vietnam?"

When they had first arrived in Hanoi, Sunhee and Myunghwa spent the night in a hotel with two beds on creaky mattresses, sheets that smelled like laundry dried in the sun, her favorite, even if it meant a rooftop in the middle of a bustling city.

Even though Sunhee had spent many hours in her LA library, perusing the photographs of any books she could find on Vietnam, nothing could prepare her for the faces, the sights, the sounds, the street food, which delighted her and Myunghwa with its herbaceous acidity from cilantro, citrus, and tamarind, delicate long-simmered broths, and succulent cuts of beef and chicken. The city further surprised her with its Old Quarter, French architecture and shady villas with dark green foliage dripping from balustrades in the mild December weather. She had always imagined Vietnam to be wet, humid, and hot, lush with the giant leaves of prehistoric plants and the cathedrals of banyan trees, but there she delighted in the architecture, the work of human minds and hands, the layers of long histories in the infrastructure which had been mostly absent in bright but dull Los Angeles, city of concrete and dreams.

She couldn't help but feel like a rebel or renegade having paid off the border agents at the airport. She received her in-clinic abortion the next day, shockingly easy to obtain. There had been no counseling or shame. The vacuuming of her uterus had been treated as a medical procedure, a bit of housekeeping. Refreshing. And she had absolutely no attachment to what she knew, indeed, resembled a tiny child, because in her mind, she had simply been undergoing menopause the entire time, and her body had been a horrid, wretched inconvenience—constipated and nauseous.

What could this baby want from this world in which it would not have a stable mother and father, mentally and financially, and its siblings would already be adults? Why would she carry it to term if the risks had been too great at her age for both herself and the unborn?

And Sunhee could not possibly be someone else's mother. She barely even knew how to take care of herself.

After the procedure, she lay in her tiny bed for a day and slept for the first time in what seemed like months. She hadn't rested much, afflicated by insomnia, since she had seen RJ outside the market in October. She worried about him at night, and perhaps her anxiety over her inability to affect the outcome of his life, or their lives, compelled her to create art. Painting offered an escape, a release from what had come to feel like the confines of living inside her husband's dreams, his aspirations. She wanted more. She needed more. So she created that world for herself.

But now she realized how quickly even all of that could be taken away and destroyed.

Life had been meant to be lived on a scale too large to be on any canvas. Here, far away from any responsibility, her children, she felt present, all five of her senses alive. She indulged in the black coffee poured over cold glasses of condensed milk. At night markets, she slurped on long white noodles in clear beef stock simmered for hours, and devoured deep-fried prawn cakes. They snuck into a slick international hotel on the river and swam in the pool, blue from drinking the color of the sky. She loved this city—its buildings, its smells, its sounds, its people. She was a foreigner there, but there was always something to see or do; life overcame you. There was a sense of both danger and friendliness everywhere, from the scooters and motorbikes that almost ran you down to the smiles of strangers who greeted or offered you a small plastic seat. Maybe America was more safe in its consistency and its rules, but in many ways it felt less human. Here she watched as a child urinated on the side of a street near a dashing young man in áo dài on his way to a wedding. And all of it made complete sense.

In their room, they lay on their backs in bed, arms splayed, doughy waistlines from all that new food, and they did not care how they appeared at all. They loved their bodies exactly the way they were, these bodies that had not only endured and survived the machinations of men and children, but had been fed and flourished under a different light, the generous gaze of themselves when free from the pressures of competition, the pitting of one against the other to prove their worth, which left them with a constant feeling of inadequacy. But they and life too could be abundance itself. The breeze from outside, the fan above, caressed their bare tan legs, which had grown ashy, but they never bothered to lotion them. Now this was how it must've felt to not be looked at, to focus on simply what one felt, the present.

"My back is killing me, but I'm so relaxed." Sunhee transitioned to the floor mat made out of a woven golden plastic that resembled traditional straw. She thought of the squeak of the mattress that she hated so much when she had first moved to America, but through the years, she had grown accustomed to its ebb and flow, the bodies tilting like canoes. How she had missed the ground beneath her, the heat of the ondol, which soothed her. She closed her eyes.

"Are you afraid you might not see him again?" Myunghwa asked, a question out of nowhere. "RJ. I hope he is okay regardless."

"Me too," Sunhee said.

"What would you do if you did run into him again?" Myunghwa turned on her side to face her. "How would you explain all that has happened?"

"I don't know."

Outside their window, two women laughed out loud and Sunhee could imagine them, arm in arm, lips painted a matching red. The neighbor's green parrots squawked at each other from inside their separate cages. Cars honked and scooters zoomed by on the street, wet with some kind of runoff from a hydrant or hose that leaked. Myunghwa did not move at all, and after a few minutes, Sunhee assumed she had fallen asleep. She adjusted herself on the floor, resting the side of her face on her elbow.

"Are you in love with him?" Myunghwa asked.

Sunhee remained suspended in the silence as if trapped in the amber of the room, its resin of dull light.

"No," she said. "I used to think I was. But it's something else."

Myunghwa didn't respond.

"He's like a brother. He made my life better. I learned a lot from him."

And there had been so much she didn't actually know about him, and never would. She remembered his face when she saw him last, the things he'd said. In reality, she probably meant less to him than he meant to her. He probably had many friends. Maybe he loved many women. But it didn't matter. She accepted this now. And she'd hold on to what he had given her forever.

What would she even say to him besides thank you? *Thank you for giving me something to look forward to other than my children. Thank you for anchoring me to the life we had. You helped build me to be this person, the person I've always wanted to be. Brave. Even if it meant I might feel so alone and misunderstood. It was all worth it in the end.*

Tears slid down the side of her face as she turned toward the ceiling where the fan spun, and she relaxed into the sometimes sweetness of being sad. She listened to the voices outside, the language of all the people who attempted to speak with her and Myunghwa as they passed by. The two of them stood out as foreigners, of course, simply by their clothing, their postures, their demeanors. They were Koreans after all.

"Do you like it here?" Myunghwa asked.

"I do."

"What do you like most about it?"

"I feel alive. Even in this tiny room."

Myunghwa laughed. "It's a good cage." She tossed her pillow at Sunhee.

"Anything is better than dead."

For a minute they paused, uncomfortable with that word suspended in the air.

"Do you feel dead?" Myunghwa asked.

"Not now. But I have. Sometimes."

"Is it that bad for you? There?"

She nodded her head.

"I am sure your family loves you. Everyone loves you."

Sunhee broke down. She couldn't help herself. It wasn't heartache but beauty that had overwhelmed her right now.

"I'm sorry you feel that way," Myunghwa said.

After a minute, Sunhee could feel a calmness and sense of clarity overtake her, as if all that crying had cleared the path between her mind and her mouth. "Sometimes I think it's guilt, guilt over the ones who died. Shame. Other times, I think it's because we work so much. We deny ourselves so much in our everyday lives. We need to survive, and yet surviving might be what is killing us."

"It's been hard for you. It's hard for immigrants."

"But I have been so lucky. I have a house, a husband, a home, two healthy children."

"I know," Myunghwa said. "But everyone is different. Not everything is for everyone." Myunghwa sighed as if unbuckling herself. "I'm happy to be here now. I'm happy to be here . . . with you."

Sunhee didn't respond.

"I feel like it was meant to be somehow," Myunghwa said. "Like we're in some kind of movie, but it's us—two fat ahjummas in Vietnam."

Sunhee laughed and could imagine the smile on Myunghwa's face now, the corner of her mouth curved.

"And when we go back home, I'll remember that we did this," Myunghwa said. "I'll hold on to this for the rest of my life."

Sunhee steadied herself, observed the beating of her heart, which she could feel in her throat. They were so far from everyone now. They had practically become different people who had rewritten their lives, even if only temporarily. Myunghwa was more than a sister. She would always keep her secrets with tenderness and care, and she expected the same. She had proven this, time and time again through the years. "There's space beside me," Sunhee said. "The floor is much more comfortable than those old beds." She held her breath. "Come here."

Sunhee wouldn't, couldn't say that ever again.

The mattress squeaked below Myunghwa as she lowered her feet to the ground. How delicate they were, tendons flexed beneath the hardness of all these years—or rather, what these years had done to us, Sunhee corrected herself. She reached forward like the branch of a tree where it found light, and touched the skin that shined with the tips of her fingers. Myunghwa kneeled beside her in the cramped space between their beds and took her hand in both of hers, as if she had been comforting someone who had been ill. Sunhee's mouth was dry. She swallowed the saliva underneath her tongue as Myunghwa lifted a knee to straddle her and kissed her, long hair undone, sweeping Sunhee's face. She grabbed the back of her head. Myunghwa collapsed onto her, as if stepping into a river without having prepared for its depth. Here on the floor, with Myunghwa, Sunhee became herself, or another self, a self that she had thought had been missing or dead. There was no longer the sheet covering their heads as in Magritte's *The Lovers*. She was the fabric itself, which she imagined drifting in the dark water. Some kind of magic kept her on the surface, rushing and rushing over stones, fallen leaves, and twigs swirling, toward an outlet—the lake, the ocean, the dam that would break at the sound of herself crying *unnie* at the end.

Leaning her head on Myunghwa's shoulder, Sunhee rocked with the gentle motions of the bus on the final leg of their journey to Dandong with her eyes closed, fighting through her nausea, the travel sickness she shared with none other than her daughter Ana. She remembered the times she had tried to hold her, as they sat in the backs of cars, fighting not to throw up. How much she longed to wrap her arms around her now, the feel of her downy hair on her face, the herbaceous smell of the shampoo she loved, her little duckling, the way her tiny bob had always curled up and out like precious tail feathers when she was young.

But in reality, Ana would not want to be held at her age now like a child. She had grown into a woman and found public displays of sentimentality to be immature and unfashionable. Perhaps when Sunhee had lost her grip on Ana and knew Ronald would be next, she had been propelled to leave her, leave them behind. With Myunghwa by her side, she felt full in a different way, that if she died today, she would know that she had endured, her truest self, even if only privately between the two of them.

She hadn't thought about art much these past several months. Art had been a safety net on which she could fall back, over and over again, but which ultimately kept her from launching herself. She didn't need the trapeze, or the circus; she needed cliffs from which to dive, to plunge into the water of desire, the truth of her feelings fulfilled. There were artists and there were people like her who viewed art as a hobbyist's escape. In order for her to become good enough to paint like her father, she'd have to practice, day after day. She'd have to work too hard, and in reality, she loved this life too much.

She loved this *love* too much. Myunghwa had made this possible.

They had started their travels two weeks ago by taxi and then transferred to the back of a covered truck which smelled, despite how hard it had been cleaned to disguise itself, of the undeniably human acridness of vomit, urine, and feces. In the darkness, Sunhee threw up into doubled-up plastic bags for six hours until they found themselves gasping for air with about a dozen others, in a dark forest where they then each clung to the the backs of motorbikes. She had regretted her decision to visit Dandong, a Chinese city on the border of North Korea, but she couldn't share this with Myunghwa, who had endured this trip alongside her. She would never hear the end of it. Besides, Myunghwa had other things on her mind since they would be leaving Vietnam for an indefinite amount of time straight from Beijing after Dandong, to take care of Myunghwa's mother in Seoul, who had become ill.

One of the dishwashers at the Chinese restaurant in Hanoi where they worked, a young man in his twenties who went by the American name of Johnny, had inspired these travels months ago. Sunhee had gone out to have a cigarette by herself in the alley behind the restaurant. In his stained white tank top and loose dark gray pants held up on his skinny frame with a leather belt, he stood there smoking one of his own, puffing interminably like a chimney, or steam locomotive. She realized she had forgotten her lighter and asked him for a match in Korean. He held the flame down low, close enough so that she could reach with the tip of her cigarette in her mouth and the heat touched her nose.

"Ahjumma, where are you from?" he asked.

"Seoul by way of Los Angeles."

"Los Angeles?"

"Yes." She laughed. A cloud escaped from her lips, stung her eyes.

"Why would you live *here*?"

"You mean, paradise?" She swept her arm toward a long brown rat that scurried at a short distance from them. "Because I'm happy," she said.

"I guess, you seem happy. You're always singing and humming and dancing. You and the other lady. Your sister? Is she from Hollywood too?" She loved the way the syllables of Hollywood sounded in his mouth: *Ho-ree-ood*.

"It's as good as it'll get." She flicked the ash from her cigarette. "What about you? Where are you from?"

"Pyeongyang."

"Pyeongyang? I thought I heard a bit of an accent," she said. "How did you get here?"

"Special delivery." He cracked a smile, but something rich and thick like sadness, or maybe even regret, beckoned from his eyes. He must have escaped North Korea through China and Vietnam. But was he stuck? Or did he love it here like herself? Why wouldn't he find a way to make it to South Korea?

"I was born there," she said. "In Pyeongyang. But my family left during the war."

"And you survived? The Americans didn't kill you?" he asked.

"No, not literally."

"We thought they murdered the people who fled, women and children, grandmothers with napalm, machine guns," Johnny said. "They have no mercy. This is why we've always hated them so much."

"Some people were killed, yes," she said. "Some were killed by Americans, some by Koreans like us. It's complicated. But war is always horrible. One person killing another. Brother against brother." She took a drag of her cigarette and held the smoke inside her lungs as long as she could until she felt light-headed. "I would like to visit one day," she said.

"There are ways," Johnny said.

She nodded as the cigarette burned down closer to her fingers. She always like the threat of the heat there.

"Do you feel *free*?" she asked.

"Not really." He laughed. He puffed on his cigarette. His boyish face reminded her of Ronald, how much he yearned to be an adult, a man, when Sunhee, internally, begged, *You'll have your whole life to be an adult. Stay small for as long as you can.* And now she wished more than ever to see him before that happened to him. He would be eighteen years old next year.

She had mailed letters to him and his sister. She had used Myunghwa's apartment, which her gallery assistant had been house-sitting, as a return address so that her husband wouldn't assume they were from her, and possibly destroy them.

But she never heard back.

She knew she should call, but what if her husband picked up the phone? And in a way she had become terrified that perhaps her son didn't want to speak with or have anything to do with her. Could he ever understand that here she could be, oddly enough, in this very foreign country, herself? She once believed she would literally do anything for her children, until she realized the one thing she would not do is surrender to the prolonged and certain death of living as someone else. But how could she explain this to them without creating doubt about whether or not she loved them?

She had tried to call him once. On his birthday.

Ronald would most likely have been off from school, but in the afternoon, the phone line had been busy. In the evening after dinner, her husband picked up, and she froze. She couldn't respond to his "hello," tired and raspy. And then, in the background, she heard Ronald's voice: "Can I use the internet when you're done?" The ordinariness of his language confirmed that they not only still lived in that house and received her letters, but that they had also moved on.

"There's a city by the border," Johnny said. "If you go through China, there's a river and a bridge. You could get very close to the North that way. If you ever want to. People swim in that river. Maybe you and your 'sister' should make a visit someday." He winked. "It's romantic like in the Dramas. I do love a good Drama."

In Dandong, Sunhee and Myunghwa checked into a hotel, and both took the longest showers imaginable because it had literally been weeks since their last bath. Her heart raced knowing how close they were to her birthplace, her ancestors. They squeezed on their matching black swimsuits, donned their largest visors to sit on the sand. Sunhee watched as Myunghwa pulled the straps of a wide, flowing dress over her shoulders, and she slapped Myunghwa's behind like a farm animal's.

"Ahjumma, you are looking nice today."

Myunghwa laughed before she blew her a kiss.

How being with each other had been the most accomplished Sunhee had ever felt in her life. How strange, even after having two children that she would feel this way. Now was her time for love, for the end of longing. The fulfillment of their togetherness. It could be true. It was true.

It had been nine months since her husband John had burned her art, since she had escaped death there. Her daughter would've graduated from college already, her son from high school soon. She had been gone that long. Her children must think she was dead. But how could she leave Myunghwa now? Even though they, immigrants and outsiders, possessed so little, dining on top of plastic crates as tables, and Sunhee worked so many hours, since she had blown through most of her mother's money and didn't want to rely financially on anyone, Sunhee felt as if with Myunghwa, the world belonged to her still. Myunghwa understood all that made her laugh, preferred sleeping and eating on the floor as they did in Korea. They didn't have time to make art and it didn't matter so much, because life itself had been beautiful, rich, and whole. Staring into her eyes before they kissed, the feeling of Myunghwa's lips against hers, her hands on her face, on her neck, ripened her into being. It had been strange to think that all the things they said about love, in stories, in the movies, could be true, that it could derange you, make you commit formidable and dangerous acts, might even kill you, but it could be worth it. Who knew she was such a romantic after all?

She would return one day to Los Angeles, but she wouldn't surrender to the same life that she'd known back then. And beforehand, she needed to at least glimpse the land behind the border—not the DMZ with its touristy rigidness and spectacle of barbed wire and weapons pointed at each other. She yearned to meet more of her people, understand how they truly lived. This felt like freedom to her.

On the beach by the river, Sunhee peeled Myunghwa mandarin orange after orange. She couldn't get enough of the fruit that they had bought at a local market. She behaved as if she had scurvy. Gesturing across the river, Sunhee asked, "How many of your family is there?"

"My brother. My little brother was too young and sick to travel with us." Myunghwa wiped the juice that had squirted onto her leg. "He stayed with my uncle, my mother's brother. So my little brother and my uncle. Who knows where they are."

"Do you think we are breathing the same air?"

"As them? We always are," Myunghwa said. "No matter how far we go."

In the sun, without any umbrella, and only their large visors on their heads, they sweated and baked. They rose, holding each other's hand for support, and dipped themselves in the water, which smelled of diesel, up to their thighs, and after a minute or two, their waists. Despite the blazing heat, the river was ice cold. Myunghwa sang "Here Comes the Sun," and they, two ahjummas, soft yet strong in their stomachs and arms, danced like drunk teenagers together. Sunhee splashed herself and they shimmered, baptized by light except there was no religion here, only the kinship of being together. They painted themselves like they had just discovered water.

Sunhee tossed her hat, which landed on the edge of its brim and rolled to safety ashore. She held her breath and dove down as deep as she could. Who knew how far she could go? But she felt pure and new as if it were her first bath.

She heard Myunghwa call her name with a strange clarity, as if her tongue filled her ear.

She opened her eyes to ribbons of light in the murky gray-brown water, part emerald with webs of algae. A school of fish darted by, glinted like a cloud of knives. A warning. Until at the cracks of gunshots and screams, she inhaled the river. She struggled to stand on her feet. But there was no bottom. Her left leg burst into flames and she screamed as she tasted blood like a child as it entered the world. Memory shredded into confetti. Her past blew away like flecks of green grass mown.

1999

"You should put it in your car and take it to work, okay?" His son held the shovel in the blue pillowcase. John had almost fainted at the sight—the stain of another man's life on it, the shame that John had brought upon this house. The anger in his son's face now, the downturned corners of his mouth.

Whenever Jung Ho had cried, his father had yelled, sometimes struck him on the side or back of his head, released sprays of stars behind his eyes until Jung Ho became too terrified to feel anything besides rage. He could never remove the metallic taste of blood on his tongue, even after his gums had receded so badly that he lost most of his teeth and wore dentures. The joints of his fingers ached, but how else to survive war—not through sadness or heartache or grief—but a never-ending cycle to feel something through a violence, detonations like freedom.

And now John, a man, had sworn he'd tried his best. Yet he had failed them all.

"Go. Now. Take the shovel." Ronald tossed it onto the ground. The sound of the handle as it hit the concrete cracked open the past two weeks, this year—no, this entire life from the day he said goodbye to himself, goodbye to Jung Ho whom he had left behind with a mother that had been his home. Memory flooded him, poured down his face, and his shirt became wet.

When the stranger said her name out loud—"Sunny. Is Sunny here?"—he could not imagine the layers of a man's life—a daughter, a family, a job—when all John could think about was his wife in the foreigner's mouth. The two syllables asserted the most painful truth, that he not only grieved people, Sunny and his mother and his siblings in the North, but that he grieved the person that he could've become if he hadn't lost them, if he had more fully known them. He hadn't escaped. He had abandoned them.

And after he had said her name, the stranger turned to flee, and Jung Ho raised, then slammed, the blade of the shovel down. The air was like a knife plunging inside his lungs. He needed only to strike once, gasped for relief, and the dark fume-filled cave of his mind collapsed. There was no light. There was only death, two men trapped—one dead and one alive named John.

Because it was still his yard. His property. RJ, the intruder.

This was America after all.

John had grabbed the shovel and the envelope on the ground near the stranger. A messenger.

He entered the garage where he found an old blue pillowcase in a tightly wrapped bundle of bedding and towels. *Sunny. Is Sunny here?* No, no, she was not. He didn't know who Sunny was. What had she been doing all those years? How had she gotten pregnant before she disappeared? How could she have gotten pregnant by this man, dirty and slumped on his side?

The week that she had disappeared, yes, she had been making Ana's favorite foods in preparation for her visit, but she had also been consuming—what else?

Miyeok guk almost every morning. He knew what that meant. How old was she? They didn't think it was possible. How many times had they had sex in those months? Once, twice?

So after their fight about Ronald, his truancy and lack of interest in school, which he partially blamed on her neglect of him, the intensity of her interest in her own art, he went outside into the garage and discovered the image only she could've made—Sunny and a man he didn't know or even recognize then.

In her final painting, she lay on a bus bench pregnant with his child, her head in his lap.

He had found an old metal trash can, shoved the canvas inside, and doused it in thinner. The noxiousness made him dizzy. Destroy the proof. A bastard. Everyone would know. He wouldn't raise another man's child. How many more humiliations could he take in this one life? He remembered a young woman who appeared to be bleeding to death from her vagina on the side of the road. Her exposed breasts covered in bruises and the blood of her face broken as she wailed, and what could he do? He could see her pulling herself along the ground toward a tree, gnarled and charred black. She had been crawling to her dead child who had been murdered. He had the urge to carry her at least to her daughter so that she could spend her final moments with her. But when he dropped his bag on the road, his father slapped him on the back of the head in an explosion of stars. He bit down on his tongue as he fell to the ground. "Idiot," his father said. "Do you want to die like her? I'll kill you if that's what you want. I'd have one less mouth to feed."

Women would always be the first casualty. Women and their useless children.

All he could've known of her might've been in the painting that he had burned, but he couldn't stand to look at it knowing that it didn't include him, that there had been no room for him inside of it. He couldn't find himself—neither Jung Ho nor John—in its story at all.

None of it had been recognizable to him, and something had exploded like a bomb inside his heart.

The man in the painting had been anonymous until this past week, when he came back into their lives again.

RJ. Ronald Jones himself.

RJ had come back for her.

His son now stood before him, gritted his teeth and fumed. "You've done enough. Unbelievable. Now all we can do is save what we have left, right? What good would it do to get caught?"

He grabbed the shovel still in its pillowcase, heavy with dirt and blood.

Inside the garage, the fumes, the mildew and mold, struck him in the face, left a smear of a disgusted expression on his mouth. He lay the shovel on the ground, and twisted the cap off a bottle of turpentine. The smell of pine, pungent and clingy, reminded him so much of both Sunny and the gas station where he had worked all those years to save and prove himself to a father that still hated him, to a country that still hated him, to a family that still hated him.

Splashing the liquid as far as he could, he knew exactly what to do.

He felt a hand on his arm. His son's face appeared so much like Sunny's now, and he tipped the thinner onto his son's shirt. Horrified, Ronald ran out of the garage.

John's head throbbed, and the walls spun around him. He could barely feel his feet anymore. He had become all knees and elbows.

Nauseous and light-headed, John emerged like a deep-sea diver, gasping for air. The CDs on the persimmon tree glinted and glared, dappling his vision with the promise of "free hours." The clock was always ticking. He couldn't get the sound out of his head now. He barely even remembered hanging the CDs up on the twiglike branches at the crack of dawn this morning to ward off any vermin.

Time would always cost something. This internet had doomed them into nothing, a zero-zero. There wouldn't even be anyone left to remember them, to study them in museums, or read their books, their stories. And he realized that years ago, when he had quit graduate school, given up on literature, he had given up on life itself. Unless she had gotten rid of them, all of his books must've been in the garage too—from his favorite Shakespeare (*Macbeth* and *King Lear*) to the occasional Russian in translation. *Crime and Punishment*. Stories about extraordinary men who had been doomed.

He stepped on his son's packet of Marlboro Lights and picked the red lighter off the ground beside his shoes, still muddy from work. He lit one of the crushed cigarettes in his mouth.

The sun in its long descent blanketed the earth in a plate of gold.

As soon as Ronald emerged, hair wet and clinging to the sides of his face, John threw his cigarette, almost down to its nub, into the garage and shut the door.

His son froze, eyes wide, the terror. *Burn it down,* he thought. *Burn this all down.* The stacks of smoke would rise like a message to all the missing. The garage, a stick of incense. Purify this space. Make it clean. The contents of the garage popped like corn. "What the fuck," Ronald yelled. He ran into the house again and returned with the small fire extinguisher they kept by the stove. John grabbed his arm as he sped past. But his son yanked himself free and kicked down the door from which he sprayed as he choked and coughed.

John wept as he sat in the dirt. His wife's burning art, the odors, the heat on his flesh, seared into his head.

Did she ever have the child? Did she raise her or him in Korea?

Did she want to come back?

He was a coward for having thrown all her letters away.

A week after she had disappeared, as soon as he had seen her writing, the painfully crafted capital letters of her hand in English, her children's names—ANA AND RONALD KIM—the postmark, he had torn the envelope in half, then in half again until he had nothing but the scraps of her in his hands, in the recycling bin. *That's where she belongs,* he thought. He didn't want to know what she had been thinking, whether or not she had been seeking forgiveness, nor did he want Ana and Ronald to find out their mother had abandoned them to birth and raise the child of another man.

Some things would be better left unsaid or unknown forever. If she wanted to repair their family, she would have to return, flesh and bone herself. She had her sister, her sister's family in Korea still. He had so little. He had no one—no siblings, no parents. He had no one but this one life he had made to break over and over again.

And she had escaped to the one place where he wouldn't chase her.

He hated that country now.

For half a year, foreign envelope after envelope arrived to be destroyed by him.

Until the summer, then the letters stopped.

And then on Ronald's birthday in June, the phone rang after dinner.

When John answered it, he heard only static and breathing on the line.

His son, who had been in the kitchen, appeared. "Can I use the internet when you're done?"

John shook his head.

"It's my birthday," Ronald said.

John waited for a few more seconds until the person hung up.

He knew it was Sunny. Ever since that day, almost six months ago, he waited, he waited for her to call again, as he watched his Korean shows in the living room. As his son now hosed down the inside of the garage and destroyed unburned contents with water, John realized that the only thing that made him an extraordinary man was the spectacular ways that he had failed. He never meant to hurt RJ, but still he would be punished. He should be punished. But how? How could he pay for his crimes without hurting his children anymore? They had been innocent, as innocent as any human in this wretched world could be. There would still be a future if we allowed them to be full-throated, full of song.

"Sunny. Is Sunny here?" John said, an echo of RJ's voice, shocking himself.

The spray nozzle clinked on the ground.

Beside his daughter Ana, Rhonda stooped, exasperated, worn down.

Ana coughed in the dark smoke and the pop of the contents like corn inside the garage. He had done this to them. When the cigarette had departed from his hand, when he had ignited the gas, the fumes inside the garage, he experienced the bluster of a fire which could be extinguished, he knew, unlike the head full of flames, the ashtray of a heart inside his chest. He had been ruined and he ruined where he went. That was why he was so tired all the time. It took a lot for a man to not love himself.

"What happened?" Ana asked.

Neither John nor Ronald knew how to explain. What did any of it matter now? His wife's art and supplies had been destroyed. Who knew what survived?

Rhonda covered her face with her hand, rubbed the space between her brows.

"Were you smoking back here?" Ana asked.

His eyes met his son's, soft and maybe forgiving. The grace of a child still in him.

"Yeah," Ronald said. How much his son yearned to save him. Tears filled his eyes. Just as John had wanted to save *his* father, the most valuable person in their family, the one who carried the knowledge, the resources to survive any government, the one who carried the family and its name, its histories, burdens, and fortunes.

"Thank God, you didn't . . . burn the house." Ana struggled to catch her breath. "Fuck. Do we need to call the fire department?"

"No, no," John and Ronald said together, a chorus.

"Are you sure it's out?"

"Yes," Ronald said, shaking his head. "I tried . . . I tried."

"I know, Ronald. I know." Ana held him close. Several inches taller than her, still he seemed to fold inside her arms. How much stronger she was than both of them, father and son. Because she always had to be, just like her mother, to keep their family together. None of this would've happened if Sunny were still here. Maybe none of this would've happened if Sunny had had the chance to name herself.

"I tried . . . I wanted to . . . I was going through Mom's stuff to find out what . . . she would've wanted back here." Ronald appeared both confused and surer of himself than he had ever been before. "I wanted to keep planting stuff for her."

Ana burst into tears. "I know how hard that was. I know it took a lot to go inside the garage." She wiped her face with the back of her hand. "I know this sounds ridiculous because you probably almost killed yourself and burned down the house but . . . I'm so proud of you?"

"Dad and I will take care of things out here. Salvage what we can."

"Priscilla will be here soon," Ana said.

Priscilla. John had forgotten about her. What had these kids been up to now? The humiliation. The clawing sensation in his chest.

How had they contacted her? What did she have to do with this? What had he done?

By going to the police station, against Rhonda's wishes, he had brought Priscilla into his life, their lives, and now they couldn't remove themselves from the mess he had revealed, the past, the history of why RJ had been fired, how he had ended up without a house and dead behind their home. His plan to prove RJ's culpability had backfired.

"Did you find anything at the library?" Ronald asked.

"Nothing." Ana coughed. The smoke from the fire irritated his lungs and eyes too. "I still don't . . . I can't understand what Mom was supposed to . . . go to Janet for. Was she supposed to drop off something?"

What could they do now to save themselves but move on? Move on from RJ, from this mess with the police. John remembered the paperwork he had begun drafting, the questions he had begun answering for his last will and testament. He would fix things there. He'd get the final word and then they'd understand what had happened, and how much he was willing to pay for it.

"*Drop off* what?" Rhonda looked confused. "At the library?"

"With Janet." Ana's voice broke.

"I thought we were looking for his book," Rhonda said.

"We were." She paused. "We are. It's just . . . oh, fuck it."

"Ana, wait—" Ronald begged.

But her words were already rushing out in a torrent. "I found this letter in our trash, torn. Your father had written it. It was a letter to my mother. Your father was . . . coming by our house . . . to pick up something. It was also asking my mom . . . to find Janet."

"What?" Rhonda appeared as if she had just been slapped in the face.

The envelope with "Sunny Kim" on it.

But it was too late for Ana to take back her words, just as it had been when she had revealed that RJ and their mother had taken her and Ronald to the Observatory as children. *Maybe RJ appreciated her. Maybe she liked her feelings. Maybe she wanted to feel something. Unlike you.*

"So my mother, she has, or *had* something of his," Ana said.

"What?"

"From what I can tell, it was some kind of evidence against Jacob, or maybe an officer, someone Jacob knows or was working with. This is what Jacob must've been looking for the night that he was in our backyard. Your father must've left it with my mother. He was traveling and couldn't—"

"And no one was going to tell me?"

"Priscilla was going to tell us. She *is* going to tell us."

"Why didn't you tell me about the letter earlier?" Rhonda said, voice trembling, tears now running down her face. "Do you still have it?"

Ana glanced at her brother and then stared straight into John's eyes, and he could sense an apology from her. She was asking him for forgiveness now. But she didn't need to, no, because she had been right all along. *They* had been right all along. It was he who should beg for mercy, some form of grace at the end of this world he had worked so hard to build.

"I saw my father rip up the letter . . . and throw it into the trash," Ana said.

She knew what those words meant. Everyone did. And there was no place to hide now.

"Where did you get it?" Rhonda asked John.

"It was, uh . . . next to your father." His legs wobbled beneath him. "On ground."

"And you didn't show it to the police? Or anyone? You just took it?"

"My wife's name on envelope," he said, gulping the saliva in his mouth. The envelopes he had intercepted for half of a year, the envelopes with his children's names on them. He destroyed those, too. "Her name on envelope. It . . . belong to me."

"No, it didn't," Rhonda said.

Ana placed her hand on Rhonda's shoulder. "I'm sorry."

Rhonda brushed her away. "All of you get to decide what belongs to you when it works for you, right? And then you throw it away once you're done. But you don't realize whose life you're fucking with when you do that. You don't realize whose life you're throwing away. My father's life. My life." She pointed to herself. "When did you get to decide that it was your letter?" she asked John. "When did you get to decide that you didn't have to tell me about it?" she asked Ana. "I thought you were helping me."

The smoke fumes from the garage spread.

"You should've told me about the letter," Rhonda said. "You weren't trying to help me. You were trying to control the story and how it made you and your family look."

Ana shook her head. It was partially true, yes, but John also knew Ana and that she genuinely did care for RJ and Rhonda. And she also loved him. She loved her father. It had been her instinct to protect him. She had made a mistake, but that didn't define who she was.

"This is my whole life you fuck with to save your precious selves. You really do think you're more valuable than us, don't you? More useful? Harder working? More deserving?"

Ana covered her face.

"Let me tell you something. All you do is work so you can prove you're something in this country, but you're left just the same as me—broken and without a family. Is this what a family is to you? Did you all just agree to the same thing, the same lie, the same things you'll ignore, to keep the peace? Peace for what? Keep your version of peace to yourself." Rhonda stepped toward John, pressed her finger in the center of his chest. He froze, unable to move, but also terrified that she'd strike him. And he deserved it. "I always knew it was you." She backed away, folded her arms across her chest. "There was something between my father and your wife. And you couldn't stand it, could you? You were disgusted. And now that he's dead, you get the final words, don't you?"

Ana cried while her brother held her around her shoulders. John slumped down onto the concrete, exhausted, unable to hold himself up. He placed his head between his knees and stared at his feet, the sneakers. What else had he taken? He had spent his whole life trying to survive by filling the emptiness inside of him, the emptiness that came from having so much of your existence determined for you. His spirit had been wiped out long ago, but he was not clean. His hands were dirty.

And he made everyone around him suffer for it.

"Hey, are you back here?" A voice rang out. "Hola. Hello? I brought you some tamales." Priscilla carried a Pyrex casserole dish covered in foil with one hand and her white cane in the other. "They're chicken and cheese . . . for the vegetarians." She shrugged.

Rhonda exhaled out loud. "Oh my God," she said, shaking her head.

"Is this a bad time?" Priscilla asked.

No one knew what to say. John's heart could take only so much.

"Rhonda?" Priscilla tucked her cane under her arm and extended her hand. "Is that you?"

"Yes."

"I have so much to tell you." Tears filled her eyes. Priscilla appeared both worn down and relieved to be there. How John had fooled himself into believing he could unburden her. *He* was the one who needed help.

"I've been . . . I want to do what your father would've wanted. And, oh God . . . I want you to know how much he loved you."

Rhonda nodded, her face full of both pain and gratitude. "I understand you've been . . . going through a lot yourself, that it hasn't been safe for you?"

"I tried to be safe all these years and look where it got me, right? Could someone get these?"

Ana took the casserole dish from her.

Priscilla gathered herself, pushed hair away from her face. "He had film and tape recordings. There was a death, the murder of a young woman. He had evidence. RJ." She shook her head.

"Tape recordings?" Ana asked.

"There was a whole group of guys, officers, for years—and no one did anything to stop them." Priscilla caught her breath. "They worked with a few landlords. They threatened people with eviction, took money from them, or even sex so they could stay . . . so that the people could stay in their homes. It was mostly immigrants, Mexican, Central Americans. A lot of them didn't know their rights, or they were undocumented so they were very afraid. All of this went as far as back as the nineteen seventies."

"Oh my God." Rhonda covered her mouth.

John's face tingled.

"The officers . . ." Priscilla continued, "they would sometimes laugh and joke about the families who lost their homes. Children." She wiped her face on her sleeve. "They called themselves the Crusaders." The word seemed to disgust her. "One day this young lady . . . was killed. They found her body in the river."

John's entire body shook. The story sounded familiar yet he couldn't quite place it.

"Everyone thought she was just another victim, you know? Another victim of one of the serial killers. It was that gruesome."

"When was this?" Rhonda asked.

"The early eighties. It was in the newspaper, the girl's death. It was a strange time and it was easy to blame such a terrible crime on all the serial killers. They seemed to be everywhere. But . . ." Her face flushed red. "But RJ had been— He'd been investigating things himself, and he was waiting for the right moment to come forward."

"While he was a janitor?"

"Yes. Rhonda, he always wanted to be a reporter, and he gathered all the evidence. He'd even taken pictures of some of the officers going into people's apartments . . . for hours. Without warrants." Priscilla closed her eyes. "He recorded one of them bragging. About torturing, killing the girl. That's how sick these guys were."

"He told you all of this?" Rhonda asked.

"I was one of a few people who had heard the guys talk about the families they bullied. One day . . . I spoke with RJ about how much I hated it all, and he confessed to me what he had overheard—and recorded. He planted a recorder in the locker room. He wanted me to be careful, to keep my distance because the murderer—"

Priscilla jumped at the sound of a car door slammed shut. Like a herd of animals, they turned at the unmistakable crunch of feet on gravel.

Detective Coleman strode into the backyard, clad in a blue polo shirt, the same shade as the pillowcase with the shovel in the smoking heap of the garage. *Shit*, John thought to himself. *Shit*. He had been wrong all along in so many ways, didn't want to listen to the truth, because it disproved every myth he had worked so hard to help build—that this country was a meritocracy and would prosecute and punish only those who broke the laws, that everyone who worked hard would be redeemed.

RJ had suffered because he wanted to do what was right. And he had been condemned to the circumstances at the end of his life because of the color of his skin, and his inability to stay quiet, to suffer in silence. His final words: *Is Sunny here?*

"What happened here?" Coleman asked as he scrunched his nose. "Christmas lights burn out? I'm surprised to see you as well," he said to Rhonda. "Merry Christmas."

"My brother was smoking," Ana said. "He's not supposed to be, and I guess he was cleaning out some of my mother's stuff."

"She was a painter," Ronald said. "I didn't know, but a bottle of that paint thinner . . . stuff got spilled."

"Lucky you didn't kill yourself," Coleman said. "Shit . . . it's a fucking mess back here."

"Is there a reason why you're here today?" Ana asked.

"What do you want?" Priscilla asked. "It's you, Coleman, right?"

"Yeah, and what are you doing here? Looking for something?"

"I'm friends . . . with John." Priscilla's words were like a punch in John's gut.

"Friends? Since when?" Coleman asked.

"You've been following me," Priscilla said. "I know it's you."

"Brought me right here, too. How convenient."

"How did you know—"

"I heard this guy over here was at Vista Park. And that the two of you had lunch or something? What was that about?"

"I . . ." John tried to answer. How could he explain that he had been attempting to figure out why the police had been so interested in RJ, that he assumed RJ had been some kind of wanted criminal from whom they should all distance themselves? He had unwittingly brought all of this, brought Priscilla and Coleman to his house, there, on the Christmas Eve before the apocalypse.

"I imagine it was about our friend RJ," Coleman said. "What is that you've got?" He gestured toward the casserole dish in Ana's hands.

"Tamales," Ana said.

"And none for you, asshole," Priscilla said.

Everyone held their breath.

"Open the garage door for me? The one for the car. I want to see what's inside there."

John yanked the sliding bolt back and forth a few times before the painted-down door sprung upward to reveal the inside full of smoke. Everyone coughed.

"Shit. Maybe I *should* burn this whole fuckin' place down. Then I wouldn't have to fuckin' kill you," Coleman said to Priscilla. "And you and you and you and you. I'd save some lead." He kicked a box of Sunny's art supplies. "Now I gotta go through all this *useless* shit. Make sure your friend didn't store anything here. He was so friendly with that guy's wife." He snickered as he pointed to John.

Coleman fondled a blank canvas of Sunny's that had survived, covered in soot. He stroked his fingertip on it, making the sign of the cross as he wiped away the gray, the inverse of Ash Wednesday. "That dumbass Hendricks couldn't get shit done. Seriously. Figured out that RJ was writing a book, a fuckin' *memoir*"—he said the last word in an exaggerated French. "Supposedly he had some tapes and film too. But he couldn't find shit. Maybe he made the whole thing up?"

"So you killed him?" Ronald asked, out of breath. "You killed Jacob?"

Coleman drew his gun from his side.

Where was John's revolver? Where had he left his revolver?

"How did you figure out . . . How did you even find me?" Rhonda asked. "How did you figure out where I live? Have you been—"

"Jacob was good for that." Coleman smirked. "There were some pages of your dad's book with your name in it. He wrote that you joined the military. Anyway, good ol' Hendricks had some friends at the VA look you up—*just* in case your dad might've finally found you and . . . ha, maybe you might've wanted to help him with his shitty little book."

"My dad's *what*?"

"Excuse me." Coleman cleared his throat. "His *memoir."*

Ronald grabbed the shovel, still in its pillowcase, and knocked him on the head.

The gun fell clumsily to the ground. John panicked. Rhonda snatched the Glock. "Son of a bitch," she said, her hands shaking.

"Shit." Ana placed the tamales by her feet.

Ronald leaned on the shovel, catching his breath. John placed his arm around his son's shoulders. His chest swelled. Was this pride?

The tip of Priscilla's cane hit Coleman's head a couple times.

"He dead?" Priscilla asked.

"What do we do now?" Rhonda asked, Glock still in her hands.

It was obvious to John.

They needed a bigger fire.

He darted toward the lighter on the steps at the side of the garage. *Burn it down*, he thought. *Burn this all down*. When he turned around, everyone screamed. Coleman pointed another gun from an ankle holster at Rhonda. The terror in her face. The exhaustion. The defeat.

John leapt with all his weight, pushed her to the ground, where their bodies crashed. And he imagined the shattering of the glass. A loud bang ripped through his chest. He cracked his dentures as he gritted down. He lay on the concrete in front of the garage, mesmerized by the blood, a shocking stream as his vision blurred into bodies, legs, and feet. *Pop.* He squeezed his eyes shut. More shots. He couldn't bear to witness his children killed. No, not his Ana, not his Ronald, who would always be babies to him. He failed.

"Holy shit," Rhonda said as she pulled herself from under him. "John?"

He was still alive. He lifted his head with all his strength to a backyard filled with the smell of rust, hands on him, his daughter's face above him, an eclipse. Dark red soaked through the blue shirt. Coleman was facedown.

And then a strange apparition: Rodriguez with a revolver, on top of a ladder in a Santa Claus suit, a cigarette dangling from his mouth.

"Holy shit," Rhonda said again, leaning back onto her hands, body tilted to the side. But she was alright.

Jesus was real, John thought. "JEEZ-us," he cried.

"That's not my fuckin' name. It's Abel." Rodriguez pointed toward someone below him, holding the ladder. "Jesús is my friend, the paletas guy."

"Hola," a voice called from behind the vines.

"You left your fuckin' car on," Rodriguez said. "I went to turn it off and found this in the passenger seat." John's gun. "My grandma used to have one like this." He frowned. "Haven't busted one in like twenty years, but I'm still good I guess."

The warm red liquid spewed. John's and Coleman's, two rivers, a lake. John's body burned as Rhonda's hand now pressed to stop his wound. His daughter cried, and yet he had been free, hadn't he? Coleman, unmoving still, on the ground. His body in the fire that no one could put out. And he felt, finally, like he had escaped—as if he could relax and breathe—because yes, he had found this way, his very own and private success. *I can go home now,* he thought. *I can go home.*

"John—"

The pain inside his chest as his heart cracked open like a seed.

"Dad. Dad."

"No, no. I want— I want home."

"Dad."

"We're waiting for an ambulance," Rhonda said. "Hold on." The sky darkened as his children hovered over him like clouds pregnant with rain, clouds that could devour the sky, the color blue itself. Birds shook the weight of their wet wings until they could fly. "John? Hold on, okay?" Her voice broke. "We *are* home, John."

His daughter dropped to her knees beside him, a bow. His son held his face in his hands. They pleaded for him to stay. But they were old enough now, weren't they? A woman and a man.

He and Sunny had done their jobs. Pride swelled inside him as the blood spurted like truth out of his mouth. He spit out his dentures.

"No, no. I want to go . . ." He muttered, but he heard his own voice, a thirteen-year-old's, with the clarity of spring light on dark soil. He heard this voice for the first time without anger or shame. His father was gone, and he was no longer terrified of him. Jung Ho was listening; he listened to himself. The faces shifted around him. How he loved to try on his father's glasses, thick lenses like the bottom of a glass that you could drink and drink from. Swallow. But he had always been thirsty, thirsty for his love, the kindness obscured and buried in the ground. And here now he felt full. He wanted his mother. He knew where she was. He knew where he could find her. The tears slid down the side of his face, the first droplets that fell before the storm. "집에 가고 싶어요."

DECEMBER 31, 1999

"I remember this fruit when I was a kid," Rhonda said to Ana. "When we were growing up, we had two of those in our backyard. I never liked the fruit much, but it was sweet and something we could pick and eat for fun. The seeds are—they're huge inside. I always wondered what the point was for fruit to be so much seed." Rhonda pinched off one of the spear-like leaves, bent it in half along the center seam. "It's weird that I could even remember that. I must've been only two or three years old, but it's so clear to me, this fruit. Or maybe it was just a dream."

Ana remembered how her father would lift her and Ronald up on his shoulders to reach the branches heavy with bunches of the yellow oval spheres. She'd lean forward onto his head, downy and soft, hair so black it appeared blue under a certain light like a crow, the color of midnight. He had been powerful, thin yet muscular then.

How much she loved him despite who he had become, who he had been. She always felt the need to take care of him, though she didn't know exactly why, and she had failed—didn't she in the end? She couldn't save him.

Splitting open a loquat revealed a slimy, hard brown seed.

As a family, they'd sit at the breakfast nook and peel the skins off together with their fingers. The meat was sweet, honeylike, but not her favorite without any real edge or acid; the effort to eat them wasn't worth the level of satisfaction. But it was the process of watching them ripen, green into gold, and that gathering the fruit had been this informal tradition once a year, an occasion that brought her delight. Her father had seemed at such peace then, when he found the time to hoist them up to the sky. Tears filled Ana's eyes.

"Do you know where they're from? The tree?" Ana asked. Last night, she had invited Rhonda to join their intimate celebration of their father's life and to honor what they had been through, which would include Peggy, Priscilla, Janet, and Jesús and his wife. She had asked her to arrive earlier so that they could discuss a private matter, the questionnaire her father had filled out for his last will and testament, which he had never completed and signed.

Now Rhonda touched the rough, gray trunk, only about nine or ten feet tall, ceiling height. "They're from Asia. China, I think," she said, approaching the persimmon tree that Ronald had planted, the sad twig with the CDs attached to the branches.

"That's kind of genius." Rhonda laughed to herself. She turned one to read the label for AOL.

"My dad."

"It's like a Christmas decoration and a way of scaring off animals, isn't it?"

"He was . . . efficient," Ana said. "We never did get to put up our

Christmas tree." There had been so much left for her father to complete. So many questions she had about him and her mother that would continue to go unanswered.

"There's this questionnaire we found." Ana inhaled, calming herself. She couldn't believe it when she had seen it herself, the pages and pages, mostly blank. She hadn't thought her father would be so fair and prescient. But the proof was in his hand, a careful cursive, much more elegant than his words out loud in English. "My dad wanted to split the house between the three of us when he died. I don't think he was planning on that happening so soon but—"

"Three of us?"

"You, me, and my brother."

"What?" Rhonda appeared legitimately confused. It was hard to say whether or not Rhonda had or would actually forgive their family, ever. She certainly didn't have to trust Ana or her word. Ana couldn't bring back RJ. No one could. Nor could she take back what her father had done to him.

But Ana hoped that honoring his final known wish could provide for Rhonda a different start, another kind of inheritance that might at least be helpful in some way. That was certainly the least they could do. Ana and Ronald still had the nursery and could figure things out.

"Are you interested in living here?" Ana asked. "Would you want to live here?"

"I mean, not really, after . . ." She turned, focused again on the tree. She held her hand above her eyes to shield them from the afternoon light. "Maybe? Seems cursed."

"I don't blame you for thinking that," Ana said. "I've kind of always felt that way about this place, to be honest." She scanned the ruins of the yard and the garage, still filled with their charred and soot-covered belongings. Prior to the police arriving on Christmas Eve, they had all agreed on the same narrative without any mention of the evidence, their missing mother, or RJ's book. Coleman had been stalking Priscilla, for reasons unknown, which resulted in both his death and John's. Rodriguez had saved them all from what would've been a massacre. He was taken into custody, but had been branded by the media as a hero. Santa Claus had saved the day. A Christmas Eve miracle.

Ernesto Coleman was a grinch. A lone wolf with a troubled past, numerous citations. Recently divorced. Zero friends. An alcoholic who didn't know his mother. Of course they blamed the mom. And ex-wife who took everything from him.

For once, the story that the media told worked in their favor. None of them could think of any reason to mention the evidence of the police's past crimes and RJ's book if they didn't possess any of those objects themselves. They would simply be complicating matters and prolonging the investigation and Rodriguez's release.

Rhonda would serve as his attorney pro bono.

Now Rhonda turned to face Ana. Her brows furrowed, mouth strained. There had been so much that she had experienced these past few weeks. How did she go on? How could any of them go on after this? All this loss? Even if the world did not end tonight, they had been left in a landscape, a life they could hardly recognize. All their parents gone. Neither Rhonda nor Ana was somebody's daughter.

"But another part of me sees what this house is, too. What it can be," Ana said. "Not simply a crime scene, but a place where things can heal and grow. I think that's what my mom was trying to do, what my dad wanted as well. I just think the healing part never happened for them. That's kind of my job now, me and my brother's."

If Rhonda wanted to live in the house, Ana and Ronald could find an apartment together. They didn't need this much space. For now.

Ana would have to find another job to supplement whatever they could make at the nursery. She had been responsible for taking care of herself almost entirely since she turned eighteen. Her father never talked about money, but she assumed from his conservative spending habits, how he purchased all his clothing at the big discount clubs, how he frequented the 99 Cents store for cleaning supplies, that he struggled still, and that their house had been the only thing he could afford to maintain—and barely, at that. But overall, owning a house had cost him too much.

"Or if you wanted to split the house, we could sell it. It'll take us a while to get everything settled, move out, maybe a year? And Rodriguez . . . I'm sure we'll all be involved for a while. But after that, I don't think my brother and I want to stay here anyways." She shook her head. "Would you even want to live here or . . . would it be too painful?"

"I'll have to think about it a bit." Rhonda closed her eyes. "What's in the garage, anyways?"

"All my mother's stuff, some of our stuff too. Mementos, things through the years. You know, the kind of stuff we didn't want to throw away."

"Your dad, and my dad . . . they could have been such different people if the world had been kinder to them, don't you think?" She kicked at a weed then bent down to twist it out of the ground.

"I believe they wanted what was best," Ana said. "He knew he was wrong. This was his way of apologizing, his only way, I guess. He took a bullet."

"I did not expect that shit at all." Rhonda laughed ruefully. "Old man was quick."

"He really was." Ana remembered her father on the ground, his last words, the gift of them. She would never get them out of her head. They were real. It was him. He had bared himself. How life could really be like theater. "I need a job soon. Maybe the library could use me. Who knows what I'm going to do."

"Nobody does," Rhonda said. "It's a trick. Every life is its own thing." Rhonda wiped the dirt off her hands. "Strangely enough, I've been thinking of my ex lately. Do you remember the one I mentioned? Up in Oakland? He's the one who wanted a family, but I wasn't ready for it yet." She adjusted the tie that held the persimmon tree to its stake. "So many years I spent, trying to find my dad. Trying to make sense of him. So many years. And for what? Every person is a mystery. Even my mother was to me. Still is."

With a pang of sadness in her chest, Ana remembered her mother's words: *I'm so proud, you.*

"It must've been the camera that reminded me of my ex," Rhonda said as she tilted her head to check the angle of the sapling.

"Camera?" Ana asked.

"Yeah, an old Canon Sure Shot."

The photograph she had taken of RJ. The feel of the point-and-shoot's shutter beneath her finger. Its power.

"It was on him when he died," Rhonda continued. "But it was empty. No film. Nothing."

RJ's words: *Hold it steady, Ana.*

"My ex used to take photos all the time too. Dabbled in art." Rhonda paused. "Is something wrong?"

"I . . . I didn't mention this before, but I . . . took that photo, the photo that Coleman had, the one my father had torn up . . . the one from the Observatory."

Rhonda widened her eyes in shock.

"When I was a kid, RJ . . . your father and my mother . . . we had all gone to the Observatory. It wasn't planned. It was spontaneous. It was like my mother was driving and she just saw him on the side of the road and pulled over."

"Wait, what?"

"That's my only memory of him, of them together."

"It's my favorite photo." Rhonda's face flushed. "I have . . . a few copies of it still."

"Do you know where he got it from? Coleman. I couldn't figure that out."

"When he came to my house after my father died, I thought it was strange he was there by himself, but I also just wanted that asshole to leave so I gave him a copy," Rhonda said. "After he left, I called up a couple friends at the coroner's office."

"Oh, and that's when—"

"That's how I finally saw him," Rhonda said, face crumpled. "That's when I also grabbed what they had of his stuff—the notebook, the library card, the camera."

"I'm sorry," Ana said.

Rhonda shook her head.

"When my mother died, the photo was in her belongings. She had this dresser drawer full of old things, and she had hidden it in a book of poems. That and some other photos of him."

Ana placed her hand on Rhonda's shoulder. "I remember him saying it was his daughter's favorite spot." *Could you do me a favor and take a picture of me, young lady? I'd like to send a photo to someone special.* "He must've given it to . . . your mother *for* you."

Rhonda inhaled with her eyes closed. "I had a feeling that was the case. He was sort of looking at the camera the way I had always dreamed he would . . . look at me." She wiped the tears off her face.

That made perfect sense to Ana.

"Isn't it amazing," Rhonda asked, "the way that people find ways to speak with each other through time? It's as if we're always . . . leaving messages for each other, purposefully *and* accidentally, of course."

"He seemed to know what he was doing," Ana said. There was still the drawing she had found of her mother's, the pencil image of her lying down on a bus stop bench. Her head in a man's lap, the loquat tree behind them. An apple in his hand.

"I bought apples for tonight," Ana said.

"Okay?" Rhonda smiled. "I noticed you cut them up nicely that first night. I guess it's your thing?"

"There's this drawing of my mother's that I found and I'm pretty sure the man in it is your father. He's holding an apple in it."

"Like Adam?" Rhonda asked.

"Who?"

"Adam and Eve."

"Oh, ha, maybe?" Ana said. "I just figured it would be a nice little nod to him. I'll have to show you the drawing inside. It's pretty weird. But shows a lot about their friendship." She turned toward the rear of the house. Her brother and Peggy were in the kitchen, preparing the meal—japchae and pancit as sides for the galbi and pollo asado they'd cook on Jesús's grill, which they'd borrow for the night. Apples, persimmons for dessert. Ana had been practicing her peeling technique with a knife. "I want to say that my mother was so lucky to have him in her life."

"We all are," Rhonda said. "Even if I didn't get to know him the way I needed to, I feel like . . . he's here with us. And I could say the same for your mom." The back door sprang open as Rhonda said, "They're proud."

In the kitchen, Ronald unwrapped the plastic from a pound of sirloin for the japchae they would make. The dried shiitake soaked in a bowl of water by the sink. With their hands busy, Ronald and Peggy hoped to keep their minds off their anxiety about the apocalypse. Even though they had seen the footage of New Year's celebrations around the world—including Down Under, eighteen hours ahead, where all the Australians had lived to sing "Auld Lang Syne"—they couldn't quite trust that they'd survive Y2K until it actually happened to them and they officially entered the year 2000.

Their father was gone. His father was dead.

The day before Christmas, Ana, Rhonda, Priscilla, Rodriguez, and himself had agreed to the same facts, omitting the question of the evidence and RJ's book.

Coincidentally, this story would be the easiest to remember.

Ronald rinsed the steak and laid it on a plate covered in paper towels, while Peggy chopped the carrots into matchsticks that she would also include in the pancit she always made for celebrations. She and her mother had rolled fresh lumpia for them last night, which they'd deep-fry closer to when the guests—Priscilla, Janet, and Jesús—would arrive at around five o'clock to honor the passing of his father.

He had been numb since he had witnessed the death of his dad, and he knew that tonight would be difficult for many reasons—the death of two fathers, Rhonda's and their own, the sullenness yet strange relief of having most of their questions answered. And now they were left alone with nothing but the mystery of themselves and how they could—despite all of this—move forward. How were human beings capable of starting again and again and again in even the most difficult times? Tears filled his eyes. If only his mother were here for them.

But for now, they'd have a feast like only she could've prepared, and send their father off, leave him behind in this strange millennium full of fury, silence, and sound.

He reached into the fridge for the mak kimchi he had made, and took a bite. Peggy opened her mouth because with her hands busy she wanted him to feed her too. She wore one of his mother's aprons like himself, cartoon strawberries and ruffles along the hems, and her skin glowed, shiny around the nose and forehead, without any makeup.

"What do you think?" he asked.

"Perfect, delicious."

He tightened the lid of the jar and shut the refrigerator door. "There'll be so many more issues down the line. Trials? Shit. I don't know. It's clear that Rodriguez saved our lives."

When Ronald fell silent, Peggy said, "Take some time off next year. You've been through so much." She split a head of green cabbage and shredded the halves with a knife as she created a large mound that spilled off the cutting board. "How could you go back to school after this? Besides, it's your senior year. Screw it. Take the GED or something. You don't have to figure it all out now. Just take a couple weeks off. There's been so much . . . death. I'm sorry, Ronald."

She paused to wrap her arms around his waist. For years he had been ashamed of his house, this kitchen with its battered and stained cabinets, the crooked and loose laminate tiles, the opposite of Peggy's life—the marble, the stainless steel appliances, the fancy pots and pans, plates and bowls that all matched. But here, now, he realized how much he had stalled their getting to know each other better, this intimacy, because of his fear that he and his life could not be lovable. She had proved him wrong, again and again. He had so much to be proud of, and his parents did too, even if they hadn't lived up to some standard that had been unrealistic for them.

This was the best they could do, and life could still be magnificent and full.

"Maybe this is why my dad wanted the world to end. So he wouldn't have to deal with all this legal shit. Fuck."

"It still might, Ronald. It still might."

He wiped his eyes with an edge of the apron, his mother's apron, which looked ludicrous on him but he didn't care. "I guess . . . I wonder what RJ would've wanted. My mom too." He burst into a sob. Was this the first time he had really cried in front of her?

"Your mom would've wanted you to stay out of this shit." Peggy smiled. "RJ would want redemption of some kind. And he's getting it. He will. I just know it. Coleman is dead and more will come to light. I am sure there were more officers involved." She handed him a napkin from the breakfast nook. "And your dad? Oh God, your dad got to die a hero. He saved Rhonda. It's like . . . I don't know, Shakespearean, his life."

"How boring." He blew his nose. "Seems like RJ and my mom got screwed the most."

"Maybe in the end, they got to lead the lives they wanted to lead. Could you imagine that? RJ wrote a freakin' book. We just don't know where it is. He found his daughter in a strange way eventually. He went to Vietnam. He wanted to help people. He was kind. People loved him. Remember, they still do. Just like people still love your mother. I couldn't think of a better way to live, honestly. To die and still have your loved ones curious about you, searching for you, searching to know more about you. That's beautiful. It means you've inspired others to seek the truth, to not . . . settle for less."

"Was that like, your college essay? Was that what it was like, because I'm sure you got into every single one—"

She punched him lightly on the chest, and he grabbed her hands and kissed her face in a way that he knew she would find annoying. She wriggled free from his grip and pretended to knee him in the groin, and he blocked her with his leg. She threw a dish towel over his head, and he laughed out loud, which he needed after the heaviness of this week, this year, this life.

"When do you find out about college admissions?" he asked.

"February." She sniffled, hands on the mound of cabbage like a crystal ball.

"What are you leaning toward? For school."

"Oh God, who knows where I'll get in. I would like to stay here though."

"I thought you wanted to go to one of the East Coast schools. Hang out with Abercrombie and Fitch models." He lifted his shirt to reveal his abs, which weren't ad-worthy, but still admirable.

"I applied just to keep my parents happy."

"They want you to leave?"

"Of course. If it means I'm going somewhere good. They've always wanted 'the best' for me. They need something new to brag about . . . always. They're like weird adrenaline junkies. But honestly, they don't really know who I even am. They're too busy with work."

"Where do *you* really want to go?" He had avoided the subject. He himself would start at a community college and hopefully transfer to a university after two years. His parents had never been able to save much for his education, and he didn't want to take on too much debt. And he also thought culinary school could be possible, really anything now that his father was dead. Who would judge his choices? His sister, the radical, that weirdo with the shaved head?

"UCLA. I want to wear flip-flops every day. Thought you knew that about me."

A rush of excitement flooded him as he realized she might stay local after all. He didn't have to live this next year alone. He hid his face by searching the fridge for the zucchini that he'd dredge with flour and egg to pan-fry, hobak jeon, one of his favorite side dishes, that he even enjoyed at room temperature, a little soggy and dipped in soy sauce and vinegar. His mouth watered as he imagined the soft squash over steaming rice.

The phone rang. He rushed to answer it before the machine might pick it up.

"It's Janet," he said out the back door to his sister and Rhonda. His heart beat through his mouth. She had news.

As they now raced toward the bottom of the stairs, Ana and Rhonda looked at him in shock. They had planned on seeing Janet tonight, since they had invited her over, but the urgency in her voice suggested something else. Was it about RJ? Or their father? Ana, Rhonda, and Ronald scrunched together to hear Janet's words.

"I know I'm supposed to see you later but . . . I found the book," Janet said. "It's here."

"What?" Ana asked.

"RJ's book. It was on a couple CDs in the poetry section of all places."

"Shit," Rhonda whispered.

"I knew it," Ronald said.

"My assistant and I literally spent all night going through each and every shelf, and it was there. I wanted to let Rhonda know before . . . I wanted to see what she wants to do with them."

"I'm here," Rhonda said. "I came earlier to speak with Ana."

"Oh good. We could . . . contact the DOJ, you know? But I've made copies too. I made copies for you. I'll bring them over today, okay? I have a couple things left to do here. The place is a wreck. I can't believe it though."

Rhonda's eyes, her entire face, lit up. A miracle. An Apocalypse Miracle. Her father had worked diligently to preserve what he knew. His story.

"It's beautiful. The book." Janet wept through her words, trembling. "I always knew it'd be beautiful. The writing. People should read this. It's written in the style of a letter to Rhonda."

He had written this for none other than her, the daughter he loved.

"He meant for people to read this, to feel themselves more, to inspire us to act on behalf of . . . ourselves. To save ourselves. I just couldn't believe it. It's written in the style of a letter to you, Rhonda, his daughter, yes, but it's also something else, a song. He had such style. I always knew he would—"

"You read the whole thing?" Rhonda asked.

"Of course. I couldn't help myself. I should've called you earlier, but after all we've been through, I couldn't put it down. I couldn't stop listening. And by listening, I felt like I was breathing life back into him. I could see him, his mind, the shape of his heart. It's sublime. Who knows what this could lead to?" Janet paused. "Maybe, finally, some healing."

In the backyard, she heard unfamiliar voices. Men and women, laugh-ter, and Mexican music, horn and drum heavy, something folksy and danceable like banda. The sound was an affirmation that yes, indeed this was Los Angeles.

She hadn't realized how much she had missed the city itself, its strangeness, not simply her family. Her neighbor Rodriguez had continued his annual tradition of multicolored Christmas and icicle string lights draped on his cacti and succulents. Mockingbirds chirped and beeped like car alarms. The smell of barbecue from every continent in the world—from jalapeños and citrus notes to sesame and soy to brown sugar, cumin, and Worcestershire sauce. The unlikely. A bizarre bazaar. Scent didn't have any borders.

Were they ghosts in the backyard now? What had happened to her family? She recognized the Eldorado in the driveway, but none of the other cars parked on the street—a Camaro, a Toyota Corolla, a Honda Civic.

Where were her children? Ana and Ronald, how much they could've changed in one year. Just as she had as well.

She now walked with a cane, planted one foot after the other, up the low slope of the driveway beside John's precious Cadillac, and on the dirty driver's-side glass, she wrote with her index finger the words "Happy New Year." She had made it this far, after surgery to replace her kneecap and months of physical therapy, during which she had lived with Myunghwa, who had taken care of her, in Seoul.

Swimming in the river, Sunhee and Myunghwa, mistaken for refugees, had nearly been killed. Together they had sweated and baked, dipped their bodies in cold water, after their arduous journey from Vietnam. Myunghwa sang, melodically, "Here Comes the Sun," in a way that had made them sway and dance like teenagers without worry or care. Sunhee tossed her wide-brimmed hat ashore, dove down as deep as she could, until she heard Myunghwa call after her, "Sunhee," her voice filled with terror. Gunshots cracked. And the image of Myunghwa, then Professor Cho, on the side of the Bukhan River, beaten to death, flooded Sunhee's mind. She panicked. Her left leg burst into flames. She tasted blood in the water.

Flailing, finally, she touched ground with her right foot, soft and silty between her toes. Her mouth gulped the open air, which smelled like rust. She glimpsed soldiers on the sand, her brothers in another life, her sons. They pointed toward the river, now dark and red, the color of midnight despite sunshine, the blue sky. For a second, she thought of Magritte's series, *The Empire of Light*. "Sunhee," Myunghwa yelled as she dragged Sunhee out of the river. Her kneecap had been shattered.

After her surgery and recovery in Seoul, a week before Christmas, she had worked up the nerve, finally, to call her children, even if their father were to pick up the phone, even if no one wanted to speak with her at all, even if they'd never forgive her. But no one answered.

She had been overwhelmed, unable to sleep at night, wondering what had happened to them, if her departure led somehow to their separation, or disintegration. Maybe Ana stopped coming home. Maybe Ronald ran away.

Maybe Sunhee was more important and powerful than she had ever known? She had left them to find herself, and yet now that, in a way, her future had been clearer than ever with Myunghwa in her life, she felt as if she had abandoned them in a state of disarray, confusion. Could something have happened to them? She'd have to return to LA herself. She needed to see Ronald and Ana. She needed to understand why they hadn't answered her letters. She needed to hold them just once more. She longed for the downiness of their heads as they rested their faces on her chest, the softness and smell of them. Would they ever know how much they meant to her, despite how much she absolutely needed to leave them when she did? All of their survival had depended upon her departure, and her return someday.

On the cab ride to the airport, Myunghwa had held her hand, fingers laced, which they often did in public, because who would suspect anything from these two older women, who could be sisters after all? Sunhee heard the uneasiness in her breath. Her silence that entire morning spoke volumes about her worries, what Myunghwa felt. Would she ever understand how grateful she had been for Myunghwa, how she cared for Sunhee this past year, how she had loved her in a way she had never imagined possible for herself before?

After Sunhee had checked in for her flight, Myunghwa, eyes glowing, finally asked, "Will you be back?"

"Don't be silly. Of course," Sunhee said.

"I wouldn't blame you if you decided to stay. Your children."

"We will find a way to make things work. I don't want to grow old without you." Sunhee laughed. "You do torture me in all the right ways." She pinched Myunghwa's arm.

"Once my mother gets better, I'll come visit you," Myunghwa said.

She nodded, zipped up Myunghwa's jacket for her. "Maybe there's a place for us in America after all," Sunhee said, and she meant it. "Consider this an exploratory visit? I'll call you every day, if I can. And if I don't, know that I am thinking of you."

They embraced each other, and briefly kissed, despite the fact that someone might see them. Neither of them cared anymore what anyone else thought. At their age, people barely noticed them anyways. They had faded out of a public life into a mostly private existence that suited them both. Sunhee squeezed Myunghwa's hands with both of hers and joked, "Don't forget me, okay. AH-MEH-RHEE-CAHN wuuuh-mahn." She pointed at herself.

She didn't know how she'd handle her husband once she arrived. She had forgiven him long ago for what he had done to her art, but she also knew that she could never live with him again in the same bed. She could take up Ana's former room for now. Be there for half of Ronald's final year in high school. After he graduated and figured out when he wanted to leave the house, eventually, if at all, she could finalize her plans for a future with Myunghwa. She could get a divorce and either move back to Korea or find a way for Myunghwa to immigrate here. Myunghwa herself had come from a wealthy family and would have enough money to establish her own gallery focusing on contemporary Korean art, which would be so valuable in Los Angeles.

Once she had landed at LAX, she had easily convinced the customs agent that she had only been in Korea for a couple weeks, and when she pretended to be confused during his additional questions, he waved her away rather than deal with her, an inconvenience. Of course, her car had been stolen in the long-term parking lot, unsurprisingly, and she rode a cab, her first time inside an American taxi by herself.

It was New Year's Eve, and even though she knew the world would not end, she would have to beg her children for forgiveness. Afterward, she must figure out a way to find RJ again. Was he in Vietnam? Where could she look for him? She wished that he had left her some kind of meeting spot, or at least a contact, in case she needed to reach him one day.

Did he still need the evidence?

The night that she had run into him outside the supermarket, after her husband had fallen asleep, she had gone out into the garage and rummaged until she found his boxes. He had said that inside would be a bank deposit bag full of film canisters and cassette tapes, and she needed to make sure that no one would ever get their hands on it. His life depended on this task.

Where could she hide the bag? It would need to be safe for a long period of time without any interference from her family, her husband especially. There wasn't a place inside the house. Her husband was methodical about flipping over their mattress twice per year. And the bag had been too large to squeeze into a light fixture or tape to the bottom of a drawer. She had already used the succulent planters up front to hide the emergency cash her mother had given her. And she shouldn't use the garage, which held too many other belongings and would be an obvious place for someone who searched.

The dirt in the backyard had been hardpan, mostly untouched since they had moved in. She could wrap the evidence in plastic bags and bury it in a corner in which no one would go—beneath the loquat tree that her husband and children would often pluck from when the fruit had become ripe, golden globes, sweet and honeyish under the skin like apricots, without the tartness. She found the shovel that they always kept in their yard that night, and in the darkness, she wet the ground to loosen it, possibly the first time they had hand-watered the tree. She drove the blade into the soil, barely chipping away at it, and forty minutes later she had dug a relatively shallow but wide hole, one-foot deep. She gently placed RJ's prized possession inside two plastic grocery bags, which she then covered with dirt. She stomped on the ground as best she could, and watered the area again to level the surface as much as possible. No one came back here. No one would plant anything for a while, if ever. She was sure of it. She leaned the shovel against the wall of the garage that night, spent but victorious.

And now as she stood still at the top of the driveway, terrified by the sounds she heard in the backyard, the voices that sounded so foreign to her; one of her cats hopped the fence from Rodriguez's yard and purred hello as she stooped down, carefully, to rub the space between its ears. A feeling of calm entered her body as she stood up straight, leaned on her cane, and remembered RJ, his leg injury that he had all those years. Would she ever find him again? He would always remain a mystery to her, roving, leaving his belongings. But even her brief encounters with him had nonetheless been inspirational in ways that he would never understand. Perhaps she would never fully know him. But it didn't matter. There had been a kinship that was unbreakable between them, unsaid through the years, and now that she had the opportunity to live the way she wanted, she trusted that he would be there one day to laugh with her about her adventures—including nearly getting killed at a border.

And maybe home was not the place where you thought *I'm here*. It was the place where you felt *I've returned*. She could smell the meat on top of a fire. When had they bought a grill? The smoke was an invitation. Was someone else throwing a party at their house? She couldn't understand. They had done nothing in the backyard, and suddenly after she had been gone for a year, this strange scene, that not even she could've dreamed, appeared before her eyes. A small crowd like a welcoming party in the dark. The paletero? The librarian? A woman with RJ's face. Was Sunhee dead or alive? Even she shocked herself with the sound of her voice as she said slowly in English, to all her guests, "I have so much to tell you."

ACKNOWLEDGMENTS

My editor, Natalie Hallak, was once again the most exceptional partner, who startles me with her ingenuity, empathy, grit, and passion for books. This novel would've been impossible without her unwavering support and dedication to the art of storytelling on every level. My literary agent, Amy Elizabeth Bishop, at Dystel, Goderich & Bourret, kept the dream team together, and I couldn't have asked for a greater advocate for my work. She has been an essential early reader and I feel blessed to have her tenacity, tact, and boundless enthusiasm in my life.

I am especially thankful for the extraordinary team at Atria Books: Libby McGuire, Lindsay Sagnette, Jade Hui, Vanessa Silverio, Liz Byer, Paige Lytle, Stacey Sakal, James Iacobelli, Laywan Kwan, Dana Sloan, Sirui Huang, Dana Trocker, Alexis Minieri, and Nicole Bond. It has been an absolute thrill to work with the incredible Lisa Sciambra, Gena Lanzi, and Emi Battaglia in publicity, marketing genius Maudee Genao, and social media maven Morgan Hoit, as well as Simon & Schuster's Sienna Farris and Imani Seymour for their expertise in multicultural publishing. Special thanks to Johanie, who illuminated these pages with her generous and precise feedback and to the brilliant Elizabeth Hitti for her incisive reading and very thoughtful, detailed exchanges which have kept me on track.

Reese Witherspoon, Reese's Book Club, and the tremendous community of readers, both on- and offline, created a busy and beautiful space for my first book, *The Last Story of Mina Lee*. I am moved by the discussions you have had about family, identity, migration, and language in response to my debut. Thank you for getting to know and welcoming Mina and Margot into your lives.

My film/television agent, Addison Duffy, is both a remarkable reader and an outstanding representative who has orchestrated some of the most exciting and creative conversations about my work.

Libraries and librarians hold a very special place in my heart. I am indebted toward the Los Angeles, Seattle, Berkeley, and Oakland public libraries, which provide a safe and quiet place to think, read, and write. Your often difficult but necessary work protects the biggest and kindest values in our society through the books, art, and culture that you share.

Independent bookstores and booksellers, in particular Marianne Reiner of La Playa Books, Lucy Yu of Yu & Me Books, and Pegasus Books, The Booksmith, Green Apple Books, Mrs. Dalloway's, Orinda Books, and East Bay Booksellers in the San Francisco Bay Area, hosted events or offered my book a sacred spot on their shelves in the Kim section, which I love to visit.

I am inspired by and in awe of fellow artists and writers who also supported my first book in a variety of ways online and in person: Amerie, Kristen Arnett, Chloe Benjamin, Tara Block, Frances Cha, Alexander Chee, Karen Chee, Alyssa Cole, Vanessa Hua, Carolyn Huynh, Randa Jarrar, Alka Joshi, Crystal Hana Kim, E.J. Koh, Jean Kwok, Marie Myung-Ok

Lee, Corinne Manning, Amy Meyerson, Etaf Rum, Gary Singh, Maya Sonenberg, Michelle Min Sterling, Catherine Adel West, and Mimi Wong.

The great Nguyễn Phan Quế Mai offered invaluable suggestions on this novel and I am deeply appreciative of her compassionate storytelling and unflinching advocacy on behalf of the victims of war and Agent Orange.

No one writes in a vacuum and I am exceedingly grateful for the teachers who make an enormous impact on both my daughter's life and my own: Yaminah, Beccah, Mary, Catie, Erna, Mckenzie, and Estefania. Thank you for the kindness and creativity you bring to the classroom every day.

I am overwhelmed with gratitude for the friends and family who have championed my books, in particular: Eva Larrauri de Leon; the Lee, Kim, Goodman, and Robin families; Talia Shalev; Naomi and Keiko Namekata; and Paula Shields. My writing group—Ingrid Rojas Contreras, Tanya Rey, Melissa Valentine, Yalitza Ferreras, Angie Chau, Amber Butts, and Meron Hadero—astonish me with their talent, humor, generosity, and magic.

My father died decades ago, and he never lived to read this book, but I hope he finds love in these pages still. I know now how misunderstood he was, that he never had the time or space to heal from the injustices of his own childhood. He survived long enough so that I could write about them. This book is one way that I carry on his search for the people and the places we have lost. I am proud of him and us.

During the course of the pandemic, my mother nearly lost her life. What we as human beings have been through collectively these past few years has really shaken us in ways that we might not understand for years, possibly never. My gratitude for my mother—who she is, was, and has yet to become—has only grown during the course of writing my first book and then another. Fortunately, I learned to fight from her.

My husband, Paul, has done the most to support me and my writing for a decade now. He is how I continue to meet my characters on the page each day. I couldn't have written two books that every version of me has needed without him and his undying belief in this thing that I do with my headphones on. Thank you (and Mr. Noodles, our dog) for giving me so many reasons to wonder, laugh, and look forward to the future.

My daughter, Moonhee, I am simply grateful for all of you, from the mischief in your smile to the dimples on your hands and your hilarious interactions with the world. I admire your limitless imagination, supernatural levels of courage, and the adorable words that you, unafraid, sing and string together in new ways. Your generation deserves so much more. I won't ever give up. And of course, I'll love you forever.

ABOUT THE AUTHOR

Nancy Jooyoun Kim is the *New York Times* bestselling author of *The Last Story of Mina Lee*, a Reese's Book Club pick. Born and raised in Los Angeles, she now lives in the San Francisco Bay Area.